other words for love

Y

Lorraine Zago Rosenthal

other words for love

DELACORTE PRESS

Text copyright © 2011 by Lorraine Zago Rosenthal
Jacket photograph (top) © 2011 by Melissa Breanne Jackson
Jacket photograph (bottom) © 2011 by Hilary Elizabeth Upton

Delacorte Press is a registered trademark and the colophon is a trademark of Random House, Inc.

Visit us on the Web! www.randomhouse.com/teens

Educators and librarians, for a variety of teaching tools, visit us at www.randomhouse.com/teachers

Library of Congress Cataloging-in-Publication Data
Rosenthal, Lorraine Zago.
Other words for love / by Lorraine Zago Rosenthal. — 1st ed.
p. cm.
Summary: In 1985 Brooklyn, New York, sixteen-year-old artist Ari learns about first love.
ISBN 978-0-385-73901-6 (hc)
ISBN 978-0-385-90765-1 (lib. bdg.)
ISBN 978-0-375-89692-7 (ebook)
[1. Coming of age—Fiction. 2. Family problems—Fiction. 3. Artists—Fiction. 4. Schools—Fiction. 5. Family life—New York (State)—Brooklyn—Fiction. 6. Brooklyn (New York, N.Y.)—Fiction.] I. Title.
PZ7.R7194458Lim 2011
[Fic]—dc22
2009053656

The text of this book is set in 12.5-point AGaramond.

Book design by Angela Carlino

Printed in the United States of America

10 9 8 7 6 5 4 3 2 1

First Edition

acknowledgments

I would like to express my heartfelt appreciation to those closest to me for their unwavering support; my deepest gratitude to my agent, Elizabeth Evans, for her dedication and enthusiasm; and my sincere thanks to all the people at Delacorte Press—especially my editor, Stephanie Lane Elliott—who contributed their talents to this novel.

other words for love

one

In 1985, just about everyone I knew was afraid of two things: a nuclear attack by the Russians and a gruesome death from the AIDS virus, which allegedly thrived on the mouthpieces of New York City public telephones.

My best friend, Summer, however, didn't worry about catching AIDS from a phone or anything else. She started kissing boys when we were twelve and wrote every one of their names in her diary, which had a purple velvet cover.

I didn't have a diary. I didn't need one because I had only kissed a boy once, in the Catskills during a family vacation between eighth and ninth grades. The Catskills boy was from Connecticut, and he turned on me after I kissed him. He claimed that I opened my mouth too wide and that I was *only a four on a scale of one to ten in the looks department.*

Don't get any ideas, he said. *You Brooklyn girls bore me. And I'm going home in two days, so we'll never see each other again.*

That was fine with me. I wanted to pretend that the kiss had never happened. It wasn't what I'd practiced on the back of my hand while imagining handsome faces from *General Hospital* and *Days of Our Lives.* None of those guys would have said I was only a four, and they definitely wouldn't have told me to watch where I was going after we bumped into each other at the breakfast buffet.

What are you doing in there? my mother asked later, while I was brushing my teeth in our motel bathroom and hoping there weren't any AIDS germs in my mouth. And I didn't tell Mom what had happened. She'd already warned me that bad things could hide in the most unlikely places.

Summer and I went to different high schools. I attended our local public school in Brooklyn, while she was a student at Hollister Prep, a fancy private school on the Upper East Side of Manhattan that charged tuition my parents couldn't afford.

Summer's parents *could* afford it, but that wasn't why she transferred there after only three months at my school. It was because some girls were spreading rumors about her, inventing filthy stories about how she supposedly serviced the entire wrestling team and went down on their coach in his office. *Summer Simon swallows*—that was what the girls wrote in bright red nail polish on a bathroom wall. Then they Scotch-taped Trojan *Ribbed for Her Pleasure* packets all over Summer's locker. That made her cry.

I peeled them off while she sobbed into her hands. *Forget it,* I whispered. *They're just jealous because all the guys like you.*

This was hard for me to say, because I was jealous myself. But Summer stopped crying and even smiled, and I was sure that I'd done something good. And she did lots of good things, too—like not ditching me after she started at Hollister and became a member of its popular crowd.

Now our sophomore year was over and Summer and I sat on folding chairs in my sister Evelyn's backyard in Queens. Toys were scattered across the grass, and Summer rolled a Nerf ball with her dainty foot.

"Eight whole weeks of vacation ahead of us," she said.

I nodded and looked at my nondainty foot. There was a callus on my heel and a scab on my ankle and I needed a pedicure, but Summer didn't. The sun bounced off her painted toenails and the long blond hair that was strategically highlighted around her pretty face. Her eyes were dark, she always wore flashy clothes, and she smelled of L'Air du Temps. She hadn't been without a boyfriend since junior high. Her latest conquest was a Columbia University sophomore she'd met last September who'd taken her virginity by Halloween. *He's nineteen, so it's illegal,* she'd told me in a giggly whisper the next day. *Nobody can ever know.*

I knew. And I was jealous. Since she'd started at Hollister, everything had been so easy for her. She rarely studied, yet her name was a permanent fixture on the honor roll. She was good at math, she was a fashion expert, and she could recite the stats of every player on the Yankees. She lived as the only child in a palatial house in Park Slope. Even her name was perfect: Summer Simon, like a movie actress on a glitzy marquee.

I wondered if her parents had planned it that way, and I wished my parents had planned better. They should have known that guys would be more attracted to girls named Summer Simon than to girls named Ariadne Mitchell. I also wished that my mother was as interested in movies as she was in literature. It wasn't a smart idea to name me after some dusty old book by Chekhov.

But Mom was a reader. She had a master's degree in English and taught sixth-grade language arts at a public school. She thought my best friend was highly overrated. According to Mom, Summer was short, she was a shameless flirt, and she was totally manufactured—all dyed hair and makeup and fake nails. Mom said I had a much better figure than Summer because I was thinner and three inches taller, and *Jet-black hair with light blue eyes is very rare. You can thank your father for that.*

"Ari," Summer said. "Patrick is looking quite gorgeous today."

My attention shifted to Evelyn's husband, who was barbecuing hamburgers at the opposite end of the yard.

Patrick was thirty years old and six feet tall, and he had blond hair and brown eyes like Summer. He also had a killer body. It was lean and muscular from lifting barbells in his basement and battling fires with the FDNY. I'd had a crush on him since we first met. He and Evelyn had a son named Kieran, whose fifth birthday we were celebrating, and now my sister was pregnant again.

"You're so boy-crazy," I answered, because what else could I say? Could I tell Summer that I knew Patrick was gorgeous and that whenever I slept at his house, I would press my ear against the guest bedroom wall to hear him and Evelyn having sex? I knew that made me a pervert.

"Take it easy, little sister," Patrick said when Mom and Summer and I were leaving, but he pronounced the last word "sistah" because he was from Boston. He also referred to the sprinkles on Kieran's birthday cake as *jimmies* and he complained that it was "wicked hot" today. He always called me little sistah, and I grabbed every chance to make fun of his accent.

"There's an *r* on the end of that word, Patrick Cagney," I told him.

"Don't be a wiseass," he said. "You criticize your father like that? He don't talk no better than me."

He *doesn't* talk *any* better than you, I thought, sure that Mom was cringing at Patrick's disgraceful grammar. But he was right. Dad did have a heavy Brooklyn accent, the accent that Mom had successfully discouraged in me but not in Evelyn. My sister's grammar was as bad as Patrick's, and she had the vocabulary of a drunken sailor, especially when she was angry.

She wasn't angry today, when we said goodbye at the front

door of her modest home, which was always messy and had wallpaper from 1972. Today she smiled and looked at me through her heavy-lidded green eyes. Bedroom eyes, that was what her high school friends used to call them. Evelyn had been as popular as Summer when she was our age. The boys in our neighborhood used to drool over her auburn hair, her delicate nose, and her pouty mouth.

"Come and spend the weekend soon," she said, hugging me tight. I felt her swollen stomach and noticed the thin layer of fat that had settled beneath her chin. Evelyn's face was still beautiful, but her first pregnancy had left a stubborn weight gain that she didn't try to lose.

I never criticized her figure out loud and neither did Mom, who wasn't in any position to criticize. Mom was thirty pounds overweight but she didn't care. She would never give up her favorite Hostess chocolate cupcakes or her homemade Sunday dinners with roasted chicken and potatoes drenched in gravy. *Food is one of life's simple pleasures,* she always said.

She lit a cigarette when she and Summer and I were in her old Honda, headed back toward Brooklyn. The windows were open because the air conditioner didn't work, and Mom's hair swirled around her head. It was shoulder-length, naturally auburn but now mixed with gray. In her wedding picture she looked like Evelyn, but her nose wasn't as small. And now her eyelids were a little too heavy.

"Are your parents at home, Summer?" Mom asked from the driver's seat next to me. I almost laughed. It was as if Mom thought we were eight instead of sixteen. But she believed that parents should be around a lot for their kids. That was why she'd become a teacher—so she could wait at the front door for me after school, so we could spend August afternoons together at Coney Island. She complained that Dad wasn't home enough, even though that wasn't his fault. He was a homicide detective in Manhattan, and the city was just so crime-infested.

"Yes, Mrs. Mitchell," Summer said, and I thought she sounded like one of Mom's students. Those kids were so intimidated by Mom, they practically wet their pants when her husky voice boomed across the classroom.

Mom stopped at the curb in front of Summer's house. All the houses on her block had double front doors, majestic bay windows, and elegantly angled rooftops. Her parents were outside, planting flowers in the tiny square of dirt that was their front lawn, and they both waved after we dropped Summer off and headed toward home.

Our house was in Flatbush, and it wasn't huge or imposing. It was similar to Evelyn's—all brick, two stories, three bedrooms, forty years old. But our house was much neater than hers, and there was a statue of Saint Anne on our lawn. She'd been abandoned by the previous owner, and I was sure she knew it. *She's the mother of the Blessed Virgin Mary,* Mom said. *So we can't evict her. That would be a terrible sin.* Saint Anne always looked like she was crying when it rained.

Evelyn thought we were nuts for keeping the statue. She also rolled her eyes and stuck a finger down her throat whenever Mom got religious. She said that Mom was a lapsed Catholic, a phony Cafeteria Catholic—one of those people who pick and choose the rules that suit them—and she wasn't wrong. We only went to church on Christmas and Easter, and we never abstained from meat on Fridays during Lent.

Once Mom even signed a pro-choice petition that a lady from NOW brought to our front door. *Women are entitled to their rights,* Mom had said after I gave her a funny look. *There are enough unwanted children in this world.*

Then I glanced at Saint Anne, standing there in a chipped blue gown with a gold shawl over her head and her baby daughter in her arms, and at that moment I thought she looked very sad.

"Is Summer seeing anyone?" Mom asked.

It was a few hours after we had come back from Evelyn's house and we sat on the living room sofa, enjoying the breeze that floated through a window screen. Illegal fireworks crackled outside, and I was polishing my toenails. There was barely enough light to see, but I didn't want to turn on a lamp because the darkness improved our plain furniture and hid the small charred hole in our La-Z-Boy. Mom had accidentally dropped a cigarette on the seat after she drank too much eggnog last Christmas Eve.

"Not right now. She broke up with the Columbia guy," I said, thinking about Summer's other ex-boyfriends. I asked her once if she missed any of them. She'd just shrugged and said, *I don't think much about guys from the past. I'm glad I knew them, but there's a reason they didn't make it into my future.* It surprised me that she could be so nonchalant, although I figured she was probably right.

"So she's actually without a boyfriend? That's shocking," Mom said, puffing on a Pall Mall. I wished she wouldn't smoke so much. I wished she wouldn't smoke at all. I didn't want her to get sick, or to end up as one of those people who have to lug an oxygen tank around. I used to beg her to quit, but she didn't even try. She was too addicted. Or too stubborn. Smoking was another one of her *simple pleasures*. So I'd given up on begging, but I silently worried. "She'll end up in trouble, if you know what I mean."

I knew, all right. Mom used to warn Evelyn about the same thing but it hadn't worked. Evelyn told our parents that she was "in trouble" during winter break of her senior year in high school. Then she took the GED, married Patrick before Easter, and gave birth to Kieran on a rainy June morning.

Later I sat in her old bedroom, which Mom had cleared out before we'd even finished eating Evelyn's leftover wedding cake. Now it was what Mom called my *studio,* the place where I sketched the faces of anyone who interested me. And I found them everywhere—in school, on the subway, at the supermarket. I only showed my drawings to Mom and my art teachers because nobody else understood. Mom noticed the details in an eye, the curve of a mouth. She believed that I had inherited her artistic gene, the one that drove her to write novels she never finished.

I could've been a writer, she sometimes said. *Or an editor at a publishing company in the city.* Then she'd look at me and smile, pretend it didn't matter, say that I was the best thing she ever created. And that I would have all the opportunities she never did.

I didn't expect an opportunity to arrive so soon. It happened after Mom and I came home from the barbecue and I went to sleep in my old canopy bed that was a hand-me-down from Evelyn. I woke to familiar noises downstairs—Dad's key in the front door, Mom's footsteps in the foyer, a midnight dinner frying on the stove.

They were talking as usual, but I didn't hear the normal words like *electric bill, plumber, that pain-in-the-ass neighbor blocked our driveway again.* Tonight it was something about a phone call and money, and Mom's voice was cheery but I wasn't sure why.

"Wait until the morning, Nancy," Dad said.

"But it's good news, Tom," Mom answered, and then she was in my room, telling me news that didn't sound good at all. "Uncle Eddie died," she said, and I saw Dad out in the hallway, Mom beside my bed, and Uncle Eddie in my mind. He was Dad's bachelor uncle who lived alone in a rent-controlled apartment.

"Oh," I said, remembering the many times I'd gone with Dad to check on Uncle Eddie. He was a kind old man who loved game shows and offered me chocolate from a Whitman's Sampler box. The thought of him watching *The Price Is Right* alone always made me sad. "That isn't good news, Mom."

My voice cracked. She pushed my long hair out of my face and glanced at Dad the way she did whenever my voice cracked. *Can you believe two tough cookies like us created such a delicate flower?* I once heard her say, and it was true, she and Dad were tough and I wasn't. But they had to be tough. Mom's parents had been alcoholics and not one of her four brothers had ever visited our house. Dad had been raised by a widowed mother who worked at a charity hospital to pay for the tiny apartment that she and Dad had shared, and he'd seen a lot of ugly things during his thirty years with the NYPD. *Kids are so spoiled these days,* he and Mom always said, and I didn't want them to say it about me. They thought that anyone who ate three meals every day and had two employed parents was spoiled.

"I know, Ariadne," Mom said, because she insisted on calling me by my full name. "But he did something nice for us. He left us his entire savings—a hundred thousand dollars. Now you can go to any college you want and we can send you to Hollister Prep in September."

I could go to any college I wanted and they were sending me to Hollister Prep in September. I wasn't sure how to tell Mom that I didn't want to go to Hollister. I knew I couldn't measure up to the girls there—girls like Summer who got sparkling report cards without opening a book and didn't leave the house if their shoes didn't match their purse. My current school wasn't great—my classmates seemed to think I was completely unremarkable—but it was nearby and at least the teachers liked me. So I hoped my parents would forget about Hollister.

I tried not to think about it when Mom and Dad were gone, when they were asleep in their bedroom down the hall and I couldn't possibly sleep. So I sat next to my window, studying the stars in the clear summer sky, shifting my thoughts to Uncle Eddie. I thought about him and his entire savings and the fact that he had nobody to leave it to except us.

two

There were more people at Uncle Eddie's wake than I expected, so that was good. Other than me and my parents, and Patrick and Evelyn and Kieran, there were a few neighbors from Uncle Eddie's building and an attractive older lady who whispered to Dad that she and Uncle Eddie used to be *special friends*.

Summer was there too. She came with her mother, who had stringy brown hair and always looked tired. She probably *was* tired, because she owned and operated a business called Catering by Tina. She made the food herself and loaded it into a white van that she drove to people's homes in all five boroughs. Sometimes Summer and I helped with the cooking and went with Tina to the parties, where we stayed in the kitchen and arranged stuffed mushrooms on fancy silver trays.

Now Summer sat next to me in a stylishly appropriate dress. I glanced at my own dress, which I'd hastily chosen from a clearance rack at Loehmann's. It was baggy and dull, but I hadn't been thinking about style when I bought it. I'd been thinking about Uncle Eddie, about the fact that he would be buried alone, not next to a wife or children or anyone that mattered. I wanted him to know that someone cared, so I wrote a note telling him how much I appreciated the hundred thousand dollars. I also mentioned that because of him I could afford to go to college at the Parsons School of Design in Manhattan, which had been my dream since I was twelve.

The note was in an envelope that I clutched between my sweaty fingers. I wanted to give it to Uncle Eddie, who was lying inside that box at the front of the room, but I couldn't. The idea of being near a dead person made my knees shake.

"What's that?" Summer asked, nodding toward the envelope.

I folded it in my lap and glanced at Uncle Eddie. "He left my family some money. I know I can't really thank him, but I wanted to, so I wrote this letter. . . ." I turned back to Summer. She was sitting with her legs crossed at the ankles, her dark eyes fixed on my face. "I'm being stupid. It's not like he can read it."

She gave me a smile. "You're not being stupid. I think you're being nice."

I smiled back. "I still can't go up there, though."

Summer uncrossed her ankles. "Why not?"

"Because he's dead. It scares me."

She threw her hair behind her shoulders. "Don't be afraid of the dead, Ari. They can't hurt you. It's the *living* you should worry about."

She had a good point. Uncle Eddie couldn't do anything to me. But I stayed where I was, bending the envelope until it was wrinkled and damp.

Summer took it out of my clammy hands. She squeezed my shoulder and whispered in my ear. "Do you want me to do it? I'm not afraid."

That didn't surprise me. Summer wasn't afraid to do anything. "*I* should do it," I said. But I stayed where I was, wishing I wasn't so cowardly.

Summer stood up and extended her hand. I remembered all the times she'd done that before. She'd done it at her sweet sixteen, when I'd hidden in her bathroom because I didn't have the guts to mingle with the crowd of Hollister students in the living room. Summer coaxed me out and stuck with me the whole night, telling everybody, *This is my best friend, Ari.* That had made me think I might not be so unremarkable.

"Come on," Summer said, looking from me to Uncle Eddie. "We'll do it together."

* * *

I didn't go home with Mom and Dad after the wake. Instead I climbed into the back of Patrick's black Ford truck. Mom thought I had spent too much time in my room over the last few days and needed a change of scenery.

An hour later, I was helping Evelyn unload the dishwasher in her dingy kitchen. The outdated appliances were bile green and the wallpaper could make you dizzy if you stared at it for too long. It was covered with orange flowers, big leaves, and metallic swirls that weaved between the petals. Patrick had started to remove the wallpaper once, but he never found the time to finish. He was always working, either at the firehouse or doing odd jobs on his days off for extra money. Installing tiles, landscaping, anything to pay the mortgage.

"Look what I got for you," Evelyn said.

She stuck a Mrs. Fields bag in my face. It was filled with my favorite chocolate chip cookies, so I knew that Evelyn was in one of her good moods today. I liked her much better this way, when she was sweet and thoughtful the way she used to be, and not cranky and mean like she'd become over the past few years. *Dirty diapers and a husband with a dangerous job can make anyone grouchy,* Mom said. *I warned her.*

The worst was after Kieran was born. Evelyn broke out in a nasty case of eczema, and she cried every day and yelled at Patrick constantly. Mom had to call Summer's father for advice—he was a psychiatrist. He'd said he believed Evelyn had postpartum depression, and he recommended we send her to New York–Presbyterian Hospital in Manhattan. We did, and she had stayed for two months.

Her treatment hadn't been covered by Patrick's health insurance. My parents had cashed some savings bonds to pay for the whole thing, and they'd agreed when Evelyn's doctors recommended that she stop having children. But Evelyn didn't listen to anyone, especially Mom and Dad. She used to fight with them all the time. They fought about her failing grades, her trampy clothes, and the bag of marijuana that Mom once found in Evelyn's room. And there was always the issue of her revolving-door boyfriends and the fact that she'd gone alone to a clinic at the age of fifteen to get a prescription for birth control pills.

The biggest fight came when she was seventeen and announced that she was pregnant. Dad's mouth shrank into a thin white line and Mom yelled loud enough for our neighbors to hear. She said that Patrick was uneducated and ignorant and low class, she couldn't stand his South Boston accent, and he was lucky that she didn't hire someone to break his legs.

I had feared for his safety, worrying that some barbarous thugs would bind him and gag him and leave him bleeding somewhere in Bed-Stuy. But Mom chose not to solicit any criminal activity, and she changed her tune after Patrick and Evelyn left for their Florida honeymoon. Mom and Dad whispered in the car as we drove home from LaGuardia Airport, talking about how they'd done everything they could and they'd given Evelyn a nice wedding, and then Mom laughed and said, *She's Patrick's problem now.*

I shot Mom a stern look when she said that, because I didn't think it was right for a mother to refer to her daughter as a problem. And I wasn't shocked when Evelyn told us about the second baby. Being a mother seemed to make her feel like she wasn't just a girl who got married too young and worked part-time as a cashier at Pathmark. Now she was a playgroup organizer, a soccer coach, the woman who'd written a scathing letter to Hasbro after Kieran almost choked on a plastic game piece. Of course there were also the incessant comments from every direction about how handsome Kieran was, how he was blessed with Patrick's coloring and Evelyn's exquisite features.

She was striking, even with the extra weight. I sat across from her on the patio that night, admiring the way the fading sunshine accented the copper highlights in her long wavy hair. She was happy now, and she smiled with straight white teeth, let out throaty laughs that jiggled her cleavage.

I heard her laughing again after the sun was gone and I was alone in the guest bedroom, which would soon become a nursery. Patrick was laughing too, and then their voices lowered and changed into murmurs and moans and their headboard smacked the wall. I hadn't been expecting that sort of thing tonight because Evelyn was more than seven months pregnant, but I'd been wrong. And it was impossible not to listen. They were so loud and Patrick's noises made my heart race. He sounded like those professional tennis players who grunt whenever they hit the ball really hard.

Maybe it was the noise that gave me a headache. Either that or it was punishment for enjoying the sound of my brother-in-law having what my classmates jokingly called an *organism,* but I was in too much pain to decide. I was at the start of a migraine that blurred the vision in my left eye and made me see freaky things. Auras, that was what my doctor said they were called. They came around whenever I was stressed or upset or exposed to loud noises. *Don't bottle up your emotions,* the doctor said. *They'll manifest themselves physically and turn into headaches.*

I didn't follow his advice. And my migraines always started out the same way, with a web of fluorescent purple light that pulsated and grew until my medication kicked in. Tonight my medication wasn't here. I had been so preoccupied with Uncle Eddie that I'd forgotten to pack it in my overnight bag.

So I went across the hall to the only bathroom in the house, where I searched through a cabinet for Tylenol. But all I found was Patrick's Drakkar Noir and the bottle of ipecac that Evelyn had bought when Kieran was younger. She'd shown me where it was just in case he swallowed something dangerous while I was babysitting. She also made me go with her to a class where I learned to perform CPR and to diagnose broken bones.

I could see clearly through only one eye, and the pain in my head was so bad that I kneeled beside the toilet, ready to throw up. When I was down there, I spotted a book on the floor called *Name Your Baby*. I flipped through it and noticed that Evelyn had circled some names, but only girls' names. She'd refused a sonogram but was positive that she had a daughter on the way.

The names, the letters, Evelyn's scribbles in bright blue ink, made me feel worse, and I left the book on the tiles before I stood up. There was no reason to stay down there because nothing was happening, not even one lousy gag. I headed into the kitchen to search for Tylenol.

"What's wrong?" Patrick said.

I turned around. Patrick stood in the kitchen doorway, shirtless, his pajama pants resting low on his waist, a gold Celtic cross dangling from a chain around his neck.

"I'm trying to find some aspirin," I said.

He raked his hair back with his fingers but it was useless. Patrick's hair was very straight and it always fell over his forehead in a silky flaxen wave. "You got one of those headaches again?" he asked, and I nodded. Then he told me to sit down, he would find the aspirin, the bottle was hidden on a top shelf where Kieran couldn't get into it.

I didn't sit down. I stood on the linoleum watching Patrick rummage through the cabinets. I watched because he had a broad chest. A six-pack stomach. I hoped he wouldn't catch me staring at him and he didn't. He found a bottle of Tylenol and pointed to the table.

"I told you to sit down," he said, which was typical. Patrick was bossy, and words like *please* and *thanks* rarely came out of his mouth. Mom said it was because Patrick came from a family of eight kids with parents who were probably too frazzled to teach their children any manners. But I always followed his orders because I knew he meant well. So I took a seat and he sat opposite me, pushing two pills and a glass of water across the table. Then he reached over and pressed his palm against my forehead. "Are you sure it's only a headache? You ain't got no fever?"

Fev-ah, he said. No, Patrick, I thought, shaking my head. I don't have a fever. You could use a few lessons in Mom's class, but I won't tell you that. I can't hurt your feelings because you're so gorgeous and your hand feels nice on my face, hard and soft at the same time.

"So what brought this on? Are you still devastated about the corpse?" he asked, and I gave him a disapproving look that made him laugh. "Oh, come on, Ari. The man was almost ninety years old."

I shrugged, studying the ice in my glass. Then I told him what I'd been thinking, about how sad it was that Uncle Eddie had died in that gloomy apartment, that he didn't have a wife or children and his neighbors in the cemetery were strangers.

"I'm afraid of that," I said. "Dying alone."

He laughed again. "How do you come up with this morbid shit? You shouldn't worry about dying. You're a young kid."

But I do worry about it, I thought. I'm not Evelyn. Boys don't ring the doorbell for me and they don't call on the phone. I might never have a husband like you or a son like Kieran, and it's really confusing because I'm not even sure if I'd want to be like Evelyn. I wouldn't want to get in trouble and disappoint Mom so much that she'd laugh when I was gone.

"Come on," Patrick said, standing up. "You need some sleep."

I stayed where I was, watching the ice melt. I didn't want to sleep. I just wanted to sit there and think. Then he clamped his hand around my elbow and marched me to the guest bedroom. I wouldn't have let anyone except Patrick do that. I was sure he meant well.

Dad picked me up two days later. It was a humid morning and my legs stuck to the leather seats in his car.

"How was your weekend?" I asked, and repeated myself when he didn't answer. Some sports program was on the radio and he lowered the volume.

"I worked," he said, and turned it up again.

Dad's eyes were blue like mine and his hair used to be just as dark but now it was totally gray. He was tall and he didn't talk much. Not to me, anyway. He was a distant father, in Mom's opinion. But she said that he was also a good father because he kept a roof over our heads and food on the table. And he worked hard, all the time; he could have retired a decade ago but he didn't because retirement would drive him crazy. He wasn't interested in traveling or golf or anything except solving homicides, so he had to keep working. At least, that was what Mom told me. I never knew what Dad was thinking.

He sped back to work after I got out of the car in front of our house. Mom was inside, slicing bagels at the kitchen counter. She turned around and rested her hands on her hips.

"You look very thin, Ariadne. Didn't Evelyn feed you this weekend?"

I should have expected that; Mom always said critical things about Evelyn. *Didn't Evelyn feed you? Evelyn lets Kieran eat too much junk. Evelyn's house is a pigsty.* I wished she wouldn't. Evelyn might not have been perfect, but she wasn't so bad. Whenever she got cantankerous and snapped at me, I tried to remember the sweet things she did—like choosing me to be the maid of honor at her wedding and letting me tag along with her and her friends to the bowling alley, even though I was only eight at the time and nobody wanted me there.

"Of course she did," I said, but Mom looked skeptical. She toasted a bagel, slathered it with cream cheese, and watched while I ate it.

I went upstairs afterward, where I closed the door and opened the window in my studio. It was a sunny day, and our next-door neighbors—the annoying ones who constantly blocked our driveway—were having a party. Balloons bounced from their mailbox at the curb and guests were double-parking their cars, carrying cases of beer to the front porch. I watched for a while, and then I sat at my easel, sketching a tree across the street. The leaves, the bark, the rays of sunlight peeking through the branches. It wasn't the best thing to draw, not as interesting as faces, but my art teacher had said that I should practice drawing everything.

An hour passed before I heard Mom's voice. I saw her standing on our lawn, talking to the lady next door. Mom was calm at first, saying "I would appreciate it" and something about our driveway and when I looked at the driveway, I saw a Trans Am parked there with a dented Buick behind it. Our neighbor raised her voice and shouted something rude and so did Mom.

"Get those fucking cars off my property or I'll call the cops," Mom said. "My husband's on the force—I can get someone over here in five minutes."

Then I heard our front door slam and pots banging around in the kitchen. None of this was unusual, because Mom was feisty. That was the word Dad always used to describe her.

I wouldn't have survived in my family otherwise, I heard her tell him once, but I didn't know exactly what she meant. Mom had only mentioned her parents a few times in my presence, using a tone typically reserved for talking about something distasteful, like diarrhea or Evelyn's eczema. Her parents were both gone now, dead for years, although her brothers were still around. One of them had called our house a while back and Mom had hung up on him. She'd told Dad that her brother was a drunk looking for a handout and she didn't believe in handouts. She was proud that she'd done everything on her own. Even her degrees had been financed by loans that had taken twenty years to repay.

"Ariadne," Mom said, startling me. "Didn't you hear the phone?"

I hadn't heard. Now I looked away from my drawing and toward Mom, who was standing in the doorway, smiling and speaking in a gentle voice. She could flip the switch so easily, just like Evelyn. One minute Mom was screaming the F-word at somebody who cut her off in traffic, and the next minute she sounded as demure as a librarian.

I shook my head and she walked into the room, stopping behind me to examine my tree. "That's extraordinary," she said. "I'm glad you took your teacher's advice about drawing everything. He knows what it takes to make it as an artist."

"Or as a teacher," I said, and Mom rolled her eyes because she didn't want me to be a teacher. She wanted me to have an exciting career, better than what she had, even though that idea made me nervous.

But the thought of teaching didn't make me nervous. I imagined teaching art as fun and quiet and far from judgmental eyes. If I tried to be a real artist, people might say I had no talent, and that would ruin everything. There would be no point in drawing anymore, and life would be pointless without drawing. I'd have no reason to memorize people's faces on the subway.

"Summer called," Mom went on, adding that Tina was catering a party tonight and she could use my help with the cooking if I was interested, which I wasn't. I wanted to stay in my room and draw another tree, but Mom thought I had practiced enough for today.

She drove me to Summer's house, where she talked to Tina on the front steps and I went inside. Summer was sitting at the dining room table, cutting strips of dough with a pastry wheel. There was flour on her face, and she blew her bangs out of her eyes.

"How's your stud brother-in-law?" she asked.

Gorgeous as always, I thought. I love it when he walks around the house without a shirt. That weight lifting he does in the basement must really work, because his shoulders are huge. But of course I can't tell you that, Summer. He's married to my only sister and it's sinful for me to think these things.

"He's fine," I said.

Summer handed me a rolling pin and a bag of walnuts. I sat down and crushed the nuts, noticing that she wasn't wearing any makeup and thinking she looked much younger this way, more like she did before she blossomed and cast a spell over everyone. Back then—before puberty and highlights and operations to fix her lazy left eye and to straighten her nose—she used to just blend in. Except during the holidays, when some kids picked on her because she had a Christmas wreath on her door and a Hanukkah menorah in her window. *Make up your mind,* they used to say, and I told them they were ignorant. I said that Summer's mother was Episcopalian and her father was Jewish, and Summer was going to pick her religion someday but for now she was both.

"Ari," she said. "I'm sorry for drooling over Patrick, but I'm dying without a boyfriend."

"*You're* dying?" I said.

She knew what I meant—that I'd never had a boyfriend in my entire life. She reached over and squeezed my arm, leaving a smear of flour on my skin. "You'll get one. Then you'll see how nice it is to make love."

She smiled dreamily and I kept hearing those last two words even when she was quiet and cutting dough. She didn't say *screwing* or *banging,* and she called a guy's you-know-what a *magic wand* instead of the four-letter words that everybody tossed around at school. But Summer was mature and smart, and she'd read most of her father's medical books in his library down the hall.

She wanted to be a psychiatrist too, and she already acted

the part. She'd explained to me years ago that schizophrenics hear voices and that kidnapping victims can develop Stockholm syndrome, and she once had a talk with a boy in our seventh-grade class who had a crush on her. He used to call her house just to hear her answer the phone, he wrote sappy poems, and we actually found him collecting strands of her hair from her jacket in the coatroom. So Summer sat him down and explained that he wasn't in love with her, that he only thought he was in love because he was suffering from something else—a psychological word that I quickly forgot. Whatever it was, she said it was similar to lust but much worse because it could get you so stuck on somebody that you'd simply lose your mind.

He didn't bother her anymore after that. Summer considered him her first cured patient and started talking about UCLA, her father's alma mater. But I didn't want her to talk about any colleges that weren't in New York. Summer had been my best friend since first grade, and the possibility that she would go so far away was depressing.

"Ari," Tina said later on, when Summer and I were chopping raw steak into cubes. She gave me a piece of paper with a name and telephone number on it and ran her hand across her forehead. Her hair was limp and she looked exhausted as usual. "Please give that to your mother. She needs the name of someone to contact at Hollister."

"Thanks, Tina," I said, and I wasn't being disrespectful. Summer's parents didn't want me to address them as Mrs. Simon and Dr. Simon. They'd told me years ago to call them Tina and Jeff. Mom rolled her eyes when she found out about it and mumbled that Tina and Jeff were *progressive*.

26

I folded the paper and stuck it in my pocket. I felt Summer staring at me. I'd told her about our inheritance and the Parsons School of Design, but I had never mentioned Hollister Prep.

"Are you going to Hollister?" Summer asked.

She looked nervous. I guessed she was worried that I might accidentally mention embarrassing things to her Hollister friends, things like her eye surgery and her nose job. They must have believed that she was born perfect.

"My mother wants me to," I said. I was still secretly hoping that Mom would forget the whole thing and let me finish my last two years in Brooklyn. But I rarely got what I wanted.

A month later, my parents and I went to Queens for a Saturday-afternoon lunch. Patrick was on duty and I was sleeping over, because Evelyn's due date was getting close and he didn't want her to be alone.

I sat on the couch as Evelyn bent solicitously over Dad, offering him one of those mini hot dog things wrapped in a flaky biscuit. She was wearing a summery maternity dress with a neck that was too low and a hem that was too high. More weight had crept onto her recently and I could see the dimples above her knees.

"Evelyn," Mom said from her seat next to me. "Did Ariadne tell you that she's going to Hollister Prep in September?"

By this point, Mom and I had talked about Hollister Prep. Yesterday I'd admitted that I was afraid. I was afraid of new surroundings and new people, and I was sure I wouldn't make any friends because I hardly had any friends now, but Mom insisted that this was completely irrelevant. In her opinion, I was an interesting, intelligent, fabulous person, and if people didn't recognize that, then they could just go and screw themselves. Besides, it was only for two years, and I had to agree when she said that Hollister would help my college chances. So I was going.

"No," Evelyn said, lowering herself into a chair. Her stomach was gigantic and her feet were too swollen for shoes. "She didn't. So how are you paying for that?"

"Oh," Mom said. "Uncle Eddie left us some money. Didn't I mention it?"

Mom knew that she hadn't mentioned it. We all knew that she hadn't mentioned it. And I could almost hear what my sister was thinking: *Uncle Eddie left you some money, you're sending Ari to an expensive school, how much will that cost, and where's mine?*

That wasn't fair. Mom and Dad had given Evelyn lots of things, like a wedding and a two-month stay at New York–Presbyterian. But she could be very selfish sometimes.

"Well, that's nice," she said in the same bland voice she used lately whenever anything good happened to me, like when I entered a boroughwide art contest last year and won a second-place ribbon. I didn't know why she had to be that way, because I was always happy when good things happened to her. I'd been happy when she married Patrick, even though I'd wished he would marry me.

Evelyn changed the subject by bringing us upstairs to the guest bedroom. It was a nursery now, with walls painted a color called Valentine Rose.

"Sort of loud, isn't it?" Mom said.

Evelyn shrugged. "It's pink. Pink is nice for a girl."

"Yes," Mom laughed. "But you don't know if you're having a girl, sweetheart."

Evelyn's skin suddenly matched the walls and her expression was one I'd seen many times when she lived with us in Brooklyn. It was as if she was about to dissolve into tears or commit a fatal stabbing.

"Evelyn," Dad said. "Is lunch almost ready? I can't wait to eat your tuna casserole."

Tuna casserole was one of her specialties—along with meat loaf and sloppy joes.

Evelyn turned toward Dad. "It has potato chips on top," she said, giving him a faint smile. "Just the way you like it."

We had her tuna casserole for lunch, with her no-bake cheesecake for dessert, and after my parents went home, I washed dishes in the kitchen. Evelyn fell asleep on the couch, and Kieran asked if he could play in the backyard.

I nodded and changed into shorts and a bikini top. After that I sat on a folding chair while Kieran ran across the grass and dove on his Slip 'n Slide as if it was the most fantastic thing ever. It made me wonder who had come up with that brilliant idea—convincing kids that it was fun to skid across a slimy sheet of plastic on the hard ground.

The sun was fading when Evelyn joined us. She carried a bag of Doritos and dragged a chair next to mine.

"Do you know how much weight I've gained from this baby?" she asked, and I shook my head. "Well, I won't tell you because it's too embarrassing. I've turned into a big fat cow."

"Don't say that, Evelyn. You always look beautiful."

She snorted. "You're such a fucking liar, Ari. I mean . . . if you asked what I thought . . . I'd tell you that you've got a good body but your boobs are small and uneven."

What had happened to the sweet Evelyn? I knew that my breasts were small, but they were uneven, too? I looked down at my bikini top and she nodded toward my right breast.

"*That* one," she said. "It's a little smaller than the other side. I can't see it much in normal clothes, but it's obvious in a bathing suit. You should stuff your bra with tissues or whatever."

Later on, when Evelyn and Kieran were asleep, I stood at the bathroom mirror putting Kleenex in and pulling Kleenex out, and after an hour I decided that Evelyn was right. My right breast really was smaller than the left. This was especially upsetting because my list of flaws was long enough already.

There wasn't anything horribly wrong with me, like a receding chin or an oversized nose. My chin was strong and my nose was small and straight. I didn't even have any acne problems. But my face was kind of gaunt and pale, and one of my front teeth slightly overlapped the other. I had thick eyebrows that I had to tweeze relentlessly. Standing in front of a mirror, examining my reflection and criticizing myself, was something I spent a lot of time doing. My latest torture session, however, was cut short by Evelyn's voice outside the door. Her water had broken early and the contractions were starting.

* * *

Sweet Evelyn emerged again on the way to the hospital. We'd had to wake up Kieran and leave him with one of Evelyn's neighbor friends. We also had to take a cab because I didn't drive yet and we couldn't reach Patrick. I'd called the firehouse and was informed that he was out. *Explosion in a high-rise,* the guy on the phone had said.

I left a message and lied to Evelyn. "It's just a grease fire in somebody's kitchen." She worried about Patrick enough; she didn't need to be worrying then, when she was in pain and clutching my hand.

I also called Mom and Dad, who met us at the hospital. Evelyn was being wheeled from the emergency room when she started talking about Lamaze, saying she needed Patrick for that, and Mom offered to take his place.

"No," Evelyn said. "Ari can come but nobody else."

This made me happy and sad at the same time. It was nice to be needed, to be part of Evelyn's inner circle—and I loved her for wanting me there—but I didn't enjoy leaving our mother out. Mom and Evelyn were very skilled at leaving each other out. *We have nothing in common,* Mom often said. *Evelyn has never finished a book in her entire life.*

Now Mom mumbled something that sounded like *Don't let me intrude,* but I wasn't sure. I was following behind Evelyn and a nurse, and we were getting too far away to hear.

We went to a room on the fifth floor that reeked of Lysol. I looked the other way while Evelyn undressed and slipped into a flimsy gown. Next there was a doctor and a needle that went into Evelyn's spine. That made me cringe and she got quiet. She drifted in and out of sleep while I watched television—a news reporter talking about the explosion in the high-rise—but Evelyn didn't notice. She was too busy with the doctor, who kept snapping on latex gloves, sticking his hands underneath her gown, and talking about centimeters.

I wished he wouldn't. It was all so stark and mechanical. How could soft moans behind a bedroom wall possibly result in needles and stirrups and K-Y Jelly? Even though I was still flattered to be a member of Evelyn's private club, I kept hoping that Patrick would show up before I had to help with that Lamaze business.

Luckily, he did. He dragged the scent of ashes with him and I read his jacket as he leaned over Evelyn's bed. CAGNEY. FDNY. ENGINE 258. He was kissing her cheek when he got yelled at by a nurse who ordered him to take a shower in an empty room next door and change into sanitary scrubs. I followed him to the hall and he laughed at me.

"Gross enough for you?" he asked as I studied the smears of dirt on his face. His hair dangled over his forehead and his firefighter clothes made him huge. The big black jacket with the horizontal yellow stripes, the matching pants, the thick boots. "I told your parents I'd send you back downstairs. And I'm warning you . . . Nancy seems pissed off."

So did Evelyn the next day, when my parents and I stopped by in the late afternoon. We'd stayed at the hospital until Evelyn gave birth, and we were so exhausted afterward that we slept until noon. Evelyn was exhausted too. Her labor had been long, she'd lost a lot of blood, and she was in a cranky mood.

"Here," she said, shoving the baby at a nurse. "I'm tired."

The baby wasn't a girl. He was a healthy boy with blond hair, a pink bedroom, and no name. Evelyn never even looked at the second half of the *Name Your Baby* book. Now she folded her arms across her chest, stared at *Days of Our Lives,* and didn't say goodbye when our parents left to get some coffee.

"Look, Evelyn," I said, lifting an elaborately wrapped box from Summer. There was a pair of baby pajamas inside, but they didn't make Evelyn feel better.

"This is for a girl," she said. "I didn't get a girl."

"It's yellow. Yellow is for a boy, too."

"Yellow is for faggots," she said, tossing the pajamas toward her night table.

They fell to the floor and I picked them up, thinking that she was being rude and ungrateful, because Summer had spent a lot of time wrapping that gift. I knew she was disappointed, that she'd wanted a daughter to dress in Easter bonnets, to sit side by side with at the beauty salon and share secrets. She probably wanted a do-over for all the fun things that didn't happen between her and Mom. But I was worried, too. She hadn't looked this miserable since Kieran was born.

three

When Evelyn had been at New York–Presbyterian Hospital five years earlier, Mom had moved into her house. She'd taken care of Kieran while Patrick was at work, and she'd taught me how to hold a baby's head and how to change a diaper and the best type of formula to buy.

Now I took Mom's place, because she'd caught a stomach virus and Evelyn was still in the hospital. We weren't sure if it was because of all the blood she'd lost or if the doctors thought she was getting crazy again, and Evelyn wouldn't tell us. We only knew that there was a new baby in the family and Patrick couldn't miss work. He had two children and a thirty-year mortgage with a ten percent interest rate, after all. And his family couldn't help. They were in Boston and his mother had little kids at home. Patrick was the oldest; his youngest brother was in the third grade.

So the baby was my responsibility. His name was Shane, only because he couldn't leave the hospital until Evelyn came up with something to put on the birth certificate. She'd gotten the name from a soap opera and I wasn't sure she even liked it.

I held my nephew on a warm afternoon in his nursery, which wouldn't be pink for long. Patrick had already bought two gallons of blue paint because we couldn't let Evelyn come home to a reminder that she didn't get a girl.

Patrick joined me in the nursery that evening, freshly showered after a rough day at the firehouse. He settled into a rocking chair to feed Shane, while I stood there thinking that he was a good father. Not a distant one, either. Patrick changed diapers, and he knew to be careful of the soft spot on a baby's head. He also spent tons of time teaching Kieran how to throw a football and watching televised Red Sox games with him, which Dad didn't appreciate. He was horrified that his grandson was being raised to hate the Yankees and the Jets. It was blasphemy, in Dad's opinion. Brainwashing, too.

"You're doing a good job, little sistah," Patrick said. He also told me that I should take a break and go to the public pool with Kieran.

"I'll just stay for an hour," I said. "Then I'll make dinner."

Patrick rubbed Shane's cheek with his thumb. "I can't wait."

He loved my dinners. The night before, I'd made pork roast and broccoli with hollandaise sauce. The night before that it was stuffed peppers and zucchini in peppercorn vinaigrette. I took the recipes from a cookbook I'd found under the kitchen sink. Someone had given it to Evelyn as a Christmas gift and it was still wrapped in plastic.

Tonight we were having southwestern burgers and twice-baked potatoes, but Patrick didn't know that. I kept the menu a surprise. Then I changed into my bikini in the bathroom. I slipped a pair of denim cutoffs over it and stared at myself in the mirror, stuffing the right side of my top with tissues. But it didn't look realistic and I could just imagine the humiliation of Kleenex floating in the crowded pool if I decided to swim. Kieran banged on the door after a few minutes, and I pulled a T-shirt over my head to hide my deformity.

I kept the shirt on at the pool, where I sat on the edge and soaked my feet while Kieran played with his friends in the shallow end. I had only been here a few times before, but Evelyn was a fixture from Memorial Day to Labor Day. She and her friends spent each summer gossiping and chomping on the salty Goldfish crackers that were supposed to be for their children.

"Are you Evelyn Cagney's sister?" a voice asked.

I looked up and nodded. A vaguely familiar woman was standing there; I recognized the excessive eye makeup and the clear braces on her teeth. Angie, Lisa, Jennifer, what was her name again? It had to be one of these, because almost every woman who lived in Queens and was between the ages of twenty and forty was named Angie, Lisa, or Jennifer.

"So how is everything?" she said. "I heard that Evelyn's having problems."

And I heard that you took a crap on the table when you were squeezing out your fourth baby, I thought. Then I looked at the other end of the pool, where Kieran was splashing around with his friends, whose mothers were talking and glancing at me. They all knew about Evelyn's first meltdown and were probably dying for another one. The phone lines must have been sizzling with discussion of poor Evelyn Cagney and her pathetic relapse.

"No," I said. "That's not true. Evelyn's fine."

"But I heard she's still in the hospital."

"Only because she had some complications with the delivery," I said, which might have been the truth.

She nodded and changed the subject. "You know, I can't believe you're Evelyn's sister. You don't look anything alike."

Insult. For sure. Whether it was directed at me or Evelyn, I didn't know. She could have meant that my face wasn't as pretty as my sister's—that my top lip didn't have a Cupid's bow and there wasn't a natural arch in my eyebrows. Or she could have meant that Evelyn couldn't possibly fit into size-four shorts.

"Well," she said. "It was nice talking to you. I really have to go and pee."

I really have to go and pee. I hated when grown women said that. They all did, though. All my sister's so-called friends who were waiting for Kieran to leave so they could rip Evelyn to shreds. They were no different from those hyenas on PBS nature shows—standing in a circle, tearing a carcass apart. I could almost see fresh blood dripping from their chins. And I thought it was sad that some women were still as mean as they'd been in high school. This was their new clique, the housewives who just loved it when one of them couldn't measure up and got cut from the team.

Evelyn called from the hospital that night to say she was coming home in two days. I wanted everything to be perfect, so I stayed up late even though Patrick told me not to. He didn't want me to knock myself out, but I did anyway. I scrubbed the bathtub and cleaned out the hall closet. It was filled with cobwebs and shredded wrapping paper that had been there since Evelyn's first baby shower.

The next morning, Patrick refused to let me help him paint the nursery. "Just take it easy," he said. "You've been killing yourself."

I didn't take it easy. He painted and listened to the radio while I changed the contact paper inside the kitchen cabinets and rearranged the dishes. I was almost finished when Summer rang the doorbell. I answered it in my cutoffs and a shabby shirt. I was completely disheveled, but of course Summer wasn't. She'd taken the subway to Queens after an appointment at a ritzy hair salon in Manhattan and she looked fantastic.

"You look pretty," I made myself say as we walked into the kitchen.

She thanked me and stood on her tiptoes to peer into a cabinet. "It's so neat around here. I bet Evelyn will be happy when she gets back."

"I did a lot of work," I said. "I hope she'll like it."

"Well, she *ought* to. She doesn't know how lucky she is to have a sister like you."

I smiled. "You can watch TV if you want. I'll be finished with the cabinets soon."

She settled into the couch in the living room and turned on *General Hospital*, but she didn't watch it for long. Ten minutes later I found her standing in Shane's nursery, leaning against his crib, twisting a lock of newly highlighted hair around her finger.

She was talking to Patrick. Flirting with him, the way she did with every attractive man who crossed her path. She seemed to think she had to do this to find out if she really was beautiful, or if she was still that mousy girl with the lazy eye and the crooked nose.

I was used to her flirting, but not when it came to Patrick. She rarely saw him, and when she did, Evelyn was always around. Now Evelyn was in the hospital and Summer was wearing a short skirt. She kept sliding her foot out of her sandal and rubbing her heel against her calf. She reminded me of a hooker I'd once seen on Thirty-fourth Street in Manhattan.

Patrick was painting the closet door. Painting and talking but not flirting. Then he noticed that the knob was loose and he turned toward me. "Go get my toolbox," he said.

"'Go get my toolbox,'" Summer repeated. "Don't you know how to say *please*?"

He looked at her, his hair dripping over his forehead, his sleeves rolled to his shoulders. "This is my house. I don't say please to nobody here."

"Well," she said. "Somebody needs to teach you some manners, young man."

Unbelievable. Shameless. I saw her staring at Patrick's arms and it made me sick. She was so nervy to flirt with my sister's husband—in my sister's house—right in front of me and Evelyn's baby! At least I tried to hide my stares. But her comment made Patrick laugh, which annoyed me even more. I stood still until he reminded me about the toolbox, and I rushed to get it from the garage because I didn't want them to be alone for long.

"Can I touch your tools?" Summer asked after I came back and Patrick was rummaging through the box in search of a screwdriver. "I'll bet you've got some really big tools."

He nodded toward the door. "I'm busy, kid. Go play."

She smirked. "Will you play with me, Patrick? Or should I play with myself?"

The radio was still on. A screeching guitar, pounding drums, Eric Clapton. Patrick shook his head and went back to the doorknob, and Summer followed me to the living room. We sat on the couch and I gave her the cold shoulder.

"What's wrong?" she asked.

I spoke in a harsh whisper. "He's my sister's husband. Leave him alone."

She sank into the couch as if I'd hurt her feelings. "I didn't mean anything by it, Ari. It was nothing."

Later on, after Summer left and Patrick and I were cleaning up from dinner, I found out that he didn't think it was nothing. "Your friend is wicked bold for a high school girl," he said as I organized dirty glasses in the dishwasher.

She was *wicked bold.* He didn't approve of her. I loved that. "Do you think she's pretty?" I asked, staring down at the glasses, bracing myself for his answer.

"She's fake," he said. "Bleached hair and shit. And don't you get influenced."

I looked up. "What are you talking about?"

He dried his hands on a towel. He had big hands. *You know what they say about men with big hands,* Summer had told me repeatedly.

"She's not a nice girl. But you are. So stay that way."

"She's a nice girl," I said automatically, because I was so used to defending her. She always gave people the wrong idea. A girl in her neighborhood even called her a dumb blonde to her face. Summer and I laughed at that because we knew better. Tina and Jeff had her tested once and found out that she had a very high IQ.

Patrick raised an eyebrow. "You know what I mean, Ari."

I knew what he meant. I nodded and he left the towel hanging from the sink, all wrinkled and lopsided. I straightened it when he went into the living room to watch the Red Sox with Kieran, thinking that he loved my cooking and he said I was a nice girl, and if he wasn't my brother-in-law I would have kissed him. I was sure *he* wouldn't say that I opened my mouth too wide.

Later that night, I went to the basement with a basket of laundry. The basement was unfinished, with a concrete floor and two tiny windows. A washer and dryer stood against a wall and Patrick's barbells were lined up across the room. He was there now, on his back, bench-pressing God only knew how many pounds as I dropped stained bibs into the washing machine. I did everything slowly because I didn't want to go back upstairs. It was nicer here, with the smell of fabric softener and the sound of Patrick grunting and groaning.

I was filling a plastic cap with Tide when he finished. He stood up, took off his shirt, and used it to wipe his sweaty face. He threw it at me as he walked toward the stairs.

"Toss that in," he said.

"I'm not your maid," I answered, even though I didn't mind being his maid.

When he was gone, I looked at the shirt. It was navy blue with FDNY printed across the front in white letters, and it smelled of him—of beer and charcoal and cologne. The smell made me want to keep it, so I smuggled it into my overnight bag before tucking Kieran into bed. I adjusted his pillows and he mumbled something that I couldn't understand.

"What was that, Kieran?" I asked, sitting on his New England Patriots sheets. Brainwashed, I thought, hearing Dad's voice. Blasphemy.

"You're better than Mommy," he said with a sleepy smile, and I felt good for a second. He probably noticed that I was a more talented cook than Evelyn and that I never yelled at him the way she did. *You have no idea what you're talking about,* she'd said last year when I asked her not to raise her voice because it could hurt Kieran's self-esteem. *All you know is what you see on* Phil Donahue.

But the smug feeling quickly changed into guilt. "I'm not

better than your mommy," I said. "I'm just different. So don't say that to her because it would make her sad. Understand?"

He nodded and I was worried that he didn't understand. But he fell asleep before I could be sure.

The next morning, Kieran went with Patrick to pick up Evelyn at the hospital. I hung a new set of curtains on the kitchen window while dressed in my cutoffs and a sleeveless blouse that I knotted under my chest, and I didn't have time to change before everybody came back.

"You could've asked me," Evelyn said, about the curtains and the cabinets and everything else.

We were standing in the kitchen with Patrick and she didn't look good—there was a bumpy rash on her chin and her hair had frizzed in the humidity on the way home.

"Sorry," I said, disappointed that she wasn't grateful. "I was just trying to help."

She scratched her chin. "There's a difference between helping and taking over. This is *my* house, not yours."

"No kidding," I said.

"Ari," Patrick said in a warning tone that shut me up and annoyed me. I hated when he took Evelyn's side over mine, but of course he did—she was his wife, she'd just given birth to his baby. I assumed she was rightfully exhausted and grumpy, so I offered to take Kieran to the park.

When we came back, Patrick was gone. He was at a landscaping job in Manhasset with one of his firefighter friends. Kieran went to the backyard to play on his Slip 'n Slide, while

Evelyn stood by the stove boiling noodles for a tuna casserole.

"Need some help?" I asked, lingering in the doorway.

"What are you *wearing*?" she said.

I was still in my knotted-up shirt and my shorts, and she stared at my bare stomach and legs like I was a stripper on a pole. She seemed to forget about the skimpy things she used to wear when she could fit into skimpy things. But she made me so uncomfortable that I untied the shirt and let it fall over my hips.

"Nothing," I said. "Just . . ."

"What are you trying to do?" she asked, stirring noodles with a wooden spoon as steam rose into her face. "Get Patrick's attention?"

She turned away and laughed to herself, as if I was incapable of getting Patrick's attention. Or any man's attention. It made me so angry and embarrassed that I couldn't keep my mouth shut anymore.

"I don't want Patrick's attention," I lied.

Evelyn laughed again. She kept her back to me as she lifted the pot from the stove and dumped noodles into a strainer in the sink. "Yeah, sure. You used to climb on his lap whenever you got the chance."

Why did she have to bring that up? And it wasn't whenever I got the chance, it was just once, and I was only ten years old. Patrick had been dating Evelyn then, and he'd been sitting in our living room while she and Mom cooked dinner and I read a comic book on the floor.

He was on the couch watching TV, and I kept glancing

over my shoulder at his light hair and dark eyes. He didn't notice me, but I wanted him to. I had such a crush on him, even back then. So I jumped up on his knee with the comic book as if my only intention was to read him a particularly funny page, and Evelyn got aggravated after she came out of the kitchen. She told me to get lost, to leave Patrick alone, but he said he didn't mind, he had three younger sisters in Boston and they always sat on his lap. Then she charged into the kitchen and returned with Mom, who also told me to get lost. *Don't hang on him, Ariadne,* she'd said. *You're much too old for that.*

I didn't want to get into this now, so I set the table while Evelyn diced an onion that made my eyes water. She didn't say a word until I was finished, when I sat down with a magazine and she stuck the casserole into the oven.

"Mom is picking you up right after dinner . . . isn't she, Ari?"

She just couldn't wait. She acted like I was nothing but a pesky mosquito buzzing around her head. After a few seconds, she suggested that I go and watch TV. She was trying to cook for her family, if I didn't mind.

Her family. And what exactly was I? Who had taken care of her kids while she was gone? Was she ever planning to thank me? Oh, and by the way, Evelyn, those friends of yours at the pool aren't really your friends. I defended you to that dingbat with the braces on her teeth.

But I didn't want to tangle with Evelyn—she was too dangerous when she was like this—so I kept quiet in the living room until dinner, when Patrick came home. I sat across from

Kieran, who spit a mouthful of casserole into his napkin and griped that the noodles were too soggy.

Evelyn went to the refrigerator. "What do you want? I'll make a sandwich."

"No," Patrick said. He was sunburned and his eyes were bloodshot. "Kieran can eat what's given to him or he can go to bed hungry tonight."

She slammed a jar of mustard on the counter. "Just because you were raised that ignorant way doesn't mean I'm doing the same thing to my son."

A vein throbbed in Patrick's neck and I knew why. He was tired, his muscles were sore from mowing lawns, and things had been a lot more pleasant around here before Evelyn came back.

She gave Kieran his sandwich and it kept him quiet until dessert was served. It was another no-bake cheesecake, and according to the box, it was supposed to be *delicious* and *delightful*. Kieran didn't agree and he complained again.

"This is disgusting," he said, singing the last word. "Disgusting, disgusting, disgusting . . ."

Evelyn stared at him from her seat, and I wished Kieran would cut it out. The cake was fine; he was acting like a brat. Maybe I had spoiled him when she was away. Maybe if I'd raised my voice once in a while, he wouldn't be saying that same word over and over and Evelyn wouldn't have tears in her eyes.

Patrick must have been thinking the same thing. His voice was stern when he told Kieran to eat his dessert and stop being a pest, but Kieran didn't stop. He smashed his fork against the cake, turned it over, and left a mess on his plate.

"This is gross," he said. "How about a Twinkie?"

Patrick made a fist. "How about this?"

I knew Patrick would never touch him, but Kieran didn't, and he was stunned. Then he sat and sulked until he decided to hurt someone.

"What's on your face, Mommy?" he asked.

She lifted her hand to her chin. "It's eczema, Kieran. Just a rash."

"It's ugly," he said. "Ugly like you."

Evelyn's skin reddened and Patrick got furious. He ordered Kieran to his room, it didn't matter that another Red Sox game was on tonight, and was he planning to play on that Slip 'n Slide thing after dinner? Forget about it. It was going back into the garage until next summer.

Kieran slammed his bedroom door upstairs and the noise woke Shane. I heard him crying and Evelyn joined him. Tears spilled from her eyes, striping her cheeks with mascara. Patrick tried to talk to her but she wouldn't listen, so he followed her to the counter, where she turned her back, cried into her hands, and shoved him away.

"Go fuck your mother," she said.

Patrick just sighed because he knew what was going on. Her hormones were a mess and she couldn't be blamed for anything that came out of her mouth. Then he reached out to touch her but she wasn't done yet. She shoved him again, narrowing her eyes into an evil squint.

"That's what your mother likes, right? Pushing out eight

kids, getting knocked up at forty-four. Stupid Irish immigrant. Doesn't believe in birth control. She can't keep her scrawny legs shut."

Evelyn's hands were on her hips. Her body shook and this time she didn't shove Patrick away. He put his arms around her, ran his fingers through her hair, and I just sat there.

I wasn't angry with my sister anymore. Now she didn't seem mean and dangerous—she just seemed young and overwhelmed. I'm sorry, Evelyn, I thought, listening to her cry into Patrick's shirt. I'm sorry that you had a hard labor and you didn't get a girl. And I know I shouldn't feel the way I do about your husband, but I just can't help it.

four

Right before school started, Summer stepped on a rusty nail in her front yard. The cut required seven stitches and a tetanus shot. She could get around on crutches but she didn't want to. She refused to be seen in public because she had a bandage on her foot and she couldn't fit into her Gucci shoes.

She was excused from school for a week, which was bad luck for me because Summer was the only person I knew at Hollister. Before her accident, she'd assured me that she would show me around and sit with me at lunch. Now I had to go to a new school all alone.

"It'll be okay," Summer said over the phone.

It was the night before the first day of school. I leaned against my kitchen counter, wrapping the phone cord around my wrist, watching it make white crinkles in my skin. "I don't think so, Summer. I don't even want to go."

"Of course you do. It's one of the best schools in the city, and it'll help get you into Parsons."

"What if I can't keep up with the work?" I asked, sighing and loosening the phone cord.

"Ari," she said calmly, the way she often did when I was nervous. "You'll do well, as usual. I know you'll be fine."

If Summer knew I'd be fine, I supposed I shouldn't worry so much. I relaxed a little, but the next morning I still wished she was around. On top of everything else I needed from her, I also wanted her fashion advice, because I couldn't count on Mom to validate my outfit. Mom said the teal shell looked fine under the black blazer and of course it was okay to wear white pants because it was still almost ninety degrees outside, but that didn't help because what Mom knew about fashion couldn't fill a thimble. And Hollister had a strict dress code. According to the student handbook, there were to be no sneakers and no jeans, not even a denim jacket. *Violators will be penalized,* I read. I didn't want to be penalized, especially not on the first day.

"Your ride is here," Mom said, and I saw a silver Mercedes parked outside our house. It belonged to Jeff Simon, who drove Summer to school every day because his office was just a few blocks from Hollister. Now he was my chauffeur too, even without Summer.

Jeff's car smelled of cigars. He was a tall fiftyish man with hair a mix of blond and gray and eyes the color of weak tea. He always spoke to me and Summer like we were his intellectual equals.

"How's Evelyn?" he asked as I sat beside him.

"She's okay," I said, although I wasn't really sure. Some days she seemed fine and other days my parents talked about spending some of Uncle Eddie's money to send her back to New York–Presbyterian Hospital.

Jeff nodded. "She's not symptomatic?"

Symptomatic. He had used that word five years earlier. *Is Evelyn symptomatic, is she displaying a flat affect?* I shrugged and he tuned the radio to a classical music station. Then we were on the bridge and I saw the skyline in the distance, below a smear of purple and orange across the early-morning sky.

"A new environment is always unsettling," Jeff said after we reached Hollister Prep and I was wringing my hands while watching a swarm of smartly dressed students file into the building. "Your mood will level out after you get used to it."

I was hoping Jeff was right when I reached homeroom, which was crowded, noisy, jammed with people who knew everyone but me. I sat in a chair against the wall, taking everybody in, sure that I wouldn't talk to anyone but that I'd definitely draw them later. The guy with his arm in a cast, a girl whose sunburned skin was peeling from her cheeks.

I leaned my head back and squeezed my eyes shut. I hadn't slept much the night before; the only thing that had helped was Patrick's shirt. I kept it hidden in my closet beneath a stack of winter scarves, where Mom wouldn't dust or snoop. I told myself that I hadn't stolen it—I had just borrowed it for a while, and nobody would notice because Patrick owned so many of those shirts. I needed it more than he did, anyway. I wore it in bed whenever I had a headache or trouble sleeping, and the smell of it relaxed me like a long hot bath.

"Damn," I heard somebody say, and I turned around to find a redhead searching through a handbag. She looked up and I saw hazel eyes, a small nose, lots of freckles, and no makeup. "Do you have any tampons?" she asked in a raspy voice. "Or some Stayfree? I'm a week early."

There were some Stayfree in my purse from last month, but now the teacher was here and she was taking attendance and I couldn't pull out a maxi pad in full view of the three guys sitting next to me. So I passed her my purse and said she could bring it to the bathroom, she would find what she needed in the left pocket.

She was Leigh Ellis. I found this out when she came back and the teacher called her name. Then the teacher said my full first name in a loud voice and I waited for stares, laughter, all the things I was used to, but nothing happened. There was just silence until I spoke up.

"It's Ari," I said.

"Why do you shorten it?" Leigh whispered in my ear, and I wondered if she had a sore throat. She sounded like she was on the verge of laryngitis.

I twisted around. She was leaning forward, resting her face on her hand. I noticed a widow's peak, a pointy chin, and tiny gold flecks in her irises.

"Why do you shorten your name? It's very pretty," she said, smiling with straight teeth, and I decided that I liked her. There was no way I couldn't. She was the first person besides Mom to say anything positive about my name in all my sixteen years. "It's the title of a book, you know. By Chekhov."

Now I liked her even better. Soon the bell rang and she was off, gliding solo down the hallway past rows of lockers. I walked past girls dressed in tailored pants, crisp blouses, antique earrings made of rubies and sapphires and pearls. Their eyelashes had only a little mascara; their lips, just a touch of gloss. There was nothing reminiscent of my school in Brooklyn—couples kissing against walls, big hair sprayed high and stiff with Aqua Net, Madonna wannabes. No fingerless gloves, no lace ribbon. Not one bustier.

I glanced down at my clothes as I walked into my next class. It was English literature, and I fit in. My light makeup, my straight hair—I was one of them, and that almost made me cry. I had never belonged at my other school, where I was ignored and dismissed as a dull, quiet girl who sat in the back of class and sketched faces in notebooks.

But I couldn't transform into one of those confident types that easily. So on my first day at Hollister Prep, I sat in the rear of each class. I ate my salami sandwich in a bathroom stall while everyone else socialized in the cafeteria. In art class I watched from five seats behind Leigh Ellis as her colored pencils moved across a sketch pad. She was drawing something abstract. It wasn't what the teacher had ordered us to do, but it was good, and more interesting than the bowl of fruit the rest of the class was copying.

I watched Leigh's freckled fingers clutch her pencils, her silver bracelet skim the paper, her thick red hair swish across her collar whenever she shifted her head. She caught me looking at her and I pretended that I wasn't, but I didn't have to pretend. She smiled, waved, pointed to herself and mouthed the word *homeroom,* as if there was any way she could be forgotten.

Jeff was a one-way chauffeur. He drove Summer to school and then she took the subway home, which I did that first day. It wasn't very crowded at four in the afternoon, but the station was warm and so was I. My skin was clammy underneath my blazer after I reached Brooklyn and walked up the steps into the sunshine and sticky air. There were people everywhere, going in and coming out of Asian food markets and Indian restaurants, speeding around on bicycles and honking horns at anyone who got in their way.

"Ariadne," I heard Mom say.

She was standing in front of me. Her hair frizzed as badly as Evelyn's in this weather, and there were dots of perspiration above her lip. She said something about waiting for me, she'd called my name three times, hadn't I heard her, and was I getting delirious from this hot weather?

I hadn't heard her. I'd been thinking that I'd chosen the right outfit that morning and my hair wasn't wrong, and nobody at Hollister had said a single thing that made me want to lock myself in my bedroom and spend the rest of my life there.

"So how was it?" Mom asked, holding her breath. She was probably hoping for something good but expecting something bad. She was more familiar with something bad, like when Summer was voted Prettiest Girl in junior high and I wasn't voted anything.

I heard Mom exhale as we were walking home and I finished telling her about Hollister. I mentioned how much I liked the fancy iron gates outside the school and the girl from my homeroom with artistic ability and knowledge of Chekhov.

Mom was happy. She smiled, put her arm around me, and gave me a squeeze as we stood at the curb and waited for a traffic light to change. She was wearing a tank top, but she shouldn't have been because her upper arms were heavy.

She and Evelyn had the same build. Now I imagined my sister at thirty, aged beyond her years, her beautiful face distorted by too many no-bake cheesecakes the way Mom's face was puffy from Hostess cupcakes. I saw Evelyn wearing a sleeveless housedress, flabby arms swaying as she washed dishes over her kitchen sink, but I didn't mention that. My first day at Hollister had gone well and Mom was taking me out for Chinese food to celebrate. I didn't need any gloomy thoughts banging around inside my head; they haunted me enough as it was. This time I refused to listen.

Leigh wasn't in homeroom the next morning. I worried that she'd never come back, that she'd moved away or transferred to a different school, which would be just my luck.

And I wished Summer hadn't stepped on that nail. I wished she'd come to school on crutches and sit with me in the cafeteria. Because if she did, I wouldn't have to eat lunch in the bathroom while thinking that Hollister wasn't so great after all. It seemed big and scary. Maybe I should have stayed in Brooklyn, where I'd spent my lunch breaks in the art room. The teacher had let me organize her supplies, and I wanted to be there, alone with brushes and paint, eating at a clean desk. Now I was eating on a dirty toilet. So I trudged through the rest of the day and barely noticed when a swish of red hair flew past at the beginning of art class.

"Hey," Leigh said, taking a seat behind me. She was in violation of the rules, dressed in jeans, Converse high-tops, and a maroon T-shirt with the words SUNY OSWEGO printed across the front. "Did I miss anything in homeroom?"

I shook my head, noticing a silver chain and matching arrowhead charm around her neck.

"Colossal waste of time," she said. "I never go."

I didn't know how she got away with breaking so many rules, but I couldn't have asked if I wanted to. The teacher started talking, telling us that this was a free drawing period and we could do whatever we wanted, as long as it wasn't potentially offensive.

"Censorship," Leigh muttered. "Nothing in art is offensive."

I agreed and she got inquisitive about where I was from and where I used to go to school. I answered her questions, adding that I was a friend of Summer Simon, and she gave me a blank stare.

"Never heard of her," Leigh said, and I was sure that she was just confused, because everyone knew Summer. Leigh sounded like she was still nursing a cold, so I decided that her head was congested and it was clogging her memory. I also decided not to mention her when I called Summer that night. The idea that someone was oblivious to Summer's existence would crush her, and I didn't want to be responsible for that.

five

I packed my overnight bag on Sunday morning. Pajamas, underwear, my migraine pills just in case. I was going to spend the day with Evelyn because Patrick was on duty again.

This was Mom and Patrick's idea. But they pressured me to pretend that I had thought of it myself, because Evelyn would get suspicious otherwise. She needed my help, and they knew what was best for her.

They'd been talking about what was best for Evelyn since Shane was born. The two of them were constantly on the phone, which didn't seem ironic to anyone but me. Everybody else seemed to have forgotten that Mom once despised

Patrick and that she'd made a huge scene after Evelyn got in trouble. Mom had picked me up from school the day after she found out Evelyn was pregnant. She drove to Patrick's firehouse and screamed and swore at him on the sidewalk. I watched from her car as she called him a lowlife and a scumbag, and I shrank down in my seat when she asked him if he'd ever heard of a condom. *You should think with your brain,* she had said. *It's in your head, Patrick. Not in your pants.*

Now they were allies. A few times Dad mumbled something about how Mom shouldn't get involved, it wasn't right to meddle, but Mom didn't listen. She said that Evelyn had two children, her nasty attitude might drive Patrick away, and a divorce would be catastrophic because Evelyn had no education or job skills.

"You have nothing to worry about, Nancy," Dad told her as he drove us to Queens in Mom's car that afternoon. The windows were open because it was warm for the second week of September, and Mom's hair floated around her head in a frizzy swirl. "I think Patrick is very much in love with her."

I thought so too. He had to be in love to put up with everything she dished out.

Mom didn't seem convinced, because she made a disgusted face and breathed a stream of Pall Mall smoke through her nose like a bull. "Listen, Tom. I've never said anything about the weight she's put on. I could stand to drop a few myself. But between that and Evelyn's mood swings . . ." She shook her head, inhaled on her cigarette, and blew a gray cloud out the window. "My point is that she's giving Patrick plenty of reasons to screw around."

Dad glanced over at Mom, who was lifting her face to the

breeze and enjoying her cigarette. I thought he might argue with her, but he didn't. He never did. He just tuned the radio to the Yankee game. That was the only sound I heard until we rang Evelyn's doorbell.

It was one of her good days. She stood in the foyer, wearing a sundress that minimized what was wrong and exaggerated what was right. The skirt elongated her legs, the belt slimmed her waist. A beaded necklace got lost in her cleavage. Her hair had been blow-dried smooth, and it framed her refined features and the rare color of her eyes.

She made lunch for us. Chips and dip in the living room, stuffed shells covered with Ragu baked in the oven, Mrs. Fields cookies served with Neapolitan ice cream on paper plates.

"I know you like all three flavors, Dad," Evelyn said, running a scooper across the vanilla and the chocolate and the strawberry. She dropped a tricolored blob on his plate and sat down with Shane on her lap, and I wondered why Mom was so worried, because Evelyn seemed fine. She looked across the table at me and asked how school was going. "Any cute boys?" she said.

Mom was swallowing a spoonful of chocolate ice cream. "Boys are irrelevant," she answered before I could open my mouth. "Ariadne is at Hollister so she can get into a good college and make something of her life."

There was a clock over the sink and I heard it ticking. Mom went back to her ice cream and didn't notice how much Evelyn's face had changed—her jaw was stiff, her mouth tight. How could Mom be so clueless? College, making something of my life, everything Mom thought her firstborn daughter hadn't done. *Boys are irrelevant*—that had been Mom's favorite phrase when Evelyn was a teenager, and I knew what Mom was thinking: You didn't listen to me, Evelyn. And look at where that got you. You're an overweight twenty-three-year-old with a GED and two kids, sitting in an ugly kitchen that your husband can't afford to remodel.

"I love your dress, Evelyn," I blurted out, hoping a compliment would help, but it didn't. She smiled dully, mumbled something about changing Shane's diaper, and disappeared upstairs until it was time for Mom and Dad to leave.

"Don't be a sourpuss," Mom told her on the front steps. "Patrick will get sick of you."

Then she and Dad were gone. Evelyn slammed the door, went to the refrigerator, and plopped on the couch with a beer bottle.

"Fucking unbelievable," she said, prying off the cap. She took a swig and rested her feet on the coffee table. I just watched from the foyer. Sweet Evelyn had vanished as quickly as she'd appeared, and now I was afraid to go near my sister. "Don't listen to what our dear mother tells you about boys, Ari," she said, raising her middle finger to a photograph of Mom on the wall. It was a framed picture from Evelyn and Patrick's wedding, and everyone was smiling. "She'd keep you in a cage if she could. Make you do everything *her* way."

I stared at the picture. I remembered that it had been a sunny day. Mom had hemmed Evelyn's dress the night before, and she had invited Patrick's parents to sleep at our house because they couldn't afford a hotel. She'd driven Evelyn to ten different florists to find the prettiest bouquet, and she'd relinquished a strand of pearls Dad had given her, so that Evelyn would have something old.

"Mom means well," I said.

Evelyn laughed. "Are you aware that she wanted me to have an abortion when I was pregnant with Kieran?"

I was, but I shook my head anyway. I didn't want Evelyn to know that I heard the conversation almost six years ago through the wall that separated my room from hers. She and Mom were yelling and Evelyn was crying, and Mom said that an abortion would be the best way to solve this mess. Then Evelyn could finish high school and go to college—even if it was just Kingsborough Community College or Katharine Gibbs Secretarial School—anything would be better than having a baby before she turned eighteen.

"What a Catholic," Evelyn said. "Only goes to church on holidays and tells her daughter to kill a baby. She's a hypocrite, you know."

I didn't agree with that. Mom wanted what was best for Evelyn. I remembered her voice behind my lilac wallpaper, saying that Evelyn was throwing her future away, she was so young and so beautiful and Mom didn't want her to end up as a dependent housewife who had to ask her husband's permission every time she wanted to buy a new pair of socks.

"I don't think that's true, Evelyn," I started, but it was all I got to say.

"It is so," she said.

She turned on the television and finished her beer while

I went upstairs to the bathroom and swallowed two migraine pills. I was glad I hadn't forgotten them this time, because a fluorescent purple web was crawling into my left eye.

Later that night, I fell asleep in the living room because I had to. The guest bedroom didn't exist anymore. I woke up on the couch on Monday morning and heard Evelyn in the kitchen, asking Kieran what kind of cereal he wanted—Frosted Flakes, Apple Jacks, or Cap'n Crunch? Next there were Shane's babbling noises and Patrick slamming barbells against the basement floor, and soon Evelyn rushed past me with the kids, saying that Kieran was late for kindergarten and I should remind Patrick that he had to drive me to school. I didn't mind going to school, because I wouldn't have to eat lunch in the bathroom. Summer was coming back today.

The front door shut and I watched from the window as Evelyn sped away in her minivan. It was warm outside. A filmy haze covered the block, and everything was quiet except for the neighbor's Doberman barking and Patrick exercising downstairs. I went into the kitchen to eat breakfast and he came in a few minutes later, sweating, naked from the waist up.

"I gotta drive you to the city this morning, don't I?" he said, and I nodded as I tried not to stare at his chest. "I'd better hurry up and take a shower. What do they do at that place if you're late? Beat you with a ruler?"

I laughed. "I think they'd go to jail if they did *that*, Patrick."

"Not when I was in school. Those nuns used to smack the living shit out of me."

"There are no nuns at Hollister," I said, and he told me that nuns were sadistic and vicious and the reason why his kids were going to public school. Then he went upstairs. I heard the shower running and thought sadly about Patrick as a young boy in a stiff uniform, being terrorized by ferocious packs of ruler-wielding nuns.

Nobody could terrorize him now—he was too tall and strong. I admired his broad shoulders underneath his shirt as we climbed into his truck at the curb. He stuck a cassette into the tape deck, Bruce Springsteen singing about the Vietnam War or something like that, I wasn't really listening. Patrick was talking about Evelyn, saying that she seemed better lately, she was settling into a routine, and did she seem okay to me?

"I think she's fine," I said, because we both wanted it to be true.

Twenty minutes later, Patrick left me at Hollister and I had to fight my urge to clutch the back of his truck as he drove away. Even though Summer was here, I would have preferred to spend the day with Patrick, to hang out at the firehouse, maybe even sit in the fire engine as it raced around Queens, but of course that was just stupid.

"I'm back," I heard Summer say when I was spinning the combination on my locker.

We weren't in any classes together, not even homeroom, but at least I could eat lunch in the cafeteria like a normal person, which I did later that day.

Summer sat beside me, nibbling a Chipwich and talking

about some guys who'd installed new tile in her parents' bathroom. One of them was from Canada and was incredibly good-looking and flirty.

"He gave me his number," she said. "Not that I'll call. I'll just add it to my collection."

She meant her collection of phone numbers, which she kept in her bra drawer with the velvet diary. Her insistence on mentioning every single man who flirted with her was getting on my nerves. "That's nice," I said, glancing around the cafeteria.

I spotted Leigh Ellis a few tables away. She was sitting alone, skimming through a novel. She'd skipped homeroom again this morning and now she left the cafeteria early, waving at me on the way out. Summer was utterly shocked.

"You *know* her?" she asked.

"She's in my homeroom," I said.

Then Summer started talking. Gossiping, really. She told me that Leigh didn't have to go to class because one of her relatives had founded Hollister Prep and her uncle was some big-deal lawyer, and she was going to graduate from this school with good grades even if she lit the place on fire and danced nude in the ashes.

"She had a boyfriend," Summer whispered. "College guy. He died in a car crash upstate last winter. I heard she was driving . . . drunk, supposedly. She was out of school for three months after that but of course she didn't have to repeat the year. She seems to have recovered, because she's got a new boyfriend already . . . I've seen him pick her up in a Porsche. He's got a nasty scar on his mouth . . . I guess he must've been born with a cleft lip."

I nodded, dizzy from information overload. The bell rang and we walked out of the cafeteria and through the hall, where Summer pointed to a bronze plaque with words underneath a man's aristocratic profile. FREDERICK SMITH HOLLISTER, it read. FOUNDER OF HOLLISTER PREPARATORY ACADEMY, 1932.

"Leigh isn't directly related," Summer said. "I think the connection is through her uncle—the lawyer I told you about. It's his wife's father or something. I'm not sure because she doesn't talk to anyone." Summer waved to a group of guys who were walking past and then she spoke into my ear. "Listen, Ari . . . I'm glad you're here. But everybody at Hollister . . . they don't know about anything that happened in Brooklyn and I don't want them to know. Understand?"

I nodded. "It's our secret."

The next day I found out that Summer had been wrong when she said that Leigh didn't talk to anyone, because she talked to me in art class. We also talked during the cool, late-September mornings when she actually came to homeroom, throughout October while we drew the bright orange trees outside our art-class window, and into November, when all the leaves were gone and the sky filled with clouds and we sketched everything in black and gray.

It was on one of those afternoons that our teacher announced a project, a paper we had to write about a modern artist. He listed names on the blackboard and said that we could work in pairs, and Leigh and I both raised our hands when he pointed to *Picasso* scrawled in lime-green chalk.

"Do you want to come to my apartment tomorrow to

start working on it?" she asked from her seat behind me, and I turned around.

She was wearing her SUNY shirt and she was touching her silver bracelet. She looked optimistic, but I let her down. I paused for too long, thinking of everything Summer had told me. The car crash. The drunk driving. I liked Leigh but I wasn't sure if she was safe outside the iron gates of Hollister Prep.

She read my mind. Her face dimmed and I thought again about the gossip. It could all be a lie or a skewed version of the truth. Summer should have known better than to spread rumors. So I accepted the invitation.

six

Summer slammed her locker door in a snit the next day. I'd just told her that we wouldn't be riding home together because I was going to Leigh's apartment, where we planned to extract Picasso information from books that we checked out of the Hollister library.

But that wasn't exactly what happened. Leigh and I were walking away from school beneath a dusky sky when she said something about Twenty-third Street. She thought she'd lost her bracelet but she hadn't—it had been found, she had to pick it up, and I didn't mind, did I? It would only take a few minutes and the bracelet meant a lot to her.

The wind bit at my cheeks as I shook my head. Then Leigh and I sat in a series of subway cars that took us to West Twenty-third Street, which was crowded with old row houses. They were narrow, four stories high, separated by just a sliver of an alley. We stopped at a building that had fire-escape ladders across the top three floors, and windows covered with plywood. I heard noise inside, rough voices and drills and hammers—construction workers, who I saw at the far end of the building after Leigh opened the door.

The place had a dank smell, mixed with sawdust that the drills were kicking up. I listened to men shout at each other about nails and bolts, and Leigh started walking up the staircase in front of us. It was slim, long, advancing into darkness. I followed her, hearing the steps creak beneath my feet.

"This is my cousin's place," Leigh said as she rapped a red door with a gold knocker. "He's planning to turn it into a dance club. His father thinks he's insane."

Her cousin opened the door and I saw his apartment— a renovated loft with exposed brick and a skylight and modern furniture, all black, leather, and glass. There was an adding machine on the coffee table, in the middle of stacks of receipts and cash.

"Ariadne Mitchell," Leigh said. "This is Delsin Ellis."

I guessed that Delsin Ellis was about twenty-four. He was stocky and average height, and he had dark hair, an aquiline nose, and eyes that were an unusual color. I couldn't tell if they were green or gray or both.

"Del," he said, extending his hand, and I took it.

"Ari," I replied, which made Leigh sigh.

"I can't believe either of you," she said. "Such distinctive names and for some strange reason you shorten them." She looked at me. "My cousin was lucky enough to be given a name that reflects our Native American heritage."

I glanced at her necklace, at the arrowhead charm. Now it made sense.

" 'Native American heritage,' " Del repeated. "A hundred years ago, maybe. And mixed with German and Irish and everything else."

Leigh crossed her arms. "We have blood from the Shawnee tribe and you know that, Del." She looked at me again. "Del's father and my mother are brother and sister. They're from Georgia originally. The Shawnee used to be all over Georgia."

"Nobody gives a shit, Leigh," Del said, and waved us over to a bookcase. He took her bracelet from a shelf and she locked it around her wrist. It was an ID bracelet, the silver one she always wore. It wasn't meant for a girl, it was made for a man, with heavy links and the initials M. G.

"Take it to a jeweler and get it shortened so it doesn't fall off again. You might lose it in the street next time instead of in my car, and I don't want that to happen," Del said as I examined his face. I saw a ropy scar that began near the middle of his upper lip and weaved its way into his left nostril like a snake.

A scar on his mouth, a cleft lip—Summer was so wrong. Leigh hadn't already recovered from her dead boyfriend. The bracelet that meant so much to her was probably his. And she didn't have a new boyfriend. All she had was a cousin.

Leigh nodded and said that she and I should go, sounding raspy as usual. I'd recently figured out that there was never a cold or laryngitis, she was just naturally hoarse.

She kept talking after Del shut the door behind us and we

were heading down the staircase. Then we were on the side-walk and Leigh was talking about Del. I'd guessed his age correctly, and she was telling me other things—that his mother had died twelve years ago, that he had a younger brother, and that he was a college dropout.

"So many strings were pulled to get him into Northwestern," Leigh said. "He didn't exactly have the grades. Then he starts a fight with some engineering student over a parking space and gets himself expelled. . . . Del knocked out the guy's front teeth, if you can believe it. My uncle had to fork over a lot of money to make that one go away."

"Oh," I said, for lack of anything better.

The wind blew Leigh's hair across her face, long copper strands against freckled skin. "I shouldn't talk badly about him. Everybody else does," she said. "His name . . . it's Native American, and it means 'He is so.' My uncle always says 'He is so stubborn,' 'He is so angry,' 'He is so stupid.' This whole thing about starting a business . . . Del bought that dump with some of the trust-fund money he got from his mother. I hope it works, because nobody has any faith in him and he needs something meaningful in his life."

"Oh," I repeated, wondering why Leigh was telling me all this. But I was the only person she ever talked to at school, so I figured she was lonely and there was nobody else who would listen.

Leigh's apartment was in a modern building on East Seventy-eighth, with a doorman who ushered us through a glass door into a mirrored elevator that played Muzak as it carried us to a small but well-decorated and bright apartment on the twentieth floor. It had fashionable furniture, windows covered with sheer turquoise drapes, and silver appliances in the kitchen.

We sat down at the kitchen table and pored over our library books, scribbling Picasso facts on loose-leaf. I was reading about one of his most famous paintings, *Les Demoiselles d'Avignon,* when I had to use the bathroom.

"Through the living room and down the hall on the right," Leigh said, pointing in that direction. She was too engrossed in Picasso to lift her head.

I walked through the living room, past a heather beige sofa, an oak coffee table the color of sand, and a Georgia O'Keeffe painting on the wall—an abstract flower, a blast of pink and orange and a light shade of turquoise that matched the curtains. Then I was in the hallway and a door at the end opened. I saw a tall, willowy young woman with spindly limbs, hair the same color as mine, and a beautiful face. She wore a short nightgown that was practically transparent.

"Hi," she said. "I'm Rachel."

"I'm Ari." I was closer now, so her face was clear. Her skin was olive-toned, smooth and flawless. Her nose was prominent but perfectly straight, her eyebrows were thin and arched, and her eyes were dark and shaped like almonds. Rachel was model-beautiful, as gorgeous as those women on the cover of *Vogue.* I couldn't imagine who she was, maybe Leigh's older sister, but they looked nothing alike.

"Do you need to use the girls' room?" she asked. "You go ahead . . . I'll wait."

I locked myself in the bathroom and took care of business quickly because I couldn't be rude and keep Rachel waiting. She slipped into the bathroom after I left. Leigh was still reading about Picasso in the kitchen when I walked in.

"We should go to MoMA," she said after I sat across from her. "To get a feel for his work. We can write about it better that way, don't you think?"

I nodded. Then I heard water running in the bathroom and Leigh heard it too. She said she didn't know that her mother was awake, and I couldn't imagine that the woman I'd just met could be anyone's mother, especially not someone as old as Leigh.

"Did you see her?" Leigh asked, and I nodded again. "She doesn't usually emerge from her slumber before five o'clock. You know . . . the fact that she's old enough to have a teenage daughter practically gives her the vapors. Not that she's really old enough to have a teenage daughter. She's only thirty-four."

I subtracted quickly—thirty-four, sixteen. Leigh was born when Rachel was eighteen. Evelyn had been three months short of eighteen when she gave birth to Kieran, but I wasn't inclined to blab my family secrets, so I didn't say anything.

Leigh told me that Rachel always slept during the day. I assumed she had some kind of night job, although I couldn't imagine what that was. She didn't seem the type to make change in a tollbooth or take care of sick people in a hospital.

"What does she do?" I asked, thinking that I was too nosy, but Leigh didn't mind.

"Hangs out at nightclubs, mostly. Studio Fifty-four was

her favorite when it was really popular. She's friends with one of the owners. He's sick now, though. AIDS." Leigh whispered the last word, like AIDS could be caught just by mentioning it. "My mother actually does have a job . . . she's a makeup artist on Broadway. It used to be *A Chorus Line* and now she's doing *Cats,* but only Tuesday through Thursday. She won't work on weekends—too busy with her social life. She's lucky that my uncle supports us or I don't know where we'd be. Living in a cardboard box on the corner, probably. Or in a trailer park in Georgia."

She said *Georgia* with a hokey Southern accent, and that was the last thing she said for a while. We went back to our books, to Picasso. We read about his rose period and his cubism period until I noticed that the apartment wasn't bright anymore.

"I'd better go," I said, glancing around for my coat. "It's late."

I'd forgotten that Leigh hung my coat in the hall closet. She brought it to me and I was closing the buttons when she said something about calling a car service to take me home.

"I'll be fine on the subway," I told her, thinking I only had a ten-dollar bill in my wallet and I was sure that wasn't enough to pay for a cab ride from Manhattan to Brooklyn.

"It's dark outside, Ari," Leigh said. "And dangerous. The subways are filled with people who've been kicked out of Bellevue too early. Don't you watch the news?" She picked up the phone and started dialing. "This is the service my uncle's firm uses and it's completely free . . . I won't take no for an answer."

I couldn't find a reason to argue. We rode the elevator downstairs, where we stood with the doorman until a glossy sedan arrived. I slid onto the backseat and watched Leigh wave goodbye through tinted windows. Then I listened to 1010 WINS while the driver sped through Manhattan, past skyscrapers and traffic lights in a swoosh of red and yellow and green.

Soon we were in Brooklyn and I saw different things—unassuming houses, Saint Anne on our lawn. The wind was so fierce that she and little Mary looked like they were huddling to stay warm.

Mom was in an apron on our steps. The front door was open behind her and I smelled our dinner from the sidewalk as the sedan drove off. I walked toward her, sure she was annoyed that I was late and that I hadn't bothered to call. Her expression was a combination of ticked off and puzzled, and she was looking down the street at the sedan, its scarlet brake lights glowing in the dark.

"What the hell is this?" she asked.

I assumed she was wondering why I'd been driven home by a chauffeur as if I was some kind of socialite, but I was thinking of other things. I was thinking of a dilapidated row house on West Twenty-third Street and a bright apartment on East Seventy-eighth, and Delsin Ellis with the Shawnee blood and the scar on his lip. I had no idea how to answer Mom's question because I couldn't explain any of it.

seven

Summer didn't eat lunch with me the next day. She was supposed to—I went to the cafeteria carrying a paper bag that Mom had stuffed with ham on rye and a Hostess cupcake—but Summer immediately said something about her friend who lived in an apartment nearby. She whispered that every so often they'd sneak over there and order a pizza even though leaving campus during school hours was a blatant violation of Hollister rules.

"Do you want to come?" she asked, chomping on a square of Bubble Yum.

I looked over her shoulder at a group of girls who

belonged in a Bloomingdale's catalog. They were standing in the doorway with Louis Vuitton purses dangling from their wrists. And they were authentic Louis Vuitton—not the fake kind with the upside-down *L* and *V* that foreign guys sell in dark alleys.

I glanced back at Summer—at her indigo eye shadow, her lips that were wet from pearly peach gloss. She wore a tight angora skirt set with high-heeled boots that made her as tall as me, and a long strand of silver beads was looped around her neck three times.

"No," I said.

Her brow furrowed. "Why not?"

Your friends scare me, I thought. I don't know enough about designer shoes and dating rituals to fit in. But I couldn't admit all that, so I just shrugged.

"Ari," she said. "I really want you to come with us. I can't leave you by yourself."

"It's okay. I'll probably find Leigh around here someplace."

"Leigh?" Summer said. "She's a weirdo and a drunk driver."

"Summer," I said, and my voice held the scolding tone that usually comes from teachers and parents. "You shouldn't talk about people like that. Or spread rumors about them."

Her eyes widened as if I'd just shouted "Summer Simon swallows." "Yeah, I know," she said, and I ate my sandwich alone after she was gone because Leigh never showed up.

I didn't see her until last period, which made me wonder if she slept all afternoon like Rachel and just strolled in for art because it was the only class that didn't cause yawning fits.

"Want to go to MoMA after school?" she said.

She was wearing her Converses again, with the SUNY Oswego shirt underneath a blazer that didn't match. And I did want to go to MoMA, but Summer wasn't happy when I told her about it later that afternoon.

"We're supposed to ride home on the train together," she said, and she was right, so I compromised. I invited her to MoMA, where she and Leigh and I looked at Picasso and at melting clocks in the Dalí exhibit.

"This is idiotic," Summer said. She'd never been an art fan.

"I think it's amazing," Leigh answered, which Summer repeated in a sarcastic tone later when she and I were inside a subway car speeding toward Brooklyn.

"She's strange," Summer said, examining her fingers. She spotted a chip in her manicure, took a bottle of polish from her purse, and executed a skillful touch-up. "I'm sorry, but it's true. Haven't you noticed the way she dresses? I've seen her wearing that shirt three times in the past week. From what I hear, Oswego is where her dead boyfriend went to school. It's probably his shirt, and that's not psychologically healthy. She has to let go."

I shrugged as lights flickered inside the subway car. I thought about the shirt, wondering if it really had belonged to Leigh's boyfriend, if she never washed it because it smelled of him, if she wore it for the same reasons that I slept in Patrick's shirt. Then Summer mentioned Thanksgiving. She asked if we were eating at Evelyn's next week the way we usually did, and I shook my head.

"My mother is cooking this year" was all I said, because

she didn't need to know that Evelyn wasn't doing well lately, that Mom kept sneaking the telephone into our laundry room so that Dad wouldn't hear her conversations with Patrick, or that Evelyn didn't cook anymore, not even tuna casserole or no-bake cheesecakes. Patrick had told Mom that there was never anything in the house but Doritos and Dunkin' Donuts.

"We'll all have a nice day today," Mom said on Thanksgiving when she was bending into the stove and jabbing our turkey with a fork. "You'll help with the baby so Evelyn can relax. Everything will be just fine."

She nodded as if that would make it so. But she seemed disappointed during dinner, when Dad and Patrick argued about football and Evelyn did nothing but eat. She drowned her turkey in gravy and devoured three slices of pumpkin pie, and from the look on Mom's face, I knew she was worried that Evelyn's weight would be an excuse for Patrick to *screw around*.

Then a button popped off Evelyn's blouse and landed on Dad's plate. I wasn't surprised—she was bursting right out of her bra.

"Goddamn it," she said, snatching the button back. Her face turned splotchy like it had been during most of her first pregnancy, when she'd cried about the squiggly purple stretch marks that left scars on her skin.

"That happens to me all the time," I lied. "Things are made so cheaply these days."

Evelyn's jade eyes shot toward me. "Who the fuck asked *you?*"

I didn't think anyone had to ask me. I was just trying to be nice, but now I didn't know why I bothered. Forgive her, I thought. Her hormones are still out of whack and she has no idea what she's saying.

Mom tried to fix things. "Evelyn," she said. "Go find something else to wear in my closet. Take whatever you want."

Evelyn went upstairs. Dad took a walk to burn off some calories, Mom disappeared into the kitchen with the kids, and I heard the clang of dishes being washed while Patrick and I sat at the table.

"Well, that wasn't very nice," he said. "Go get me a ruler."

"For what?" I asked.

"So I can smack some sense into my wife."

I giggled. I loved him for being on my side. He was gone a few minutes later, off to work his shift at the firehouse, leaving Evelyn and the boys for Dad to drive back to Queens later on. I fed Shane his bottle on the couch while Kieran spread out on the carpet with a coloring book and a box of Crayolas.

"Mom," I heard Evelyn call from upstairs. "Can you come up here, please?"

Her tone was urgent, and I was worried that she couldn't find a single thing that fit. I was wiping formula off Shane's lips when Mom came out of the kitchen in her apron and slippers and headed up the stairs, and I'd just turned on the TV when she called my name.

I climbed the steps with Shane in my arms. The hall was

dark except for the light coming from my room, and my knees got wobbly when I saw Evelyn sitting on my bed with Patrick's T-shirt draped across her thighs.

Mom was in the doorway. Evelyn stood up and took Shane away from me. One of her curls smacked my right eye as she turned back to the bed. I felt sick. I had never expected that Evelyn would go rummaging through my closet.

"What's wrong?" I said, blinking the sting out of my eye, shocked at how calm I sounded. Nobody could possibly know that I was close to puking on Mom's terry-cloth slippers.

"Nothing," Mom said. "Evelyn found Patrick's shirt in your closet and she was wondering how it got there."

Evelyn rolled her eyes. "I *know* how it got there, Mom. Ari stole it from my house."

"Who gave you permission to snoop through my things?" I said.

"Why can't I snoop through your things?" Evelyn asked. "What are you hiding?"

"Evelyn," Mom said. "Patrick must've left that shirt here accidentally. Remember when he helped Dad paint the kitchen last spring? I know I did some laundry for him then, and it probably got mixed in with Ariadne's clothes."

"Yeah," I agreed, because this was such a reasonable, innocent explanation.

"Oh, please," Evelyn said, glaring at me. "You know he makes you cream your pants."

I despised that expression. It was so crude, so crass, the type of thing that Evelyn's low-achieving friends used to say while they smoked Marlboros on street corners instead of going to school. "You're disgusting," I said, clenching my fists so tightly that my nails dug semicircles into my palms.

"Girls, girls," Mom broke in before Evelyn could lunge at my jugular. She sat on the bed, stuffing Patrick's shirt into the front pocket of her *Kiss the Cook* apron. "Evelyn, you shouldn't talk to your sister that way. Patrick is your husband, and Ariadne would never do anything inappropriate. The idea is just ludicrous."

"Even if she did," Evelyn said, lifting her chin, "it wouldn't matter. Ari could strip naked in front of him and he wouldn't go for it. He isn't turned on by flat-chested teenagers, you know. Patrick only loves me."

The truth hurt. It hurt more than the worst migraine that ever festered inside my head. For a moment I hated Evelyn, sitting there all smug and haughty, the proud owner of Patrick's love. The worst part was that she was right. He did only love her, and he loved her so much that he overlooked the extra weight and the eczema, her roller-coaster moods and tuna casserole.

Then Shane started crying, which was good because it took the attention off me. But Evelyn got upset because his diaper was clean and he was fed, so there was no reason for him to be crying.

"I always get the criers," she said, pacing the floor while patting his back. "Kieran was exactly the same."

"They *all* cry," Mom told her.

"My friends' babies don't cry for nothing," Evelyn insisted, and she started crying for nothing too. She wiped her runny nose with her hand and I didn't hate her anymore. Don't listen to your friends, I thought. They're lying. Their babies cry too. Those horrible women want you to fail so they'll have something to gab about at the pool.

"I'll take him," I said. "Why don't you lie down on my bed for a while and relax?"

"Good idea," Mom chimed in. "Isn't that a good idea, Evelyn?"

Red lines marred the whites of Evelyn's eyes and she looked sorry for what she'd said before. She smiled; Mom and I closed the bedroom door and went to the living room with Shane. Dad took Evelyn and the kids back to Queens a few hours later, and I waved from the sidewalk as they drove away. It was cold outside, and crispy orange leaves spun in clusters on the cement. I turned back to the house, noticing Saint Anne watching me from the corner of her painted eye.

Inside, I hung my coat in the hall closet and felt Mom behind me. She gave my hair a sharp yank that made me lift my hand to my head, feeling for a bald spot.

"What was *that* for?" I asked.

She didn't answer. She smiled, holding up Patrick's shirt with her left hand. There was a laundry basket in her right. "I'll wash this and give it back to him."

Please don't, I thought. You don't know how much I need it. "Okay," I said, but my voice wasn't as steady as it had been in the bedroom, so I tossed my hair and cleared my throat to cover any sign of weakness.

"I figured you wouldn't mind," Mom went on, jamming the shirt into the basket along with gravy-stained dish towels and Dad's boxer shorts. "You've outgrown it, haven't you? You really should have by now."

At that moment I knew Mom hadn't forgotten the one time I sat on Patrick's lap. It was so humiliating that I wanted to disappear. And I thought about how Mom was a talented ringmaster, orchestrating everything in our circus of a family, trying to keep us all on the right track.

"Of course I have," I answered, wondering if I ever would.

Jeff's Mercedes was in front of my house on Monday morning. While Summer examined her face in a compact, I sat in the back and noticed that our neighbors had been busy over the weekend. All the Thanksgiving decorations were gone, replaced by wreaths and bows tied on mailboxes and lampposts.

"How is Evelyn doing?" Jeff said.

I shrugged. "Not great."

"Is she seeing anyone?" he asked, meaning a psychiatrist, and I shook my head.

When we reached Hollister, Summer went to her home-room and I went to mine. Leigh was actually there, dressed in an oversized SUNY Oswego sweatshirt. I wondered if it belonged to her boyfriend, but I couldn't ask.

"You're invited to a party," she said. "A week from this Saturday."

I turned around. Leigh's hair was pinned back. The arrow-head charm grazed her sweatshirt and her bracelet rested on her hand instead of her wrist because it was still too big. I thought she should hurry up and take it to a jeweler before it got lost forever.

"What party?" I asked.

She explained that her uncle was having his annual Christmas bash. It was at his apartment, a hundred people were invited, and he always let her bring a guest.

"Is your cousin going to be there?" I asked.

She knitted her brow. "You mean Del?"

Who else could I have meant? I nodded, thinking about his name. Del. Delsin Ellis. It was just as distinctive as Leigh had said.

"He'll be there," she said, then lifted her thumb to her mouth and chewed on her nail. She looked like there was something she wanted to tell me but wasn't sure she should. "He thinks you're pretty, you know."

I didn't know. I never would have thought that—compliments were hard to come by. Del's made me think about him all morning, through calculus and American history and even during lunch, while Summer babbled about an engagement party.

"Do you want to do it?" she said, but I was clueless. I wasn't listening. I was staring across the cafeteria at Leigh, who was flipping through *ARTnews*. I wanted her to look at me so I could wave her over to sit with us, but she probably wouldn't have, anyway. Summer hadn't exactly been charming when we'd been together at MoMA, and she was even less appealing now that she didn't have my undivided attention.

"You've got no idea what I'm talking about, do you?" she said, to which I meekly shook my head. Then she got huffy and spoke in a loud voice as if I was deaf or stupid. She told me that Tina was catering an engagement party next weekend and they could use my help if I was available.

I wasn't available. I'd been invited to a party at an apartment that was big enough to fit a hundred guests, with an older guy who allegedly thought I was pretty. I wanted to tell Summer, to brag the way she would, but I didn't. I lied. I told her I was spending the weekend in Queens, which was an acceptable excuse. I was sure she'd get huffy again if she heard the truth. It would devastate her to find out that I'd once again jilted my best friend for a girl who wore the same shirt three times in one week.

The next day Leigh gave me an invitation to her uncle's party. Even though the party was going to be at his home, the invitation had been mailed from his office. It was made of thick red paper, tucked inside a gold foil envelope with printing on the back. ELLIS & HUMMEL, P.A. EMPIRE STATE BUILDING. 350 FIFTH AVENUE. 98TH FLOOR. Leigh's uncle's name was Stanford Ellis.

I'd never been inside the Empire State Building and neither had my parents or Evelyn, because Mom said that real New Yorkers never did those touristy things. But I imagined that a man who owned a law firm on Fifth Avenue and whose Christmas-party invitation ended with the words *Black tie optional* expected his guests to wear something special.

"Can I get a new dress in the city?" I asked Mom the weekend before the party. It was Saturday morning, and she and Dad were sitting at our kitchen table reading the newspaper over a coffee cake. Mom was already smoking a cigarette, and she gave me a look like I had suggested a trip to Mars.

"In the city?" she said, as if the city wasn't only a few miles away. She looked at Dad and they let out a simultaneous laugh, went back to the newspaper, and left me standing on the tiles.

But I couldn't go to Stanford Ellis's party in some old clearance-rack rag from my closet. "The party is a semi-formal, Mom. Black tie optional."

"Well," she said. "La-di-da."

Dad laughed and I almost cried. Didn't these people understand anything? Didn't they notice that I never went anywhere interesting or did anything exciting? I wanted to tell Mom that I had to look decent at the party because someone who might be attracted to me was going to be there, but I was smarter than that. *Boys are irrelevant,* she'd probably say.

We compromised. We went to a local Loehmann's, where she promised to buy me a dress that was practical and sensibly priced.

"This big-shot friend of yours," Mom said as we browsed the racks. "She might invite you to some other parties, so pick out something you love. I'm not buying a new dress every time, Ariadne. You're not Princess Diana."

I knew I wasn't Princess Diana. And Leigh wasn't a big shot. But I also knew Mom would make me leave the store empty-handed if I argued, so I didn't. An hour later we were back in the Honda, where I clutched a shopping bag, grateful for what was inside—a knee-length black velvet number that had been on sale for twenty percent off. A little black dress. Summer always said that every girl should have a little black dress.

I carefully packed it in a garment bag on the night of the party, and searched my dresser drawers for a pair of panty hose while Mom watched.

"Is your homework done?" she said.

"Yes," I answered, trying not to sound snotty even though she'd asked me that same question three times already.

"And Leigh's parents . . . they'll be at home?"

I was going to Leigh's apartment so we could get ready and take the car service to the party together, and I knew Rachel would be there, but the word *parents* threw me off. Leigh had never mentioned her father, and it would have been rude of me to ask. "Her mother will," I said.

"Her mother," Mom said. "What about her father?"

"I don't know, Mom. They're probably divorced. Just about everybody's parents are divorced."

She grunted. I didn't want to look at her, so I kept rummaging through the drawer. Then Mom gripped my arm and I had to look. Her eyes were puffy, and I wished she would dye her hair soon. She was so negligent about her hair.

"Be back by midnight, Ariadne. Not a minute later."

Midnight was fair. I agreed, and then I rode in the sedan that Leigh had ordered for me. The driver took me to Leigh's apartment, where Rachel opened the door. She was dressed in another nightgown, and her long hair cascaded over her shoulders.

"Can I tell you something?" she said a few minutes later. I was sitting beside her on the couch and Leigh was in a chair across from me, shaking her head.

"Oh, Mama," she said, which was weird. Everyone I

knew called their mother Mom or Mommy or Ma. The way Leigh said it reminded me of an old Elvis Presley interview I'd seen on television once. Mama and Daddy, that was how Elvis referred to his parents, and I guessed it made sense, because he was from the South too.

Rachel's accent was slight. I heard it after she ignored Leigh and spoke to me. "Ari," she said. "You have beautiful eyes. But honey, you're not tweezing those brows right. Let me fix them and I'll make you gorgeous."

Leigh seemed insulted. "Mama," she groaned. "What's wrong with you? Ari didn't ask for a makeover."

But I didn't mind. I couldn't pass up the opportunity for a professional makeup artist to make me gorgeous.

Rachel clicked her tongue. "*You're* the one who needs a makeover. I haven't seen you in lipstick for almost a year."

I'd never seen Leigh in lipstick either. Or mascara or anything else. Leigh's boyfriend had died almost a year ago, and I wondered if makeup didn't matter to her anymore.

"I'm fine," she said.

"You're not, but we'll discuss it later," Rachel said, and the next thing I knew, I was sitting on the edge of a bathtub and she was crouched in front of me with a look of intense concentration, as if she was performing microsurgery instead of plucking my eyebrows. When she was finished, she turned to Leigh. "See?" she said. "Wasn't I right?"

Leigh smiled and admitted that my arch was perfect. "You really opened up her eyes."

"Just keep her away from Del," Rachel said, then turned back to me. "He's a runaround like my father was. I swear he wants that club so he can have a bar full of girls just a staircase below his bedroom."

I guessed Leigh wasn't kidding when she'd said that everybody talked badly about Del. She and Rachel left me alone to get dressed for the party, and I stared at myself in the mirror, thinking that I looked better. My eyebrows were artfully sculpted and they ended in tapered points at the outside corners of my eyes, which seemed bluer somehow. I stared for a while, zipped up my dress, and stepped into heels that made me much taller than Leigh.

She wore flat shoes. No makeup. Her dress was plain, the same color as a paper lunch bag and just as wrinkly. Rachel told her to find something else, she had a whole closet filled with more attractive things, but Leigh didn't listen and Rachel didn't argue. She was too busy working on her hair and her face and her dress, which was made of sequin-covered white satin that twinkled inside the sedan on our way to the party.

We weren't in the car for long. Stanford Ellis's apartment was only a few blocks away, in a tall building with a concierge and a granite floor in its lobby. We got into an elevator that played a symphony through invisible speakers; there was a leaf-shaped sconce on the wall made of frosted glass. Rachel pressed a button and we rode to the top floor, where the doors opened into what I thought was a shared hallway but was actually a private foyer.

We were standing on granite again. I felt heat from flames burning low in a fireplace and I smelled the greenery that covered a round table in the middle of the room. The walls around us were dark wood. We walked into a carpeted living room with floor-to-ceiling windows that boasted a breath-taking view of Manhattan.

I'd never seen the city from so high; I didn't think this place was really an apartment. It was a penthouse. It had a big kitchen and a formal dining room and a wide staircase of creamy pearl marble with an intricate iron railing. There were people sitting on the stairs wearing expensive suits and classy dresses, holding wineglasses and scotch glasses and cocktail napkins, probably because there was nowhere else to sit. The couches and chairs were filled with other people who were drinking and talking and laughing, and I noticed a man weaving his way through the crowd, spending just a moment with each person, like a bee pollinating flowers.

"That's Uncle Stan," Leigh said, pointing a freckled finger in his direction.

We were eating mini-quiches that we'd snagged from a gloved waiter's tray. We sipped Perrier and leaned against a wall and I watched Stanford Ellis, who wasn't what I expected. He wasn't as old as my parents and he wasn't as young as Rachel. I decided that he was in his forties and as handsome as any actor.

Leigh introduced him a few minutes later. He was Rachel's height and they had the same nose. His wheat blond hair was thick and his skin was tan. He didn't spend any more time with us than he did with his other guests, but he filled every second with smiles and charm.

"What's the matter with you, Leigh?" he said in a fading Southern accent, his dark eyes fixed on me. "Bringing such a pretty girl to the party. I'll have to lock up my sons."

He probably didn't mean it. But when he was gone, I

pretended he did and it got me all happy and excited and I kept sipping my Perrier, hoping Leigh wouldn't see that I was desperate for a compliment. She didn't seem to notice. She started talking about Del, who had just arrived and was working the crowd as expertly as his father.

We ran into him in the kitchen before dinner was served. The caterers were dropping sprigs of parsley on plates and Del was mixing his own drink.

He wasn't wearing a tie. The top of his shirt was open underneath his blazer and he smelled of cologne and tobacco. He smiled at me and Leigh with his scarred lip.

His eyes were greener than the last time I'd seen him. I hadn't realized until now how sharply his nose hooked downward at the tip, and I decided that he wasn't nearly as handsome as his father, but he made me much more excited.

"You ladies want a drink?" he asked.

I shook my head. I'd never had more than a Budweiser, and tonight wasn't the time to start experimenting. I needed to keep my wits about me so I wouldn't do anything stupid or embarrassing or both.

Leigh folded her arms. "We're underage. Not everybody breaks the law, Del," she said teasingly, and I remembered the engineering student with the missing teeth.

"Funny," he said.

She smiled, leaning against the counter. "Where's your brother?"

Del's drink was in his hand and he shook it to spin the rum inside. "Blake's upstairs. He's studying for finals like a good little boy."

Blake didn't join us for dinner, which was a buffet set up

in chafing dishes on the dining room table. Everyone loaded their plates and Leigh found an empty spot on a soft leather couch, where I settled down between her and Del and barely touched my food because I had to avoid getting spinach stuck in my teeth and dribbling marinara sauce down my chin. I couldn't humiliate myself, especially not with Del so close that his knee was touching mine.

His pants were smooth. He wore a gold bracelet and a diamond pinkie ring. He left twice to get more food and three times to refresh his drink, and I worried that I was boring and he wouldn't come back, but he always did.

"I'm opening my club on New Year's Eve," he told me. "You should come."

"I don't think I could get in," I said, because the minimum age for those clubs was twenty-one and I didn't have a fake ID. Del laughed and I felt a trickle of sweat roll down my back.

"That was cute," he said. "And don't worry. I won't let anyone keep you out."

I smiled and sat there talking to Leigh and Del until Rachel told us it was time to leave. Del walked with us to the foyer and Rachel looked at him after pressing the elevator button on the wall.

"Give me and your cousin a kiss goodbye, delinquent," she said.

He smirked and obeyed, then the elevator doors opened and he got close to me when Rachel's and Leigh's backs were turned. He whispered something in my ear, something that sounded like "Merry Christmas," and I felt the stubble on his chin as he kissed my cheek.

It was just a regular kiss. It was the same kiss he gave his aunt and cousin, the same nothing kiss that all the guests were giving to each other as they filed out of the party. But he clutched my shoulder and rested his hand on the small of my back, and it made me breathe faster because nobody had touched me that way since the Catskills boy.

"Leigh," Rachel said when we were in the car. "Did you see Blake tonight?"

Leigh shook her head. "Del told us he was studying."

"Hiding, more likely. Stan tells me he's still upset about that girl."

What girl? I wondered, but only for a moment. Rachel and Leigh were quiet now and I pressed my forehead against the window, watching lights whiz by while Del's kiss simmered on my skin.

When I walked into my house later that night, Dad was asleep and Mom was in the living room, smoking a Pall Mall and scribbling on a notepad.

"Are you working on a novel?" I asked.

"Aren't I always?" She ripped three pages from the pad, crumpled them in her hand, and told me to sit down. "I'll get a snack and you can tell me everything."

She went to the kitchen, came back with a plate of sandwiches, and handed me a warm glass. It was filled to the rim with milk and I didn't want it, but she wouldn't take no for an answer. Mom always forced milk on me and Evelyn to make our bones strong or whatever.

"I heated it up," she said. "It'll help you sleep tonight."

I was too excited to sleep. I kicked off my shoes and Mom and I sat cross-legged on the couch, where I told her about the fancy elevator and the penthouse. I mentioned Leigh's uncle but not her cousin, because Stanford Ellis was safe—I could talk about him the way I would any unattainable older man, like Don Johnson or Tom Selleck. But Del was twenty-four, like Patrick when he got Evelyn in trouble, so I kept him to myself.

eight

I slept late the next morning. I would have slept even later if Dad wasn't so noisy when he climbed a ladder next to my window to line our roof with Christmas lights. I saw his feet on the rungs as I looked outside. I also saw a dusting of snow on Saint Anne's tranquil face. Mom was next to her, searching through a box marked *Extension Cords*.

There were more boxes in the living room. They gave off the scent of candles and the aerosol stuff that Mom always sprayed on our artificial tree to make it smell like real pine. The house reeked of Christmas and it boosted my mood, which was good already because I still felt Del on my cheek. I felt him while Mom and Dad were shouting at each other about whether they should use white or colored lights on our hedges, while I toasted a Pop-Tart, and even after the phone rang and I heard Patrick's voice.

"Evelyn has the flu," he said. "And I gotta go to work."

So we had to go to Queens, where I only got to see Patrick for a minute. He was waiting at the front door and he rushed past us without so much as a hello kiss because he was late for his shift.

This was the first depressing thing. There were many others, like the sound of Evelyn puking in the bathroom, the pile of dirty dishes in her kitchen sink, and the mountain of withered tissues that she hadn't bothered to clear from her coffee table. And even worse was the obnoxious blue Muppet that Kieran was watching on TV in the living room. I felt a headache starting and I didn't have my migraine pills, so I asked if he could watch something else, but he ignored me.

"Kieran," I said. "Please change the channel."

Dad was reading the newspaper in the kitchen, Mom was washing dishes, and Evelyn sneezed on the couch. She wiped her nose with a Kleenex but she didn't do a very good job, because when she looked at me, there was a sickening shimmer of snot above her lip.

"That's his favorite show," she said.

"It's giving me a migraine, Evelyn."

Her throat was filled with phlegm and she sounded like an old woman dying of pneumonia. "Oh, poor you. Go back to Brooklyn if your ears are so damn delicate."

She raised the volume on the TV and scratched her eczema, and I wanted to grab the tissues and use them to smother her. I wanted to tell her that she was nasty and rude and that I had come here to help even though I would rather be at home. I would rather be drawing or reading and not listening to some puppet sing a stupid song that was worse than nails drilling into my skull, but I didn't say that. I just went to the kitchen, where I complained to Mom.

"I know," she said. "But we have to be careful around her."

We had to be careful. I couldn't kill my sister. All I could do was set up a cot in the nursery and rest in the dark with Shane while Mom drove to the store to pick up some aspirin, Evelyn went to sleep in her bedroom, and Dad played with Kieran in the living room.

My blanket smelled of Patrick, which made me feel better. I stayed wrapped up in it until I heard a shrill noise and I went downstairs, where Kieran was rubbing his hair and crying.

"He hit his head on the table," Dad said in the airy tone adults use to convince children that they're not really in pain. But Kieran kept bawling and Dad put him on his lap on the couch while I watched from the bottom of the stairs.

That was what depressed me the most. More than the messy house and the puking and the snot. It depressed me because I only got that from Dad once, on a summer day when I was six years old. I accidentally slammed my finger in a drawer while Mom and Evelyn were at Pathmark. He came rushing into my bedroom, and after he checked that my finger was still attached, he scooped me up and told me in a soothing voice that everything was okay until I believed him.

That was the one and only time. There were other times

I wanted that kind of attention again, lots and lots of times, like when I came home from junior high with a tear-stained face because Summer had been voted Prettiest Girl. But Dad was working on his car in the garage and he just stared at me from ten feet away like I was ridiculous and said that Mom would be home soon.

At that moment I decided that I really was ridiculous, because I was twelve and my breasts were growing and my hips were curving, and I figured that breasts and hips were the things that made you a grown-up and grown-ups weren't supposed to cry to anyone. They weren't really supposed to cry at all, but if they did, they had to do it alone, locked in a bathroom or in the car when nobody else was there, and if anyone noticed their bloodshot eyes, they had to shake it off and be all stoic and say *Oh, I'm just fine.*

I believed this for a few years. I believed it and bravely accepted it until the first time I saw Evelyn cry to Patrick and he held her and stroked her hair, and I thought it was the most hopeful thing I'd ever seen.

Summer rushed to my front door on Monday morning, carrying a Bloomingdale's shopping bag. Her hair poked out of a fuzzy pink hat and there was a matching scarf around her neck with pom-poms that bounced against her black coat. She smiled, pulled a box out of the bag, and shoved the box at me as she stepped into my front hall.

"This is for Evelyn," she said. "For the baby, I mean. It's an outfit my mother and I bought at Bloomingdale's yesterday. . . . It's so precious that we just couldn't resist."

I considered telling Summer to bring the precious outfit back to Bloomingdale's for a refund because Evelyn was on Santa's bad list this year and she didn't deserve a baby gift. But I just thanked her and put the box under our Christmas tree.

"And here's something for *you*," Summer said as I turned around. She dug into the bag, took out a cedar box, and handed it to me. I saw EMPIRE STATE FINE ART SUPPLIES engraved in the wood. "My mother and I passed by there on our way to Bloomie's and I *had* to go in."

I opened the box. "Summer," I said with a gasp, running my finger across a row of pencils and charcoals, taking in their brand-new smell. "They're beautiful. But that store is expensive . . . you didn't have to spend so much money on me for Christmas."

"Oh, this isn't a *Christmas* present," she said. "It's just because you like to draw."

I closed the box and gave her a hug. We went outside and Jeff drove us to school, where Leigh didn't show up for homeroom or even art class. She must have gone to at least one of her classes, because I saw her in front of Hollister when Summer and I were leaving that afternoon.

She was walking across the street, heading toward a charcoal-colored Porsche with a young man leaning against it. He wore a long black coat and was smoking a cigarette, and it took me a second to figure out that he was Del.

Summer groaned. "There's the weirdo and her ugly boyfriend. Doesn't he look like an Indian? I heard somewhere that she's an Indian, so it makes sense. Maybe she's his squaw."

She laughed but I didn't. "Native American," I said, thinking that she sounded like a racist and wondering how someone who had the patience to psychologically counsel her own stalker could turn into a completely different person in matters relating to Leigh Ellis. It was such a change from this morning. "*Native American* is the proper term."

Summer seemed thoroughly insulted. "Whatever," she said, but she pronounced it "what-ev-er," breaking it into syllables as if the syllables were separate words.

"And she's only part Native American," I went on. "From way back."

We headed toward the subway, and for some reason Summer kept talking about Del.

"I think he looks like an Indian," she insisted. "His hair is so dark, and did you see his nose? And that hideous scar on his mouth? If Leigh marries him and has babies, they could get the same thing. I saw a picture in a medical book of a baby with a cleft lip—it was like a big wet gaping hole in the middle of the kid's face. I almost puked. That's a genetic birth defect, you know."

"My hair is dark," I said. "Lots of people have dark hair. And he has light skin and light eyes—and she's not going to marry him, Summer. He's her cousin."

She stopped walking. "How would *you* know anything about his eyes?"

Because I saw them when I was at his apartment, I thought. I also saw them at a penthouse party in the city on Saturday and I spent an hour last night mixing paint to match his shade. But I can't tell you that, Summer. I'll conjure up something believable and considerate to answer your question. You think I was in Queens instead of Manhattan on Saturday night and I wouldn't want to hurt your feelings, even though you're becoming so shallow it scares me.

A few days before Christmas vacation, when Summer sat with me during lunch period and she was all cheery because she'd reconciled with her Columbia guy, I caught Leigh's attention as she glanced up from *ARTnews*.

"Why did you have to do that?" Summer said after I waved across the cafeteria at Leigh, who closed her magazine and walked in our direction.

She settled down next to me; Summer was across from us. Leigh acted friendly and Summer sat stock-still in her chair like an absolute prig. Then Leigh started talking about Del and his club and the opening-night party on New Year's Eve.

"He told you about it, didn't he?" Leigh said, and I nodded and stiffened, feeling Summer's eyes sear holes in my face. "You can come, Summer . . . if you want to."

She did want to. I wasn't sure if it was because she liked the idea of being the private guest of a Manhattan nightclub owner—even one with a birth defect—or if it was just spite. And during the subway ride home that afternoon, she didn't ask where or how I had spoken to Del. She pretended that the entire issue was unimportant, which was even worse.

"I'll bring Casey," she said. "Leigh told me that I could bring a guest."

Casey was the Columbia guy. He was blond and good-looking and the mention of him reminded me that I didn't have a guest to bring, but I didn't feel bad. Normally I would have—I would have felt inadequate and unattractive and I would have spent hours pondering my uneven breasts—but this time I decided to be positive. I was going to see Del next week and he had kissed me and touched the curve in my back, and any guy who did such a thing to a girl had to have at least a smidgen of interest in her, didn't he?

But Mom couldn't know about that. I only told her that I wanted to go to a nightclub on New Year's Eve and that Leigh's cousin owned the place, and it was all perfectly safe because Leigh's mother would be there and I wouldn't have a single drink.

She puffed on a cigarette while I argued my case and then she demanded to meet *This Leigh Person,* as if I was five years old. But I agreed and Leigh stopped by on Christmas Eve so we could exchange gifts.

I gave her a sweater and she gave me an Eighty-eight-Shade Pro Eye Shadow Palette. It came in a glazed black case with a built-in mirror. She told me that Rachel had chosen this particular set because it was the appropriate match for my skin tone.

"Leigh is very nice," Mom said after she was gone. We were in the living room while Dad slept upstairs, and she handed me a plate of homemade butter cookies. "You can go to the club as long as you come home at a reasonable hour."

What a relief. I smiled and selected a cookie in the shape of a star.

The next day, Evelyn came to Brooklyn with Patrick and the boys. She'd lost seven pounds from the flu; her face was thinner, her eczema was almost gone, and she wore a royal blue dress with a Christmas present from Patrick—eighteen amethysts that formed a teardrop and hung from a gold chain around her neck. She whispered in my ear that they couldn't afford anything extra this year, but she'd been feeling so low lately that Patrick wanted to give her something special, so he just put it on their MasterCard.

I fawned over the necklace. I smiled after Mom whispered in a relieved voice that Patrick and Evelyn were getting along better. I snapped a Polaroid of them on the couch as Patrick's hand squeezed Evelyn's leg and Evelyn's head rested on Patrick's shoulder. And when they kissed under the mistletoe that hung from our kitchen doorway, I cheerfully agreed with Mom that they were a beautiful couple. Then I hid in the bathroom for a while. I was so jealous that I almost cried.

nine

It was New Year's Eve and there was a party downstairs. Summer and I were in her bedroom, and she was frowning at my outfit.

"It's just too boring, Ari," she said, glancing at the imitation satin blouse that was my Christmas gift from Patrick and Evelyn. Then she reached into her closet and started tossing things on the bed until she found something supposedly appropriate—a black suede miniskirt and a bustier similar to the one she was wearing. "I hate to be so critical, but you usually want my advice and I'm only trying to help."

I knew that. But I couldn't wear a bustier. Hers was pink with jeweled lavender florets and underwire that hiked up her breasts; I couldn't imagine leaving the house in such a thing. "I can't, Summer. That top wouldn't look right on me."

"Well, maybe not. I know you're uneven up there. But it's barely noticeable."

She turned back to her closet and I felt the blood drain from my face, thinking that it couldn't possibly be *barely noticeable* because she had noticed it. And Evelyn had noticed it. And God only knew who else. Now I wanted to forget this whole thing, but Summer distracted me by latching a pearl choker around my neck.

"There. It's flashy but preppy. I know you love the preppy crap, Ari."

Preppy crap. That made me feel fabulous. I felt even better when she said my pants were too loose and my shoes were dull, but I took her advice because she did have a lot of fashion sense. So I ended up leaving her bedroom wearing my blouse, her choker, the suede skirt, and a pair of black pumps that she never wore because they were too big.

"You're going now?" Tina said.

Summer and I had just pushed through a crowd of guests on our way to the kitchen, where we found Tina staring through the window of her oven. The house smelled delicious and Tina looked exhausted.

"The car is outside," Summer said. "I won't stay out too late."

Tina pursed her lips and swung around to the counter. She peeled a sheet of wax paper from a tray of deviled eggs and shook her head. "I'm letting you off easy tonight, Summer.

But the next time I have a party at home or an event to cater, I expect your help."

"You don't have to work so hard," Summer said. "Dad makes plenty of money."

Tina was arranging eggs into a perfect circle on a plate. "Money has nothing to do with it. . . . I have a business and responsibilities. I have a reputation, you know."

They got into a tiff that lasted until Jeff and the scent of cigars joined us. He said that everyone was asking for Tina. Tina said she would be there in a minute and she didn't say anything else to Summer, so we left.

Once we were in the back of the sedan, Summer gave the chauffeur her boyfriend's address. I had to move to the front when Casey got into the car, but it was better that way, because as I checked my makeup in my compact, I saw the reflection of Casey and Summer kissing and groping. She only brushed his hands away after they reached her bustier.

"Wait until later," she said. "You're so pushy."

He was? She had never told me that. But I didn't think about it for long, because soon we were on West Twenty-third and there were so many cars and people in front of Del's building that the chauffeur had to drop us off way down the street. Summer was between me and Casey as we walked toward the club, and she kept saying "Isn't this exciting?" while the wind blew her hair into my face. It slapped my nose, but I didn't mind. Summer was right—this was *very* exciting. A strobe light flashed behind the windows in the two lower floors of Del's building, and we bypassed an endless line of people who gave us the stink eye while they waited behind a velvet rope.

The entrance wasn't the front door, which Leigh and I had used the last time we'd been here. It was on the side of the building. Summer and Casey and I waited there for Leigh so she could get us past the sinister-looking bouncer with the shaved head who was in charge of letting people in.

"What's the club called?" Summer asked.

"Cielo," Leigh said, suddenly behind me. "It means 'sky' in Spanish."

That was an appropriate name. Before Leigh had gotten here, I'd been staring at the pointed roof of the building, thinking that it nearly skimmed the moon, wondering if Del watched the stars through the skylight in his loft on clear nights.

Leigh spoke to the bouncer. He stepped aside and ushered us in, and the music was so loud I thought my eardrums might burst as I listened to Modern English—drums and a synthesizer and a male voice singing with a British accent. Lights pulsated in bursts of blue and yellow through smoke-filled air, and guys and girls were lifting their arms and grinding against each other on the dance floor. I thought I'd made a smart move by taking my migraine pills before I left home tonight. The lights and the noise would have given me a massive headache otherwise.

Summer, Casey, and I followed Leigh through the crowd until we reached a crescent-shaped bar surrounded by people sitting on stools covered in faux zebra skin. There were lit candles on the bar, a mirror behind it, and bottles of Stolichnaya and Johnnie Walker Black that were poured by three bartenders.

Leigh said something to one of them, I couldn't hear what, and the next thing I knew we were behind the bar, going through a door into a dark room that I guessed was an office because it had a desk and a phone, and then there was Del, standing in front of us in black pants and a silk shirt with the first three buttons undone.

Leigh made the introductions. Del shook hands with Casey and with Summer. He kissed Leigh and he kissed me and I felt his hand on the curve between my back and my rear end, which got me all shivery.

"No underage drinking, please," he said. "I'll lose my liquor license on my first night."

We nodded and Del said he had some things to do so he would see us later. Leigh and Summer and Casey and I went back to the club, where Casey found an empty barstool and stayed there because he wasn't a dancer.

The rest of us were. We carved out a space in the crowd, and we danced to the blare of Wham! and Duran Duran until our feet were sore and we had to take off our shoes and dangle them from our hands. Summer kept taking breaks to visit Casey, but Leigh and I were afraid to lose our spot, so we stayed right there.

I saw Del in the distance, working the crowd, and I also spotted Rachel, who looked beautiful in leather pants and a metallic halter top, dancing with various men. I caught her eye and she waved, jangling a jumble of bracelets on her wrist.

"Who's *that*?" Summer asked.

Her breath smelled of alcohol. I glanced across the club at Casey, who'd been sitting there all night with a glass in his hand, and I guessed that the glass had been refilled several times with something that wasn't Pepsi. He probably had a fake ID and was sharing his drinks with Summer. I was sure that neither one of them cared about Del and his liquor license.

"Leigh's mother," I said.

Her eyes grew big and round. "Really? Jesus."

We kept dancing and Summer kept crossing the room to be with Casey, and soon she started laughing too much and I knew she was drunk. Then she and Leigh and I got tired of dancing, so we stopped and found seats next to Casey at the end of the bar.

"Why did your cousin name this place Cielo?" Summer asked, yanking on her bustier, which had begun a downward slide.

Leigh was sipping a mock Pink Lady with an orange slice stuck on the rim. "His girlfriend is Spanish. She gave him the idea."

Summer nodded and touched up her lipstick, Leigh ate her orange slice, Casey ordered another drink, but for me the party was over. Del had a Spanish girlfriend and I was such an idiot.

"Hey," Summer said, reaching across me to tap Leigh on her sleeve. "Did Ari tell you I thought Del was your boy-friend?"

Leigh shook her head. What Summer said after that wasn't meant to be cruel—she was probably trying to be sym-pathetic and use her counseling skills when she said she was sorry that Leigh's boyfriend died, losing someone in such a tragic way must be horrible, blah blah blah. Summer's eyes were glassy and her face was flushed, and she didn't shut her mouth until Leigh opened hers.

"I think you've had enough to drink," she said, and Summer looked even more offended than she had when I'd told her that *Indian* wasn't the proper term. "You're not supposed to be drinking anyway. My cousin asked you politely, as I recall."

Leigh turned her head, gazing across the club. Summer was quiet at first. I knew she was formulating a good response, the way people do during the whole car ride home after they've been insulted at a party and they make a lengthy mental list of clever comebacks.

"*You're* one to talk," she said finally, as her bustier slid down and her cleavage bounced up. "At least I'm not planning to drive my boyfriend home tonight."

Leigh's face went pale and I thought I saw her lip quiver. "Fix your top," she said. "You don't want people to think you're a slut."

She shouldn't have said that. Leigh didn't know about the condoms on the locker or the nail polish on the bathroom wall. But Summer had never forgotten, and now her chest heaved up and down as she leaned across me again.

"Not that it's any of your business, Leigh . . . but I've only slept with one guy. And I haven't killed him."

I cringed. Leigh's eyes filled with tears. She jumped off the stool and shoved through the crowd toward Rachel while Summer muttered the word *bitch* and Casey put her coat over her shoulders.

"We'll get a cab," Summer said. "Right, Ari? Let's leave."

I watched her button her coat. I didn't want to leave. I

wanted to find Leigh and make sure she was okay. Summer was angry and flustered, and she seemed to think I was too. I just sat there until she stopped buttoning and looked at me.

"Right, Ari?" she said again. "Let's get out of here."

I touched the choker she'd given me. "I don't want to leave yet, Summer. I want to talk to Leigh before I go."

Her mouth fell open. "*Leigh?* Why would you talk to her after what she said to your friend?"

What about what you said to her? I thought. But I didn't say it; Summer was upset enough already. "She's my friend too. I can have two friends, can't I?"

Summer closed her mouth. She looked like I'd punched her. "You've never had two friends. *I've* always been your friend. You've always *needed* me to be your friend."

I didn't know what to say. There was a straw on the bar; I picked it up and started bending it in different directions. Now I knew why Summer had hated Leigh from the beginning—because it made her feel important to be my only friend. She was right when she said I had always needed her, and I supposed she wanted to be needed. I supposed everyone did.

"I never abandoned you," Summer went on, shouting over the music. "When I went to Hollister . . . and I made other friends . . . I never ditched you. I was always there for you."

I tossed the straw back onto the bar and looked at her. Her eyes were glistening. She was right again—she hadn't ditched me, even though most people would have. She had still invited me to her sweet sixteen and hadn't let me hide in the bathroom all night. She'd even stood next to Uncle

Eddie's coffin with me and put my thank-you note in his cold hand.

The strain between Summer and Leigh had worn me out. The music was deafening and I was tempted to jump in a cab and go home, but I couldn't do that to Leigh. "I know," I said tiredly, reaching over to squeeze Summer's shoulder through her coat. "I just want to stay for a while longer, that's all. It's New Year's Eve . . . and you know I never get to go anyplace."

Summer tugged pink gloves onto her hands, looking at me disdainfully from the corners of her heavily made-up eyes. "Why aren't you on my side?"

"There aren't any sides," I said, thinking that having two friends was more complicated than I'd ever expected. "I don't want there to be."

She shook her head. "There are *always* sides, Ari. And I *hope* you're only staying because it's New Year's Eve."

I was sure we both knew that wasn't the reason, but we didn't talk about it anymore. Casey said goodbye, and he and Summer walked away, pushing past people as they headed to a bright red Exit sign. I looked over the crowd and saw Rachel and Leigh across the room. Rachel hugged Leigh and led her away, and I watched until I couldn't find them in the shimmery sea of people.

Then I watched Del. He was weaving in and out of the crowd, shaking men's hands and kissing women's cheeks, and every time he kissed a woman, he rested his hand on the small of her back. It was enough to make me wish I was back in Flatbush, eating Mom's leftover cookies and waiting for that stupid ball to drop over Times Square.

* * *

I wasn't sure how I ended up in the front hall, walking toward the staircase that led to Del's apartment. I had spent a long time alone at the bar, watching people dance and kiss and gaze longingly into each other's eyes while nobody gazed at me. Nobody except the sleazy overweight guy who kept offering to buy me an Alabama Slammer.

I didn't deserve that. I didn't deserve to be hit on by someone like him. I had shiny hair and well-groomed eyebrows and I was thin and above average height. I might not have been as sexy as Summer or as exotic as the image of Del's girlfriend that I'd spent the last hour concocting, but I was better than this fat creep with his three chins and his tacky pierced ear.

So I had bolted. I had given up on finding Leigh. I'd forced my way through the crowd until I saw a door that I hoped would lead to fresh air and a cab ride home. But of course I'd chosen the wrong door, and now I was in the front hall passing the staircase.

"It's all right, baby," I heard a voice say, and it was Rachel, huddling with Leigh on the lower steps. Leigh leaned her face against Rachel's neck and Rachel spoke in a comforting voice. They made me think of a widow and her child who'd been evicted by a greedy landlord. The two of them against the world.

It was a private moment, so I tried to sneak past. But when I heard my name, I turned around. Neither of them moved. They kept their arms around each other while Leigh apologized for ditching me.

"I'll call a car to take us home, Ari," she said, then turned back to Rachel. "You go inside, Mama. You were having fun before I ruined it."

Rachel held Leigh's face in her hands. "You didn't ruin anything, baby."

Leigh insisted. Rachel left and Leigh looked at me. "Let's go use Del's phone."

I didn't want to use Del's phone. I didn't want to see his loft with the exposed brick and the skylight with its amazing view of the stars. I wanted to forget about him, because how could I have expected that somebody like Del would be interested in me? The whole idea was preposterous. I just wanted the night to end.

I couldn't tell Leigh that, so I went. She had her own key, which she used to unlock the red door; then she picked up the telephone and I sat on a couch.

There were no partitions between the rooms. I stared at Del's bed on the far side of the loft. It was lacquered black with a mirrored headboard and rumpled sheets that dripped suggestively to the hardwood floor. There was a window next to it, and I saw gargoyles on the neighboring building. Or maybe they were dragons. I couldn't make them out from where I was, so I walked to the window and pressed my forehead to the glass, but I didn't see dragons or gargoyles. I saw spooky angel faces with apple cheeks and rosebud lips like Evelyn's.

I looked away, around the room, because Leigh's back was turned and she was still on the phone, and I had a chance to snoop. I slid open a bureau drawer, where I saw cigarettes and a pair of frilly panties that I was sure belonged to the Spanish girl. She probably had straight teeth and a cute accent and perfectly even breasts.

"Our ride will be here soon," Leigh called across the loft.

I closed the drawer. "Okay," I said, and felt Leigh's hand on my arm a minute later.

She sat on the bed and I sat with her. "Listen," she began, and I was uncomfortable. I couldn't stop imagining what had made the sheets so disheveled, and I wondered what it would feel like to lie down right here with Del next to me instead of Leigh. "You should know a few things," Leigh was saying.

Then she told me about her boyfriend. She said that he was a nineteen-year-old zoology major who had planned to become a veterinarian. She also said that whenever she had visited him in Oswego, he had let her drive his car for practice. She'd never so much as made an illegal turn until one Saturday last December. That night, they were driving back to his dorm after a movie when she skidded on an icy road. He hit his chest on the dashboard and was gone before the ambulance came.

"He had internal injuries," she said. "It was a freak accident. So people at school can tell all the stories they want . . . but that's the entire truth."

I believed her. The gossip was probably one of the reasons why Leigh rarely came to class. She probably walked around in her boyfriend's clothes because she felt him inside them. And I supposed there was no point in getting fixed up when the only guy you loved would never see your face again.

"Summer has no idea what she's talking about," Leigh said. "I didn't kill my boyfriend—it wasn't my fault—and

I never even slept with him. I made him wait because I was afraid of ending up pregnant. I was afraid he'd run off and disappear, because that's what happened to my mother. He was so understanding and patient but I made him wait anyway and it was the worst decision ever. Now I'll never get a second chance. And I'm not sure if I'll ever want anyone else. Most guys are jerks and phonies."

I rolled my eyes. "I know. They pay you compliments they don't even mean."

Leigh stared at me for a moment. "Are you referring to Del?"

I shrugged. I hadn't meant to give myself away, but the words just fell out of my mouth.

She leaned into the white ripples of the sheets. Then she told me that Del and his girlfriend had split up for a while and had gotten back together just a few days ago, and she shouldn't keep criticizing him but she was going to because I should hear the facts.

"He's a pig, Ari. You don't want him. Trust me."

"He's . . . ," I started to say, not sure if I'd heard her right.

"A pig," she said. "He's my cousin and I love him, but he really *is* a runaround. He cheats on his girlfriend constantly— he's always got a different chick up here." She patted the bed. "*Putas,* that's what Idalis calls them. They're just a bunch of skanky whores who get kicked out onto Twenty-third in the morning."

Who was Idalis? And I couldn't believe that every one of the girls Del brought up here was a *puta.* Some of them had to be regular girls who thought Del cared about them. That idea brought a disturbing image into my head. I pictured a pretty girl in high heels and smeared makeup stumbling on the sooty sidewalk after a night on these temptingly soft sheets. I saw her as a Christmas tree that got left on the curb with garbage cans and ratty old rugs like it had never been any better than the rest of the trash.

"Idalis?" I said.

She nodded. "His girlfriend. And he doesn't even protect himself. He caught an STD two years ago—I'm not sure which one—I heard my mother and Uncle Stan talking about it. It was cured with penicillin, but Del could end up with AIDS if he doesn't watch out. It's not just a gay disease, you know. A raging heterosexual like Del can get it too. I mean, when you sleep with one person, you're sleeping with everybody that person has been with and . . . it's like . . . endless."

"Yeah," I said, because I'd heard it all before in Sex Ed. But I wasn't sure if the rest was true. A part of me suspected that Leigh was sparing my feelings, like when a girl in junior high hadn't invited me to her birthday party and Mom had said, *You don't need that uppity little snob and her goddamned party. Who does she think she is, anyway? Her father spent two years in prison for tax evasion, from what I hear.*

But another part of me believed everything. And that part felt relieved, as if Leigh had snatched my hand away from a dog that was really cute but had razor-sharp teeth that could disfigure me for life.

ten

When the holidays were over, I banished Del from my mind and focused on things that were supposed to be important, like grades and drawing and the practice SAT exams in a thick book Mom had picked up at Barnes & Noble.

At Hollister I ate lunch with Summer and without Leigh, who stuck to the opposite end of the cafeteria. But I talked to Leigh in homeroom and art class. I gave each one of my friends special attention to make up for New Year's Eve. I decided that Summer was oil and Leigh was water and they were both valuable in their own way, but they just couldn't mix.

I spent the first Saturday in January browsing at Bloomingdale's with Summer and the second at the Guggenheim with Leigh. The next day I accompanied Leigh to a Sunday-matinee performance of *Cats* at the Winter Garden Theater because Rachel got tickets for free. I warned Mom to keep my whereabouts a secret if Summer called while I was gone.

"Oh, Ariadne," she said with a laugh. "Is that really necessary?"

"Definitely, Mom," I told her. "Summer would be upset."

"Jealous, probably. She isn't used to sharing you."

That was a keen observation on Mom's part. I kept it in mind when January sixteenth came and Evelyn wanted to host a family dinner at her house for my seventeenth birthday. I invited Summer and not Leigh. Summer had been a fixture at my birthday dinners for years and Leigh knew nothing about them, so I wasn't snubbing anybody. At least, that was what I kept telling myself.

"I hope you like it," Summer said.

We were sitting on Evelyn's couch amid a field of tattered wrapping paper, and Summer's gift was my last. Mom and Dad had given me a garnet birthstone ring, and Patrick and Evelyn had bought me an imitation-angora sweater. Kieran's present was hilarious—a necklace he'd created in kindergarten, made of uncooked pasta. I wore the necklace because it made him happy. The rigatoni hung around my neck while I opened Summer's gift—a gold heart charm engraved with #1 FRIEND. She said I was her "best friend ever," which was really sweet. She had also brought cookies from Tina. They were arranged in a fancy container with a big bow and her new business card, which said CATERING BY TINA. TELL YOUR FRIENDS.

I filed the card in my wallet. Then we all sat around the kitchen table and ate the cookies and a cake that Evelyn had bought at Carvel. There were edible daisies on the outside and vanilla ice cream with those little chocolate crunchy thingies on the inside, and I thought that Summer wasn't the only one who was being sweet today.

Evelyn was in a good mood. She had lost more weight, she looked pretty, and she'd even served us dinner earlier—salad and garlic bread and lasagna. The lasagna was delicious, even though it was the kind that comes frozen in a box.

"Don't you want a cookie, Evelyn?" Summer asked.

Sabotage. That was exactly what sprang into my mind. Evelyn was on a diet—what was Summer trying to do, keep my sister chubby? Maybe Summer was hoping for a chance with Patrick, who sat across from me looking gorgeous, with his blond hair and those big hands that I was sure matched other big body parts.

"I can't," Evelyn said. "Weight Watchers, you know."

Summer nodded. "I can tell. You've lost a lot already."

That was nice. I was too suspicious. Summer excused herself to the bathroom, and Dad and Patrick went into the living room to watch the Rangers play the Bruins. Evelyn ate an apple, and I was proud of her—she was sticking to her diet. I wanted her to get thin enough to fit into her old high school clothes that were buried in our basement. There were tube tops and a Diane von Furstenberg knockoff dress and Jordache jeans that Mom couldn't stand. *They're so tight, I can see all your business,* Mom used to say. *You'll end up with a yeast infection worthy of the medical journals, Evelyn.*

She never got an infection. And those jeans were a decade

out of style now. But if Evelyn could fit into them, she might be inspired to get a new wardrobe that Mom and Dad could buy with some of Uncle Eddie's money. That might boost Evelyn's confidence enough for her to take some classes that would teach her to do more than ring up groceries at Pathmark.

"Evelyn," Mom said, finishing her second slice of cake. She grabbed a cigarette and I wanted to tell her to lay off those things, but I knew I'd be wasting my breath. "Did you know that your sister is on the honor roll again?"

I cringed. Why why why why why did she have to bring that up? Evelyn shook her head and Mom flicked her Bic and talked behind a billowy, menacing fog. She talked about my A in calculus and my A in English, and I thought she might have an *organism* when she brought up my art teacher.

"At the parent-teacher conference," Mom said, waving her hands around dramatically, holding her Pall Mall between two fingers, "he told me that Ari is loaded with talent and that she'll have no problem whatsoever getting into Parsons. No problem whatsoever."

No. Problem. Whatsoever. That was how she said it. And I was amazed that someone with a graduate degree could be so dense. Had she forgotten that we had to be careful around Evelyn and that talk of good grades and talent was the same as calling her a big fat stupid failure?

"That's nice," Evelyn said with a stiff grin, the way people do when they meet an ugly baby. *How cute. How adorable. That's the most hideous thing in existence but I'll just smile and tickle the unsightly creature because it's the polite thing to do.*

I wanted to change the subject, and I was struggling to

come up with one when Summer returned. She sat next to me, and Kieran started talking about his new racetrack set.

"Come and play with my cars, Aunt Ari," Kieran begged, tugging on my hand.

"Not now. I'm visiting with everyone," I said, but he didn't understand. He clung to me. He whined. He yanked at the rigatoni around my neck.

"Leave Aunt Ari alone, Kieran," Evelyn said. "I'll play with you later."

Then the worst thing happened. It was one of those *if only* moments—the kind of thing that makes you retrace your steps to pinpoint the exact second you could have averted the disaster. *If only I hadn't sat around in that wet bathing suit, I wouldn't have this kidney infection. If only I hadn't waxed the tiles, poor old Grandpa wouldn't have slipped and broken his neck. If only I had played with Kieran and his cars, he wouldn't have snapped at Evelyn like he was the spawn of Satan.*

"I don't want *you*," he said. "Aunt Ari is better than you."

Everyone was quiet. I heard Dad yelling at the television about a penalty, and Mom told Kieran to go and play in his bedroom. Her voice was low and husky and she wore the intimidating face she used with her students. It made Kieran skulk out of the room as she crushed her cigarette in an ashtray.

He was so moody. Maybe he got it from his mother, but that didn't matter right now. All that mattered was Evelyn. Last summer I had warned Kieran not to say I was *better* and I hadn't been sure he'd understood, so I had just let him fall asleep on those blasphemous New England Patriots sheets.

"He didn't mean that, Evelyn," Mom said. "Kids say the strangest things."

Evelyn's fingers shook as she cleared dishes from the table. Mom pointed at me and at Summer and nodded toward the living room.

Then Summer and I sat on the couch and watched the rest of the game with Dad and Patrick. Summer cheered and booed at the appropriate times, but it was just a blur to me. I had more important things on my mind, like the fact that Evelyn probably hated my guts and that an aura was floating around my left eye and my migraine pills were at home.

I sat in my studio the next Saturday afternoon, drawing hands with a pencil from the cedar box Summer had given me. I drew a man's hand and a woman's hand, intertwined. The man's was rugged, with veins that stretched from the wrist to the fingers like the pattern on a leaf, while the woman's was delicate and smooth as ivory.

"How beautiful," Mom said from the doorway.

She startled me. I'd been staring at my work, thinking that the hands were romantic. I imagined the feel of that strong hand against my palm, his fingers lacing into mine, fitting as perfectly as puzzle pieces.

That was probably because I'd seen Summer holding hands with Casey, who had picked her up from school every day last week in his BMW. He locked his hands into hers while she kissed him, and she waved to me from the window as they drove away.

It was sickening. But I couldn't let her know that I was

dying of envy, that I wished some handsome guy would whisk me away from school while my admiring classmates watched, and I couldn't complain about riding home alone on the subway. It was one thing for Summer to gripe about Leigh, but placing a boyfriend above everyone else was expected. It was the female code or whatever.

"I'm just practicing," I told Mom. "I'm terrible at extremities."

She lingered behind me. "On the contrary. You're very good."

I didn't think so. I flipped to a blank page in my sketch pad and Mom started talking about Queens. She said that Evelyn was desperate for a break from the kids, Patrick wanted to take her out tonight, and someone had to watch the boys.

"Oh," I said, sure that my birthday dinner had been forgiven and forgotten and Evelyn needed me. "What time are we leaving?"

"Well," Mom started, sitting down on a chair. She looked like she was about to tell me something important and was searching for the right words. She'd done the same thing years ago when she'd explained my *monthly visitor*. Now her eyes scanned the room as if the best words were written on the curtains or the walls. "Here's the thing . . ."

Here's the thing. That was the phrase Mom used to begin unpleasant conversations. It was what she'd said when Dad's mother died. Now it was the first sentence Mom chose when she told me that she and Patrick had decided it would be best if I didn't go to Queens for a while.

I knew Mom didn't mean Queens in general. She didn't

mean Shea Stadium or Flushing Meadows Park. She said Queens because she thought it sounded better than just coming right out and telling me that I wasn't welcome at Patrick and Evelyn's house.

"You mean they don't want me there?" I said. "Are you kidding? I've always tried so hard to help them."

"Of course you have," Mom said in that *You're not really in pain* tone. "But you know how Evelyn is. We want what's best for her . . . don't we, Ariadne?"

She spoke like I was too much of a delicate flower to handle this and she had to pretend everything was fine so I wouldn't start crying or get a migraine, and she was probably right. I almost did cry, and my head started to throb. We want what's best for her, I thought. I knew that *we* was Mom and Patrick. Of course he would sacrifice me for Evelyn. I might have been an excellent cook and a very nice girl, but Evelyn was his wife and the mother of his children. I was expendable.

eleven

Hollister was stingy with its snow days. This I discovered two days later, after a Sunday-night blizzard that closed Mom's school the next morning but not mine.

Mom stood outside our house dropping rock salt on the front steps while I jammed my feet into a pair of boots in the foyer. I was zipping them up when Jeff's Mercedes arrived, and as I knotted a scarf around my neck, I saw him heading toward Mom.

What was he doing? Our storm door muffled their voices, and when I went outside, they clammed up and stared at me until I got the message and walked to the car, where Summer sat in the front seat.

She was wearing her fuzzy pink hat and she was happy, which was so obnoxious. She'd become one of those people who waltzed through life without so much as a split end, and I was still one of those people who changed diapers and babysat for free but still got treated like a rented mule.

"Studying?" Summer said, looking at the SAT book on my lap after I climbed into the back.

I nodded. "How about you? Did you get one of these books?"

"I don't need it," she said, tapping her forehead. "It's all up here."

That was obnoxious too. Of course she didn't need an SAT book, because she wasn't going to study. She never studied. I knew she planned to take the test without opening a book or enrolling in one of those tedious prep courses that met on Saturday mornings. Then the scores would arrive and hers would be stellar and she would go off to UCLA, where she'd fit in with blond surfer girls and glamorous Hollywood types and forget that I had ever existed.

Fine, Summer, I thought. Go to California. Leave me here like poor lonely Saint Anne on my lawn. Look at her, all covered in snow. She's getting so old and the paint on her face is cracking from the weather and I'm the only one who cares.

"He's giving your mother the names of a few psychiatrists in Queens," Summer said, pointing to Jeff and Mom. "She called him yesterday. I guess Evelyn is having problems again?"

I didn't know that Mom had called Jeff yesterday. She'd probably done it from the laundry room, where she whispered with Patrick about things she couldn't mention to me, especially since I'd been expelled from the inner sanctum.

"Yeah," I said. "She is."

Summer reached back and squeezed my hand. "You can't help what your nephew said, Ari. It wasn't your fault."

It wasn't? But she made me feel a little better until that afternoon, when she rushed to Casey's BMW with her hair flowing and they locked hands and kissed, and then I rode the subway to Brooklyn by myself.

The next day, I sketched in my notebook during homeroom until I felt a tap on my shoulder and heard a raspy voice in my ear.

"What's the matter with you?" Leigh asked. "You look sad."

I told her the truth. I told her about Evelyn and about Patrick, and she listened intently before inviting me to another party. This one was at the theater where we'd seen *Cats*.

"You need a night out, Ari. The party is a farewell for one of the cast members. My mother's planning it. It's supposed to be on Friday, but it might not happen because the caterer she hired just canceled. She's looking for another one."

I thought of Tina's *Tell Your Friends* card, pulled it out of my wallet, and gave it to Leigh. "I know you and Summer don't get along, but this is her mother's catering business, and she's very reliable."

Leigh shrugged. "We'd hire a mass murderer at this point."

A mass murderer would have been better. Because later

on, when it was nearly midnight and I was studying for the SAT at my kitchen table while Mom and Dad slept upstairs, the phone rang and it was Summer, who wasn't happy that Rachel had hired Tina for the farewell party.

"Are you retarded?" Summer asked.

Retarded. That was worse than calling Del an Indian. "Am I—" I began, thoroughly confused, but she cut me off.

"Retarded," she said. "I think you must be if you expect me to wait on Leigh Ellis like I'm some Puerto Rican maid."

She needed a few courses in respecting ethnicities and disabilities if she wanted to be a psychiatrist. And making her work as a maid wasn't what I'd meant to do at all.

"Summer—"

"Ari," she interrupted. "If a person is a true friend, she doesn't associate with people who'd disparage her best friend of many years by calling her names that are written on dirty bathroom walls and spoken aloud only by low-class individuals."

"Leigh isn't a low-class individual," I said as Mom and Dad walked into the kitchen with messy hair and the worried expressions they often wore after late-night phone calls. I suddenly got the feeling that Mom was right—Summer didn't want to share me. She preferred it when I sat at home on Friday nights while she was on dates and at parties.

Then I listened while Summer told me that she had plans with Casey on Friday and she wasn't going to the Winter Garden no matter how much Tina ranted and raved, and I should find my own way to school tomorrow.

"I told my father you're sick," she said. "I'm so mad right

now that I don't feel like riding to school with you for a few days. He thinks you're staying home for the rest of the week . . . and don't you dare tell him anything different or I'll never speak to you again."

I heard the dead hum of the dial tone. I hung up the phone while my parents stared at me, and I knew what they were thinking: Was that Patrick? Did something terrible happen and are we going to be visiting Evelyn at New York–Presbyterian Hospital soon?

They both relaxed after I explained that it was just Summer. Dad went upstairs and Mom sat across from me and asked me what Summer wanted; then she lit a cigarette and I told her everything.

"Well," Mom said. "I think I'll call Jeff and let him know that you're perfectly healthy."

"Do me a favor and stay out of it," I said, and the mention of Jeff got me thinking about psychiatrists in Queens and about Evelyn. I asked Mom what was going on and she sighed.

"Evelyn's seeing a shrink again. But you shouldn't worry about any of that."

"Of course I'm worried, Mom. I'm not welcome in my own sister's house."

She opened the window beside the table and tapped her ashes into the air, where they turned into fiery speckles before vanishing in the wind. "It's just for a while, Ariadne. Evelyn is in a delicate state right now and there's some jealousy going on . . . you know the crazy things she comes up with."

I felt guilty, thinking that not everything Evelyn came up

with was crazy and Mom knew it. But Evelyn had no reason to be jealous of me. She was the one with the refined features and the green eyes and the handsome husband who did things in their bedroom that made her moan and gasp.

"She shouldn't feel that way," I said. "I don't have anything Evelyn wants."

Mom shrugged. "Some people don't know what they want."

On Friday night, Leigh sent a car that took me to the Winter Garden Theater, and I decided to have fun even if it killed me. I forced myself to forgive Patrick for keeping me out of Queens. I was sure that the situation was only temporary. Evelyn's new psychiatrist would probably recommend an innovative medication, and soon she'd be buying me Mrs. Fields cookies by the dozens. So I was going to have a good time tonight. A fantastic, spectacular time with interesting theater people and Tina's deviled eggs.

This idea lasted approximately five minutes. Leigh met me at the front door and I followed her into the theater, where we walked beneath a gaudy gold ceiling past rows of empty chairs and through a big red curtain. Then I heard jazz music and voices and I saw Summer.

She was serving truffle canapés on a tray and she looked miserable. Her mouth was stiff and her feet dragged, and Rachel made everything worse. She ordered Summer around in a sharp, condescending tone, and I knew why. It was Summer's fault that Rachel's *baby* had cried on New Year's Eve, and this was payback.

"Summer," Rachel said, towering over her in a pair of silver stilettos and a matching dress. "Every party has a pooper, but I don't pay to have one at mine. Put on a happy face, sweetheart. And clean up that mess over there—stage right. My guests are getting tipsy and spilling their drinks."

Summer glanced around. "Right *what*?"

I heard someone laugh. Rachel did too, as if the entire world should be familiar with stage directions.

"*Stage* right," Rachel said, pointing a spindly finger. "Right, left . . . get it?"

Summer got it. She grabbed some napkins and crouched down on the floor, and I pitied her. Rachel acted like she was royalty and Summer was a peasant, and Tina only cared about her business—*I have a reputation, you know.* She expected Summer to be polite no matter what. I was glad I'd brought my medicine, because I had a headache. So I found a bathroom, stuck my mouth under the faucet, and swallowed two pills.

Leigh was standing by the door when I came out. "My bracelet's missing," she said.

I was sweaty. I wanted to go home because this whole mess was my fault, but I couldn't go anywhere. Leigh's ID bracelet was gone and she was panicking.

We looked everywhere—backstage, on the stage, in every row of the theater. We were searching the lobby when Rachel came in, wondering why we had ditched the party.

"I can't find my bracelet," Leigh said, and started to cry. I wished she'd brought that thing to a jeweler like Del had suggested.

"It's not here, baby," Rachel said after another search, and then she and Leigh and I went backstage, where everyone tried to help. Finally Tina told Leigh not to worry, she and Summer were going to clean up after the party and if the bracelet was here, they would find it.

Leigh's eyes shot toward Summer, who was standing *stage left* with a tray of Gorgonzola popovers in her hands, obviously eavesdropping on our conversation. Leigh's lip was quivering as she looked at Tina. "What if *she* finds it?" Leigh asked, nodding toward Summer.

Tina glanced over her shoulder and then back at Leigh. "You mean my daughter? She'll let you know if she finds it. Why wouldn't she?"

The story was too long to tell, and we wouldn't have shared all the sordid details with Tina anyway. Leigh shrugged and Rachel said that she and Leigh should go home, but Leigh shook her head.

"I'm always ruining your fun, Mama. You stay here. We'll go over to Uncle Stan's for a while. I just need to use the bathroom first."

She walked away and I dashed across the stage, where Summer was leaning over a table and refilling her tray.

"Summer," I said, lingering behind her. "You'll let Leigh know if you find her bracelet, won't you? I think it belonged to her boyfriend, and it means a lot to her."

She straightened up and put a hand on her hip. "Of course I will, Ari. What kind of person do you think I am?"

A few minutes later, the chauffeur was driving me and Leigh away from the Winter Garden while Leigh brushed tears from her face and I obsessed about Summer. I kept quiet as the chauffeur took us to the Upper East Side, where we found Leigh's uncle in the foyer of his luxurious penthouse. He was wearing a suit and he was all smiles, like last time. I addressed him as Mr. Ellis and he didn't correct me.

"Is Blake here?" Leigh asked.

"He's studying," Mr. Ellis said.

She made a sour face. "He needs to relax."

"He needs to stay on the dean's list, and he will. Blake knows I've had my share of disappointment—he won't give me more."

I was sure he meant Del. I thought of the fight with the engineering student and the college expulsion and the STD, whatever it was. I also thought of Evelyn, and I wondered if Blake and I had something in common. We were both trying to make up for things we hadn't even done.

"Where are you going at this hour, Uncle Stan?" Leigh asked, and he said something about work and a client. Then the elevator doors shut and she led me to the kitchen, where she sat at the table and sounded desperate. "That bracelet belonged to my boyfriend. If I don't get it back . . . I swear I'll kill myself."

"Stop it, Leigh," I heard someone say, and I turned to find a young man behind me. "Don't ever say that again."

"I can't help it, Blake," she said as tears dripped from her eyes.

He sat next to her. I was surprised that this was the studious Blake, because he didn't look studious. He wore jeans and a T-shirt over a body that was average height with muscles that rivaled Patrick's, he had a shock of deep brown hair that stood up from his head, and his eyes were a much brighter blue than mine.

"Are you all right?" he said after Leigh stopped crying, and I wanted him to say something else because his voice was so soft and smooth. Leigh nodded and excused herself to the bathroom, and we were alone. "Blake Ellis," he said, reaching his hand across the table, flashing a boyish grin worthy of a Colgate commercial. "Please pardon my family drama."

His two front teeth were slightly longer than the rest, and there was something cute about that. I was suddenly embarrassed by my own flawed teeth, but what did they matter? Blake was probably no better than Del, and I wouldn't have a chance with him even if my teeth didn't overlap. So I shook his hand and smiled back.

Mom didn't listen to me when I told her not to call Jeff about my perfect health. She did it on the sly, and the next thing I knew, it was Monday morning and Summer and I were sitting on the couch in my living room. Mom stood on the carpet with her arms folded while Jeff advised me and Summer to *work this thing out like adults.*

I wanted to work it out. Summer put on a big phony act. She pretended to understand that I had only wanted to help Tina when I gave her business card to Leigh, and she hugged me after the conversation ended, but it was the fakest thing ever. It was worse than an air kiss or those people who said "Let's do lunch."

Then she and I were at Hollister and I remembered

Leigh's bracelet as we passed the iron gates. I asked Summer if she had found it, and she looked at me with the disgust she usually reserved for chewed-up gum on the soles of her Gucci shoes.

"Did I find what, Ari?"

"Leigh's bracelet," I said.

"Oh, that." She took out her compact and examined her lip gloss as we walked through the entrance and past the plaque of Frederick Smith Hollister. "It wasn't in the theater. We checked everyplace. Leigh must've lost it somewhere else."

"Are you sure?" I said.

Summer snapped her compact shut and stopped walking. We were standing next to a row of lockers and a crowd of students maneuvered around us.

"Yes, I'm *sure*," she said, her dark eyes blazing. "What are you implying?"

She looked so offended that I felt guilty for bringing it up. Maybe she was right—I'd known her forever, she had her flaws, but she wasn't that kind of person. I shouldn't have accused her of stealing a dead boy's bracelet.

"Nothing," I said before heading to homeroom.

A few days later, I was sitting with Leigh in the cafeteria. Summer was eating pizza at her friend's apartment and I hadn't been invited.

"Are you really sure Summer doesn't have my bracelet?" Leigh asked.

"Positive," I said. "I know she can be sort of flaky

sometimes, but she doesn't mean it. She's a good person underneath. She wouldn't do something like that."

Leigh let out a heavy sigh. "So I guess it's gone and I just have to accept it." Then she started talking about California, and I almost choked on my sandwich.

"You're leaving?" I said, wondering if it was my destiny to be alone.

Leigh nodded and told me that her uncle owned a condominium in some city called Brentwood, and she and Rachel were moving there in June. Mr. Ellis also had a close friend whose aunt was the principal of a private school where Leigh would be accepted for her senior year, and another friend was a movie producer with connections who could get Rachel hired as a makeup artist at Warner Brothers.

"I need a new atmosphere," Leigh said as I noticed that she wasn't wearing anything printed with SUNY OSWEGO, which was a good thing. So I smiled and listened while she told me that she'd be going to UCLA because her family had donated money there and she would get in for sure.

UCLA. Of course. I imagined UCLA surrounded by palm trees and sidewalks with famous people's names carved into the cement. I saw it as a giant magnet with the power to drag my friends across the country. But I didn't say anything negative because Leigh seemed excited, and she changed the subject by asking about my college plans.

I mentioned Parsons and it sounded boring. But maybe *I* was boring because I wasn't interested in Brentwood or anyplace other than here. I didn't want to be far from my parents, and I couldn't move away from Patrick and Evelyn and the boys, even if they never wanted to see me again.

"Uncle Stan knows people at Parsons," Leigh said. "He can get you in. Do you want to work in art?"

"Sort of. I want to teach. But you're going to be a real artist, aren't you?"

"No," she said. "Art is mine."

That made sense. Her art was hers and my art was mine, and I wanted to keep it hidden in my studio like a newborn baby because nobody would ever love it the way I did. So I nodded and Leigh started talking about teaching on the college level, something about getting a master's and a PhD, and she suggested that I become an art professor.

"That's what Idalis is planning to do. And you're much smarter than she is, Ari."

I had no idea who she was talking about until she reminded me: Idalis, Twenty-third Street, the *putas* in Del's bed. According to Leigh, Idalis was finishing her master's in Spanish literature. She was going to start her PhD in the fall, and I could meet her and get some career advice if I went to Mr. Ellis's apartment for dinner on Saturday night.

"You *have* to come, Ari," Leigh said. "It won't be any fun without you. Del will be there, but who cares? You don't want him, anyway."

Not really. Maybe a little. But Del was a pig, so I started thinking about other things—things like very blue eyes, a Colgate smile, a smooth voice that gave me goose bumps. The possibility that Blake would be at the dinner too made me accept Leigh's invitation.

twelve

Idalis Guzman was older than Del. I found out—over a four-course dinner served by two maids in Mr. Ellis's penthouse—that she was twenty-six, she was from Venezuela, and she wasn't serious about her boyfriend.

"I can't marry this guy," she said in perfect English with an accent that was even more appealing than I expected. "Then my name would be Idalis Ellis."

She had Rapunzel hair. It was honey brown and down to her waist, but not the kind that gets chopped off on those daytime talk shows where women neglect themselves and need a makeover. Hers was shiny and stylish. Her face wasn't the prettiest, but her skillfully applied makeup compensated for that. She wore classy clothes and expensive jewelry, and she carried herself like she was somebody special.

"If you want to teach," she said to me as we were eating our second course, which consisted of something I'd never seen before called sautéed leeks, "the university level is the way to go. Once you get tenure, you make good money and you have a flexible schedule, so you can work and still have time for a husband and kids. You can have it all, as they say."

I could have it all. I imagined myself as a professor: I would stand in a classroom and give lectures about Picasso to eager college freshmen. Then I would zip home to Brooklyn, where I would live in one of those elegant Park Slope houses, which I would be able to afford on my salary, and I'd be greeted at the door by my loving children, who would be as adorable as their father.

That idea got me excited and hopeful and it made me shift my gaze from Idalis to Blake. He sat opposite me, not eating his leeks, and his eyes reminded me of a marble that I had owned when I was nine years old. I'd had lots of others, but this one was my favorite, because it was transparent with a brilliant streak of sapphire blue that I would stare at and hold up to the sun. Then one day it disappeared. Mom took me to Woolworth's to find a match, but I didn't search very hard—I knew that something so beautiful only came around once.

"You don't need all that butter on your bread, Stan," Rachel said after the main course was served. "And slow down. You're eating too fast."

Mr. Ellis sat at the head of the table. He was digging into a slab of beef and he sounded annoyed. "I have to go out soon, Rachel. I'm meeting with a client."

Idalis laughed. "A client, sure. I think you've got a few lady friends stashed around Manhattan. And you should listen to your sister. You don't want another heart attack."

"That was three years ago," he said. "It won't happen again."

He still seemed annoyed and so did Blake, between dinner and dessert. I was in the bathroom upstairs when I heard his voice and Del's in the hallway. They were arguing, and I pressed my ear to the door.

"Tell your girlfriend to watch her mouth," Blake said.

Del laughed. "Why? You know she's right. Daddy keeps that apartment downtown for whoever he happens to be screwing at the moment. He can pretend he's faithful to Mama's memory all he wants, but that's just his usual hypocritical bullshit."

Daddy and Mama. That reminded me again of Elvis, even though Del and Blake both spoke like native New Yorkers. I listened while Blake said Del had no respect for their father and Del said their father led Blake around on a leash, and then Del started talking about some girl in Georgia.

"You've got nerve to criticize Idalis," Del said. "She's better than that little bleached-blond piece of trailer trash you banged for two years."

How scandalous. And interesting. The polite part of me wanted to turn on the faucet to drown out the conversation, but the nosy part was dying to hear what would happen next.

So I stayed where I was while Blake got angry and Del got angry.

"Don't talk about her," Blake said.

"Why?" Del asked. "She drops you with no explanation—she disappears without so much as a phone call—and you still defend her? It's pathetic, Blake. Get on with your life and stop moping about that chick. Be a fucking man, for Christ's sake."

And that was it. I heard footsteps on the stairs and I washed my hands and joined everybody in the dining room, where one maid was filling coffee cups and the other was lighting crème brûlée with a mini butane torch.

Blake didn't eat anything. Del devoured his dessert and swallowed two cups of coffee while I compared him to his brother. They were identical in height, and they both had dark hair and the exact same hands. Del was outgoing and a slick dresser, while Blake was quiet and wore casual clothes. His face wasn't quite as handsome as his father's, but it was much better than Del's. Blake's nose didn't hook down at the tip and there was no scar on his mouth. There was no way Summer could accuse him of having a birth defect.

"What's the matter?" Leigh asked Blake when she and Rachel and I were in the foyer with him, slipping into our coats. He shook his head and she patted his cheek, told him to cheer up, and suggested that they go skating at Rockefeller Center tomorrow.

"I love Rockefeller Center," I said, surprised at my boldness. I was fishing for an invitation, even though I shouldn't have because I had a chemistry test on Monday. Chemistry made my mind go numb. I had to work extra hard in that class to stay on the honor roll, so I'd been planning to study tomorrow, but Blake needed cheering up and this was a good excuse to see him again.

Leigh looked between me and Blake. "Oh," she said. "Do you want to come too, Ari?"

More than anything. I nodded, and Leigh told Blake we would meet him at noon. Then I was in the back of a sedan with Leigh and Rachel, and Rachel pointed at me.

"Blake would be perfect for this one," she said, and I was embarrassed to have been so transparent. But Rachel seemed to think the idea was her own.

Leigh glanced at me and back at Rachel. "Ari doesn't want your dating advice."

"Now, Leigh," Rachel said calmly, smoothing Leigh's hair. Leigh had a perturbed look on her face and her lips were puckered. "All three of you can be friends. I'm sure Ari wants to be friends with you *and* Blake."

That's right, I thought. I want to be friends with both of you. All three of us can be friends and I do want Rachel's dating advice, so shut up, Leigh.

Rachel turned toward me and started talking like a gossipy matchmaker. "Blake's a good boy, Ari. He doesn't prowl around the way Del does. And he's smart, too. He's a sophomore at NYU."

"He's nineteen, then?" I asked.

"Twenty," Leigh said, and I wondered if Blake hadn't started college right after high school, if he was one of those people who bummed around Europe for a year to find themselves. But she explained that he'd broken his leg when he was eight and was out of school for a while, and he'd had to repeat the third grade because he went to a school where the Ellis family hadn't donated any money. I was surprised that such a place existed.

"Del broke Blake's leg," Rachel said.

Leigh gave her a shove. "Don't say that, Mama."

"It's the truth, isn't it?" Rachel asked, then looked at me. "It was after their mother died. They got into a fight and Del pushed Blake down the stairs. That's the kind of temper he has."

Leigh told the driver to turn on the radio and we all got quiet. He dropped Leigh and Rachel off at their building, then drove me home, where Mom was waiting in the living room. There were sandwiches and warm milk on the coffee table and she wanted me to tell her everything. So we sat on the couch and I described the crème brûlée and the four courses, and asked if she'd ever eaten a leek.

"Once," she said. "At a swanky anniversary party."

Then I brought up my new plans. I talked about teaching college and becoming a career woman who could also have a husband and children and a house in Brooklyn with a flower garden and a hammock tied between two shady trees in the backyard, and I kept closing my eyes to see all of it. But when I opened them, Mom had a blank expression on her face, and that was so disappointing.

"Why would you want to live in Brooklyn?" she asked. "And being a college professor isn't what you think. Positions are hard to find, and nobody makes any money until they get tenure, which doesn't always happen." She stood up and brushed crumbs from her bathrobe. "Don't be in a rush to have children, either, Ariadne. Just look at Evelyn. She isn't exactly the portrait of fulfillment."

Mom went to bed and so did I, but I was too miserable to sleep. I switched between staring at the ceiling and through my window, wishing I could be what Mom wanted. I wished I could be like Summer, who wasn't afraid to go to UCLA or to put a note in a dead man's hand. She'd probably do all sorts of adventurous things that scared me, like move out of Brooklyn forever and travel solo around the globe. She'd probably become one of those independent women who didn't care about adorable children and flower gardens and hammocks.

There was an old pair of ice skates in our basement. I searched for them the next morning, remembering that they'd been a fourteenth-birthday gift from Mom and Dad to Evelyn, and Dad had said they were a goddamned waste because Evelyn had only worn them once.

They had to be here somewhere, lurking inside a cardboard box or buried in one of the plastic bins stacked against the wall. I was looking through a box marked EVELYN when I heard footsteps on the stairs.

"What are you doing?" Mom asked.

The skates weren't in the box. I saw a macramé purse, a container filled with seashells, and a pair of Jordache jeans that made me sad. But my mood was lousy anyway because Mom had crushed my dreams last night, and now I didn't want to look at her. I mumbled that I needed to find Evelyn's ice skates, and she started searching with me.

"Is it just going to be you and Leigh today?" she asked, pulling a hideous paisley dress from a box. "You didn't invite Summer?"

"Summer's always busy with her boyfriend," I said, watching as she held the dress against herself. It was a size eight, and I thought Mom should face reality and donate it to Goodwill. "You know that."

She must have read my mind. She tossed the dress onto an exercise bike that nobody ever used. "And all your homework is done?"

"Yes," I said impatiently, and Mom put her hands on her hips. I wasn't looking in her direction—I was bent over, digging through a box filled with musty old clothes—but I saw her from the corner of my eye and I wished she'd just go and eat something.

"Don't be so snippy, Ariadne. You want to get into Parsons, don't you?"

I straightened up. "Leigh told me her uncle has connections there."

Mom found the skates. There wasn't a scratch on them, but they weren't exactly what I remembered. I thought they were white or tan, or something less ridiculous than silver with rainbow shoelaces and purple lightning bolts stitched into the leather.

She pushed them at me. "What do you mean, her uncle has connections?"

No wonder Evelyn only wore those skates once. They

couldn't have been stylish even in 1976, when teenagers walked around in bell bottoms with combs sticking out of their back pockets. So I jammed the skates into a box and turned to Mom. "Leigh's uncle knows people at Parsons. He can get me in. My grades probably don't even matter."

I might as well have told her that I was "in trouble." That was how horrified she looked. "We," she said, pronouncing the word in a virtuous tone, as if she was about to say *We Kennedys* or *We Vanderbilts,* "don't need anyone's connections. We stand on our own two feet in this family and you know that."

I did know that. I felt like a shallow sloth who wanted an escape from those brain-frying SAT practice tests, and that just wasn't who I was raised to be. So I nodded. I was about to go upstairs when Mom grabbed the skates and held them in the air.

"Forget something?" she asked, and I couldn't say that I wouldn't wear those ghastly things, because my parents had bought them with their hard-earned money and it didn't make sense to pay for rented skates at Rockefeller Center when these were practically brand-new.

They were snug, though. Painful, even. I forced them onto my feet an hour later as I sat on a bench at Rockefeller Center with Leigh. She had spotless white skates with matching laces, and she was too nice to say anything critical about mine.

When Blake showed up, he sat next to me. I slid my feet under the bench, hoping he wouldn't see my stupid lightning bolts.

I saw other things. I saw his outrageously blue eyes and the wind sweeping through his hair as he leaned over to tie his skates.

"Aren't you coming?" he asked.

"I have a headache," I lied. I told him and Leigh to go without me and they disappeared into a swarm of people gliding on the ice, listening to piano music from those Charlie Brown holiday specials.

I acted fast and unlaced my skates, stuck them in my knapsack, and put on my boots so I wouldn't be humiliated in front of Blake, although I wasn't sure why I cared. He was skating laps around the rink without ever stumbling or stopping to tie a wayward shoelace, and I felt like I had as much of a chance with him as I did with Del.

I watched anyway, as he zoomed by the United States flag and the Japanese flag and other flags I couldn't name, but I stopped watching when I heard a dull thump.

There was a boy on the ice just a few feet away from me. He was about ten years old, and he had fallen on his arm. Someone skated over his hat after it fell off.

"Are you all right?" I said, jumping off the bench. I stood over him, offering him my hand, and hoisted him up, which wasn't easy because he was a chubby kid. "Did you hurt your arm?"

"Yeah," he said, rubbing it with a gloved hand.

"Are you here by yourself?"

He nodded. "My mom went over to Saks. I promised I'd be careful, but now look at what I've done. My arm is probably broken." He was getting all worked up.

"Don't worry. I can check your arm," I said, remembering the class Evelyn had made me take a few years ago, the one where I learned about CPR and diagnosing broken bones. So I checked for swelling and bruising and asked if he'd heard a snap or a crack when he fell. He was shaking his head when Leigh and Blake came back. "You're fine," I said, zipping his jacket to his chin.

He sat with us until his mother appeared at the side of the rink, looking worried and carrying shopping bags. She thanked me before she and her son left, and Blake smiled after they were gone.

"You're good with kids," he said.

He was next to me on the bench again. His eyes were on my face and that made me edgy. I worried that my mascara had pooled into my tear ducts or that there was an unbecoming smear of lipstick across my overlapping teeth.

I shrugged. "My sister has two. I'm just used to them."

He raised his eyebrows. He seemed interested. I assumed he was just making conversation and that he'd go back to skating with Leigh, but he didn't.

"Don't you guys want to skate with me?" she asked, standing on the ice, her eyes darting between me and Blake. "Isn't your headache better yet, Ari?"

No, Leigh, I thought. My fake headache isn't better. And I really like you, but I like your cousin more. "Not yet," I said.

She chewed on her nail, looking disappointed. "Are you sure? Do you want to find a drugstore and get some aspirin? I can take off my skates and we can run across the street to—"

I cut her off. "No, I'll be fine."

She nodded and skated away with a sulky look on her face. Then I was alone with Blake, listening to the tinkle of piano keys and the flapping of flags in the wind.

"Is Leigh okay?" I asked.

He shrugged, watching her drag her feet at the other side of the rink. "She's been through a lot lately . . . and she's by herself too much. It's good she has you to hang out with. She needs a friend, especially someone who's got so much in common with her . . . I mean the art and everything," he said, and I suddenly felt bad that Leigh was skating alone. Then Blake changed the subject. "You mentioned your sister . . . how old is she?"

"Twenty-three. She has a five-year-old and a baby," I said without thinking. Twenty-three minus five—now he'd know that she was a teen mother. But Rachel was too, and he didn't seem to be subtracting. He was smiling and looking at the cloudy sky.

"Nice," he said wistfully. "It's good to have your kids when you're young."

Not *that* young, I thought. Then he said Leigh had mentioned that I had a brother-in-law who worked for the FDNY. Blake said that he'd always wanted to be a fireman, which was very ironic, in my opinion. People who lived on the Upper East Side didn't usually become firefighters.

"Firemen don't go to NYU," I told him.

"No," he said. "Lawyers do."

"So you want to be a lawyer like your father?"

He smiled, but it wasn't a happy smile. It was a wry smile

that lifted just one corner of his mouth. "Not exactly. My father wants me to be a lawyer like my father."

I got it. And I was right about the two of us having something in common. I realized, as we sat on the bench and talked while Leigh did laps and figure eights around the rink, that Blake had to compensate for Del the way I had to compensate for Evelyn. Mr. Ellis and Mom were cut from the same cloth. They wanted what was best for us, but they never asked what we wanted.

"My mother expects me to become an artist," I said after Blake told me that he was supposed to take over Ellis & Hummel someday. "As if *that's* a practical goal."

He smiled. This time he used both corners of his mouth. "Well, maybe it is. You should show me your work sometime."

I nodded at the same time the sun peeked out from behind a cloud. A ray struck Blake's right eye, and I decided that my lost marble finally had a match.

thirteen

We were in the last days of March. The temperature was rising, and pea soup–colored grass burst through the melting snow, reminding me of prickly stubble on a bald man's head. The winter had eroded most of Saint Anne's nose. It was all so depressing that I never looked at our lawn anymore.

"What do you think?" Summer asked.

Dad was downstairs watching the Sunday-afternoon Knicks game. Mom was at Evelyn's house, helping to take care of Shane because he had the chicken pox. Or at least, that was what I thought she was doing. The flow of information had fizzled to a trickle since I'd been barred from Queens.

Now I looked at Summer, who had opened my curtain. I'd been keeping it closed lately to block out the gloom on the lawn. But she had the gall to open it so she could show off the red rose that had been tattooed on her ankle while she was in Key West with Casey for spring break.

"Pretty," I said, because it was. But I felt so blah and my voice came out that way.

"Our initials are on the petals," she said, pointing to an *S* and a *C* written in calligraphy. "Isn't it romantic?"

Casey was still in Florida. He was staying there for a few extra days, and I knew Summer was here because she was bored without him. The only contact we had lately was in Jeff's Mercedes every weekday morning, and romance wasn't a good topic for me right now. Weeks had passed since Rockefeller Center, and Blake had never asked to see my drawings or anything else.

"Sure," I made myself say.

"And the *C* will be easy to change when we break up."

I blinked. "Why would you get the tattoo if you're planning to break up?"

"Ari," she said in a sensible, psychiatrist-type voice. "The chances that Casey and I are going to live happily ever after are slim, don't you think? Besides, I'm not about to settle for the first guy who comes along. I need experience. And getting the rose was an experience too."

I studied the tattoo, imagining a sharp needle injecting the red ink and the black ink and the green ink beneath her skin. "It must've hurt," I said.

"So does sex the first time you do it, but I didn't let that stop me."

I sighed. This was such old news. "I know. You've told me fifty times already."

She sat on my bedspread. "Well, I'm just warning you in case you ever get a boyfriend."

I pulled the chair out from my desk and sat down, feeling limp and despondent and in the mood to denigrate myself. "Yeah . . . hopefully I'll get one before I turn all wrinkled and hunchbacked."

She gasped and covered her mouth. "I didn't mean it that way, Ari. That came out wrong. I always say things wrong. You know I meant *when*. *When* you get a boyfriend."

Whatever. I watched her zip her boots while my mind shifted back to her tattoo. It made me think of dirty needles and AIDS and people in hospital isolation units, wasting away with sores that blistered every inch of their bodies. I was about to ask if the tattoo parlor had taken the necessary precautions when she changed the subject.

"That Rachel Ellis is an even bigger bitch than her daughter. 'Stage left, stage right . . . ,' " she said, imitating Rachel by pointing her finger. "But my mother is all gushy about her because she got us a new account. A law firm or something."

"You mean Ellis and Hummel?"

She nodded. "We'll be handling their business meetings and stuff starting later this spring. I think it's in the Empire State Building."

Ninety-eighth floor, I thought. Then I got nervous because Summer might meet Blake, who probably wanted another bleached blonde to replace the one in Georgia, and I didn't stand a chance against Summer Simon. I wished she had never given me that *Tell Your Friends* card, because it had led to nothing but disaster.

I was glad when Summer went home, passing Mom on the front steps. Mom was carrying a grocery bag filled with marshmallow ducks, jelly beans, and eggs, which we dyed in the kitchen later on.

I dropped a yellow PAAS tablet into a cup filled with a combination of water and vinegar and watched it fizz. I'd already colored a dozen eggs and I was planning to do a dozen more. Mom and I always gave Kieran a huge Easter basket, and now we had to give one to Shane, too, even though he was less than a year old and mostly toothless.

"Is Shane better?" I asked, drawing a rabbit face on a fuchsia egg.

"Oh," Mom said. "He's fine."

I was drawing whiskers. I stopped because her voice sounded funny. It sounded like she was trying to keep something from me. "Well," I said, certain that my exile would be suspended on holidays. "I guess I'll find out next week."

"Ariadne," she said. "Here's the thing."

That was when I found out I wasn't going to Easter dinner in Queens. Mom acted like this was no big deal, it was a one-time occurrence. Evelyn had lost eleven pounds since my birthday, her psychiatrist was fantastic, and we wanted what was best for her, didn't we?

Mom was being a ringmaster again. I nodded and went back to drawing because I didn't want to talk about Evelyn anymore. What was the point, anyway? I'd just come off as spoiled and weak and a wimpy delicate flower if I complained that nobody ever put me first, not even Mom. I wasn't in the mood now for jelly beans or colored eggs, but I forced myself to organize them in Kieran's and Shane's Easter baskets. It wasn't their fault they had a very selfish mother.

On Monday I complained to Leigh about Easter. There was no other choice. I couldn't talk to Mom and I never talked to Dad, and Summer was too involved with herself to care. She rarely ate lunch at Hollister nowadays, Casey always picked her up from school, and she was constantly meeting with guidance counselors. She wanted to convince them to let her take extra classes next fall so she could graduate in January instead of in June, which just figured. Leigh would be gone soon and Summer probably would too, although it seemed as if she was far away already. *What do you care if I don't eat lunch in the cafeteria?* Summer had said last week. *You've got Leigh.*

"Well," Leigh said as we sat together in homeroom. I was surprised that she'd actually shown up, and I hadn't seen a SUNY Oswego shirt for weeks. Now she wore a dab of lipstick, a white eyelet blouse, and her chain with the arrowhead charm. It was a sunny morning, and she looked a lot more cheerful than I felt. "You'll just have to come to my place for Easter."

"I don't want to impose," I said.

She picked up her charm and pulled it back and forth across the chain. "Now you're being ridiculous. It's no imposition at all. We'll have plenty of food . . . my whole family will be there. I really want you to come—I'll even send a car to pick you up. Please come."

Her voice was tinged with desperation. Her face was close to mine, and there was a mix of hope and sadness in her eyes that made me nod, just so she wouldn't say please again. I also did it because I knew what it was like to be unpopular, because I knew how important it was to have at least one friend, and because I remembered that Leigh's *whole family* included Blake.

"Don't let this bother you, Ariadne," Mom said the next Sunday afternoon. We were standing on our front steps while Dad loaded the Easter baskets into his car.

"It doesn't bother me," I said, because I had to. My parents didn't think that missing one lousy Easter dinner was a big deal—they went through much worse when they were my age. *Kids are so spoiled these days.* Mom once said that her father had usually passed out drunk before the ham was served, and it was no secret that Dad's mother had spent every holiday emptying bedpans. So I pretended I didn't care.

Then a sedan arrived. It took me to the apartment on East Seventy-eighth, where I settled down at a cramped dining room table. Mr. Ellis sat at the head; Rachel was at the opposite end. Leigh sat next to me, and Blake and Del were across from us. I was surprised that I felt so comfortable eating Easter dinner with a family that wasn't mine.

"Pass that over here, sugar pie," Rachel said, gesturing to

a disposable aluminum tray beside Blake's elbow. Her accent was very Southern today, and so was the food. There were no maids or leeks or desserts set on fire. We had potato salad and pork chops and collard greens, and I ate the collard greens even though I'd never heard of them before. Rachel had cooked everything herself, and it wasn't exactly a penthouse party. It was the same kind of simple family gathering that was going on in Queens. There was another similarity too— I had to hide my Blake stares just like I hid my Patrick stares.

Blake ate more than he had at the penthouse. He dug into the potato salad and left four bare pork-chop bones on his plate. As we ate, he talked to me across the table. We talked about school and about grades, and at one point Mr. Ellis chimed in.

"A-plus on the Intro to Business Law midterm," he said proudly, patting Blake's shoulder in a way that was supposed to be affectionate, but he did it so forcefully that it probably hurt.

Rachel clapped her hands. "Congratulations, nephew. Now you get an extra piece of hummingbird cake." She turned to me. "You're not allergic to hummingbirds, are you, honey?"

Hummingbirds. Those were the little things with the thin beaks and the speedy wings. *Hummingbirds are of the* Trochilidae *family,* I remembered one of my science teachers saying. *They're the only birds that can fly backward.* I didn't re-member her mentioning that hummingbirds were edible, but maybe it was a Southern thing. A delicacy or whatever.

"Aunt Rachel," Blake said. "Don't do that to her."

It was only a joke, thank God. Rachel went to the kitchen

and came back carrying a four-layer cake covered with cream-cheese frosting and chopped pecans. It tasted heavenly. Blake was cutting his second piece when Mr. Ellis rose from his chair.

"I have to get going," he said. "There's a trial next week and work on my desk."

Rachel twisted her mouth. "You push yourself too hard, Stan. You should get some of your associates to help you."

He smacked Blake's shoulder again. "This boy right here will be working for me over the summer. That'll be all the help I need."

Rachel offered to walk him to his car, adding that it was a beautiful day and we should all take a spin around the block to burn off dinner. Blake and Del shook their heads but Leigh sprang out of her chair and grabbed my hand.

"Come with us, Ari," she said.

I didn't want to. I wanted to stay here with her cousins, so I unlatched my hand from hers. "You go ahead, Leigh. Have a nice walk."

She stood there looking disappointed, like she had at Rockefeller Center. Her clinginess annoyed me a little, but I didn't want her to know, so I got up and went into the bathroom. When I came out, she and Rachel and Mr. Ellis were gone.

I went back to the dining room, where I sat at the table with Del and Blake. They made the room smell musky and masculine, from the things they drank or smoked or slapped on their skin, and I liked it, whatever it was.

"That was rude," Del said. He struck a match and lit a

cigarette. "Daddy leaving early, I mean. Who works on Easter?"

Blake ran a hand through his hair and it stood up straight. "You know he's busy."

"Yeah. Too busy to see my club. It's been open for three months and he hasn't shown up once. And neither have you." A long stream of smoke came out of Del's mouth. He pushed his chair back and it scraped the wall and that annoyed him. "This apartment is so fucking small. Why doesn't he get them a better one?"

"Del," Blake said. "There's a lady in the room. Watch your language."

That's okay, I thought. Nobody in my family watches their language, but thanks anyway, Blake. I'm flattered that you care. Del muttered an apology and Blake told him that Mr. Ellis paid Rachel and Leigh's rent and their bills, and wasn't that enough?

Del didn't seem to think it was, because he screwed up his face and started clearing the table. I watched him and tried to find the green in his eyes, but I only saw gray.

"You'd defend Daddy if he slit their throats," he said before disappearing into the kitchen. I heard water running and trays being crunched into the trash. Blake let out a heavy sigh.

"Sorry," he said. "Another family drama."

That's okay, I thought again. I'm familiar with family drama. Then I remembered the way Del had talked about Cielo and I felt sorry for him. "Your brother's club is nice . . . I was there for the opening-night party."

"I skipped that," he said, sliding his hand beneath the

neck of his shirt to rub his shoulder. I wondered if it was sore from when Mr. Ellis had pounded on it. I caught a glimpse of bare skin, and I also saw a silver chain. Then Blake turned slightly in his seat and I noticed something dark on the top of his back, near his shoulder. "So how old are you, Ari? Leigh's age, right?" He stopped rubbing and his shirt fell back into place before I could figure out what the mark was.

"Right," I said.

He smiled. "Then you're old enough to get into R-rated movies."

"Yeah," I said, wondering where he was going with this. "I'm old enough."

"You want to see one with me?" he asked. I couldn't believe it—Blake had just asked me on a date. Suddenly this was a very good Easter.

He called on Wednesday night. The phone rang when I was curled up on the couch with my calculus homework, and Mom answered it in the kitchen. Then she came into the living room with a puzzled expression on her face.

"It's for you," she said. "It's some boy."

She looked so surprised that a boy would deliberately dial my number, and that really irked me. Then she lingered in the kitchen while I talked to Blake. She opened and closed cabinets, pretending to search for cinnamon. She also rummaged through the refrigerator, checking the expiration dates on the milk and the sour cream and the butter, even though she knew good and well that they were all perfectly fresh.

She was even worse on Saturday night. I heard a car's engine at the curb and I flew down the stairs from my bedroom, calling "I won't be home too late," and I thought Mom would have the sense to stay inside, where a mother belongs, but she didn't. I was at the curb when I heard her husky voice behind me.

"Don't I get to meet your friend?" she said.

Go away go away go away, I thought. Blake is twenty years old and he drives this beautiful black Corvette convertible and you have no idea how much you're embarrassing me. Then Blake was on the sidewalk and he shook Mom's hand. Next he answered her probing questions with "Yes, ma'am" and "No, ma'am" and "I go to NYU, ma'am." She loved that *ma'am* business. She waved goodbye when I was in the car, and I watched her reflection in the rearview mirror as Blake drove away.

"I apologize," I said. "For her, I mean."

The Corvette had the scent of leather and plastic and other unknown substances that make a car smell new. It was a stick shift, and I marveled at how expertly Blake changed gears.

"Don't worry about it," he said. "I don't blame her. When I have a daughter, I plan to interrogate every guy who comes within a hundred yards. I'll probably get a polygraph machine and stick bamboo shoots underneath their fingernails."

I laughed. I wasn't embarrassed anymore. And I decided that Blake was different. He was better than the guys Evelyn had dated before Patrick, the ones who honked their car horns impatiently and rolled their eyes behind Mom's back and gave Dad weak handshakes. None of them ever said *ma'am*. I wondered if Blake's good manners were a sweet Southern thing, like Rachel's hummingbird cake.

He drove us to a movie theater in Manhattan, where he held every door for me, and the next thing I knew, we were eating dinner in a Little Italy restaurant with red-and-white-checkered tablecloths and a waiter who called me *Signorina*.

Blake seemed comfortable. So was I. The food was good and the atmosphere wasn't formal or fancy, which was fine with me. Our table was near the front door and I felt the cool April air, heard it rustling a tree outside, and saw Blake's Corvette parked across the street.

"You have a nice car," I said.

He shrugged. The waiter had just brought two bowls of chocolate gelato and Blake lifted his spoon. "My father gave it to me for Christmas. Total waste of money."

I wasn't sure how to answer, so I didn't. I lifted my own spoon and swirled it around the gelato, and Blake asked if I was seeing anybody else.

"No," I said. "I was dating someone for a while. It's over now."

It was a massive lie but I had to say it. I couldn't let Blake know the humiliating truth that this was my first real date. For some strange reason he didn't doubt me.

"Same here," he said.

I nodded and conjured up a vision of his bleached-blond girlfriend. I imagined her in a mobile home in Georgia, trying to make the place presentable by hanging up a wind chime and growing flowers in plastic containers out front. I saw Blake inside, having sex with her on a foldout couch while rain beat down on a metal roof, and I thought she was lucky even if she did live in a trailer.

"Who were you dating before?" I asked, as if I didn't know.

"A girl in Georgia," he said.

I acted all surprised. "Georgia," I echoed. "Do you go to Georgia much?"

"I used to. My grandmother lives down there. She has a little house far away from everything, underneath these big oak trees that were planted before the Civil War." He leaned his chair back and smiled at the ceiling. "I want a place like that someday."

I laughed. "But you live in a penthouse."

The check came. He tossed some cash on the table. "That's my father's taste," he said, popping a Life Saver into his mouth. "And Del's. I'd rather live in your neighborhood."

We were back in my neighborhood an hour later. It was dark now, and Blake parked the Corvette in front of my house as butterflies fluttered in my stomach. I remembered when Evelyn was a teenager and she would sit in parked cars on our street with her boyfriend of the month, while Mom paced the living room saying things like *She'll end up with trench mouth* and *I hope the neighbors don't see.*

I was looking out the window, checking for neighbors and hoping to give them something to see, when I felt Blake's hand on my chin. I looked at him, at his straight nose and his perfectly carved lips, feeling his finger move slowly back and forth on my skin. Don't ask me, I thought. Just do it.

He lifted my mouth to his and it was so much better than that stupid Catskills kiss. It was nice and gentle and he squeezed my shoulder and smoothed my hair, and he didn't get grabby with my off-limits-on-a-first-date areas or turn all critical when it was over.

"You want to sit over here?" he asked.

The only place to sit over there was on his lap. The invitation was so enticing and his voice was so soft that it made goose bumps pop all over me. I nodded and Blake smiled, hooking his arm around my waist, pulling me over the stick shift. Then I was on his thighs, and I loved it there, where I smelled aftershave and stayed wrapped up in his arms. He kissed me again, harder and deeper this time. I felt his tongue exploring my mouth and tasted a trace of his Wint-O-Green Life Saver. I wondered if he knew that they made tiny blue sparks if you crunched them in the dark.

"You're too pretty," he said when we were done.

I was? Those three words sent me floating over my lawn. The grass was growing in thick and green, and Saint Anne didn't seem lonely and old and chipped. Her dress was bright blue, her shawl was sparkly gold. She and little Mary looked like they were having a good day.

fourteen

Mom was waiting on the couch. She made sandwiches and she heated milk, but I didn't want to tell her anything. The memory of tonight was as unblemished as new-fallen snow that I had to protect from careless footsteps. I just talked about the movie and the restaurant as Mom stared at me with her heavy-lidded eyes, waiting for something that never came.

"Don't you even want a sandwich?" she asked.

I shook my head. I heard her in the kitchen while I was brushing my teeth upstairs; she was tearing a sheet of aluminum foil to cover the sandwiches. I might have felt a lot guiltier if I wasn't so happy.

My happiness hindered my sleep. I stared at my bedroom ceiling later on, thinking about Blake, remembering the way he had touched me. He was careful and gentle, as if I was something fragile and important, like I was that soft spot on a baby's head.

He called on Sunday night. I wished there was a phone in my room. Evelyn used to have one, a powder-pink princess model that Mom and Dad bought after she whined and cried and nagged for weeks. Its cord had been woefully tangled and the dial had nearly fallen off from constant use, but she had still lugged it to Queens along with her Pet Rocks and Peter Frampton poster.

I'd never asked for a phone, and that was a mistake. If I had one, I could get some privacy from Mom and Dad, who were watching *60 Minutes* in the living room while I leaned against the kitchen counter, surprised at what came out of my mouth—girlish giggles and a flirty voice that made me wonder if I'd been possessed by Summer.

"What are you so cheery about?" Summer asked the next day as we strolled by Frederick Smith Hollister. You have a very handsome grandson, I thought, giving the plaque a puckish sideways glance.

"I went out with Leigh's cousin," I said.

Summer stopped walking. She made a noise like she'd just found a hair in her soup—*blech* and *ick* and *ugh* all rolled into one. "You mean that hideous Indian-looking guy with the messed-up lip?"

That was mean. She seemed to have forgotten that she hadn't always been flawless. Besides, Del wasn't hideous, and he couldn't do anything about his lip. I didn't want to talk about Blake anymore, but Summer said "Tell me tell me tell me" until I gave in.

"Leigh has another cousin you haven't met. He's Del's brother and he's adorable," I said.

She laughed. "Sounds like you've got quite a little crush brewing there, Ari."

I'd suffered through so many crushes. There was Patrick, and boys at school, but none of them had amounted to anything except a painful ache. They'd never resulted in what happened the next Saturday night—a handsome guy at my front door who willingly came inside and gave Dad a firm handshake and chatted politely with Mom before taking me to another movie and a dinner that he paid for with an American Express card.

Later that night, Blake and I sat in the Corvette, which he'd parked a block from my house, this time next to a vacant lot where another house used to be. The owners had torn it down with plans to build a bigger place because they'd won Lotto or risen in the ranks of the Mafia. Our neighbors were gossiping, but nobody was sure of the truth.

"Why did you park here?" I asked.

"Because," Blake said, "I can't go on kissing you in front of your house. That isn't nice, and I was brought up to be a gentleman. I want your parents to like me."

I like you, Blake, I thought when his mouth was on mine and his arms hugged my waist and our fingers laced together as perfectly as the ones on my sketch pad.

"Ari," Blake said, and I glanced at the clock on his dashboard, shocked at how late it suddenly was. "I should take you home now."

"Why?" I asked.

"Because it wouldn't be nice if I didn't," he said.

Nice. It wasn't nice to kiss in front of my house and it wasn't nice to kiss for too long. I wondered where all this niceness came from. It definitely didn't exist in Brooklyn guys or Connecticut boys who vacationed in the Catskills. I finally decided that it came from somewhere else—a faraway place where people ate collard greens and lived beneath pre–Civil War trees.

The next afternoon, a meteorologist on TV said the temperature was record-breaking. It was so warm that our obnoxious neighbors were sunbathing in their driveway and everybody else on the block was washing cars or mowing lawns.

I drew the lady next door as I watched her from the open window in my studio. She was spread out on a lounge chair, shiny from Coppertone, holding a foil collar beneath her double chin. Then I turned to a blank page in my sketch pad, but I wasn't motivated. I didn't even want to be here, with my pencils and my paper and my oil paints in their squashed tubes. I wanted to be outside soaking up the sunshine and the cut-grass smell, or on my driveway packing the car with Dad for a visit to Queens. But mostly I wanted Blake, who told me last night that he had an Intro to Business Law exam on Monday and planned to study for hours today.

"Ariadne," Mom said after I dragged myself to the kitchen. "What are you going to do while we're gone?"

I flopped into a chair, thinking that it was hot in here and why didn't this house have central air? All we had were noisy old window units that Dad hadn't taken out of the garage yet.

"Nothing," I said, watching as she put a tray of cupcakes in a cardboard box. They had homemade icing and multi-colored sprinkles, and I knew Patrick would enjoy them because he was a big fan of *jimmies.*

"You can study for the SAT," she suggested.

I rolled my eyes. Studying for the SAT and sketching in my studio seemed like death compared to keeping my eyes shut while Blake's tongue wandered inside my mouth.

Then my parents were gone. I watched television on the couch, listened to a group of kids play stickball on the street, and ignored my SAT book. Mom had left two cupcakes on a plate in the refrigerator, and as I bit into one, the phone rang. Blake was on the line.

"Leigh and my aunt Rachel convinced me to blow off studying today," he said. "We're driving out to the Hamptons. . . . I'm renting a car since we can't all fit in the Corvette. We'll pick you up in an hour if you want to come."

Of course I did. I wanted to go to the Hamptons more than anything in the world, even though I'd never been there before. So I ran upstairs and showered and shaved my legs.

Next I stood beside my dresser drawer and pulled out a bikini the color of a plum, which would have to be covered with a T-shirt because if Blake saw my uneven breasts, he might stop calling. The thought of that was too dismal for words.

He showed up right on time. Rachel jumped out of a black Toyota in a bikini top that wasn't covered by anything and a sheer sarong that was wrapped around her hips. A big pair of sunglasses—the same kind that Jackie O wore around Manhattan—rested on the bridge of her nose. She ushered me into the front seat next to Blake.

A couple of hours later, we arrived at a massive white house that resembled something out of *Miami Vice*. The walls inside were white, and there were endless windows and a balcony over the first floor. The furniture was modern, and Leigh showed me the indirect lighting in the five bedrooms and four bathrooms before whispering in my ear that the house belonged to her uncle.

"He has parties here during the summer," she said. "With his clients and stuff."

I nodded and followed her outside to the pool. It was four feet deep at one end and nine at the other, and was covered on the inside with sea green tiles except at the bottom, where black and yellow tiles formed the image of a scorpion.

I teetered at the edge of the pool to see a curvy tail, and then Leigh was next to me.

"I guess my mother was right about me and you and Blake. We can all be friends. We can do stuff like this for the next few months until I go to California," she said, glancing at the pool and the patio and the house. "I like to draw, but

I can't stand another spring alone in my apartment with my colored pencils."

I knew what she meant—I couldn't survive another spring locked in my studio, either.

"Sure, Leigh," I said. "We'll hang out together for the rest of the spring."

She smiled, crouched down, and moved her hand back and forth in the water to check the temperature. "Del and Idalis will be here soon. I'd like some ice cream before then."

So we went for a walk. Rachel sauntered down the road, waving at admiring male neighbors while Blake and Leigh and I trailed behind like baby chicks. We stopped at a quaint ice cream parlor near the beach that had a striped awning and smelled of roasted peanuts. Rachel ordered a cup of frozen yogurt, Leigh asked for vanilla ice cream in a waffle cone, and Blake and I both got a scoop of lemon sherbet. He paid for everything even though I took out my wallet. It didn't seem right that Blake should pay every single time we were together; it was 1986—the whole equality thing was supposed to have been settled years ago.

"Put that away, honey," Rachel said, jamming my wallet into my purse before Blake saw it. "A Southern man never lets a woman pay for anything. He wouldn't be a gentleman otherwise."

"But Blake isn't really a Southern man," I said.

She lifted a black eyebrow. "He was raised as one, and that's what matters."

* * *

Del and Idalis were at the house when we got back. She floated around the pool on an inflatable raft with a piña colada in her hand, and she talked to Del in a mixture of Spanish and English while he sat at a table on the patio with his adding machine and a stack of receipts.

"Hey, *latoso*," she shouted. "You planning to sit there all day?"

He didn't answer and she yelled the question again. "I'm working, goddamn it," he said without looking up, and she got huffy and said a few things in Spanish that I didn't understand and something in English that I did.

"You can just lick me, then," she said, sticking out her tongue.

"Don't you wish," Del muttered over his receipts.

I laughed to myself. I knew they were talking about the thing that a lot of Catholic girls did instead of having sex because it was just bending the rules, not breaking them. It wouldn't give them a fatal disease or get them knocked up; they wouldn't become a disgrace to their rosary-carrying mothers. I didn't blame them, but it seemed to me that skirting the rules was a dirty trick and possibly more sinful than everything else.

Del wasn't dressed for the pool, he was dressed for work, and I got the impression that an afternoon in the Hamptons hadn't been his idea. Rachel became a mother hen and said things like "Oh, now, now" and "Mind your manners," and Leigh tried to help by dragging a volleyball net out of a shed and suggesting that we all play. Del ignored her and Rachel didn't want to wreck her nails, so the game turned into Leigh and Idalis against me and Blake.

"Are you keeping that shirt on?" Leigh asked. "I'm

wearing mine. I burn easily, in case you couldn't tell from my gazillion freckles."

"Same here," I said, grateful that she'd come up with an excuse before I had to. Then we sat at the edge of the pool while Blake installed the net and Idalis smashed a ball across the water in a way that told me she was one of those competitive girls I avoided in gym class.

"I have an idea," she said. "Ari can get on Blake's shoulders and Leigh can get on mine and we'll play that way. It's more challenging."

Leigh and Blake agreed, and I just nodded to go along. I waited while Blake finished setting up the net. His shirt was already off, and I saw that the silver chain I'd seen during Easter dinner had the same arrowhead charm that Leigh wore. The mysterious dark thing I'd seen was a tattoo on his left shoulder blade—a circle with a cross in the middle and three feathers dangling from the bottom.

"Hop on," he said a few minutes later.

He was crouching in four feet of water. I slid my calves over his shoulders, and I was glad I hadn't forgotten to shave my legs that morning. He gripped my ankles and I held on to his neck. His skin rubbed against my skin, and it was going to be hard to concentrate on this volleyball nonsense.

Leigh hit the ball with her fist and it came barreling toward my head. I ducked and Blake laughed, but Idalis didn't seem happy because she was probably expecting a real game. I stayed on Blake's shoulders while he retrieved the ball. That was the best part—just being close to him, clutching his strong shoulders with my bare thighs.

He gave me the ball and I tossed it back, but I had to do

that four times before it cleared the net. Idalis was frustrated and she switched positions with Leigh, which made me nervous. She was just about to hit the ball when Blake called a time-out because his father was standing on the patio.

"What are you doing here?" Rachel asked.

She was on a lounge chair. There was a blazer draped over Mr. Ellis's arm, and he loosened his tie. "I came to make sure the people I hired to clean this place were doing their job. I didn't know there was a party going on." He shaded his eyes and turned toward the pool. "Isn't there a test tomorrow, Blake? You should have your nose in a book instead of a girl on your shoulders."

"Come on, Daddy," Del said. "Let him have some fun for once."

"Nobody asked *you*," Mr. Ellis said sharply before directing a suave smile and a goodbye wave at the pool. I watched through a wall of windows as he went into the house, and then I heard a car start up and fade away in the distance.

"*Pendejo*," Idalis called to Del. "Get some shorts on. Let's do boys against girls."

I wasn't sure what *pendejo* meant, but it couldn't have been a compliment because Del's face was darker than that scorpion in the pool. He kept punching numbers into his adding machine. Then Blake jokingly tossed the volleyball across the patio. It was wet and it landed on Del's receipts. Del grabbed the ball and shot it in Blake's direction, but it hit me right in the mouth.

Thick red droplets fell on Blake's chest. Next I was on the patio, surrounded by frantic people. I kept insisting that I was fine and I heard Del apologizing. Blake sneered at him.

"Fucking moron," he said.

He shouldn't have broken his *Watch your language around a lady* rule. It was just an accident; I could see that Del was sorry. Blake led me into the house, and I watched Del over my shoulder as Rachel wagged her finger and Leigh shook her head and Idalis screeched in Spanish.

I didn't hear her anymore after Blake took me to a bathroom and closed the door. It was completely white inside, with a granite countertop and towels emblazoned with the letter *E.* Blake ruined one of the towels by pressing it against my bloody lip.

He doted on me. He kept the towel on my mouth until the bleeding stopped, he soaked a cotton ball in iodine to clean what turned out to be just a minor cut, and he scoured the entire house for a Band-Aid. The one he found was the kiddy kind with a picture of Snoopy on it, but that was okay. Everything was okay because this was the best I'd ever felt.

Kindergarten. That was what was in my mind after Rachel and Leigh caught a ride home with Del and Idalis and I sat next to Blake as we sped down the parkway. The car windows were open, the sun was setting, and I thought that kindergarten was the last time the sun had looked so golden and the air had smelled so fresh. Little things had made me happy back then—little humdrum trivial nothing things, like polish on my toenails and strawberry shampoo and a crisp new dollar that I could spend on the Good Humor man. As I got older I'd noticed that nail polish chipped, and shampoo burned if it got in your eyes, and the Good Humor man's ice cream was no different from the stuff in the freezer case at Pathmark. The color slowly drained from everything and it was all just boring and pointless or both.

But tonight, when I got out of the car in front of my house, I could have sworn that Saint Anne was smiling. My neighborhood trees looked leafier than usual, the whole block smelled of a barbecue, Blake's face was more handsome than any I'd imagined while I was kissing my hand, and I felt like I was in kindergarten again.

It was getting dark and the air turned cool. Blake leaned against his car, draping his arms around my waist.

"Listen," he said. "Can we just say we're a steady thing?"

The lady next door was lugging her trash can to the curb. Crickets chirped and kids played stickball and I nodded. Then I saw Blake's Colgate smile. He held my face in his hands and kissed my forehead, and I was sure it meant something. A guy who didn't care about you just wanted to feel you up and feel you down, and Blake hadn't tried any of that. Only a guy who really cared would give a girl something as sweet and innocent as a forehead kiss on a dreamy April night.

My parents weren't home yet. I closed the front door after Blake was gone and walked around the house smiling and aimless, like I was giddy on champagne. I touched my Band-Aid, inventing a reason why it was there, because nobody needed to know about my amazing day in the Hamptons.

"You were fortunate, Ariadne," Mom said later that night, after I pretended that I'd tripped on a stair and bashed my mouth against the railing. I also pretended that the Snoopy Band-Aid had been in my dresser drawer for years and I didn't want it to go to waste. "You could've lost some teeth."

I was more fortunate than she knew—Del was good at making people lose their teeth. I held in a laugh and followed her to the kitchen, where we sat at the table and she handed me a Polaroid. It was a picture of Evelyn, but I thought it was an old one because her cheekbones were showing, and she was wearing a short skirt and there weren't any dimples above her knees. Her legs were thin and her hair wasn't frizzy, and she was leaning against Patrick with a seductive smile.

The Polaroid wasn't old. It had been taken just a few hours earlier. Mom told me that Evelyn had dropped twenty pounds since my birthday, her new medication was working, and I was invited to Queens next month for a Memorial Day barbecue. Then she lit a Pall Mall.

"Did you have a good time on your date last night?" she asked, to which I nodded and said that I really should do some SAT studying, but she wouldn't let me leave. She gripped my wrist and stared at me. "Look," she began, and stopped when Dad strolled in to raid the refrigerator. She kept quiet until he left with a sandwich to eat in front of the TV in the living room. "Blake seems very nice," she said. "But they all seem nice at first. You have to be careful."

Shut up, I thought. Please don't ruin this. "Careful?" I said.

She blew a smoke ring into the air. "You're sensitive. Men can be cruel. I don't want you getting upset or distracted from the important things."

The important things. I was sensitive. She wanted to lock me in my studio because a delicate flower is prone to wither. "We're going steady now," I said.

There was a flash of displeasure in her eyes that she smothered with a blink. "Steady," she said. "You know what *that* means, don't you?"

I thought so. I thought it meant that a guy actually liked me. "Sure, Mom. It means we're only seeing each other."

She laughed as if I was stupid. "It means he's looking for a regular screw and you could end up pregnant just like somebody else we know."

At that moment I wondered how other women spoke to their daughters. Did they refer to sex as a *screw,* and did they tell their future sons-in-law not to think with what was in their pants? This was one time I wished she could be more Catholic, that she could be one of those devout ladies who deluded themselves into thinking their daughters were going to save themselves for their wedding night. Those women would never initiate a conversation like this.

Why did she have to spoil everything? This was the first time a guy had shown the slightest interest and she had to go and get practical. I didn't want to hear about realistic things like ending up pregnant.

"We're not doing anything" was all I could say.

Mom scrunched her mouth into a skeptical smirk. "Not at the moment. But a twenty-year-old who looks like *that,*" she said, pointing toward the dishwasher as if Blake was standing there, "isn't exactly a virgin."

I made the same noise that Summer had when she

thought I was dating Del—the *blech* and *ick* and *ugh* combination. "Really, Mom," I said, amazed at how casually she used embarrassing words. But I couldn't argue because she wasn't wrong.

"Ariadne," she said. "I was young once too. I know what goes on. Now, if you want to go out with Blake, that's fine with me as long as you keep your grades up and you don't get serious. But remember, high school will be over before you know it and there are plenty of fish in the sea—you don't want to get stuck with the first one."

She was so sensible, so cynical, it was really depressing. I wanted to say that I'd love to get stuck with Blake, that I didn't care about the other fish in the sea, but there was no point. She'd just tell me that I was young and naive and that she knew best. Don't be so pessimistic, Mom, I thought. Things don't always turn out wrong.

"Besides," she went on, "you've taken Sex Ed—you know about AIDS. There's no way to tell who's got it. So you just make sure he keeps his jeans zipped and everything will be fine. He'll respect you more that way, anyhow."

AIDS, respect . . . she really knew how to complicate things. I just nodded and Mom smiled, reaching across the table to rub my cheek. She did it sort of the way Blake did—like I was something special.

fifteen

The rest of April and half of May drifted along as innocently as the old Andy Hardy movies Dad watched on TV, starring Mickey Rooney as the boyfriend and Judy Garland as the girl-friend, holding hands in an all-American town with picket fences and cherry blossoms. Blake and I saw each other on Friday and Saturday nights but never during the week, because he had to stay on the dean's list and I couldn't fall off the honor roll. We went to the movies and to dinner, and the amount of time that Blake considered it *nice* to kiss kept growing.

Then it was the middle of May. Finals were coming and Hollister cut the school day in half on Wednesdays so we'd have time to study, although it seemed that I was the only one who actually did.

Leigh rarely showed her face at Hollister anymore—I figured she was busy getting ready for her move to California—but I saw her when she came to art class and when I went to Ellis family functions with Blake. Summer wasn't around much either, because she always sped off in Casey's BMW to activities that were more fun than studying.

It was on one of those Wednesdays that Blake parked his Corvette outside Hollister's iron gates. I didn't even see him at first. I was carrying a heavy stack of books and chatting with Summer; she stopped and gazed out at the street.

"Ooh," she said. "Who is *that*?"

I squinted from the sunshine and noticed she was looking at Blake like she wanted to tear off his clothes and slide underneath him. Or climb on top of him. Or let him get behind her, because she had told me she'd tried that position with Casey and it was *strangely exciting*.

"That's Blake," I told her, smiling and fighting the urge to skip.

"Oh my God you're kidding me," she said.

I shot her a hurt glance. *Oh my God you're kidding me.* She said it really fast, as if the six words were only one. "What's that supposed to mean?" I asked, even though I knew. She meant that Blake was filet mignon and I was Spam, and those two things couldn't possibly go together.

"Nothing," she said, squeezing my arm like she was sorry.

"That came out wrong. I just mean he's really cute. You're a lucky girl all of a sudden."

The sun was behind her head and it lit her hair into a golden halo. Her eye shadow sparkled, her lip gloss shimmered. She was gorgeous and it made me nervous. I didn't want her anywhere near Blake; I was sure she could take him away if she wanted to.

We walked toward the street, where Blake was leaning against his car in jeans and a Yankees T-shirt.

"This is my friend Summer Simon," I said, pretending I wasn't the most insecure person alive. "She's a big Yankees fan."

"Don Mattingly," she said. "*Love* him."

They started talking about other Yankees—Rickey Henderson and Mike Pagliarulo and whoever else. I couldn't join the conversation because I knew nothing about baseball.

"Pleasure meeting you," Blake said when Casey's car showed up.

Summer smiled. "You too. We'll have to do a double date sometime."

Don't count on it, I thought when Blake and I were in the Corvette. "What did you think of Summer?" I asked, trying to keep my voice free of envy, worry, and all the other pathetic emotions I loathed myself for feeling.

He stopped at a red light. "She seemed nice."

I nodded. He hit the gas and I looked out the window, at the Metropolitan Museum with its giant columns and sweeping steps.

"Do you think she's pretty?" I asked. I used a casual voice, like I didn't care about the answer.

"Yeah," he said. "She's very pretty."

I stared through the windshield. "I know. Everyone thinks so."

I kept thinking about Blake and Summer, how they might get to know each other better at Ellis & Hummel while Summer and Tina catered Mr. Ellis's business meetings and forget all about me. Then Blake reached over and turned my face toward his.

"You're much prettier," he said. "Than she is, I mean."

I almost said *You're full of crap,* but I didn't think he was. And I had never thought I'd find someone who would tell me that I was prettier than Summer Simon. So I didn't say anything—I just kept quiet and enjoyed it.

"Where are we going?" I asked a few minutes later as we were leaving Manhattan.

"You still haven't shown me your drawings," he said.

So we went to my house. My empty house. Mom was at school and Dad was at the precinct or collecting evidence or whatever it was he did to nab murderers. I opened a few windows on the first floor since Dad still hadn't installed those air-conditioning units, but Blake didn't seem to mind that the place was stuffy or that we didn't have our own elevator. He seemed comfortable. So I felt comfortable giving him a full tour of the living room and the dining room and the kitchen, where he saw Evelyn's Polaroid. Mom had taken more pictures that day—Kieran riding his tricycle, Shane in his crib—and they were stuck to the refrigerator with Mom's magnets that had corny sayings such as BLESS THIS NEST and SHOOT FOR THE STARS.

"Those are my nephews," I said.

"They're beautiful," Blake answered, and he mentioned again that it was a good thing to be a young parent.

"Evelyn was barely eighteen when she had Kieran," I said, because I'd known Blake long enough to stop keeping my sister's secrets. "That's way too young."

He nodded. "Twenty isn't, though. I'll be twenty-one in November and I'm wasting my life at NYU while I could be enjoying all of this." He waved his finger at the Polaroids.

"You're not wasting your life," I said.

He smiled at me. He smiled as if I made him feel good. He also cradled my face in his hands and asked again to see my drawings.

Then we climbed the stairs. I opened the windows in my studio as the floor creaked beneath our feet and an ambulance siren wailed in the distance. I felt nervous and twitchy and afraid that Blake might think I had no talent. Or he might tease or criticize, and that would just pulverize me into dust.

"I don't want to bore you with this stuff," I said, turning toward the door.

He caught my arm. "You're not boring me, Ari. Let me see."

I went slowly. Blake sat at my easel and I pulled things out of the closet—big sheets of paper and paint-splattered canvases. I showed him what had won me the second-place ribbon in the boroughwide art contest and even the hands on my sketch pad, because he was attentive and interested and that filled me with trust. He agreed with Mom that I could become a successful artist and I shook my head.

"You have to be extremely talented for that," I said, leaning against a wall.

He tilted backward in his chair. "And what do you think *you* are?"

I was flattered. Then we talked. I told him about my college plans and my career plans, and he said he just wanted to be a fireman with a comfortable little house and a bunch of unruly kids, and he hated the thought of working at Ellis & Hummel this summer. He'd rather quit college right now and take the FDNY entrance exam.

"So why don't you?" I asked.

"Because certain things are expected of me. And family is important," he said, which I completely understood. I nodded and we talked for a while longer, and then we were both startled by a deafening noise.

It was those stickball-playing kids. They had broken a window. Blake and I rushed down the hall and saw shattered glass covering my bedroom floor. I looked outside and saw three boys scatter in different directions. Two of them were in Mom's class and they were probably scared to death.

"They're in for it now," I said, picturing them cowering in corners when Mrs. Mitchell called their parents tonight. Then I crouched down and examined a long, jagged shard.

"Don't touch that," Blake said. "Where's your vacuum?"

I pointed to the hall closet. He used the vacuum to suck up the countless broken pieces, conscientiously checking the carpet for strays because he didn't want me to get a nasty surprise while I was barefoot.

He cared about me. I was sure of it. I thanked him and

he said he should leave because Mom might be home soon and if she found us alone together, she'd think it wasn't *nice*.

"She won't be back for another two hours," I said, draping my arms around his neck. I kissed him and he kissed me and the next thing I knew, I was lying on my neatly made bed and Blake was lying on me. I wrapped my legs around his waist. I heard sparrows chirping outside and nothing felt wrong, not even when he unbuttoned my blouse. He slid his hand inside and everything still seemed *nice* until his fingers moved to the clasp on my bra. I remembered my defective breasts and my talk with Mom, and I pushed him away.

"I can't," I said.

Our eyes were open now. His cheeks were flushed and he spoke in a patient voice. "Why?" he asked.

I held my shirt closed. "Because I'm kind of . . . uneven. Up here, I mean."

"No way. You're perfect."

I was not. But he made me feel a little better. "I still can't," I said, and I told him about Evelyn and about Mom. I also mentioned the shadowy virus that hid in unknown places and dragged people six feet underground. "I want you to respect me," I added, which was as true as everything else.

He nodded and sat up, and I sat next to him. "What about your other boyfriend?" he asked, and I had to stop myself from saying "What other boyfriend?" I just shook my head and he assumed things. "So it wasn't like that, then. Because most girls today . . ."

"Yeah," I said. "I know. Unfortunately I'm different from most girls."

I fiddled with an embroidered rose on the new bedspread that Mom had bought for me at JCPenney last week. I was waiting for him to leave, to go out and find a girl like Summer—a girl who had experience with various positions. But he just pushed a wisp of hair from my eyes and smiled.

"You're better than most girls. And all of this," he said, glancing at my bed, "it's okay if you love somebody. So I can wait until you feel that way."

All of this. He knew how to talk about sex a lot more delicately than Mom did. What he didn't know was that I loved him already.

There was a murder on Memorial Day. An entire family in Hell's Kitchen. The precinct called Dad at noon and he rushed off to work. Mom wasn't happy about it. We were in the middle of loading her Honda with a Budweiser-filled cooler and she got surly. She cursed and mumbled under her breath while we drove alone to Queens, as if those six people had some nerve to get stabbed to death on a holiday.

Blake was supposed to be here. The guest list for Patrick and Evelyn's party included their neighbors and Patrick's firefighter friends, and Blake had been invited too, but he had called last night and said he'd be a few hours late. Mr. Ellis was throwing his own party and Blake couldn't get out of it.

"That was a shitty thing to do," Mom said. "Bail out at the last minute."

She was in a rotten mood. But I wasn't the least bit upset about Blake. I couldn't criticize a guy who looked like *that* and was willing to wait for what he could easily get from any number of girls every day of the week.

I'd given in a little. I was sure that he cared about me and respected me, so it seemed okay to sneak him into my bedroom on Wednesday afternoons, where we talked and laughed and kissed on my bedspread, and I didn't push his hands away when they went inside my shirt. But that was as far as I would go, and Blake never did anything that made me say *I can't.*

"He didn't bail out, Mom," I said. "He's still coming. His father is having an important party in the Hamptons with clients and other lawyers from his firm. . . . Blake had to be there."

"Oh," she said in her *la-di-da* tone. "The Hamptons. How hoity-toity."

I dropped it. I was happy and I wasn't going to let her get me down. The week before, Mom had asked if the prescription for my migraine pills needed to be refilled and I had shown her the bottle, which was nowhere near empty because I hadn't seen an aura for quite a while. It made me wonder if feeling cheerful and pretty and cared-for all the time was a downright miracle cure.

"Hey there, little sistah," Patrick said as I stood on his front steps twenty minutes later.

He was so tall and tan, and I still felt something when he planted a peck on my cheek. But it was just a tiny tremor compared to the earthquake that came from Blake's kisses. I almost laughed, remembering how I used to eavesdrop through the bedroom wall and sleep in Patrick's shirt, and it was sort of like looking at an old toy and thinking: That doll sure is cute, but I'm way too grown up for it now.

"Hi," I said as Mom walked past us with the cooler. She opened the back door and went out to the yard, which was crowded with guests. I was heading in that direction when Patrick caught my elbow and spoke into my ear.

"You ain't mad at us, are you, Ari? I hated to keep you away."

I paused for a moment, studying the wave of hair that fell over his forehead. "Yeah," I admitted. "I was mad. Who wouldn't be?"

He smiled sympathetically, draped his arm around my shoulders, and led me to a quiet corner. "I don't blame you. But I have to put your sister first. Isn't that what you want?" he asked, and I nodded because it really was what I wanted. I couldn't stand it if Evelyn was married to some callous bum who put her last. "And you know I'm not big on saying thanks . . . but I appreciate what you've done for us, helping with the kids and everything. Please tell me you know that."

"Now I do, since you finally brought it up. But I'm not sure how much I can take . . . Patrick Cagney saying please and thanks all in one day . . . Somebody should call the *New York Times*."

"Wiseass." He laughed, leaning in close. "Evelyn's much better now, too—you'll see."

I saw her a minute later, standing at the kitchen counter, wrapping mini hot dogs in Pillsbury dough. She was thin and pretty and she was wearing a white sundress, white espadrilles, and a gold anklet with an engraved pacifier-shaped charm. MOMMY, it read.

"Is that something new?" I asked, lurking awkwardly in the doorway.

191

She looked away from a cookie sheet covered with pigs in blankets and down at her ankle. "Yeah . . . Patrick got it for me."

"It's beautiful," I said, noticing the care she'd taken with her eyeliner and her mascara, the polish on her nails. It was as if the old Evelyn had returned, and I was so happy to see her that I was willing to put everything behind us. "He really loves you," I added, and it didn't bother me to say it because now I had someone who might love me, too.

She wasn't angry anymore, I could tell. I wasn't either. She smiled, putting her arms around me. Her hair was blow-dried smooth and felt soft against my cheek. It almost made me cry, and I thought that Evelyn was also on the verge. We both sniffed and laughed when we stepped away from each other, and I knew that everything was better now.

"So," she said. "Where's this boyfriend of yours? I'm dying to see him."

She saw him later, when the sun cast an orangey gold hue over the house. Blake ate three hamburgers as if he hadn't had a morsel in the Hamptons. He fed Shane his bottle, played catch with Kieran, and settled into a chair beside mine.

"I saw your friend today," he told me.

"Summer?" I said.

He nodded. "Her mother catered the party. She handled a few meetings at the firm and now she'll be doing all my father's parties. Personally, I thought the food was way too salty."

I knew he hadn't eaten much at that party. And I felt nervous, panicky, the way I had the first time Blake and Summer met. I imagined her flirting and laughing and talking about Don Mattingly, literally charming the pants off my boyfriend. But I remembered what he'd said in his car that day—that I was prettier—and I convinced myself that worrying was stupid.

"Do you want a beer?" I asked. It was a good subject-changer.

He shook his head. "I already had one. I don't drink much . . . I'd rather not turn into a lush like my brother."

"Del's a lush?" I asked. A pig, a lush, what was next?

"I guess it's a matter of opinion." He shrugged and threw one arm over the back of his chair. "This is exactly what I want," he said, taking in Evelyn and Patrick's modest house like it was the Taj Mahal. "Don't you?"

I loved that Blake knew what I wanted and didn't act as if it wasn't enough. "Yeah," I said. "But a nicer house. In Park Slope. With a hammock in the yard and a teaching job at a good college in the city."

He nodded. "My father has connections at schools in the city."

I sat there and tried to figure out why Mom was so anti-connections. I was starting to believe that connections were a good thing, because they could get you what you wanted without toil and drudgery and practice SAT exams. Then Blake stood up to get a soda and I watched him and Patrick on the patio.

They were getting along and I was thrilled. He and Patrick discussed football and baseball and the FDNY entrance exam, but I didn't get to hear everything because

Evelyn snatched me from my chair and coaxed me into the nursery, where she closed the door and clenched my hands.

"Holy shit," she said. "He's simply fetching."

I had never in my entire life heard Evelyn say the word *fetching*. I couldn't imagine where she'd found it other than in a half-read romance novel. But it was an accurate description, so I agreed and answered her questions about how Blake and I met, and then she asked his age.

"Twenty-one in November," I told her.

"Twenty-one," she said musingly. "So are you two doing it?"

She was worse than Mom. I shook my head as if I'd never even considered *doing it*.

"You're a liar, Ari. I know what's going on. Look at you, all glowing and crap."

I was glowing? I didn't know. And I hadn't expected that I'd want to talk to Evelyn about this, but I did. I couldn't talk to Mom and I didn't talk to Summer, and I wouldn't confide in Leigh—she was Blake's cousin, after all. And suddenly, standing in the middle of blue walls decorated with Red Sox pennants, I was grateful to have a big sister.

"I'm not lying," I said after telling Evelyn about my Wednesday afternoons. "We're really not doing anything."

"But you will," she said. "I'll give you my doctor's number. She works at a clinic in Brooklyn on Fridays. . . . They don't ask for insurance there, so you won't have to tell Mom . . . and you can get a prescription for the Pill. We don't want you getting knocked up, do we?" She laughed and then she scribbled on a piece of paper that she pressed into my palm.

"Evelyn," I said. "The Pill doesn't always work, does it? I mean—you—"

She interrupted me with a different sort of laugh. It was cunning and coarse and she lowered her voice. "They work if you take them every day. But I wanted to get out of Mom's house, so I skipped a pill here and there. I mean . . . Patrick always loved me, but he loved me more when I was carrying his baby. Guys are funny that way." She winked and put her hands on my shoulders. "Listen, Ari. There are all kinds of diseases out there, and I don't just mean AIDS. Make sure Blake doesn't have anything before you sleep with him. You should find out how many girls he's been with if you don't already know."

I only knew about the Georgia girl. But all I could think about now was how desperate Evelyn must have been to get out of Mom's house . . . and how Kieran was no accident.

sixteen

I loved June. It was nothing but bright sunshine, fresh air, Wednesday afternoons on embroidered roses. I loved the music-box song that came from the Good Humor man's truck as he cruised my block after dinner each night, the smell of marshmallows roasting on our neighbors' barbecues, and the letter A written in encouraging red ink on my final exams.

"You're the most promising student I've seen in years," my art teacher said.

It was the last day of school. The classroom was empty. The windows were open and everybody milled around outside, talking and signing each other's yearbooks, and I listened to their voices until my teacher said something about a summer job. Then he handed me an index card printed with a Brooklyn address and the words CREATIVE COLORS.

"What kind of job is this?" I asked.

"It's a program for adults with mental disabilities," he said. "Down syndrome . . . brain injuries . . . that sort of thing. They do art therapy. A friend of mine owns the place and he needs some help, so I thought of you. Somebody with your talent should spread it around. You could do a lot of good there."

My talent. Did he really say that? The words repeated in my mind and I practically skipped to the subway station. Then I decided to stop by Creative Colors on my way home.

It was a few blocks from my house, on the first floor of a three-story Victorian with Doric columns and a wide porch. My teacher's friend's name was Julian; he was thirty-something, and he sported a brown goatee and wire-rimmed glasses. He said that I came highly recommended and he hired me right on the spot.

Mom wouldn't stop blabbing about my new job during dinner that night. "These people recognize talent when they see it," she said. "And you want to waste yourself on teaching." She held her hand out for my plate, overloaded it with macaroni salad, and turned to Dad. "This one just goes off and gets a job on her own. Remember when Evelyn was Ariadne's age? I begged her to find a summer job, but she wouldn't even fill out a Burger King application."

Mom was proud of me and that was great, but I didn't want compliments at my sister's expense. Evelyn had been so sweet lately—she always asked about Blake when we talked on the phone. And it had been considerate of her to hook me up with her doctor, even though it turned out I couldn't take birth control pills.

I'd found out a week ago. I had scheduled a secret appointment at the clinic, and I endured the humiliating exam with the flimsy gown and the latex gloves and the frigid instrument that could double as a shoehorn or a medieval torture device, and when it was over I felt like I'd crossed a finish line. I sat up from the examining table in that paper-thin gown, remembering a PBS program about these African boys who went through a ceremony and got their faces sliced with a razor and scarred for life because that was their rite of passage. So while the doctor sat on her stool and reviewed my medical history, I thought: This is my rite of passage. Now I'm no different from Summer or those other girls who see gynecologists regularly and swallow birth control pills faithfully, and I'm a member of the I've Got a Boyfriend Club.

Then I saw the doctor flipping through forms and scratching her head. She was a fleshy middle-aged woman who said she hadn't realized that I was a migraine sufferer and *The Pill isn't a good idea for you, Miss Mitchell. It'll only make your headaches worse.* Next she gave me a few pamphlets about pregnancy and STDs and birth control—as if I hadn't read the exact same things in Sex Ed at school—and said, *It's better if your boyfriend uses protection, anyway. You can never be sure of a man's sexual history, no matter what he tells you.*

So I'd worn that stupid gown for nothing. And Blake hadn't told me anything because I hadn't asked.

* * *

This was my first time at Delmonico's. I was sitting next to Blake on the Saturday after school ended, and I knew he wasn't comfortable. He was dressed in a suit—so was Mr. Ellis—and he kept tugging at his collar as if he couldn't breathe.

"Get used to it," Del said. "You'll be wearing a tie for the whole summer."

Rachel and Leigh and Idalis were there too. We all sat at a round table on leather chairs in a room that was dark even though the early-evening sun was blazing outside. There was a crimson carpet and a glitzy chandelier, and the waiter handed me a menu with prices that blew my mind.

I leafed through the menu as a basket of bread was being passed around the table. When it reached Leigh, she kept it beside her.

"Can I please have the bread, Leigh?" I asked, and even though she was sitting next to me, she didn't seem to hear. She was buttering a roll when I repeated my question.

"It's right *there*," she said without looking at me. "Get it yourself."

"Leigh," Blake said sharply. He was on my other side and he seemed as surprised by her nastiness as I was. "Don't talk to Ari like that."

"Blake," Rachel said from across the table, in the same chastising tone he'd used on Leigh. "Don't interfere. It's between the girls."

What was between the girls? I wondered as Blake reached

over Leigh's plate and snatched the bread away. He and I glanced at each other in confusion and shrugged it off. Then the waiter came back with a pad and pencil. Blake ordered a steak called the Classic and I ordered the same because I didn't know what else to do. Everybody was asking the waiter for things like *foie gras* and *au poivre,* which was baffling because Delmonico's wasn't even a French restaurant.

Mr. Ellis had a steak that cost more than fifty dollars. It was so rare that I had to look away after he cut into it. The meat was almost raw, and the sight of it turned my stomach.

"So will you miss us, Stan?" Rachel asked. "California is awfully far away, you know."

That was why we were here. Rachel and Leigh were leaving tonight on a flight to LAX out of JFK, and this was their farewell dinner.

"I won't miss paying your rent," Mr. Ellis said, and then he thanked me for recommending Catering by Tina. "Tina's food is excellent. And her daughter's a beautiful girl. She's your friend, isn't she?"

"Yes," I said, thinking that Mr. Ellis must like too-salty food, and that he'd called me a pretty girl the first time I met him but had never once said I was a beautiful girl. He never really spoke to me at all, other than hello and goodbye. I wouldn't have been surprised if he didn't know my last name.

"And what does her father do?" he asked.

"He's a psychiatrist," I said, which seemed to impress Mr. Ellis.

"I see. And what does your father do, Ari?"

"He's a cop. A homicide detective."

"How honorable," he said.

I wasn't sure he was still impressed. But I chose to take *honorable* as a compliment. I also tried to forget that beautiful is better than pretty and I focused on Blake, who was so handsome in his suit. But I could tell that he just wanted to tear it off.

After dinner we rode to the airport, in a limousine that Mr. Ellis arranged for us as if this was prom night. Del and Idalis had finished a bottle of wine by themselves during dinner and now they were loud and obnoxious. Blake was quiet, so I asked him what was wrong.

He whispered in my ear, "My mother died today."

He said it as if she had died this very day, this morning or this afternoon, instead of a long time ago. "You mean today is the anniversary?"

He nodded. "Thirteen years. We went to the cemetery this morning."

His voice was sad. I held his hand. Soon we were at JFK, where the chauffeur unloaded luggage from the trunk and everyone got out of the car. I wanted to give Leigh a goodbye hug even though she'd been so quiet in the limo and so touchy at the restaurant, but she was ignoring me.

"Leigh," I said, dashing ahead and catching her arm as she headed toward the airport's automatic doors. "Aren't you going to say goodbye? You have to give me your new phone number and your address so we can stay in touch."

She turned around. Her mouth was open. She looked like I'd just said something highly offensive. "Are you kidding?" she asked, and started walking.

"Leigh," I said again, following her. "What's wrong with you?"

She faced me. Then she grabbed my wrist and led me to an empty square of sidewalk, out of her family's earshot. I looked at the gold flecks in her eyes, the brown freckles on her skin. She was right—there were a gazillion of them.

"Why would you want my phone number?" she asked, perching her hands on her hips. "You won't use it. You didn't even call me when we lived across the bridge from each other. You said we'd hang out until I moved to California. Remember? In the Hamptons you said we'd hang out for the rest of the spring, but I ended up alone in my apartment as usual. I only see you at school or when you're with Blake and I just happen to be there. And he went to that Memorial Day party at your sister's house. But *I* didn't get an invitation. How come *I* didn't get an invitation?"

I was stunned. She was speaking quickly and raising her voice, and people walking by with suitcases and garment bags were staring. "W-well," I stammered. "I know we haven't seen each other much lately, but I thought you were busy getting ready to move."

She rolled her eyes and scoffed. "That's a weak excuse. As soon as you met Blake, you didn't care about me anymore. You used me to get to him . . . and it's not the first time this has happened. Lots of girls are interested in my cousins, and they don't care who they step on to get what they want. I didn't think you were like that . . . I thought you were different. I thought it would be okay to have you around them, that we could all be friends—but I was wrong. You dropped me and you didn't even notice."

I had a flashback to a four-course dinner and crème brûlée. I remembered standing in the penthouse, weaseling my way into an invitation to Rockefeller Center so I could see Blake again. I remembered Leigh telling Rachel not to give me dating advice when Rachel said Blake would be perfect for me. "I never meant to—" I started, but she raised her hand like she didn't want to hear any excuses. And maybe I was lying—maybe part of me really had meant to. I felt horrible, thinking about how friendly she'd been on my first day at Hollister, how I had let her ice skate alone, and I was shocked to realize that I was just like Summer. I'd put my boyfriend above everyone else and let Leigh sit at home on Friday nights. It was my fault that she'd spent the last few months alone in her apartment with nothing but colored pencils. It was even worse to think that this had happened to Leigh before, and that she considered me a girl who didn't care who she stepped on. I had never thought of myself as that sort of girl. "I'm so sorry," I said.

"Those are just words," Leigh said. "Do they make you feel better?"

Not at all. I wanted to make Leigh feel better, but I supposed it was too late now. "I guess you'll be back to visit soon?" I said meekly, hoping for another chance. "I mean . . . we can get together and maybe . . ."

"Yeah," she said, folding her arms. "I'll be back soon . . . to visit my *family*."

I got the message. I nodded, listening to car doors slamming and people saying "Have a safe trip." "Well . . . are you going to give me your new phone number? I promise I'll call you."

"Don't do me any favors." She spun around and stomped toward the terminal.

I knew I didn't deserve her phone number or her friendship. But I decided I would make it up to her somehow. I would ask Blake for Leigh's new address and send her a letter apologizing for everything. Maybe that would mean more than just saying I'm sorry.

I watched her walk toward Rachel, who was checking her suitcases curbside with a guy who had a Russian accent. I climbed into the limo with Blake, Del, and Idalis and just sat there thinking about Leigh.

"Can you give me Leigh's new address?" I asked Blake.

"Sure," he said. He reached into his pocket, took out his wallet, and started digging inside. The address was written on the back of an Ellis & Hummel business card that he pressed into my hand. "She didn't give it to you already?"

"I guess she forgot," I said, sticking the card in my purse, thinking it was nice of Leigh not to tell Blake that I was a person of questionable character. The fact that she hadn't made me feel even worse.

Blake nodded. "She was so snotty tonight. That's not like her. Maybe she's nervous about moving."

He hadn't noticed that I'd ditched her either. We'd been too busy with each other to give Leigh a second thought, even though we both knew how much she needed a friend. I just nodded at Blake and leaned my head against the window, watching Mr. Ellis as he tipped the guy who was taking Rachel's and Leigh's suitcases away.

The car door opened and Mr. Ellis slid onto the seat next

to Blake. "You have to give these people a good tip," Mr. Ellis said to nobody in particular. "Otherwise they'll put your bags on a plane to Moscow just to get even."

"Yeah," Del said. "Fucking commies."

He was drunk. But it was supposed to be a joke and I felt bad when Mr. Ellis didn't laugh. He turned his back on Del and spoke to Blake about starting at Ellis & Hummel on Monday, and I looked out the window because I got the feeling it was a private conversation.

Mr. Ellis stayed in the limo after the rest of us got out on the Upper East Side. He said something about work and a client and the car took him away. Then Blake and Del and Idalis and I were in the elevator and I tried not to watch as Idalis pushed Del into a corner and kissed him like they were alone.

They kept it up at the penthouse. I didn't think they would, because Del popped a movie into the VCR in the living room and we all sat together on the couch, but they started fooling around again during the opening credits. Blake had enough.

"Let's take a walk," he said, clutching my wrist.

Idalis disconnected her lips from Del's long enough to reach over and grab my arm. "Yeah," she said. "Why don't you take a walk upstairs to Blake's bedroom?"

Upstairs to Blake's bedroom. She said it long and slow, in a sultry voice that embarrassed and insulted me. I was sure I knew what she was thinking—that I was a sexless Debby Boone snoozefest and she was an erotic Madonna peep show. Blake pulled me up from the couch and Del rolled his eyes.

"Leave her alone, Idalis," Del said, and I adored him for it.

Then Blake and I were on the sidewalk. The sky had clouded over and I heard thunder in the distance. Blake was quiet as we walked to Central Park, where people started clearing from the grass after the sky lit up with an ominous spike of bluish white lightning.

Blake led me to a bench and we sat down. He pulled off his tie, took out his wallet, and showed me a yellowing picture of a young woman. She had big blue eyes and long blond hair that was parted straight down the middle, like a Wella Balsam ad from the seventies. Her skin was tan and her bone structure was regal, and she looked as if she was someone who never expected anything bad to happen to her.

"Is this your mother?" I asked.

He nodded and stared at the buildings in the distance before telling me that she had died while Del was playing Little League baseball. Blake and Del and Mr. Ellis had gone to the game and she'd stayed at home. Del had found her on the kitchen floor when they came back.

"Brain aneurysm," Blake said. "The doctor who did the autopsy said there was nothing anybody could've done. But Del thought it was his fault . . . he said we could've saved her if we'd been there. He never wanted to play baseball anymore after that. He was good at it too."

I wondered if anyone had ever told Del that it wasn't his fault. "I'm sorry," I said. "I bet she'd be proud if she could see you now."

He smiled. Thunder crashed, lightning ripped across the

sky, and we stayed on the bench with our arms around each other even though rain fell in heavy drops around us. I didn't mind getting soaked because it felt as if Blake needed me, and I wanted him to.

It was a Friday in late August when my boss, Julian, admitted that most of his employees quit after less than a week. The place was a downer for them because of the people who went there. They were called students, even though they were in their twenties and thirties, but they were really just being babysat until their parents came to pick them up at night, and they were easily entertained with crayons and finger paints.

One of them was named Adam. He was twenty-two and had cute dimples, and I was sure that he'd been a popular boy in high school until he got rammed in the head during a football game five years ago. Now he was mildly brain-damaged and he stuttered sometimes, and the highlight of his day seemed to be the pictures I sketched for him—pencil drawings of lakes and mountains. That was what he wanted because he used to hike and fish upstate, and I didn't mind drawing those things over and over if it made him happy.

"Do you have a boyfriend?" he asked.

"Yeah," I said, thinking that I'd answered the same question six times already, and if he hadn't gotten into that accident he could have chosen any girlfriend he wanted.

"You're pretty," he said. "You look like Snow White."

I almost cried. I convinced myself that helping Adam

with his painting would stimulate his mind and he might get better someday if I just kept trying.

Blake thought that this was a nice thing to do. He told me so that night, when I met him at work. It was six o'clock and we were standing beside a mahogany reception desk with the words ELLIS & HUMMEL printed across it in shiny gold letters.

"Leaving already?" we heard a voice say.

We both turned our heads and saw Mr. Ellis, who was holding a stack of papers in his hands and walking toward us.

"I left copies of the cases you wanted on your desk, Daddy," Blake said.

Mr. Ellis smiled and smacked Blake on the shoulder. A few minutes later, Blake and I were in the Corvette, where he said he wanted to stop at home to change before dinner. He went to his bedroom at the penthouse and I waited on the couch, admiring the skyline. As I was sitting there, I heard the elevator doors open. I looked toward the foyer and saw Del, who told me that he had come by to pick up an earring that Idalis lost the last time she'd been here.

"We broke up," he said, taking a seat next to me. "I was sick of her shit, anyway."

I wondered if that was true. I studied his eyes while he talked, thinking that they were much more green than gray tonight. "Oh, well," I said. "You're better off, I suppose."

He smiled. The scar on his lip curled. Then Blake was on the stairs and Del mentioned Ellis & Hummel. "Do you know what your boyfriend does at work?" he asked, and I shook my head. "He helps our father and his partners raid companies so decent people can lose their jobs."

I glanced over at Blake. He looked tired. "Cut it out, Del," he said.

Del didn't listen. "You know what else they do, Ari? They file frivolous medical-malpractice lawsuits. And they win. That's why health insurance costs so much and people dying of cancer go bankrupt."

"Enough already," Blake said, grabbing my arm. The next thing I knew, we were in the Corvette and Blake was saying he didn't want to stay in Manhattan. "Let's go to the Hamptons and order in. I've had enough of this city."

I didn't argue. He was quiet for the entire drive and when we ate a pizza at the kitchen table. Blake drank a beer and stared into space, and I knew what was wrong.

"You don't have to work there," I told him.

"I *do* have to work there, Ari. I can't let my father down."

I knew how he felt and I wanted to cheer him up. So I suggested that we sit on the lounge chairs by the pool because it was a nice night, but Blake wanted to swim instead.

"I don't have a bathing suit," I said, and he told me that Rachel had left one upstairs.

It was a hot pink bikini with a bottom that tied in a bow on the left hip. I found it in a dresser drawer along with T-shirts and sarongs, in one of those bedrooms with the indirect lighting. Then I stood in front of a full-length mirror on the white carpet, examining my thin legs and my narrow waist and my chest. The bikini crowded my breasts together into a small semblance of cleavage, and I didn't think they were perfect, like Blake said, but they weren't all that horrible. So I decided to go to the pool wearing only the bikini and leave Rachel's shirts in the drawer.

I held my breath all the way down the stairs and across the patio, and I didn't exhale until Blake smiled at me. Then he picked me up and tossed me into the deep end.

"Jerk," I said, even though I didn't mean it. I rubbed chlorine out of my eyes as he dove into the pool, and everything was still blurry when he pulled me into a corner and I put my arms around his neck.

"You look much better in that bikini than Rachel does," he said.

His hair was slicked back. The lights beneath the water were reflected in his eyes, and I remembered lifting my favorite marble to the sun.

"I can't compete with Rachel. She's beautiful."

"*You're* beautiful," he said.

Beautiful sounded so much better than *pretty*. I smiled, fiddling with his arrowhead charm. "You and Leigh have the same necklace."

"My grandmother gave one to all of us . . . me and Leigh and Del. He never wears his, though."

"Have you spoken to Leigh lately?" I asked, thinking of the letter I had sent her at the end of June. I'd spent a half hour at Hallmark searching through *I'm Sorry* cards. The one I chose had a cartoon cat with forlorn-looking eyes and a daisy in its paw. I sat at my desk for a long time that night, writing *I didn't realize what I was doing* and *I hope you'll forgive me* and *Please give me a call so we can talk*. But Leigh had never called or written back, so I guessed she still hadn't forgiven me. I really couldn't blame her. Maybe she thought the card was stupid too. *I'm Sorry* cards were so sappy.

"Yeah," Blake said. "She called me the other day. Haven't you heard from her?"

"Not lately," I said casually. Then I looked at the tattoo on Blake's back and changed the subject. "What is this exactly?" I asked, tracing the circle and the cross and the three feathers with my index finger.

We treaded water while he explained. It was called a medicine wheel and it was a sacred Native American thing. It was also supposed to bring good luck. He'd gotten it from some old Shawnee man down in Georgia.

"Don't mention it to my father," Blake said. "He knows about the tattoo, but he wasn't happy when he found out, so I don't talk about it. He's been running from Georgia his whole life . . . he wants to forget that we have any Shawnee blood in us at all."

I wasn't surprised. I thought of Ellis & Hummel and the penthouse and Blake's mother with her aristocratic father. I imagined Mr. Ellis struggling through school and winning lawsuits so that he could afford to live on the Upper East Side and pretend he'd never eaten a collard green or a hummingbird cake.

"But he gave your brother a Native American name," I said.

"He didn't want to. That was his father's name and it was expected. So he did it." Blake leaned his head into the pool to soak his hair. He raked it back with his fingers and I watched water droplets collect on his cheeks. "Anyway . . . just don't mention the tattoo. Jessica has the same one—he didn't appreciate that very much, either."

I'd never heard of Jessica before, but I knew who she was when Blake apologized and said that it isn't nice for a guy to talk about an old girlfriend.

He was right. It wasn't nice. It made a queasy lump of envy rise from my stomach to my face. I saw blond hair and a trailer with flowerpots and Blake sleeping with Jessica for two whole years.

"What happened with her?" I asked, as if I had no clue.

"I don't know," he said. "She stopped returning my calls. I even went down there to see her, but she was just gone. No explanation."

That was a cruel thing to do and he didn't deserve it. "Oh," I said. "I'm sorry."

He shrugged as if he didn't care, but he was a bad actor. Then we kissed. The water in the pool was warm and so were Blake's lips and tongue as they touched mine. He untied my top and slid it off, and then his mouth was on my chest in a way that made me worry about the neighbors. But Mr. Ellis had a lot of property, so I doubted that anyone could see from two acres away.

"We have to stop now," Blake said suddenly. "Or I won't be able to stop."

I hated stopping. It was grating on my nerves. But I came to my senses when my top was back on and we were drying off on the patio. We rested on lounge chairs and Blake read the *New York Post* while I decided that he was smart to stop what we'd been doing in the pool. There were things to consider before I could have what he used to give to Jessica.

"Blake," I said.

He was reading the sports section: YANKEES CRUSH KANSAS CITY. "Yeah?"

"How many girls have you been with?"

There. I did it. I'd been wondering ever since Evelyn had brought it up on Memorial Day and I needed to know, because terrible things could dwell in the most unlikely places.

He rested the newspaper on his lap. "It isn't nice to talk about that."

"We have to. These days, people have to talk about it."

He nodded. Then he held up two fingers.

"Really?" I said. "Jessica and who else?"

"Somebody older. That was the first time." He rolled his eyes. "I barely knew her . . . I met her at a bar in the city that Del dragged me to when I was sixteen and it felt like she was going to the bathroom on me. That's how sex is if you don't care about each other—it's no good at all." He sat up and swung his legs over the side of the lounge chair. "Listen, Ari. I don't have AIDS or anything else. I'll get a blood test so you don't have to worry."

I wasn't worried anymore; he didn't need a blood test. I shook my head but he insisted that he'd see his doctor, and then he checked his watch and said that we should head back to the city.

I went upstairs. The bikini was dry now and I stood in front of the mirror again, studying my body. The door was open, and when I saw Blake's reflection pass by in the hall, I called his name. He joined me on the carpet and I waved my hand in front of my chest.

"Can you tell?" I asked. "I mean . . . that I'm uneven?"

He held his fist to my cheek. "You *aren't*. If you say that one more time, I'll make you sorry."

I laughed and we kissed again, even though Blake warned me that it was close to nine and we had a long drive ahead.

So what? Mom wanted me home at *a reasonable hour* and there was still plenty of time before the reasonable hours were gone. I distracted him from the clock by lying on the bed and crooking my finger. Then it was Wednesday afternoon all over again, this time on a white comforter stuffed with feathers that felt as soft as a field of cotton puffs.

"Ari," Blake said. He was lying on top of me and he still hadn't put a shirt on. His naked chest, the muscles in his stomach, and the trail of hair that began at his navel and disappeared inside his shorts got me all shivery, and I wasn't sure how much longer I could worry about being *nice*. "I love you."

I gasped. I wanted to say the same but he wouldn't give me a chance. He told me not to say it until I was ready and that I shouldn't say it unless I meant it, and I was about to ask him to shut up because I *was* ready and I *did* mean it. But I couldn't say a word because he kissed me again, and his hands were on that bow on my hip.

It was loose now, and I was nervous as his hands moved to my waistband. I felt it sliding south and I thought of Idalis floating in the pool and Del saying *Don't you wish*.

Blake was edging lower on the bed and I knew what he was about to do. It was the thing that people other than Idalis kept quiet or giggled about, the thing that was supposedly safe since it wouldn't get me pregnant, the thing that supposedly bypassed all the Catholic rules.

"Don't be scared, Ari," he said. "It won't hurt, I promise."

Then the bottom half of my bikini was lying on the carpet. Blake was between my legs and it definitely didn't hurt. I felt his lips and his tongue and his thick hair brushing against the soft inside of my thighs, and after a while there was a warm burst in the center of my body that flowed to my head and made noises come out of my mouth. They were like the sounds I heard through Evelyn and Patrick's bedroom wall, but I buried my face in my arm so that they wouldn't be as loud.

I kept my eyes shut against my arm, thinking that this was amazing and incredible, like devouring an entire box of chocolate all alone. It was sweet and delicious and I just couldn't help myself. But if anybody found out, I'd have to pretend that I could never ever ever do such a sinful thing.

seventeen

One of the four bathrooms had a showerhead that looked like a mail slot in somebody's front door. It was a metal square with a rectangular opening and I almost expected a Con Edison bill to fall out.

Water flowed over me in a steady stream as I listened to Blake banging around in the bathroom next door. I'd rushed in here from the bedroom, saying I was saturated in chlorine and I needed some shampoo immediately, even though that was just a lame excuse.

I couldn't look at him. I couldn't speak. I was excited and elated and embarrassed all at once.

But I couldn't hide forever. I lingered in the shower until my hands wrinkled, then I wrapped a towel around myself and tiptoed down the hall. I ran into Blake, who was wet from the shower too. A towel was tied around his waist and his necklace skimmed his bare chest. He was so handsome, but I still couldn't look at him, even when he pressed his forehead against mine.

"You make such cute little noises," he said.

My cheeks flushed. I could have died. "I have to get dressed," I told him, but he caught my elbow as I walked away.

"Hey," he said gently. "What's wrong?"

He smelled of Irish Spring. I just stood there. "Nothing," I said.

He lifted my chin. "You think we did something bad?"

Yes. No. Maybe. "I don't know."

"Ari," he said with a laugh. "We didn't. And I wouldn't do it for just anybody. I don't get involved with someone unless I see a future."

A future. The idea that what happened tonight could lead to a Park Slope house and a hammock and kids with the bluest eyes made everything seem okay.

So I relaxed. I smiled. I danced alone around the bedroom while I changed into my clothes. Then we were in the car, where the top was down and my hair flowed in the breeze and everything felt perfect.

I thought I came home at a reasonable hour. It wasn't quite as reasonable as the time I usually came home, but it wasn't all that late. I didn't expect Mom to ambush me.

"Where were you?" she said.

I had just walked through the front door into the living room and I was startled at the sound of her deep voice in the pitch dark. I heard the click of a lamp and there she was, sitting on the couch with her arms folded and her legs crossed.

My eyes nervously searched the room. I saw the hole in the La-Z-Boy, a sealed pack of Pall Malls on the coffee table. "Where's Dad?" I asked.

"Where do you think? They pulled a body out of the East River tonight and he had to go to Manhattan." She reached for her cigarettes. "So where were you?"

I shrugged. I wondered if I was glowing and she'd figure everything out. "With Blake," I said.

She peeled plastic from the Pall Malls, slid out a cigarette, and tossed the pack onto the table. "I know that. Where exactly were you with Blake?"

"In the Hamptons," I said, and my voice sounded weak and small.

Mom flicked her lighter. "And what were you doing there all this time?"

"Nothing," I said.

She dragged on her cigarette and patted the couch. I sat beside her even though I just wanted to go upstairs and think about Blake.

"You're getting too serious," she said.

Here we go, I thought. Then I got defensive. "Why don't you like him?" I asked.

"I never said I didn't like him," Mom answered calmly. "He's very nice. He's respectful. I can see that he was brought up well. But you're my daughter and my concern is for you. You're too young to be serious about anyone."

Too young. Too serious. Too everything. "He thinks we have a future together," I said, and I thought I sounded mature and rational, but Mom didn't—she laughed as if I was an idiot.

"Ariadne, he has no idea what he wants. He's a young boy."

"He is not. He'll be twenty-one in November. You were only twenty-three when you married Dad."

"But that was 1957. It's a different world now . . . women have much more opportunity today. You," she said, pointing a finger at me, "have much more opportunity than I ever did. You don't know how lucky you are. And Blake better not be filling your head with all this *future* shit. It's just a ploy to get you in the sack." She leaned forward, staring into my eyes like they were two crystal balls. "He hasn't gotten you in the sack, has he?"

I wondered what she could see. Roses on a bedspread, a soft white comforter, a pool with a scorpion lurking at the bottom. "No," I said, and I didn't think it was a lie because *in the sack* meant going all the way, and Blake and I had only gone part of the way so far.

She settled into the couch and puffed on her cigarette. "Good. I'm glad to hear it. Because guys Blake's age are flighty—they'll tell you anything to get laid and then they move on to the next victim. There are some girls who can handle that—Evelyn, for example. She used to break up with one and find another without batting an eyelash. But you're not like Evelyn, and if this kid does anything to hurt you, I'll chop off his nuts and shove them down his throat." She snuffed out her cigarette in an ashtray. "And you tell him to bring you home earlier from now on. Understand?"

I understood. I understood that I would never tell her anything about Blake again and that my head hurt for the first time in months. "I'm going to bed now, Mom. I think I'm getting a migraine."

She wouldn't let me go to bed. She brought me to the kitchen, where she watched while I swallowed my medicine. Then she gave me a glass of warm milk and kissed my cheek.

"Good night," she said, and when she was gone, I wiped my cheek with a napkin and poured the milk down the sink.

Summer invited me to her house the next afternoon, which was surprising. I hadn't seen her once since school had ended, and she hadn't returned the four messages I'd left with Tina. But I missed her enough to forget all that and to ask Dad for a ride from Flatbush to Park Slope.

He dropped me off and waved to Tina before heading to work. I walked past her as she crouched on her little lawn, wearing a sun visor and plucking weeds.

"Hi, Ari," she said. "Long time no see. Go ahead inside— Summer's upstairs."

I slipped into the foyer and peeked into Jeff's library with its crowded bookshelves and Tiffany lamps. I heard Fleetwood Mac and I followed the sound to Summer's bedroom, where she was sitting in a chair with one foot perched on her desk. She was polishing her toenails and didn't see me.

I stood in the doorway and glanced around at her bed-room. It looked like it had been completely redecorated since the last time I'd been here. It was so fancy, so elegant. There was a paneled bed made of bleached wood set between two antique-looking night tables, a matching wardrobe chest, and taupe wallpaper speckled with shiny silver roses. The wall-paper matched the comforter on the bed, which had decora-tive pillows in the shape of circles and squares. Everything was perfect, like something from a fairy tale, and I wished I could sleep in a fairy tale instead of on Evelyn's rickety old canopy bed from when Lyndon Johnson was president.

"Your room is fantastic," I said, even though I had to force the words from my throat.

Summer looked up from her toes. She was wearing a short denim skirt with a pink halter top and indigo eye shadow, and she was as stunning as the room. But I remem-bered that I had Blake and he thought I was *much prettier,* which meant more to me than a fancy bedroom.

"Thanks," she said. "Sorry I haven't called lately. I've been busy."

I guessed she'd been busy with Casey, so I accepted the ex-cuse. Female code and all. "No problem. I've been busy too."

She leaned back in her chair. "I broke up with Casey last week."

Surprised, I took a seat on her windowsill and watched as she pointed to the tattoo on her ankle. The *C* had been changed to an *S* so that now she was wearing her own ini-tials.

"They did a good job," I said. "But I hope they used a clean needle."

"Of course they did, Ari. I got it done at a very reputable place on Bleecker Street a few days ago. I went there after a meeting that my mother and I catered at Ellis and Hummel," she said, and I tried not to react. I just nodded and crossed my legs as she flopped on her bed and hugged a pillow to her chest. "I think your boyfriend's father is gorgeous, by the way."

And my boyfriend's father thinks you're beautiful, I thought. But I didn't say it because she had a mischievous look on her face that didn't need encouragement.

"Forget it, Summer. He's old."

She rubbed one leg slowly across her comforter. "Not really. He's forty-seven."

"How would *you* know?" I asked.

"He told me. I talk to him all the time. . . . Stan's a friendly person."

She called him Stan. *I* didn't even call him Stan. He must have given her special permission, and I guessed he only did that for girls he considered beautiful. "Right," I said, and Summer flipped over onto her back and stared at her ceiling fan.

"Ari," she began. "Are you sleeping with Blake yet?"

I looked out the window; Tina was lugging a fertilizer bag down the stairs. "Why are you asking?"

She shrugged. "I was just wondering about . . . what he does and . . . what's normal for most guys. I mean . . . I dumped Casey because he was losing respect for me. He wanted a certain position all the time, not just once in a while, and I don't think that a guy really cares about you if he doesn't even look at your face while you're making love."

That image made me uncomfortable. "But you said that position was strangely exciting."

Summer shifted onto her stomach, resting her face on her fists. "Not every single time."

"Oh," I said.

"I'll bet Blake looks at your face. I've talked to him a few times at Stan's parties and I think he's a real gentleman. He always holds the door for me and he never even swears. He treats me with respect . . . like a man is supposed to treat a lady."

"That's how he is," I said proudly, and for the first time in my life, I knew that Summer envied me, that I had something she wanted. I felt victorious, but I tried not to act that way. She'd given herself to a guy who wouldn't even look at her face; she didn't need to get her feelings hurt again. "But the other stuff you asked about . . . I don't know. We haven't gotten that far."

"Jesus," she said. "After all these months? He really *is* a gentleman . . . Casey demanded sex after just a few dates."

I'd never known any of this—that Casey wasn't a gentleman, that he demanded things. Now I wasn't sure what to say, but it didn't matter because she changed the subject. She opened a dresser drawer, took out a letter from Hollister, and told me that she'd been approved to graduate early and was going to work full-time with Tina from January until college started next September. Then Tina called Summer from downstairs, asking for help with the twisted garden hose, and I was alone.

I walked around the room, examining Summer's pretty things: the carvings on her headboard, the old jewelry box with the spinning ballerina on her dresser. I glanced inside the drawer that she'd left open. I saw a lacy black bra, a purple velvet diary, and a silver bracelet engraved with the initials M.G.

Leigh's bracelet. The one she'd lost at the party at the Winter Garden. I couldn't believe it. I was furious. Leigh was desperate for that bracelet, and Summer had been holding it hostage all this time. I knew that Summer could be inconsiderate, but I'd never suspected that she was utterly heartless. I'd even defended her to Leigh. *She wouldn't do something like that.* I snatched the bracelet out of the drawer, holding it in my sweaty fist. My head was pounding and I was tired all of a sudden. A minute later Summer came back, smiling, completely unaware that she'd been found out.

"What's this?" I asked, dangling the bracelet in front of her.

"Oh, yeah," she said. "It turned up last week. I was going to tell you."

She wasn't going to tell me. And I was sure that she'd found it eons ago, the night of the Winter Garden party. Still, she stayed cool now, concocting a story—something about the bracelet getting tangled in a tablecloth that Tina hadn't used for ages.

"You're lying," I said. "You did this because you hate Leigh."

She slammed her drawer. "Why shouldn't I hate her? Remember what she said when we were at that club in the city? *You don't want people to think you're a slut.* I had enough of that crap in public school. And *you*," she said, pointing an acrylic nail at me. "You betrayed me, Ari. I always stuck by you, and I was always there for you when you needed me, but you weren't on my side against that weirdo and her bitch mother. It's unbelievable that they're related to Blake, because they're nothing like him."

I supposed she had a valid point about sticking by me and all, but I ignored that. I was so annoyed by the adoring look in her eyes when she spoke Blake's name that I couldn't be reasonable. "Stop talking about him," I said. "You don't know anything about him."

She folded her arms and let out a snarky laugh. "Neither do you."

"He's my *boyfriend*," I said. "I *love* him."

Now she really laughed. "Oh, please. You don't love him. You barely know him. You haven't even slept with him. It's just a case of limerence, like that silly boy in seventh grade who kept a collection of my hair."

Limerence. That was the word I couldn't remember. The fact that she'd compare me to a poem-writing, hair-collecting seventh grader was just too much.

"Well," I said. "I wonder what Blake will say when I tell him what you did to his cousin. I know you have a high opinion of him, but I'm sure he won't think very much of you."

She chewed on her lip, staring at me for a second. Worry spread across her face but it quickly changed into disgust. "I don't know who you think you are," she said. "You've got this idea that you're something special because you landed a guy who's completely out of your league. But you won't have him forever, Ari. He'll figure it out."

She had hit a nerve, and it hurt. "Figure what out?" I asked as an aura crawled into my eye.

"That you're boring. That you're dull and boring and *average* in every possible way."

I was speechless. Maybe I should have shrugged it off. But I thought that it might be true, that I might be even less than average, and I fought back tears.

"You can't stand it that I finally have someone," I said after a moment, choking out the words as my throat closed up. "I never had a boyfriend, and I only had one friend, but you had everything . . . and that made you feel like you were better than me."

She tossed her hair. "I *am* better than you."

I couldn't talk anymore. My eyes were stinging and my face was burning. I rushed outside, past Tina, who was spraying shrubbery with her hose.

"Bye, Ari," she said, but I didn't say anything back.

I walked all the way home to Flatbush. I was exhausted by the time I opened my front door. I smelled potatoes roasting and Mom came out of the kitchen, drying her hands on a towel.

"You're home early," she said.

I thought I might faint. Mom looked distorted, like a reflection in a carnival mirror. "I'm done with Summer, Mom. And don't call Jeff about it."

She stared at me for a moment. "All right, Ariadne," she said finally.

The phone rang and it was Blake. He said he couldn't wait to see me at Evelyn and Patrick's Labor Day barbecue next week. After I hung up the phone, I sealed Leigh's bracelet in an envelope, wrote her Brentwood address on the front, tossed my #1 FRIEND charm and my cedar box filled with art supplies in the trash, and fell asleep on my embroidered roses.

eighteen

On the Friday afternoon before Labor Day, I got dressed for my last day at Creative Colors while Dad showered for work and Mom shopped at Pathmark. I was on my hands and knees, trying to find a pair of matching shoes in my closet, when the phone rang. There was a pile of shoes around me and I didn't feel like answering the phone, but I ran to the kitchen anyway and picked up the receiver.

I heard a raspy voice, and it surprised me. "Hi, Ari," Leigh said as I leaned against the dishwasher, nervously wrapping the phone cord around my finger. "I'm only calling because I got the bracelet. It was in the mail yesterday."

That was the only reason she was calling. I supposed I shouldn't expect anything more. And I imagined that she was going to hide the bracelet in a chest or a drawer and never look at it again until she was ready. She might wait for years and years, until she was married and had children, and one day she'd take it out to show her teenage daughter and say something like, *This was from a boy I used to know. He was very special to me but that was so long ago.*

"Good," I said. The tip of my finger was turning red so I loosened the cord. "I'm glad."

"Who found it?" she asked.

"Summer." That was all I said. It was enough that Summer and I were done forever and that the #1 FRIEND charm had been taken away by a garbage truck. Even though I'd threatened otherwise, I had decided not to tell Blake about the bracelet. He might inform his father that Summer was a thief and a liar, and his father might fire Tina. For her sake, I didn't want that to happen. She worked so hard to uphold her reputation.

"I also got your note," Leigh said.

I remembered my *I'm Sorry* card with the dumb cat and the daisy. I expected her to say more, to say she'd forgiven me, but she didn't. And the flat, unfriendly voice she'd been using left me feeling very awkward. "Good," I said again. "So . . . do you like California?"

"It's okay so far. Some of my neighbors are our age, and they're much nicer than most people I knew in New York," she said, and I guessed I was one of those not-nice New Yorkers. Then she started talking about another neighbor, a guy our age from Vermont who'd moved the same week she had. "We're exploring Los Angeles together. He's a friend."

From the way she talked about him, I thought he might become more than a friend. She sounded happy all of a sudden and that made me happy, even though she was probably still mad at me and she cut our conversation short. I was glad that I'd gotten the bracelet back to her.

A few minutes later, I went outside into a sunny day. I walked to Creative Colors, past girls drawing hopscotch boards on cement. By the time I reached work, my muscles ached and I was tired even though I'd slept for nine hours the night before. I had no idea what was wrong with me. I wondered if I was seriously out of shape or if I was getting sick.

"Will you be back next year?" Adam asked.

It was the end of the day. We'd had a farewell-to-summer party—Dunkin' Donuts, and Kool-Aid in Dixie cups that I couldn't drink because my throat was sore. Adam was looking at me, his handsome face filled with hope, and he made me sad.

"Sure," I said, and my voice cracked.

He smiled. "What are you doing for Labor Day, Ari? Seeing your boyfriend?"

My boyfriend. He remembered. And he spoke without a stutter. It made me think that my work with Adam had actually done him good—that maybe all the painting had repaired his neurons or whatever was wrong inside his head. Maybe he was better off because of me. Believing that made me happy again.

Blake was on time for Evelyn and Patrick's Labor Day barbecue. He even brought an autographed Red Sox baseball for Kieran. When the sun began to set, I fell asleep on his shoulder as we cuddled together on a wicker patio sofa that Evelyn had ordered from Sears.

"Ari," he said, shaking me.

I opened my eyes. I wasn't sure how long I'd been asleep, and Blake looked worried. My hair stuck to the perspiration on my forehead and he pushed it away, asking why I hadn't eaten a thing all day.

"I'm not hungry," I said. "And my throat hurts."

"Then you should see a doctor."

"I don't want to. Tongue depressors make me gag."

"Baby," he said teasingly. "And speaking of doctors . . . I have something to show you."

He led me to the front of the house, where his car was parked at the curb. We climbed in and he took a piece of paper out of the glove compartment.

It was covered with words from Sex Ed—*chlamydia* and *gonorrhea* and *HIV*, plus a few others that my teacher had neglected to mention. They were listed on a chart and each one had a very good word next to it—*negative*.

"Did they stab you with a big needle?" I asked, scanning the chart, wondering which one of those filthy diseases Del had caught underneath his skylight. I despised needles and blood tests because I always ended up getting stuck at least five times. *Bad veins,* the nurses and phlebotomists always muttered while they turned my arm into swiss cheese.

"Needles don't bother me. And I'm not trying to pressure you with this, Ari. I just don't want you to worry about anything."

I smiled, folded the paper, and put it back in the glove compartment. "I'm not worried," I said, and he leaned over to kiss me but I covered my mouth. "Don't, Blake. You'll get sick."

"I don't care."

Later we went back to the sofa and watched Kieran and his friends skid on the Slip 'n Slide. I kept wondering about Del and I couldn't stop myself from whispering, "Which one of those diseases did your brother have?"

Blake's eyes widened. "Where did you get *that* from?"

I shrugged. "A little bird told me."

"Yeah . . . a little bird with red hair, I bet."

He didn't answer my question. I looked around the backyard at Patrick barbecuing hamburgers and Evelyn gossiping with her housewife friends until I couldn't stand it anymore and I asked again.

"Ari," Blake said. "It isn't nice to talk about that."

Nice, nice, *nice,* why did everything have to be so nice? "I won't tell anybody. I promise."

He sighed before whispering in my ear. "Syphilis," he said.

I gasped, remembering everything I'd learned in school about syphilis, like how it made people go blind. I couldn't think of anything worse than being blind. "That's a bad one, isn't it?"

"It's only bad if it doesn't get treated. Anyway . . . this isn't a polite topic of conversation, so let's drop it. My blabbermouth cousin never should've mentioned it to you. I talked to her last night, actually. She said you found her bracelet."

"Summer did," I said. "Summer and I aren't friends anymore, by the way."

"Really? I thought you two went way back."

An unexpected sadness rushed over me. We do go way back, I thought. But she's not the person I thought she was, and now you're my only friend. "These things happen," I said, then changed the subject because I didn't want to think about Summer. I just wanted to put my head on Blake's shoulder and pretend that this was my very own Sears sofa in my Park Slope backyard and that the giggly kids on the Slip 'n Slide belonged to us.

I felt strange the next morning. I was light-headed and warm, and even though my sore throat was gone and my empty stomach rumbled, I had no interest in Mom's blueberry waffles or her fruit salad with the made-from-scratch whipped cream.

"Eat something, Ariadne," Mom said.

She was standing beside the kitchen table, wearing her *Kiss the Cook* apron and a smile. Dad sat across from me with his eyes on *Newsday* and his fork moving from his waffle to his mouth, and I told Mom I wasn't hungry but I shouldn't have. She looked disappointed and I didn't blame her—she had woken up at the crack of dawn to make this first-day-of-school, *It's the most important meal of the day* breakfast for me.

Then she got worried. "You're not sick, are you? You're very pale."

I was always very pale, but I was definitely sick. Still, I

didn't want to see a doctor who would poke me with needles and drain my blood into glass tubes.

"I'm just excited," I said. I had no idea where that had come from. It was as if my body had been inhabited by a clever spirit who knew the right thing to say.

"Of course you are," Mom said. "I'm excited too. I mean, it's your last year of high school and college will be here before you know it."

I didn't think about college that morning. I rode the subway alone, feeling really tired. And I thought about Blake, especially when I spotted Summer at the other end of the hall while I was walking to homeroom.

She was chatting with a group of girls and she looked blurry. She laughed and I wondered if she was laughing at me, if she was telling her friends about that weird Ari Mitchell, who was suffering from a serious case of limerence and believed she was in love with a guy she hadn't even slept with yet.

But I wanted to sleep with him. I thought about Blake all day, through homeroom and Calculus II, and while I read meticulously typed syllabi that were hot from the copy machine. I thought about him on the subway that took me back to Brooklyn and when the walk from the train station to my house seemed so long that I wasn't sure I'd make it.

Then I conked out on my bed. Dad was at work and Mom was at a faculty meeting that would keep her away for hours. When I woke up, the house was so quiet I could hear the freezer making ice cubes.

I stared at the ceiling, listening to ice fall into a plastic container. I didn't feel tired anymore—I felt beyond tired, sort of spacey and giddy. I got up, went to the bathroom, and looked in the mirror at a reflection that wasn't pale. My cheeks were ruddy and I probably had a fever, but I didn't feel sick. I looked reasonably pretty, and that made me decide to freshen up and go to Manhattan so I could surprise Blake at Ellis & Hummel.

I made my plans behind the shower curtain. I lathered my hair and watched water bead on a stomach that was disturbingly concave from lack of food. It didn't matter; I would eat later, someplace in the city with Blake, and afterward we would go to a nice hotel or to the penthouse if Mr. Ellis wasn't home. Then I would give Blake what he'd been so patient for, what I could do now because his tests were negative and he loved me and that made it okay.

I left the house an hour later. It was cloudy and a scorching wind blew through my hair, and Saint Anne seemed immersed in a radiant peace. I walked past her, rode the subway to Manhattan, and reached the Empire State Building at five o'clock, when swarms of people were flooding out of the lobby. The Catering by Tina van was parked on the street.

Tina didn't notice me because she was busy loading the van with chafing dishes. But Summer noticed. She looked through me as if I was nobody, as if she'd forgotten elementary school and junior high and my birthday dinners, and I pretended it didn't hurt. I turned away, rode the elevator to Ellis & Hummel, and filled my mind with Blake instead of Summer.

I asked for him at the front desk, where a gum-chewing

receptionist pointed toward a conference room with glass doors. I saw Blake inside, standing with Mr. Ellis and a few other men beside a long polished table. Mr. Ellis kept smacking Blake's shoulder and jokingly grabbing him in a chokehold, as if Blake was a first-place trophy or a prize racehorse that he wanted to show off.

Blake saw me. He waved me over and broke away from his father; then we stood by the doors inside the conference room while Mr. Ellis filled the other men's glasses with liquor. I heard them talking, something about a "gentlemen's club," and the rest of the men laughed when Mr. Ellis said, "We're all gentlemen, aren't we?"

"What are you doing here?" Blake asked.

He was happy to see me. He smelled of aftershave. The darkness of his suit coaxed out the blue in his eyes, and just the sound of his voice gave me a warm shudder.

"I thought we could . . . ," I began, not sure how to finish. *I thought we could spend some time together. I thought we could have a romantic dinner. I thought we could go to your apartment and have passionate sex until the sun rises in the morning.*

But I didn't say any of that because Mr. Ellis was suddenly beside us and so were the other men, and Mr. Ellis introduced me to them as "my boy's little girlfriend."

"This is Ari . . . ," he started, and looked at Blake for help.

"Mitchell, Daddy," Blake said. "Ari Mitchell."

I knew it. I knew he didn't remember my last name. And being called Blake's little girlfriend didn't exactly boost my self-esteem. A little girlfriend, a little crush—why did everybody have to take something that seemed so big and squash it into a tiny speck of nothing?

"Of course," Mr. Ellis said, summoning his charming smile. "Forgive me, Ari. I'm getting close to fifty and the memory's the first thing to go."

Everybody laughed. Mr. Ellis put his son in another chokehold, rubbed his knuckles against Blake's scalp, and told him not to take too long. He and the other men would be waiting in the lobby.

I was so disappointed. "Where are you going?"

Blake seemed uncomfortable, and not just from his suit. "Dinner at Delmonico's. And some bar later on."

I folded my arms. "What kind of bar?" I asked, imagining a place where cheap, desperate girls in G-strings would grind on his lap for a twenty-dollar bill.

"It's just business, Ari. I'm not interested in those places. My father always takes his clients there. I have to go. You understand, right?"

I didn't want to understand. But I nodded and he hugged me. He said that I felt really warm, I should see a doctor, and I couldn't ride the subway back home all alone. He told the receptionist to call the car service and then we took the elevator to the lobby, where I left him with Mr. Ellis and got into a car that whisked me away from all my beautiful plans.

I fell asleep in homeroom the next day. My teacher tapped my shoulder and I lifted my head to find the entire class staring at me. Then I went to the school nurse and she asked if I was on drugs, which was hilarious. I'd never even smoked a cigarette or been drunk, and I wouldn't have any idea where to find drugs, unless Evelyn had left a stash of marijuana in the basement with her Jordache jeans.

The nurse called Mom, who took me to my doctor's office, where a phlebotomist tied a rubber tube above my elbow. I looked away as his needle pricked my arm seven times to find a vein. When I looked back, he had filled so many vials with blood I was surprised to still be alive.

I only felt semi-alive. I was exhausted and my muscles ached, and the doctor said he couldn't be sure until the tests came back but he was almost certain that I had mononucleosis.

"You know where you got this," Mom said.

We were in her Honda, heading toward Flatbush. "Where?" I asked.

"*Where?* From Blake, where else?"

I should have known she'd say that. I had felt her eyes on me when the doctor was talking, explaining that mono was common in teenagers because *adolescents are typically involved in intimate behavior.*

"Blake isn't sick," I said. "I didn't get it from him."

"He doesn't have to be sick, Ariadne. Didn't you hear the doctor? He said that some people carry the virus but never show symptoms. It's called the kissing disease. Didn't you hear the doctor?"

How many times was she going to ask me that? I was fed up with the sound of her voice, but I still had to listen to it when I was in bed later and she called my school from the phone in the kitchen. She told the principal that I had mono and I had to stay home for eight weeks, and that she was very concerned because I was planning to attend the Parsons School of Design next year, so I couldn't veer off track.

I didn't want to veer off track. Blake and I had a future together that couldn't be delayed. So I was glad when Mom came to my room and said that everything had been worked out. She was driving to Manhattan tomorrow to pick up my books. My teachers were going to write down my assignments every week and fax them to Mom at her school, and I could go back to Hollister in November as if nothing had ever happened.

She left me alone after that. I rested in bed, listening to the end-of-summer sounds outside—the Good Humor truck making its final rounds, people setting off firecrackers left over from the Fourth of July. I was inhaling the smell of a neighbor's barbecue when I decided that this mono thing might not be so terrible. My best friend was history, Leigh was in California, and I didn't have anyone to sit with in the cafeteria anymore. Now I wouldn't have to spend the next two months eating lunch in a bathroom stall.

I did have mono. The doctor called a few days later to confirm his diagnosis. But Blake didn't have it. I insisted he get another blood test to prove Mom wrong.

He came to my house the next week while she was at school and Dad was at work. He surprised me, driving to Brooklyn after his last class on a Thursday afternoon.

I let Blake in, and he followed me upstairs and settled into bed with me. I was on my side, his arm was around my shoulders, and I wanted to fall asleep with him. But Mom would be home in a few hours, so that just couldn't happen.

"I should teach you to drive," he said.

"You have to be eighteen to get a license in New York," I answered.

"You'll be eighteen in four months, Ari. You can get a permit now. I can give you driving lessons."

I didn't want driving lessons. Driving lessons were dangerous. I could skid on an icy road and Blake could hit his chest on the dashboard. I shrugged and he turned my face toward his, trying to kiss me. I pulled away and jammed my lips into my pillow. "You can't, Blake. I'm diseased."

He laughed. "You are not."

"I am too. I don't want you to get sick—you'll miss school. Your father would be mad."

"Let him be mad, then," Blake said. "So what?"

So what? I smiled into my pillow, thinking I'd been right a few weeks ago when I decided it was okay for me and Blake to sleep together. If he was willing to risk catching mono and missing school and letting his father down, then he meant it when he said he loved me.

But I still didn't want him to get sick—I couldn't be responsible for him feeling as tired and achy as I felt. "You can't kiss me, Blake," I said when he tried again, even though I was dying to kiss him. "I have germs in my mouth."

He laughed, moved my hair, and kissed my bare neck.

He ran his tongue from the base of my skull to the tip of my spine. It sent waves of electricity through me. "You don't have any germs right here, do you?"

"No," I said. But even if I did have germs, I couldn't have told him to stop.

He came back the next Thursday, and he brought gifts—books and magazines, so I wouldn't go stir crazy. He came to visit me every Thursday, and each time he brought presents, like boxes of dark chocolate from a fancy candy store in the city.

We'd stay in bed for hours. He'd put his arms around me and kiss the back of my neck, and sometimes I wondered if he'd try to do more than that. My parents weren't home and I wouldn't have objected, even though I was sick and contagious. I knew that most guys would see an empty house and a willing girl as an easy opportunity, but Blake didn't. And that made me love him even more.

"How are you feeling?" he asked one day. I was on my side in bed; he snuggled up next to me and draped his arm across my shoulders.

"Not good," I said, hearing early-October rain tap my window. "My whole body's sore . . . especially my back. It feels better if I lie on my stomach."

"Then lie on your stomach."

I shifted on the bed and pressed my face into my pillow, listening to the rain. It was getting heavier now and sounded like rocks hitting the roof. I also heard Blake moving, and then he was straddling me, massaging my back through my shirt, gently kneading his fingers into my skin and my aching muscles. His thighs felt warm and strong as they squeezed my hips. I thought I might melt into the sheets.

"Is that better?" he whispered into my ear as his cheek skimmed mine.

"Much better," I mumbled. I was falling asleep.

Blake touched my face and spoke in a louder voice that snapped me out of my trance. "You're really warm," he said, reaching over to my night table. He picked up a bottle of Tylenol and shook it. "This is empty, Ari. Do you have any more?"

I blinked and turned around. His eyebrows knitted together like he was worried.

"I don't know," I said, stretching and yawning, flattered that he was worried.

He went across the hall to the bathroom and I heard him riffling through the medicine cabinet. When he came back, he grabbed his leather jacket, which he'd chucked across my bed earlier.

"Where are you going?" I asked, sitting up halfway.

Now he was next to my desk, picking up his wallet. "To the drugstore to buy Tylenol. You need to get rid of that fever."

I looked outside. I saw water spilling down the window, and a tree across the street. Its leaves were deep orange and bright yellow, and they were sagging beneath the steady rain.

"You can't go out, Blake. It's pouring." I didn't want him to go anywhere, not even just down the street. I wanted him to get under the covers with me and massage my back again. So I sat up all the way and moved to the end of the bed, kneeling on the mattress. "Stay here," I said, feeling cold all of a sudden. I glanced at the mirror above my dresser; I saw pasty skin and dark circles around my eyes. I was so gory-looking lately. "My mother can pick up the Tylenol when she gets home from work."

He shook his head. "She shouldn't have to go out again in this weather."

That was a considerate observation. He was more considerate of Mom than I was. Then my teeth started to chatter. Mono was crazy—broiling one minute, freezing the next.

"I hate it when you leave," I admitted.

A smile spread across his lips. It was a lazy, sensual smile. "You hate it when I leave?" he said, like he wanted to hear it again. I nodded, and then he gathered up my bedspread and wrapped it around me as I looked into his eyes and absorbed his smell—leather and aftershave and toothpaste.

He gently pushed me back down to the pillows and kissed my entire face. He kissed me everywhere—my forehead, my cheeks, my mouth, my jaw, my chin, the space between my eyes. I was flattered again. I had thought I was too hideous and clammy to be kissed.

"Get some rest," he said afterward. "I'll be back soon."

I couldn't argue with him anymore, because I needed the Tylenol. The chills were the worst. So I put my head on my pillow and listened to his footsteps on the stairs, his car pulling away from the curb, and the rain beating against my house. It was so nice to be taken care of, especially by him.

* * *

Mom wasn't impressed by Blake's presents. She saw me eating the chocolate and accused me of deliberately slowing my recovery. She wanted me to drink milk and eat meat so I'd regain my strength. She was particularly skeptical of my favorite gift—a pure white teddy bear covered with velvety soft fur. She shoved the bear aside one night when I was filling out an application for Parsons and she was dusting my dresser.

"Blake gives you cheap gifts," she said. "Especially for a rich boy."

I scoffed. "That bear isn't cheap, Mom. It's from FAO Schwarz. Besides, I thought you weren't impressed by money."

Touché. I got her good on that one. She rolled her eyes and changed the subject, telling me for the tenth time to request applications from a few other schools.

"You'll get into Parsons," she said. "But it's smart to have some backups just in case."

I nodded and returned to my application, but I had no intention of requesting anything from other schools. I knew I didn't need backups because I had something better: connections.

It seemed to take forever for me to recover from mono. The truth was, I wasn't sure I *wanted* to recover, because it was nice to do my schoolwork at home and to lie in bed with Blake's arms around me every Thursday. It was Halloween when my doctor said that I was healed, that I should rest for another week and then get back into my normal routine.

Mom was happy, but I wasn't. I tried to think of pleasant things, like Blake's twenty-first birthday party, which was scheduled for the following Friday at the Waldorf Astoria. Mr. Ellis had invited two hundred people and the party was black tie optional. I was excited, but Mom was worried because the party was the night before the SAT.

"You'd better come home early, Ariadne. And don't even think about asking me to buy another dress. You have a perfectly good dress in your closet that you've only worn once."

I didn't ask for another dress. I wasn't going to have it on for long, anyway. I had decided that I was going to give Blake a very special birthday gift, something I'd been saving for what felt like forever.

"Can we get a room here tonight?" I asked.

The party had just started. Blake and I stood inside a reception hall at the Waldorf among lots of men in suits and women in dresses. Blake was sipping a Heineken and his forehead crinkled.

"Why?" he said.

I whispered into his ear, "Because I love you."

He got it. He smiled. I wanted to kiss him but I couldn't because Mr. Ellis came by. He took Blake away and led him around the room, smacking his shoulder and tousling his hair, introducing him to people as "my boy Blake" while I sat alone.

I watched them move through the crowd. After a few minutes I saw two familiar faces. I should have expected that

Tina and Summer would be here—it seemed as if Mr. Ellis's guest list included every single person he and Blake knew, and everybody but Rachel and Leigh had accepted.

"Having fun?" Del said, sitting down next to me.

He was in a suit, wearing his pinkie ring, and he smelled of tobacco and cologne. We started talking and he got me feeling the way I had at the Christmas party last year—excited and nervous. I had to stop feeling like that and I had to stop trying to figure out what color his eyes were, because Blake was my boyfriend, Del wasn't nearly as handsome, and I was going to be his sister-in-law someday.

But Del was seated at table three for dinner, like me. I walked with him to a room with ornate chandeliers and flower arrangements. He sat on my left and Blake sat on my right. Other people joined us—women escorted by men who Blake told me were his father's partners at the firm—and then Mr. Ellis was there, and suddenly the two seats next to him were filled with Tina and Summer.

"Hi, Ari," Tina said, waving across the table, her stringy hair brushing the collar of her plain gray dress. I wondered what Summer had told her, what story she'd crafted to explain why I never called anymore. "Look, Summer," Tina said, smiling and pointing at me the way parents point when they take their kids to the zoo. *Look, there's a giraffe, there's a bear, there's an average boring girl.* "It's Ari. Did you see Ari?"

"I saw her," Summer said, unrolling the silverware in her napkin. She mumbled a greeting across the table that I returned, only because we were in public and I had to be civil.

"Why is *she* at this table?" I whispered to Blake.

He shrugged. "My father handled the seating arrangements. You don't mind, do you?"

I shook my head. I pretended not to mind. I ate my salad even though it was made with a kind of lettuce that was more suited to rabbits than humans.

"Who's that floozy?" Del whispered into my ear.

"She's not a floozy," I whispered back. "She's an ex-friend of mine. She and her mother cater your father's parties. You've met her before, actually—at your club on New Year's Eve."

"Oh, yeah. I forgot." He picked up his drink and finished it off. It was his third, but he asked the waiter for another. "My father loves introducing Blake to chicks like her. There are two kinds of women, he always says. The nice ones you marry and the cheap ones you screw. He thinks that guys need a lot of cheap girls before they end up with a nice girl."

I felt my stomach drop as I realized that Mr. Ellis was more like Mom than I'd ever imagined. *Guys need a lot of cheap girls before they end up with a nice girl. There are plenty of fish in the sea. You don't want to get stuck with the first one.*

I wished Del hadn't opened his mouth. Now I was concerned about Mr. Ellis, who was smiling at Summer like she was the most adorable thing in the room. I thought back to the day before I'd found out about the mono, when Blake had *had* to go to a strip club with his father. How long had Mr. Ellis been introducing *cheap girls* to Blake? And what did he think about his father's philosophy?

I tried not to think about it during dinner. I tried to enjoy the melon wrapped in prosciutto, the grilled pork tenderloin with the caramelized apples, and the butternut squash. Blake

held my hand beneath the table and when the meal was finished, he slow-danced with me to a Spandau Ballet song. My
heartbeat quickened when a cake with HAPPY 21ST BIRTHDAY
written on it arrived, because the party was winding down
and soon we'd be alone.

"Here's something for you, son," Mr. Ellis said while I was
eating my cake. He crouched between me and Blake and
handed him a wrapped box that Blake opened. There was a
gold watch inside. Blake thanked him and Mr. Ellis slapped
his cheek. "Just keep making me proud," he said.

Blake lied to him when the party was over. He said that
he was going out with some friends and he wouldn't be home
until late, and then he brought me to a room with a queen-
size bed, beige curtains, and a matching carpet covered with
rows of brown squares.

"My gift isn't as nice as this," I said, stroking his watch.

He left it on a night table. "Your gift is much nicer than
this."

I smiled and started thinking about practical things. "I can't
take the Pill because I have migraines," I said, because I
couldn't think of a better way to mention the practical things.

"Since when do you get migraines?" he asked.

"Since always. I haven't had one for a while. But I'm still
considered a migraine sufferer," I said, which he found funny
for some reason. He laughed and I kept babbling. "So do you
have—you know—"

"Protection?" he said with another laugh.

I nodded and he told me that he'd been carrying protection in his wallet for months. Then we went to the bed, where
he slipped off his tie, unbuttoned his shirt, and dropped them

on the floor. I was still in my dress but not for long. Soon it was next to Blake's shirt, resting on those neatly lined-up squares. I reached over and turned off the lamp. The only light in the room came from behind the curtains, from the building across the street. I heard car horns honking, voices traveling up twelve floors, and my own breath.

There was enough light to see Blake. He leaned over me and I trembled at the muscles in his arms, the pearly glimmer of his smile. His pants joined the rest of his clothes on the floor and he guided my fingers below the path of hair on his stomach, where he felt long and warm inside my palm, hard but soft, like Patrick's hands. Then his mouth was all over me and noises came out of my mouth, little panting sounds like the ones I'd made in the Hamptons, but they didn't embarrass me this time. Nothing did. Nothing seemed dirty or sinful or wrong, even though I was about to break a major Catholic rule. I kept my eyes closed until I heard paper ripping and a snapping noise.

"Don't be scared," Blake said.

I felt his weight on me and I was definitely scared. "Wait," I said. "You didn't make a promise like you did in the Hamptons."

I saw a sympathetic smile in the hazy light. "I can't promise that."

He kissed my forehead before pressing his groin into mine, and I heard talking in my head—my voice saying that Summer's tattoo *must've hurt* and her voice saying *So does sex the first time you do it, but I didn't let that stop me.*

Summer was right. But I wasn't going to let it stop me

either, and the painful part passed quickly and turned into something fantastic. Blake gripped my hands and held them flat on the bed, his chest rubbing mine as he moved with slow thrusts, while I absorbed every part of him and he took every last inch of me.

"Are you okay?" he whispered.

I nodded, feeling a fiery jolt in the middle of my body that rose to my head. I guessed that Blake was feeling the same thing, because he made those tennis-player-hitting-the-ball noises and tilted his head back. Then I knew that I was much better than okay, and I couldn't imagine feeling any other way.

nineteen

I hadn't planned to fall asleep. I'd known I wasn't going to get home early like Mom wanted—I assumed I might sneak in at one or two and still have time to get some rest before the SAT—but I'd never expected to wake up at the Waldorf with my head on Blake's stomach. I looked at his rising and falling chest, his slightly parted lips, and the sheet that started at his waist and ended at his feet. The sight of him made me ignore Mom and the SAT.

I kept looking until Blake opened his eyes. He smiled and pushed my hair out of my face, and I thought that Mom had been wrong when she said *They'll tell you anything to get laid and then they just move on to the next victim.* I knew he wasn't going anywhere.

Then I glanced at the digital clock on the night table. It was after seven and the SAT was at nine. I panicked, gathered the sheet around my body, and slid to the edge of the bed.

"What's the matter?" Blake asked.

"I'm supposed to take the SAT this morning. I'll be late."

"You won't be late," he said. "I'll drive you straight there."

"But I have to go home and change . . . I can't show up like *this*," I said, reaching down to the carpet to pick up my dress. "I need to take a shower and wash off my makeup, and eat something. . . . I can't screw up the SAT. I have to get into Parsons."

He laughed, grabbed my arm, and pulled me toward him. "Don't worry so much, Ari. The SAT is no big deal. My father will get you into any school you want. You know that."

I still wanted to do well on the test. A low score would disappoint me and devastate Mom. I could already hear all the critical, cutting things she'd say if I blew it.

But it was hard to tear myself away from Blake. I stayed in bed with him for a while longer, wrapped in his arms while he kissed the back of my neck and made me feel like I had nothing to worry about anymore, like I wasn't a four out of ten in the looks department and I wouldn't die alone and I didn't have to fight and struggle for everything the way Mom did.

* * *

It was eight-thirty when Blake dropped me off at my house. He wanted to come in with me, to second my story that we'd gone dancing at Del's club and lost track of time, to convince Mom that we hadn't done anything that wasn't *nice*. But I wouldn't let him because I was afraid of the humiliating things Mom might say, things like *You should think with your brain. It's in your head, Blake. Not in your pants.*

I ran to the front steps as Blake drove away, and Mom opened the door when my key touched the lock.

"What the hell is going on here?" she yelled in my face.

I was in the foyer as she slammed the door with a deafening bang that made me flinch. I stood there in my wrinkled dress, feeling like Evelyn in high school, strolling in after one of her late nights with God-knows-who doing God-knows-what.

"We went dancing after the party," I said. "I lost track of time."

"Dancing," Mom said. "Where? On the backseat of Blake's car?"

"Corvettes don't have backseats, Mom."

I regretted that sentence as soon as it came out of my mouth. It sounded snotty. Mom stared at me like I was someone else, like I was a big disappointment, worse than Evelyn. But what Blake and I had done wasn't wrong, and I couldn't let her tell me that it was, so I kept on lying. I swore that nothing happened and that I was sorry for staying out late without calling and it would never happen again. Then I felt really guilty because she believed me.

"Wash your face and brush your hair," she called after me

as I raced up the stairs toward my room. But there wasn't any time for that. I tore off my dress, threw on jeans and a sweatshirt, and rushed outside into a cold day. Mom had already started the car.

I took the SAT at my old school instead of Hollister because Brooklyn residents were allowed to take the test in their own borough. Summer did the same thing. She sat one row away from me and six seats ahead, looking well rested in a white turtleneck and designer jeans while I looked positively mangy. She turned around and glanced at me once, obviously aghast at my messy hair and the black mascara smeared under my eyes. Then she went back to pretending I didn't exist.

For a moment I wished I could talk to her, that I could tell her what had happened last night. Last night was the kind of thing that a girl wants to share with people like sisters and best friends. But Evelyn and Patrick had driven to Boston with the kids this weekend for a Cagney family reunion, I wouldn't have discussed it with Leigh even if we *had* patched things up, because it wouldn't be *nice* to discuss sex-related things about her cousin, and of course I couldn't talk to Summer anymore. So I focused on the test, on the verbal section, the endless analogies.

I was exhausted and my head was killing me. The words on the page blurred together—*medicine: illness:: law: anarchy; extort: obtain:: plagiarize: borrow; tenet: theologian*— What exactly was a tenet? I'd seen that word when I was taking practice tests, but now I couldn't remember much of anything.

We took a break before the math part and I watched the back of Summer's head while I invented my own analogy: *real* is to *fake* as *love* is to *limerence,* and you had a lot of nerve to tell me that I have a *little crush* on Blake, Summer. I love him and he loves me and now you can't say that I barely know him and that I haven't even slept with him because none of that is true anymore.

I wanted to sleep. I wanted to eat. I wanted to think about Blake and last night. But after the break, I just sat and held my forehead in my hands, reading about *Susie,* who had to *visit towns B and C in any order.* There were lines on a diagram, and I was supposed to figure out how many routes she could take, *starting from A and returning to A, going through both B and C, not traveling any road twice.*

I couldn't possibly have cared less about Susie or her routes.

Summer, on the other hand, looked like she knew exactly how Susie could go through B and C without traveling any road twice. I stared at her while she breezed through the questions, twirling her hair as she filled in the answers with a pencil. She was done before anyone else, so she closed the exam book, leaned back in her chair, and examined her perfectly manicured nails.

I wanted to grab her pencil and plunge it through her heart. This wasn't fair. She never even studied. But she'd probably had the sense to go to bed early last night and to eat a healthy breakfast this morning. My stomach was growling and time was running out, and I knew I was bombing the SAT even though I'd aced so many practice tests, while Summer hadn't taken a single one.

When it was over, I found Mom waiting outside. "I hope you did well," she said nervously as she drove us back home. "Do you think you did well?"

I stared through the windshield, mustering up the strength to lie. "I think I did okay."

Mom's head snapped toward me. "*Okay?* What does *that* mean?"

"Nothing," I said, feeling queasy.

We stopped at a red light and I listened to her wedding ring tap the steering wheel.

"Well," she said, "if you didn't score as high as you should have, you can take it again."

I guessed that made her feel better. I just nodded and kept quiet. My headache was getting worse and my mind was racing with thoughts of last night. I was worried about the test, but I remembered what Blake had said this morning. I told myself that the SAT didn't matter because Mr. Ellis was going to get me into any school I wanted.

Mr. Ellis wasn't at home the next weekend when Blake brought me to the penthouse and took me upstairs to his room. I'd never been in there before and it was surprisingly small, with an old shag rug and lots of textbooks scattered across a desk.

His bed was pushed against a wall and his wool blankets scratched my skin while we made love for the second time. We went there every chance we could find, through Thanksgiving decorations coming down and Christmas lights going up. Mr. Ellis was never home. Sometimes we had sex and sometimes Blake repeated what he did in the Hamptons, and I didn't hide my face in my arm anymore. Then there were other times when all we did was stay in bed for hours with our arms around each other, and it was as nice as everything else.

"I've been thinking," he said.

It was two days before Christmas and one of those nights when we just kissed and talked while we were wrapped up in woolly blankets. There was snow on the ground outside and the temperature was brutally low, and I loved being in his hideaway of a bedroom, where we were safe from the entire world.

He told me that he didn't want to go to law school. Spending the summer at Ellis & Hummel had been proof that he couldn't stand wearing suits and that legal work bored him to tears. But he couldn't come up with a way to break the news to his father, so he was going to finish college, take the firefighter exam, and tell Mr. Ellis when the time was right.

"You have to do what you want," I said. "I've figured that out lately."

He smiled, pulling off his clothes and mine. I felt his lips on my skin and his breath on my neck.

"Blake," I said afterward. "Everything we talked about—the house and the kids and the future—you don't mind waiting for a few years, right? I mean . . . until I'm done with college and grad school? Because I want those things . . . but I won't be ready for a while."

"I'd rather have it now. But for you . . . I'll wait." Then he said that he had an early Christmas present for me and he put on a pair of shorts, walked across the room to his desk, and returned to bed holding out a tight fist. He uncurled his fingers to show me a big square ruby attached to a gold chain. "This belonged to my mother," he said. "I want you to have it."

His mother. I realized that he loved me even more than I'd thought, because he wouldn't give such a precious gift to just anyone.

Blake fastened the chain around my neck and got under the blankets with me, where we quickly passed out. I wasn't sure how long we'd been asleep when I heard a cough—and opened my eyes to find Mr. Ellis standing in the doorway, wearing a suit and an unhappy face.

It was so humiliating. My bra had been flung wantonly onto the carpet and Blake was cuddled up behind me, his arm draped over my bare shoulders. I nudged his ribs to wake him, and Mr. Ellis said that he wanted to see Blake downstairs.

I got dressed in a flash after they were gone. I heard voices: a thick New York accent and a light Georgia twang. I couldn't understand a word, so I tiptoed into the hallway to eavesdrop, but I still couldn't hear anything except footsteps. I dashed into the bathroom, closed the door, and stayed inside until Blake knocked.

"It's okay," he said. We were in the hallway now and he saw that my face was flushed. "I'll take you home, all right?"

"I'll take her home," Mr. Ellis interrupted from the bottom of the stairs. "I have some errands to do anyway. Is that okay with you, Blake?"

I wanted him to say that it wasn't okay. I stared at him, hoping he could read my mind, but he didn't seem to have the strength. The next thing I knew, I was sitting next to Mr. Ellis in a Porsche like Del's, struggling to act dignified, pretending that he hadn't just caught me naked in bed with his son.

The radio was on, 1010 WINS. *You give us twenty-two minutes, we'll give you the world.* The leather seats were heated, and a medallion swung from the rearview mirror. FORDHAM LAW, it read. CLASS OF 1964. I absentmindedly touched the ruby on my neck with one hand and nervously twisted my hair with the other.

Mr. Ellis saw my necklace. Our eyes met for a second but he didn't say anything. I tucked it beneath my shirt, thinking that my gift belonged to his poor dead wife and he probably didn't want me to have it.

He didn't act that way, though. He flipped the charm switch and engaged me in polite conversation about the weather. Next he started talking about how he'd spent years toiling at some sweatshop firm in Midtown to repay his student loans and to get enough experience to open his own place. It was all for his kids, he said. Too bad Blake was the only one who appreciated it.

"My son told me about your college plans," he said when we were close to Flatbush. "I can help you with that. I know quite a few people at Parsons."

I hoped he'd be able to tell them my last name. "Thank you, Mr. Ellis."

He ran a hand through his hair. "Is there anything else you want, Ari? I mean . . . is there anything I can do for you?"

We were a block from my house and he parked next to that lot where Blake and I used to sit in the Corvette and kiss. It was still vacant; the latest rumors were that the owners had either squandered all their Lotto money or gone to jail for killing some Mafia kingpin.

I was confused. Why had he stopped the car and what was he talking about? I shook my head and he asked if I was sure, because there were many things he could do, like finance my college education and buy me any kind of car I wanted.

"I don't need anything, Mr. Ellis," I said.

He turned in his seat and I got a clear view of his face. He was so handsome, better-looking than either of his sons, but I felt afraid of him suddenly, of what was behind that suave smile and those deep brown eyes. They were so dark that I couldn't find the pupils.

"You know something, Ari," he began. "Blake's been acting very strangely these days. His grades are dropping and he's preoccupied . . . and last week I found an application for a firefighter exam in his room. You don't know anything about that, do you?"

I wanted to run home. Instead I shook my head and listened to him talk about how Blake had acted this way once before, when he was dating a girl in Georgia, and he had even considered quitting school and moving down there to marry her and work at some dead-end blue-collar job, and could I believe that?

I could believe it. I felt sick. I remembered the night at the penthouse when Del and Blake had talked about Jessica. Del had said that Blake was with her for two years and she lived in a trailer and she'd dumped him without so much as a phone call. She probably didn't have a cent and hadn't been able to resist when Mr. Ellis asked if there was anything he could do. He'd probably done a lot to get rid of her so that she wouldn't spoil the plans he had for his prize racehorse.

But I wasn't Jessica. I didn't need anything except Blake. Mr. Ellis kept asking what I wanted, saying that he'd buy absolutely anything for me and my family.

"My family and I have everything we need," I said.

He stared at me for a second, as if his eyes could melt my will. When that didn't work, he turned away, started the car, and drove me home. He didn't say another word until we were across the street from my house. Dad was on a ladder, twisting bulbs on a string of lights that lined the roof, trying to identify the one that had caused the rest of them to die.

"Is that your father?" Mr. Ellis asked. "The detective?"

I nodded and reached for the door, but he stopped me.

"Ari," he said. "I'm sure you wouldn't want him to know what you've been up to. I mean . . . spending time alone in a young man's bedroom doing things that could cause a lot of trouble. You wouldn't want your parents to know about that, would you? I'm sure they have a high opinion of you—you wouldn't want anything to spoil it."

He'd switched from bribery to blackmail, and my face flushed again because he was staring right through me like he could see everything that Blake and I had done in his bedroom. I sprang out of the car, raced past Dad, and ran upstairs, where it took me hours to fall asleep.

Blake called the next morning as if nothing had happened. Of course, he didn't know what had happened. Mr. Ellis wasn't going to mention our conversation, and I didn't rat him out. I couldn't shatter Blake's illusions by informing him of the cold hard truth that his father was a snake.

Blake invited me back to the penthouse for Christmas Eve, and Rachel was standing in the foyer when I walked in. She looked as beautiful as ever, holding a glass of cider in her hand and saying goodnight to a man who was putting on his coat. She wore a black knit dress with a slit up the thigh, and I felt nervous when she glanced in my direction. I wondered if she thought I was as bad as Summer for hurting Leigh, and I worried that she'd tower over me in her high-heeled suede boots, pointing a skinny finger.

I dashed by her. I had almost made it to the living room when I felt someone touch my arm.

"Ari . . . aren't you going to say hello to me, honey?" Rachel said in her faint Southern accent, and I turned around. I played it cool, pretending I hadn't even seen her.

"Hi," I said, clenching my fists and waiting for something awful to happen.

"Leigh is here," Rachel said, nodding toward the living room.

I thought she was about to say that I was a selfish, scheming user and that I didn't deserve a friend like Leigh. But she just put an arm around me and bent her head toward mine.

"I think you two should patch things up," she whispered. "You didn't know what you were doing. A girl can lose her head when she has feelings for a guy. I've been there, God knows. And like I've said before . . . all three of you can be friends. Isn't that right?"

I let out a relieved sigh, nodded, and veered around wine-drinking guests in the living room until I found Leigh. She was standing by the floor-to-ceiling windows, holding a red mug and staring at Manhattan. I tapped her shoulder and she turned around.

"Ari," she said with a serious face that looked prettier than I'd ever seen it. Her hair was pulled back, and Rachel must have done her makeup. It was all the right colors—apricot-hued lipstick, sparkly gold eye shadow. She wore a green velvet dress with a silver belt cinched around her waist.

I was nervous. I tugged on one of my fingers, trying to crack the knuckle. "Merry Christmas," I said, looking at the miniature marshmallows floating in her hot cocoa.

She leaned against the window. "Merry Christmas," she said coldly.

That disappointed me, but I decided to give my apology a try. "Leigh," I began. "You didn't deserve what I did to you. I know that saying sorry doesn't mean much, but it's all I can do. I'd really like to be friends again."

The city lights blinked behind her as she sipped from her mug. I thought she was ignoring me, that Rachel was wrong, that it was hopeless. So I turned away, but then she grabbed my elbow.

"Okay, Ari. I accept your apology. But don't ever treat me like that again."

"Promise," I said, sticking out my hand to seal the deal. She hugged me instead.

I saw Mr. Ellis later on. What a phony. He was all smiles and charm and "Merry Christmas, Ari. So glad you could come."

I smiled back, deciding that I'd be just as fake as he was and that I wouldn't let him or anyone else take Blake away. I wouldn't accept bribes and I wouldn't be blackmailed, even if he'd been clever enough to place hidden cameras all over the Hamptons house and the apartment. I wondered if he had X-rated evidence that he planned to show my parents if I didn't disappear, like videotape of me topless in the pool or of Blake's head between my thighs or of the two of us going at it on those scratchy blankets.

That was paranoia, I told myself. Or maybe it was a story-line from *Days of Our Lives*. But after last night, I wouldn't have put anything past Stanford Ellis. He could call Mom and Dad to expose me as a liar and their second letdown of a daughter, and even though I prayed that wouldn't happen, I told myself it didn't matter—because it was okay if you loved somebody.

"Want to see what I got for Christmas?" Blake asked.

We were sitting on the couch with Del and Rachel and Leigh. Leigh had told me that the guy from her building was her boyfriend now, and her face lit up every time she mentioned him, which made me think the California move had been a good idea.

"Blake got a stereo system from our father," Del said. He'd been drinking and he was slumped on the couch with a cigarette in his hand. "And you know what I got, Ari? I got turned down on a loan for my club. Now I have to go to the bank and get raped on a fucking ten-percent interest rate."

"Watch your mouth," Blake said. "And don't expect Daddy to bail you out every time you get in trouble. It's not his fault that your business isn't doing well. He warned you not to open that place."

"He'd bail *you* out," Del said. "He'd do anything for you."

Blake didn't answer. He must have known it was true. Then he took my hand and led me upstairs, where he showed me an expensive stereo system and looked disappointed when I wasn't enthusiastic.

"What's the matter?" he said.

"Nothing," I answered, stepping closer to kiss him. I asked if he would come to my house for Christmas tomorrow but he said he couldn't, one of his father's partners had invited them for dinner and he couldn't get out of it. "Oh, come on," I whined. "Can't you blow it off for me?"

And he did. He showed up at my house the next afternoon with gifts for the kids and a Lindy's cheesecake for dessert. I had a gift for Blake. I gave him a bottle of his favorite aftershave. It wasn't special and precious like what he'd given me, but he seemed to appreciate my Christmas present as much as I treasured his.

"It's huge," Evelyn said after dinner when she and I were washing dishes, Mom was playing with the boys, and Dad and Patrick and Blake were watching TV in the living room. Evelyn was looking at the ruby that hung over my shirt and she whispered into my ear, "Is *he* huge too?"

I nodded and held my finger to my lips when she let out a raunchy laugh. I had told her everything about me and Blake—about the Waldorf and the time we spent in his bedroom—and she'd promised to keep it a secret from Mom.

An hour later, we ate Mom's butter cookies around the dining room table and Blake blended in like he was a member of the family. It made me think that Blake would learn to stand up to Mr. Ellis the way I was learning to stand up for myself. If he'd turn down Christmas with his father to spend it with me and my family, then he was definitely making progress.

"I love my gift," I said, twirling the ruby between my fingers.

Everyone had moved to the living room and Blake and I sat together on the couch, where he took off his NYU sweatshirt and gave it to me because I was cold. It smelled of him and it was going to keep me warm in bed tonight. I was glad I didn't have to hide it under the scarves in my closet.

twenty

$Mr.$ Ellis had his second heart attack at his partner's Christmas dinner. Leigh called my house to tell Blake, and he and I rushed to St. Vincent's Hospital in Manhattan.

Leigh and Del and Rachel were waiting for us in the emergency room. Rachel's cheeks were striped with tears, and when Blake saw her as we ran through the automatic doors, the frightened look on his face made me regret the moment in the car when I'd wished that this Christmas would be his father's last.

The hospital allowed two people at a time into Mr. Ellis's

room. *Just family,* a nurse said. The only reason I wanted to go in was to be with Blake, who I saw through a window in the door. He was sitting in a chair next to the bed and Rachel was sitting next to him, rubbing his back. I wished I could rub his back. He looked so sad. His eyes were on Mr. Ellis, who had a tube in his arm and another up his nose and a ghostly pallor covering his skin.

I stood in the hallway as Rachel came out and Del went in and Del came out and Leigh went in. The only constant was Blake, who finally left the room when a doctor wanted to speak to everybody. Then I listened to the doctor tell us that Mr. Ellis had gotten to the hospital in time, that he had to stay at St. Vincent's for a few days, but he'd be all right if he watched his diet and stopped working so hard and avoided stress.

Rachel breathed a sigh of relief. She put her arm around Leigh and they went back to the room, and then I was alone with Blake and Del. Del looked at his watch.

"This poor girl has been standing here for hours," he said to Blake. "I'll take her home."

I thought that was very considerate but Blake didn't. His face turned stormy and his voice was peevish when he told Del that nobody had asked him to take me home. Ten minutes later, Blake and I were back in the Corvette. I didn't say a word as we drove from Manhattan to Brooklyn because Blake didn't seem interested in talking.

"I should've been there" was the first thing he said.

We were parked in front of my house and he didn't look at me. His eyes were fixed on the windshield, through which

I saw piles of snow on the sidewalk and intoxicated people leaving Christmas parties.

"Your father will be fine, Blake. The doctor said so. You couldn't have done anything if you'd been there."

"But I would've been there, Ari."

He never said he blamed me. He didn't have to. I didn't get a good-night kiss, and that said it all.

Blake didn't want to welcome 1987 together. He called a few days after Christmas and said his father was home from the hospital and it wouldn't be right to leave him alone on New Year's Eve. He also said that Rachel was helping out, but she and Leigh were itching to go to Times Square and Del was working at his club, so the only one left to play nurse was him.

"You understand, don't you?" he asked, and I pretended I did. I told myself that it didn't matter, that Mr. Ellis would recover soon and Blake and I could pick up where we had left off on those scratchy blankets.

Then I went with Mom and Dad to spend New Year's Eve in Queens, where my positive thinking evaporated. I sat on the couch in a funk while Kieran raced his Matchbox cars in the basement with Evelyn, and Dad and Patrick played poker in the dining room. Mom plopped down next to me. She tore open a pack of Pall Malls, turned on the television, and watched *It's a Wonderful Life* as I stared into space and caressed my necklace.

"This isn't a cheap gift," I said.

Mom grabbed the remote control and lowered the volume. "What was that?"

"I said this isn't a cheap gift. You accused Blake of giving me cheap gifts and this is an expensive gift."

"Of course it is," Mom said. She put her arm around me, pried my hand from the necklace, and squeezed my fingers in hers. "It's a lovely gift. And I'm sure that Blake would've spent tonight with you if his father wasn't sick. But he has his life to lead and you have yours. Believe me, this time next year you'll be in college and you'll look back on tonight and laugh."

For a minute there I had thought she understood. I'd thought she was going to tell me that everything would be fine with Blake and that I had nothing to worry about . . . but instead she dismissed him as somebody I'd barely remember in twelve months.

And why did she have to bring up college? I was sure that I hadn't exactly aced the SAT, and I hadn't applied anywhere other than Parsons. If Mr. Ellis could get me in, he could probably keep me out. Our conversation in his car had made it crystal clear that he wouldn't give me something for nothing. Now I understood why Mom was so anti-connections.

Leigh called on New Year's Day and invited me to the penthouse, which was strange. It wasn't her penthouse, and Blake should have done the inviting. I asked where he was and what he was doing, and there was a pause before she answered.

"He went to some deli on the other side of town to buy chicken noodle soup," she said. "Uncle Stan is very picky about his chicken noodle soup."

Her tone was sarcastic, and I imagined Blake shivering in the cold outside Katz's or the Carnegie Deli and trying not to spill a container of scalding hot soup as he rushed home. This made me even angrier at Mr. Ellis than I already was, but my mood wasn't too terrible, because I assumed that Blake had told Leigh to call and everything was fine.

So I fixed my hair and makeup and rode to Manhattan in a car that Leigh sent to Brooklyn. It left me at Blake's building, where I took an elevator to the top floor. My heart sank when I reached the penthouse and he wasn't there.

"He'll be back soon," Leigh said. "He had to pick up some deposition transcripts . . . Uncle Stan won't stop working no matter what the doctors say."

She told me that Mr. Ellis was resting upstairs and Rachel was asleep in the guest bedroom because she'd been out clubbing until six that morning. She led me to the living room, where Del was sitting on the couch smoking a cigarette and watching a football game. Leigh sat down next to him, so I sat next to her and stared at the television, thinking that the penthouse didn't feel the same. It seemed empty and boring and grim without Blake.

He came home an hour later and I rushed to the foyer. There was a stack of spiral-bound documents in his hands and a dusting of snow on his coat, which I brushed off.

"Look," I said, raising my index finger to show him a snowflake. "They say no two are alike. Isn't it amazing?"

He didn't say anything, just smiled a half smile, as if it

wasn't amazing and he pitied me for thinking it was. "I guess Leigh invited you," he said, and this gave me a chill because I'd convinced myself that he wanted me there.

"Of course I did," Leigh said from behind me. "I figured you forgot to do it yourself. A guy wants to spend New Year's Day with his girlfriend unless he's made a resolution to become a total bastard."

So Blake hadn't wanted me there. And Leigh had definitely forgiven me—she was looking out for me even though I'd pushed her aside. We sat back down on the couch, where Del and Leigh paid attention to the game and Blake didn't pay attention to me.

"Let's go upstairs," I said into his ear, because I was sure he was in a bad mood from being an errand boy all morning and I could cheer him up.

"Upstairs?" he said. "But my whole family's here. It wouldn't look nice."

Nice, nice, nice, I didn't *care* about nice. And I doubted that anyone would notice. Rachel was still asleep and Mr. Ellis's bedroom door was shut, and Leigh and Del were arguing about whether a penalty on the Jets was deserved. So I pouted and whined until Blake brought me to his room, where he acted like his old self again. He kissed me and I kissed him back, then he was on top of me on the bed and I started to undo his belt because I craved him so much that I couldn't stand it anymore.

"Don't," he said.

"It's okay," I whispered. "We'll be quiet. Nobody will know."

He shook his head, sat up, and rubbed his temples as if he

had one of my migraines. I sat next to him and asked if something was wrong, because he'd been acting so funny lately.

"Here's the thing," he said. "I think we should cool things off for a while."

He wasn't looking at me. He was touching his knee, scratching a bleach stain on his jeans as if scratching would do any good. What he said felt like a thousand bee stings all over my body. Then he said something about falling off the dean's list last semester and about law school, and when I reminded him that he didn't want to go to law school, he reminded me that his father needed him and he couldn't let him down, especially now that he was sick and stress could make him sicker.

I wished that Mr. Ellis *would* get sicker. I wished that he'd have another heart attack and not make it to St. Vincent's in time, and I didn't care if that was a sinful thing to wish because he was ruining everything.

"I'm sorry," Blake said, looking at me with a tired face. "I didn't want to tell you until after the holidays. It's just that I'm not sure what I'm going to end up doing, so it's better for me to be alone for a while to figure things out. And I can't keep lying to my father."

"I lie," I said. "I lie to my mother all the time. I've told her so many lies about us that I can't even remember them anymore. And you shouldn't be so eager to please your father— he's not as perfect as you think."

There was a flash of anger in his eyes and he broke his *Watch your language around a lady* rule again. "What the hell is that supposed to mean?"

It means that he threatened me, I thought. It means that

he tried to bribe me and he did the same thing to Jessica. She didn't disappear on her own, you know. Stanford Ellis made that happen so he could have you all to himself. But I didn't say anything because I could barely talk. Blake had never raised his voice to me before, and his tone brought tears and an aura to my eyes.

"Nothing," I answered, and my voice cracked.

He noticed and it softened him. He reached out and ran his knuckles across my cheek, and I gripped his wrist to keep his hand where it was. "Don't be upset," he said. "I don't want to hurt you, Ari. We'll just see what happens, okay?"

I nodded, trying not to cry, wanting him to put his arms around me so I could bury my face in his chest, but he didn't. He led me downstairs, where Leigh and Del were getting into their coats. They said that Leigh wanted to go back to her hotel and Del had work to do at the club, and a car was waiting for them outside.

"Take Ari with you," Blake said. "She needs to go home."

Now it was much harder to keep myself from crying, but I managed somehow. I stepped into the elevator with Leigh and Del while Blake stood in the foyer with his face as blank as a soldier's. He didn't kiss me goodbye. Then the doors slammed shut and he was gone.

Downstairs in the lobby, the doorman ushered us into a miserable day. The snow had turned to rain, and our driver must have had the flu because he kept sniffing and coughing. His cough was so deep I felt it in my chest.

"Are you all right?" Leigh asked in her raspy voice. She was sitting between me and Del, and I guessed she was asking because I hadn't said a single word in the last fifteen minutes. She didn't know it was because I was afraid I'd break into a fit of sobs if I dared to open my mouth. So I nodded and she kept looking at me, studying my face with her hazel eyes, and she said that Blake had been acting weird since Christmas. "He's all mixed up in his head, Ari," she said quietly, so Del couldn't hear. "He'll get over it."

I nodded again, hoping she was right. The sedan parked at her hotel, and as she got out she said that she and Rachel would be back in New York next month. Del told the driver that the next stop was West Twenty-third and we were off again, riding over slick streets, past mountains of filthy gray snow that I wished would melt because they were depressingly ugly.

"I'm not contagious, you know," Del said.

At first I thought he was referring to the syphilis. But of course he wasn't. He'd been cured, and he didn't even know that I knew about it. He just meant that I was sticking to the opposite side of the car. I was still afraid to talk, so I forced a smile and slid a few inches toward him on the seat. He asked if it would bother me if he had a cigarette. I shook my head and he rolled down the window to blow smoke into the rain. We were both quiet and I kept glancing at his hands because they came from the exact same mold as Blake's.

When we reached Cielo, Del tossed his cigarette into the gutter. Then he leaned across the seat to put his hand on the curve in my back and to kiss my cheek, wishing me a happy new year. A raw gust of wind blew into my face as he opened the car door and I had a sinking feeling this wasn't going to be a happy year.

twenty-one

January was awful. I went back to Hollister, where I had nobody to talk to or to sit with during lunch. Just about every day I tossed Mom's homemade sandwiches and her Hostess cupcakes in the trash because the sight of food was sickening. I knew this was a disgraceful thing to do, especially since people were starving in Ethiopia, but I couldn't help it.

I kept thinking of the Ethiopians, sitting in the merciless African sun with flies crawling into their eyes and up their nostrils. It wasn't fair that they had to suffer so much, but of course nothing was fair. I guessed that compared to them, my problems weren't important. People without food didn't lose sleep over a boyfriend who had stopped calling.

Blake's silence drove me to start making deals in my head, deals like *He'll call if I wear his mother's necklace every day* and *If I get an A on the Calculus II exam, he'll send me a birthday card that says he can't live without me.* But nothing worked, and the mailman brought only my dreaded SAT scores on the morning I turned eighteen.

Mom tore the envelope open before I could get near it. She was in the foyer when I was coming down the stairs, and she stood on an area rug in her slippers and apron, shock on her face. I wanted to tiptoe backward and pretend I hadn't seen her, but she caught my eye before I could move. Her expression changed to anger—her eyes narrowing and her mouth tightening—and I knew I was about to get chewed out.

"Very *nice*, Ariadne," she said, shoving the score report at me. I looked at it and my results were so low, so pathetic, I almost cried. "I can't believe that a girl as smart as *you*," Mom went on in her husky voice, "could do *so* badly on a test *this* important that you spent *months* studying for. This is your *future* we're talking about."

I had known she'd say cutting things. I turned around and started up the stairs to escape, but she followed me.

"That's what happens," she said, "when you make stupid decisions . . . when you run around Manhattan right before a test and dance at a club all night with a damn *boy*."

I wasn't dancing, I thought. I was sleeping with that *damn boy*, and he doesn't seem to want me anymore. I sniffed, holding back tears, and headed to my room. Mom trailed behind me the whole way.

"What do you have to say?" she asked when we reached my door. "Don't you have anything to say?"

I turned to face her. A tear slipped out of my eye and I wiped it away. "What do you want, Mom? I'm sorry. I know I've ruined everything."

Another tear rolled down my cheek and I dried it with my sleeve. I guessed she remembered that I was sensitive, because her face softened and so did her voice. She stopped talking like a teacher.

"Okay," she said. "It's okay. It's your birthday . . . I shouldn't yell at you."

I didn't care about my birthday. I just wanted to go back to bed.

But Mom kept talking. "I guess it isn't *that* bad," she said, like she was trying to convince herself. "You can just retake the test, that's all. You'll study some more and get a good night's sleep . . . and I'll make sure you have a decent breakfast. You'll do much better next time. Right, Ariadne?"

The thought of taking that horrid test again made me want to hurl myself down the steps. But Mom looked hopeful and she was trying to be encouraging, so I couldn't tell her the truth.

"Right, Mom," I said, walking into my room. I closed the door behind me, leaving her alone in the hall.

That night, Patrick and Evelyn drove to Brooklyn with the boys. Mom didn't mention the SAT again. She pretended that everything was fine. She cooked dinner and ordered a cake from the bakery, and Kieran gave me a picture frame made of bottle caps. Everyone kept telling me how pretty I looked and there were big phony smiles on their faces, the same kind people use when they're trying to cheer up somebody with a terminal illness.

They meant well, so I went along with the act. I forced cake down my throat and played a board game with Kieran. He'd brought the game in a schoolbag filled with other stuff, like Play-Doh and an Etch A Sketch. Then he pulled out the autographed Red Sox baseball that Blake had given him, and my head started to pound. I excused myself and pretended I was going upstairs to take my migraine pills, when I was actually planning to lie facedown on my bed until tomorrow.

Patrick came out of the bathroom as I hit the top step. His hair swept across his forehead and he looked handsome, but not as good as Blake.

"Are you okay?" he asked, and I nodded unconvincingly. Then he got back into the *Let's cheer up Ari* routine by reminding me that I was eighteen now and could get my driver's license, which made me feel worse.

"Blake offered to teach me how to drive," I said. My voice broke on the last word, and that wasn't lost on Patrick.

"I'll teach you how to drive," he said.

He was such a good guy. But I couldn't think about driving. All I wanted to do was vegetate in my room, which I did for an hour before Mom and Evelyn crept in and surrounded me on the bed.

It seemed as if they were a team suddenly, a more unlikely match than the Nancy Mitchell–Patrick Cagney pairing. It got me wondering if they had secret conversations about what was best for me. And I didn't bother to lift my face from my pillow when Mom made pleasant suggestions. She said that the three of us should go shopping next weekend, maybe in the city, and it would be a "girls' day out."

I thought I must be really bad off if Mom was proposing a shopping trip to Manhattan. It didn't sound like fun to me—nothing did anymore—so I just mumbled an excuse into my pillow. Then Mom mentioned Blake.

"Is that what's been bothering you lately?" she asked. "Is it all because Blake dropped you?"

Now I looked at her. "He didn't drop me. We're just taking a break for a while."

That was what I'd been telling myself. In my mind, the proof was that he hadn't asked for his mother's necklace back. I brought this up as evidence, but I didn't convince anyone.

"Ari," Evelyn said. She grabbed an elastic band from my night table and used it to knot her hair into a bun. "You have to snap out of this. Don't let that jerk upset you."

"He's not a jerk," I insisted. "I thought you liked him. You said he was good-looking. *Fetching,* you said."

She rested her hand on my shoulder. "Any guy who doesn't treat my sister right is a jerk. And you know what? Guys are no different from buses. If one drives past, you just wait for the next and hop right on. So if Blake wants to be a prick, then he can rot in hell as far as I'm concerned. You don't need him."

I knew she was trying to make me feel better, but it didn't work. Mom had been right—Evelyn wouldn't bat an eyelash over this. And Mom had been right about me, too. I wasn't like my sister and I didn't want to hop on another bus.

* * *

I never expected I'd lose interest in drawing, but that was exactly what happened. Not once since New Year's Day had I even thought of walking into my studio.

I'd be lucky if I earned a C⁺ in art this semester. I'd be lucky if I earned a C⁺ in any of my classes because I had stopped striving for good grades. What did they matter, anyway? Everybody knew that the second half of senior year made no difference. The college-acceptance letters were practically in the mail.

I even took the SAT again like Mom wanted. I went to bed early the night before, I ate her blueberry waffles for breakfast, and I forced myself to try, only because she'd go nuts if I didn't. But my mind was foggy so I couldn't remember definitions and formulas, and there were more of those impossible logic questions that made me choose answer C over and over again. *When in doubt, choose C*—that was what everybody at school always said—but it was bad advice. When my scores came back, they were only slightly higher than last time.

I was starting to wonder if Mom and my teachers were wrong about me. Maybe I wasn't so bright, maybe I wasn't a good student, and maybe I'd somehow managed to fake it throughout my entire academic career. The look on Mom's face when she saw my results made me think she was wondering the same thing.

College-acceptance letters were supposed to arrive by the end of February, and I hoped for a miracle. I hoped that Mr. Ellis had put in a good word for me at Parsons. Or maybe he'd put in a bad word for me, or maybe he hadn't said anything and I'd get in on my twelve years of good grades alone. Or maybe I wouldn't get in and I'd have nobody to blame but myself.

I put the whole sickening mess out of my mind on a cold Tuesday afternoon toward the middle of February, while I sat in the library at Hollister and pretended to study. I couldn't study for real; basic addition and subtraction had become impossible and there was no point in trying to remember historical facts and all that meaningless drivel. Information just poured in and flowed out of my brain like it was a strainer.

I couldn't go home, either. Home was where Mom tiptoed around me as if I was a soufflé in danger of falling. She was trying so hard to make me feel better, it was exhausting to watch.

Unfortunately, the library closed at four on Tuesdays. A librarian wearing sensible shoes reminded me of that in an unfriendly way when I was still there at four-fifteen. So I gathered my books and went outside. I stood by the iron gates, trying to come up with a destination. I couldn't go back to Brooklyn and I didn't want to go to Queens—but Blake's penthouse wasn't far away. Maybe I could take a stroll past his building. Maybe he'd be on his way home from NYU and we'd cross paths on the sidewalk, and he'd tell me that he missed me and that we should go upstairs and make love in his bedroom like we used to.

This idea seemed ingenious until I actually got to the Upper East Side and saw Tina's van parked at the curb. Summer had graduated early, according to her plan, and I assumed that she was working with her mother. She was probably at the penthouse flirting with Blake—and with Mr. Ellis, if he was feeling better.

Summer was welcome at the penthouse and I wasn't. Even if she was just an employee, the thought of her up there made me want to scream or cry or both, yet I couldn't do either. I just stared at the building and the van until I heard a car door slam and felt a tap on my shoulder. I smelled cigarettes and I turned to find Del behind me.

"What are you doing here?" he asked. "Did you and Blake get back together?"

So he really had dropped me. We weren't just cooling things off for a while and I was a fool. "No," I said, and the word came out so faintly that Del got the picture and seemed sorry for opening his mouth. "I have to go," I told him. "I have to go home."

"How are you getting there?" he asked.

"I don't know," I said, because I didn't. My mind was so sluggish lately.

A scarf hung from my shoulders and he wrapped it gently around my neck. "You have to think of these things, Ari. It's freezing out here."

He offered to drive me home. I got in the Porsche, where Del tried to make conversation as we headed to Brooklyn. All he got in return were one-word answers because I didn't have the strength for anything more.

"You should know something," he said when we were a few blocks from my house. "Blake is seeing that friend of yours. The blond chick."

I wanted to die. I stared through the windshield while Del went on, telling me that Mr. Ellis thought Blake needed more experience and Summer was just the kind of girl to give it to him.

Then we were in front of my house and Del turned to me. I stared at the scar on his lip while he spoke. "Maybe I shouldn't have told you," he said, most likely because my chin was shaking. "But you don't care, do you? I mean, a girl like you . . . you've probably got another boyfriend already."

I shook my head. He changed the subject to Leigh and Rachel, who were flying into JFK this weekend. He said that they were all going to Cielo for Valentine's Day, so I should stop by. And Blake might be there too, but I would come anyway, wouldn't I?

I nodded after he passed me a little red square. It was a piece of paper printed with the name of his club and VALEN-TINE'S DAY SPECIAL. HALF-PRICE DRINKS FOR ALL LADIES. FRIDAY, FEBRUARY 14.

He smiled, leaned toward me, touched my back, and kissed my cheek. For a while there I had thought that Del's kisses meant nothing, but now I wasn't so sure.

When Summer was voted Prettiest Girl in junior high, I had thought it was the worst thing that could happen. But I was only twelve, and was clueless about all the bad things that could happen. That was just a scratch compared to the stab wound I'd been nursing ever since Del told me about her and Blake.

I couldn't stop thinking about the two of them together. I saw them in the Corvette and in the penthouse and in the Hamptons, all day long and in my dreams. I imagined Summer sneaking Blake into her fairy-tale room and I figured he liked it better there than on my crummy JCPenney bedspread. I especially thought about them on Valentine's Day, while I sat by my bedroom mirror with wet hair and my Eighty-eight-shade Pro Eye Shadow Palette.

A few days earlier, I had made a decision. I wasn't going to look like a Hollister student anymore, with simple hair and preppy pearls, because simple and preppy hadn't gotten me anywhere. Simple preppy girls wasted their youth and got dumped by their boyfriends, while flashy sexy girls lived it up in Manhattan, where they dished out *experience.* I decided that I was going to be someone else—someone glamorous and sophisticated, someone who wasn't dull and boring and average, someone who wasn't afraid of doing sinful things.

I outlined my eyes in black and smeared them with gray, then chose a lipstick the color of a ripe cherry. My clothes were waiting on the bed—a satiny bustier I'd picked up at one of those trendy stores where women who wear five-inch heels tend to shop. I also bought snug leather pants, stiletto pumps, and dangly earrings that grazed my shoulders.

My hair hung straight and dark around my face. I couldn't let it stay that way—it was nothing but *preppy crap*— so I grabbed a pair of scissors and cut a long bang that brushed my left eye. I threw some hot rollers into the rest and sprayed everything with Aqua Net after I took them out, and when I was in my bustier and my leather pants and my heels and my ruby necklace, I barely recognized myself. I looked like what I was—a girl whose parents were at a second cousin's third wedding in Yonkers, tricked into believing that their daughter was spending the night with her calculus books.

So what if I lied? Being good didn't get me anywhere. I'd spent my entire life being good, studying and babysitting and trying not to hurt anyone's feelings. I was through with being nice.

I didn't exactly have a plan for that night. All I knew was that Blake might be there and that Del would definitely be there, and I wasn't sure which one of them I wanted to see.

At first I only saw Leigh, who was wearing a tweed cap and matching coat and waiting for me in the cold. There was a bouncer beside her who handed me five of the half-price drink coupons.

"Are you in disguise?" she asked, looking me up and down.

"No," I said. "I'm new and improved."

Her forehead wrinkled. "Why? You were fine the way you were before."

"Not quite," I said, and started walking toward the door.

The club was just the way I remembered it—smoky air and flashing lights, music so loud that I had to read Leigh's lips. She pulled off her hat and nodded at the coupons in my hand. "Those will be wasted on us . . . you can give them to my mother if you want to."

"I don't want to," I said, because I wanted to try drinking and forget everything.

Leigh clutched my arm and spoke into my ear. "Ari," she said. "I don't like the way Blake's treated you, and I hope this *new and improved* stuff isn't for him. You're better than that."

This was the last thing I wanted to hear. Leigh was being practical, like Mom, and I wasn't in a practical mood. So I ignored her and walked toward the bar. It was a cinch to get the first drink, and the second and the third, because the bartender was so busy staring at my chest that he didn't bother to ask for ID. It was probably too dark to notice that I wasn't exactly even.

I felt like I was levitating. The floor blinked in yellow and red and blue while Rachel and Leigh and I danced, but after a while I ran out of steam and Rachel got all motherly.

"How much did you have to drink, honey?" she asked.

I shrugged. I had ordered a beer and a wine cooler and two White Russians that I downed quickly because they tasted as harmless as chocolate milk. Rachel shook her head and wagged her finger and told me to get a big glass of water. So I sat on faux zebra skin at the bar, guzzling Evian and watching bartenders juggle bottles.

I was there for a half hour before I saw Blake, who was at the other end of the bar. He was dressed differently than usual, similar to Del, in a dark blazer and a shirt with the top few buttons undone, and he was talking with two girls. Neither of them was Summer, but they were so much prettier than me. Then I looked around at all the pretty girls in the club. There were tons of them, swarming like a million ants on a discarded piece of candy. I couldn't even count them all. Why would Blake want me when he could choose any of them?

It was so depressing. I sat on the stool watching him, even though he didn't notice. He walked away a few minutes later and I stalked him through the club. He disappeared into the men's room and I waited outside, thinking this was my chance and I had to take it.

He didn't recognize me when he came out. He walked by and didn't turn his head until I called his name. "Ari?" he said, like I was wearing a Halloween costume.

He looked down at me and I smiled up at him. "Hi," I said as my heart pounded.

"What's all this?" he asked, motioning to my clothes and my stiletto heels.

"I don't know," I said, flirtatiously lifting a bare shoulder. "Don't you like it?"

He shrugged. "I don't know."

I wanted to talk to him. I wasn't sure what I was going to say. But it was too loud to hear myself think, so I nodded toward the men's room. It was empty and we locked ourselves in a stall.

I pressed my back against the partition that separated our stall from the next. Blake stood opposite me, leaning into the wall.

"You've been drinking, haven't you?" he asked. "I can smell it on you."

I shrugged and tried to be flirty again. "Maybe a little."

"You don't drink," he said, moving his eyes from my heels to my hair. "This isn't you."

"Good. I don't want to be me." I looked down at the tiles beneath my feet. They were ceramic, the high-quality kind.

I was sure that Del had spent a lot of money on this bathroom, but nobody respected it. They just scribbled on the walls and left empty toilet-paper rolls on the floor. "Anyway, I thought you'd like my outfit. It's the kind of thing Summer wears. You two are close friends now, from what I've heard."

He sighed. "We aren't. I don't care about Summer."

"Then why did you sleep with her?" I asked. "I thought you were a gentleman. I thought you didn't sleep with girls you didn't care about. You told me it wasn't any good that way."

"I don't want to talk about it. She was a mistake," he said, and that wasn't the denial I craved. So I just stood there in a stony silence until he opened his mouth again. "I miss you, Ari. I think about you constantly."

"Liar," I said. "You don't care about me anymore."

"I care about you too much. That's the whole problem."

That wasn't a problem. That couldn't be a problem. A rush of hope flooded through me and I forgave him for everything as I threw myself across the stall and into his arms, where he kissed me and I kissed him back.

I heard the bathroom door creak, men's voices over the faucet running. They were talking about money in hushed tones: I was probably eavesdropping on a drug deal, but it didn't matter. It didn't matter that Blake and I were in a filthy bathroom, kissing beside a toilet. The only important thing was that we were kissing.

It was comforting and familiar—his smell, his taste, his tongue on my skin. His hand went down my bustier and I hooked one leg around his waist and then he said, "We can't. I don't have anything with me."

I knew he was talking about protection and I started to think crazy things, desperate things, like Evelyn saying that Patrick had loved her more when she was carrying his baby, and I thought that Blake might love me again if I was carrying his. *Guys are funny that way.* So I stayed where I was and I moved my hand downward to feel him through his pants.

"Stop it," he said. "We can't."

I dropped to my knees and unbuckled his belt. "Can we do this?"

I didn't even sound like me. I sounded like some other girl who was used to wearing trashy clothes and tempting men by getting on her knees. Blake gripped my arms and pushed me away.

"Don't, Ari."

"Why? I want to."

"Stop it," he said again, sharply this time. He yanked me to my feet, adjusted my bustier because it was falling off. I tried to kiss him but he wouldn't let me, and that didn't make sense because he missed me and he thought about me constantly. So I kept trying until he held my wrists to make me stop. "Look at where we are, Ari. This isn't you. You're a nice girl."

"I don't want to be a nice girl," I said, sliding my hand to his groin.

He stepped back. "Don't talk like that."

Nothing I did was right. "How do you want me to talk? I'll do whatever you want."

Blake took off his jacket and put it over my shoulders. "I want you to go home," he said. "And keep this on. You shouldn't be walking around in that getup. People will get the wrong idea."

I started to cry. Softly at first, and then harder, until I could barely see through my tears and I lost it. I screeched at Blake that I couldn't think straight anymore and that I didn't care about school or life and I would never love anybody but him and I just wanted to die.

"Don't say that," he said. "I'm not worth it."

But I thought he was worth it. So I said it again and again and then his palm cracked against my cheek. It was the kind of slap that people use to wake someone from a fainting spell or a fit of hysterics.

"I'm sorry," he said. "Just calm down. Please. I can't stand seeing you this way."

He couldn't stand seeing me this way? It was his fault that I *was* this way. My cheek was stinging and I felt angry suddenly. I sniffed, wiped my nose, and struggled to compose myself.

"Summer stole your cousin's bracelet, you know." I had stopped crying and now I stood there with my chest heaving and my hands on my hips. "She kept it hidden for months even though she knew how much it meant to Leigh. And if you're wondering why Jessica ran off, ask your father. He's the one who made her dump you. He bribed her. He probably tried to blackmail her too—that's what he pulled on me, but I didn't fall for it."

I was so proud of myself for saying that, but I didn't feel proud when I noticed how Blake was looking at me. It was like he didn't believe me, like I was nothing but a pathetic liar. It made me angrier and I ripped off his mother's necklace, threw it at his feet, and stormed from the bathroom into the smoky air.

Five minutes later I was alone, crying into my hands on the steps that led to Del's apartment. I wished I hadn't come here. I wished I hadn't thrown the necklace at Blake. I wished I'd never been born.

My head was killing me and the noise from the club made it worse. The thought of taking my migraine pills before I left home tonight hadn't even crossed my mind. I heard the jingle of keys and I turned toward the banister, hoping that whoever was coming would just keep going. Then there were feet in front of me and I heard a deep voice.

"What's the matter?"

I looked up and saw Del. "Nothing. I've got a headache. I have to go."

He crouched down and touched my arm. I glanced at his hand and it was the same as Blake's except for the pinkie ring, and that made me cry again.

"You're not crying about my brother, are you?" he asked. "He's just a stupid kid."

"He is not," I said.

Del sat next to me, watching tears pour down my face. Then he massaged my aching temples with his fingertips. It surprised me and it felt really nice. It felt even better when he put both arms around me and I leaned my head against his strong shoulder and his silky shirt that smelled of cigarettes.

"It's okay," he said. "Don't cry. Blake doesn't deserve you."

My mascara was melting onto my cheeks and I couldn't stop bawling, but Del didn't make me feel ridiculous. He held me the way Patrick held Evelyn, the way I wanted, and I hoped he wouldn't let go because there was nothing else keeping me together.

The next thing I knew, we were walking up the steps and into his apartment, where I saw his skylight and the waning moon. Del tossed his keys onto a table and we sat on his messy sheets. I was sniffling and shaking and he dried my face with his hands, which felt almost as good as Blake's kisses on my neck.

"You like me, don't you?" he asked. "You've always liked me."

I nodded, thinking that his eyes were very green tonight.

"I've always liked you too," he said as he traced my jaw with his finger.

That weakened me. I missed being touched, especially by someone who might not stop me from touching him back. I heard myself breathing, felt my heart pounding again. Del wasn't Blake but he was as close as I could get, and I was thinking more crazy things.

"Really?" I said.

He nodded and I blinked because there were still tears in my eyes. The dark room looked dim and blurry, yet I saw his face getting closer to mine. He paused when our mouths were almost touching, as if waiting for me to back away, but I didn't. I let him kiss me and I felt his scar. It was like a thick piece of twine against my lip. Soon he was lying on me and Blake's jacket was on the floor and the top of my bustier was down at my ribs. I kept my eyes shut and I didn't stop him from doing anything, even when he slid off my pants and tossed them away.

They landed on the hardwood with a thump and that woke me up. The music downstairs seemed louder, my vision was clear, and Del's eyes had somehow changed to gray. Then I heard his belt buckle open and I was scared.

Del didn't tell me not to be scared. He didn't kiss my forehead. "Del," I started, but my voice was so faint that he didn't hear me and it was too late. I'd already let this go too far—we'd gone all the way. And it didn't feel good anymore. It felt wrong. It felt like nothing. Now Del looked ugly—the gash on his lip, the downturn of his nose.

I was about to push him away but I didn't need to. Everything had happened so fast, he was done already. He slumped against me, then rolled off and stared through the skylight as he tried to catch his breath. I looked around the room, at the bachelor-pad furniture and the mirror on the headboard. It all seemed tawdry and disgusting and what was I doing here? I should have stayed at home and studied calculus. I never should have said that I didn't want to be a nice girl. Nothing felt worse than not being a nice girl.

I was getting queasy. I had a migraine, and what I'd just done made me want to jump out the window, to fly through the glass toward those creepy angels on the building across the alley. I wanted to pretend that this hadn't happened. I wanted to erase it like my miserable first kiss.

I pulled up my bustier, slid into my pants, but didn't pick up Blake's jacket. "Don't you ever tell your brother about this," I said, standing over Del. "Don't you ever tell anybody."

He looked up at me from the bed, and I actually felt sorry for him because my voice was cold and he seemed hurt. Then I remembered Leigh and Idalis and the parade of *putas* that came in and out of here. I remembered Evelyn getting in trouble and STD pamphlets and Leigh saying *Del could end up with AIDS if he doesn't watch out.*

"Did you use anything?" I asked. It sounded so crass but I had to know.

He was getting dressed. He zipped his pants and buttoned his shirt. "No," he said. "I figured you were on the Pill or whatever."

I rushed down the stairs, thinking he had filled me with something toxic that could destroy my life or end it with a gruesome death. I'd been so careful before, I was always so careful, but this one moment might ruin me forever.

Del was behind me, calling my name down the stairs. I ignored him and ran through the front door into the frigid night, stumbling in my tacky shoes. I glanced around for a cab but instead I saw Blake and Rachel and Leigh at the curb.

They were probably waiting for one of those glossy sedans to take them home. I didn't want them to see me but they glanced in my direction at the sound of Del's voice. He was here now, asking what was wrong like he had no idea. Blake looked at him and looked at me with my messed-up hair and my mascara-stained face, and then he charged toward Del.

"What did you do to her?" he demanded.

"Nothing," Del said. "Mind your own business."

Blake's face was red and he yelled and swore. He shoved his brother, who stumbled backward on the sidewalk. Then Del straightened up and punched Blake square in the face. Blood gushed from Blake's nose and Del shouted at him.

"You had that coming," he said. "You only dumped her

because of Daddy. You didn't have the guts to choose her over him."

It was so quiet. Leigh and Rachel were staring at me from the curb. Blake didn't answer, and I guessed he was surprised that Del wasn't as dumb as everybody thought.

twenty-two

I dove into a cab, escaping the commotion, and watched Rachel through the window as she searched her coat pockets and then held a handkerchief to Blake's face. A big part of me wanted to jump out of the car and help him, but the rest of me thought Del was right. Blake did have that coming.

When I got home, Saint Anne pierced me with her reproachful gaze. My parents weren't back yet, the house and the front yard were dark, and I squinted across the lawn. Don't look at me like that, I thought. Not everyone can be as perfect as your daughter.

I hurried past Saint Anne, locked myself in the house, and dry-heaved over the toilet. Mom and Dad came back and soon Mom was banging on the bathroom door. She wanted to know if I was sick. The stomach flu was going around, she said.

The knocking was like a hammer crushing my skull. She had no idea how sick I was—that I was just a sick excuse for a human being. I was sick for getting into bed with Del and I was sick for practically begging to go down on Blake in a public restroom, and now I might get morning sickness or syphilis or an incurable virus that could put me in a box that Mom and Dad would buy with Uncle Eddie's money. *At least poor Ariadne got to use that money for something,* I imagined Mom saying.

The thought made me vomit. Mom knocked on the door as a half-digested dinner mixed with wine and beer and Kahlúa spewed from my mouth. I gripped the toilet, wishing she'd go away. She kept telling me to unlock the door, but I couldn't. I couldn't let her see me until I got rid of my outfit.

She finally gave up and I stripped off my clothes, burying my underwear in the trash can beneath crumpled tissues and frayed dental floss. Then I stepped into the shower, where I scrubbed every bit of myself in scalding hot water that I hoped would sterilize me. I wanted everything to disappear—the makeup, the Aqua Net, the smell of cigarettes in my hair.

I let my mouth fill with water and I spit into the drain, over and over, trying to purge the millions of microscopic germs that Del had probably left.

* * *

An hour later, I walked down the hall toward my bedroom wearing a bathrobe and clutching my clothes in a ball. I remembered rumors I'd heard about foiling a pregnancy with things like soda or vinegar and I considered trying both, but I quickly changed my mind. Those were ignorant myths; someone who had taken Sex Ed should know better.

"Ariadne," Mom said. "Are you all right? You were in there for so long."

She came out of nowhere with a pungent tuna sandwich and I stifled a gag.

"I'm fine," I said. "Just leave me the hell alone for once."

She looked stunned. I couldn't have cared less. I walked away, shut my door, and collapsed into bed, where I watched numbers change on my clock and stared at the teddy bear on my dresser.

Blake. I thought of him and of the past year. I thought about when colors had been outrageously bright and the air had smelled incredibly good and when I had forgotten how it felt to be sad. Now I remembered, and I thought Blake was no better than some street-thug heroin dealer. He had gotten me hooked on him and then he'd cut off my supply. I'd heard that addicts would do anything, would degrade themselves in every way to get another fix, and now I understood how that could happen, because it was happening to me.

I wished that tonight had been just a bad dream. I wished that Blake had some backbone. I wished he'd chosen me over his father, but he hadn't, and now all I had left was a stuffed animal and an NYU sweatshirt. The sweatshirt was tucked inside my night table, and I took it out and wrapped it around myself. It was the only thing that could get me to sleep.

* * *

Leigh called at noon. Mom came in and shook my shoulder to wake me up.

"I don't want to talk to her," I said, because last night wouldn't have happened if it wasn't for Leigh. It was her fault that I had met Blake and Del. Of course, I could have been a good friend instead of chasing after her cousins. And I was going back on my word too. On Christmas Eve I'd told her that I would never treat her badly again. Maybe now I was getting what I deserved, but I couldn't tolerate any more blame. It was too heavy for me to carry alone.

Mom just assumed I was too sick to talk on the phone. She walked away and I heard her telling Leigh that I had the flu or whatever was going around. I went along because it was convenient—sick people get to stay in bed all day, and I wanted to stay in bed all day. A minute later, Mom hung up the phone and yelled from the kitchen that Leigh said she'd call me the next time she was in New York. I didn't care if she ever called me again.

I went back to sleep, and stayed in bed for most of the day and most of the next week, faking the flu so I could skip school. I didn't change out of the NYU sweatshirt and I didn't shower and I only left the house once. I went to the library, where I hid between bookshelves and shuddered as I skimmed the pages of a medical dictionary and worried that Del's STD wasn't really cured.

Untreated syphilis can cause damage in the brain, spinal cord, heart, and other organs, I read. *Signs and symptoms of late-stage syphilis include paralysis, numbness, gradual blindness, and dementia. This damage may be serious enough to cause death.*

Blindness scared me more than everything else, including death. I imagined seeing absolutely nothing and depending on Mom to dress me and brush my hair and she wouldn't do any of it right. I'd get old and my hair would turn gray and she'd hardly ever dye it, and I'd probably end up doddering around Brooklyn with dark glasses, banging the sidewalk with a cane like some shriveled old witch who would frighten the neighborhood kids.

Then I decided I needed a pregnancy test and a blood test immediately, even if I had to get poked fifty times to find a vein.

"Do you have a faculty meeting tomorrow?" I asked Mom that night.

She nodded from her seat on the couch, where she was smoking a Pall Mall and trying to write a novel based on some idea that had come to her while she was scrubbing the kitchen sink. She smiled down at her notebook. She'd bought a spiral-bound one with a perky pink cover, like a student with high hopes for a new school year. "It would be nice if this novel works out. But I probably won't finish."

"Probably not," I said, because I knew the odds were against anything working out. Mom's smile dimmed, but it was the truth, so I didn't feel bad.

She put the notebook aside. "Are you going to take a shower someday? Your hair is greasy. I don't know why you cut those bangs . . . they're always in your eyes. And you've been wearing that sweatshirt forever."

Mom was right about the sweatshirt. I was turning into Leigh. But it was much easier for her, because M.G. hadn't left her on purpose.

"So what?" I asked. "Nobody cares how I look."

"I care," Mom said.

That seemed irrelevant. So I didn't change my clothes or do anything about my hair the next day. I had an appointment at the clinic at three. When I got there, I gave my name to a woman with coffee-colored skin and cornrows. She flipped through a book and asked if I was sure I hadn't made the appointment somewhere else.

"No," I said. "I called here."

She figured out that I had called there, but when I'd asked for a Friday appointment, she had thought I meant next Friday. So I was turned out into the street for another week of paranoia.

That night I sat at the kitchen table with Mom and Dad. My plate was filled with mushy mashed potatoes swimming in thick brown gravy and meat loaf covered in a crispy ketchup glaze that reminded me of dried blood. Mom didn't seem to think I had enough food, so she shoveled three spoonfuls of fried onions onto my plate and filled a glass with milk.

"Eat up," she said. "You're so thin, Ariadne. You really have to gain some weight back. You need your strength for school."

I kept my eyes on my food, made tracks in the potatoes with a fork, and wondered if starvation could cause a miscarriage. A miscarriage would be better than the stirrups and the instruments and whatever else doctors used to fix a big mistake.

"I'm not going back to school," I said.

"Of course you are. You're not sick anymore."

That was what *she* thought. I ignored her and hid a piece of meat loaf under my napkin when nobody was looking. Dad wasn't looking because he was busy reading the newspaper. Mom accused him of having bad manners. She said that dinnertime was when people were supposed to talk to each other.

He paused for a moment, searching for something to talk about. "I ran into someone today," he said.

"Who?" Mom asked.

"Summer Simon. I had to see a potential witness in the Empire State Building and Summer was walking out when I was walking in."

Dinnertime conversation was so overrated. The mention of that name and the Empire State Building made me nauseous, so I headed to my room. I was on the staircase when I felt Mom's hand on my elbow.

"Get off," I snapped.

"What's the matter with you?" she said in her stern teacher voice. "Why are you acting like this?"

I didn't tell her. She'd warned me and I couldn't stomach an "I told you so."

Later, when Mom and Dad were watching TV downstairs, I took a bubble bath because I was nervous and restless and I couldn't come up with anything else to do. TV didn't interest me and schoolwork didn't interest me and drawing was stupid. It was nothing but a useless hobby, I couldn't do anything with it, I would never become an artist, and the idea of teaching had suddenly lost its luster.

I tried not to think about anything when I was in the bathtub, covered with suds up to my neck. I closed my eyes, listening to water swishing and the canned sitcom laughs coming from downstairs. Then there was a knock at the door and Mom walked in even though I didn't give her permission.

"What are you doing?" I said. "I'm naked in here."

"Oh, please. I can't see anything." She sat on the toilet-seat lid and her tone was much nicer than the one she'd used on the staircase. "What's wrong, Ariadne? You've been acting so strangely."

Just go away, I thought, closing my eyes again. "Nothing is wrong, Mom. I'm fine."

She didn't believe me. I listened to her say that I was sulky and irritable and that I never drew anymore. Then she mentioned Summer and I wanted to slide down the drain and into the sewer with the rest of the filth. That was where somebody who would get on her back for her boyfriend's brother belonged, anyway.

"What exactly happened between the two of you?" she asked.

"Nothing," I said again.

She was quiet for a moment and I heard her slipper tapping the tiles. "Did it have something to do with Blake?"

My eyes sprang open. "Of course not. It had nothing to do with him. Absolutely nothing."

I should have stopped at *Of course not.* I had protested too much and she didn't believe a word.

"You know what?" she said. "I should call that boy and tell him what I think about the shitty way he's treated you."

"Don't you dare," I said, but she didn't pay any attention.

"Who does that little prick think he is? Just because his father is some big-shot lawyer and he lives on the fucking Upper East Side doesn't mean he can get away with upsetting my daughter. Look at what he's done to you, for God's sake—you haven't been yourself for weeks, and you're getting worse. I really ought to go into the city and tell him off in person."

"Don't you dare!" I said, shouting this time, and I sounded as psychotic as I had in the men's room at Cielo. "Don't you dare call him or go anywhere near him. If you say one word to Blake . . . I swear I'll kill myself."

I was definitely turning into Leigh. Mom stared at me. She stared at me as if she could see everything I'd tried so hard to hide.

"What's going on?" she said. "What happened? Something must have happened to make you act like this."

"Nothing happened," I said through my teeth. "Just go away."

She stayed where she was. "Ariadne, was your relationship with Blake more serious than you let on? I can't imagine you'd be this distraught if all the two of you did was hold hands. I mean . . . did he . . . did you let him . . ."

Did he? Did I let him? That sounded awful. Obscene. Sleazy and vile and foul. She kept asking, my head was pounding, and I didn't care anymore if she knew.

"Yes, Mom," I said, sarcastic and loud. "He did. I let him. I let him do anything he wanted whenever he wanted and you were right—he lied and he dumped me and I hope you're happy now."

I hope you're happy now. I said it four times in increasing volume and shrillness while she begged me to calm down. Then I grabbed a towel, wrapped it around myself as I sprang from the tub, and ran down the hall, leaving soggy footprints on the carpet. I slammed my bedroom door so hard that it shook the walls and my bear tumbled from the dresser. I left it on the floor while I listened to Mom and Dad out in the hallway. Mom said I was hysterical and she didn't know what to do, and Dad said I'd yelled loud enough for the whole neighborhood to hear and he had never expected something like that from someone like me.

Later that night, I heard my parents whispering and Mom talking on the phone to Evelyn, who'd surely broken her promise not to tell Mom anything. I guessed that Evelyn had to tell her everything now, since I was losing my mind and all. At that moment I thought that things couldn't get worse, but they did the next day when our mailman delivered a tellingly thin envelope from the Parsons School of Design. I got rejected and had to admit to Mom that I hadn't applied anywhere else.

I knew she wanted to yell and scream and tell me how disappointed she was and how idiotic I'd been to rely on connections, but she didn't say anything. I guessed she thought a delicate flower whose petals were barely hanging on couldn't withstand a harsh wind. Then she brought up Hollister, saying I could stay at home for another week and I should spend a few days in Queens because a change of scenery might do me good.

I didn't think so. Queens was just as miserable as Brooklyn, and I couldn't stop thinking that all my studying and drawing had come to absolutely nothing, that it was all just a colossal waste of life. And I was turning out even worse than Evelyn, because at least she was married. Marriage was a respectable place to hide from her failures, a place where she could organize playgroups and be admired for her beautiful children. I had nowhere to go and nothing to do, and that made me want to swallow my entire bottle of migraine pills, which I considered the next morning while I stood in the bathroom and scrutinized the label. ACETAMINOPHEN, it read. BUTALBITAL.

Butalbital sounded nice and lethal. But I didn't have the nerve to do it, and the fact that I was a coward on top of everything else made me hate myself. I decided that I might try again later and I took two pills like I was supposed to, and then I sat in Mom's Honda as she drove me to Queens in silence. I wondered if this was how my sister had felt when she left home with her pregnant stomach and her princess phone.

Soon we were at Evelyn's house, and she rushed down the front steps with her auburn curls flowing behind her. She hugged me on the stairs as Mom drove away, and I held on a little longer than usual. It was a relief to be with someone who knew what it was like to be the object of Mom's disappointment.

Evelyn set up the cot in Shane's room and arranged two dozen Mrs. Fields cookies on a paper plate after lunch. She and Patrick and the boys and I were sitting around the kitchen table when she pushed the plate toward me.

"No thanks," I said.

"You love these, Ari. I got them especially for you."

"No thanks," I said again, and I felt awful because I kept letting everybody down.

She sighed, turning her attention to Shane in his high chair, and tickled him. She laughed when he did and she kept saying "I love you I love you I love you."

I watched them. They made me remember my imaginary Park Slope house and my imaginary husband and my imaginary kids, and knowing that all of it would never be anything but imaginary brought tears to my eyes.

Patrick noticed. "Come on," he said. "Get up. I'm giving you a driving lesson."

I didn't want a driving lesson but I had no choice. He pulled my chair from the table while I was still sitting in it, took me by the arm, and told me to put on my coat. I followed him out to his truck even though I just wanted to sleep until the new millennium.

I sat in the driver's seat and it felt uncomfortable and confusing there. "I don't even have my learner's permit," I said. "It's against the law to drive without a learner's permit."

Patrick snorted. "Who gives a shit? We won't get pulled over. Now stick the damn key in the ignition and let's go."

"I can't," I said, and saw tears dropping onto my jeans. I didn't want to cry, so I fought it by sniffing and wiping my nose, but nothing worked.

He handed me a tissue from his glove compartment. "You know something, Ari?" he said. "Most guys are assholes."

I guessed we were talking about Blake. I wondered if Mom and Evelyn had told him everything. I couldn't even imagine what Patrick would think of me if he ever found out about what happened with Del. And I wouldn't blame him if he was disappointed, because I hadn't taken his advice about staying a nice girl.

"*You're* not," I said.

He smiled, put on his sunglasses, and told me again to start the car. Then I had my first driving lesson, and I couldn't have asked for a better teacher. We went back to the house an hour later, where I sat on the couch and nobody asked me to do anything, not even help with the boys or set the table for dinner.

We all went upstairs early that night, and Patrick made love to Evelyn at nine o'clock. I heard them when I was on the cot in Shane's room. But I didn't want to listen. And I didn't feel jealous. I bent a pillow around my ears to block out the noise and all I felt was lonely.

I stayed in Queens for another four nights. Patrick took me home on a windy Friday morning. He was driving away when I noticed a silver Mercedes parked at the curb, and it gave me the urge to clutch the back of Patrick's truck and spend the day in his fire engine.

But he was already halfway down the street. I was too tired to run, so I just sat on the front steps with my chin in my hand until the door opened and I smelled cigars. Then I looked up at Jeff Simon and wondered if he was about to handcuff me and haul me kicking and screaming to New York–Presbyterian, where I'd fit in with the rest of the loonies. *Are you Evelyn Cagney's sister?* people wearing straitjackets would ask. *You sure don't look like her, but you're obviously just as nutty as she used to be. Seems like you both inherited the wacko gene.*

"How are you feeling?" he asked.

I turned my eyes to a brown leaf that somersaulted across our dead lawn, thinking that Jeff had a lot of nerve to inquire about my well-being when it was partially his daughter's fault that I wasn't doing well at all.

"I'm not one of your patients, Dr. Simon . . . even if my mother wants me to be."

I called him Dr. Simon to sound rude and distant. It worked. He stared at me for a moment, scratched his head, and sighed.

"Don't be difficult," he said. "Tell me how you're feeling."

I gave up. "Not good," I said, and he suggested that I "talk to someone," which was a lousy suggestion. I didn't want to talk and I didn't want a prescription for the kind of pills that Evelyn took. But I said I would think about it so he'd leave me alone.

"I told Nancy that postponing college until next year is the best thing for you," he said. "It's my professional opinion that you need a break, Ari. Don't you agree?"

I agreed. I nodded. "Thank you," I said.

Jeff got into his car and drove away; then I went inside, where I found Mom sitting on the couch with a cigarette.

"How are you feeling, Ariadne?" she asked in a delicate

way. She acted like I'd explode into bits and pieces if she wasn't careful.

"Fine," I said blandly, and headed for the stairs.

"If you need your medication," she called after me, "I've got it."

I turned around and she was smiling as if she could trick me, as if neither one of us had the slightest inkling that too much butalbital could be fatal or that she'd stolen my pills while I was in Queens. It was probably something else Jeff had advised.

twenty-three

I hated March. March was when I worried about my *monthly visitor* because it hadn't shown up. It still hadn't come by my Friday-afternoon appointment at the clinic.

A young nurse kept saying "Sorry, I'm new at this" as she used my left arm as a pincushion. I wanted to tell her that it wasn't her fault and that I had bad veins, but I was too tired to bother. She hit the right spot on the sixth try and handed me a plastic cup.

"Pee in this," she said, and I thought she could have been more professional. A nurse should use better terminology than Evelyn's brainless friends. "The restroom is down the hall. Bring your sample back here when you're finished."

I walked past a waiting room, jammed with knocked-up teenagers, toward a bathroom the size of a broom closet. It had one of those dreary old-person safety rails on the wall, and I was so nervous about blindness and blisters and my late period that I couldn't fill the cup. I thought of things like waterfalls and rainy days, and that worked until someone banged on the door.

"Just a minute," I said, and I felt rushed and sweaty and the minute turned into much longer. Then I finally had my sample and I wondered how I was supposed to get it back down the hall without anyone noticing, but I didn't have much time to think because the banging started again. So I put the lid on the cup and stuck it in my purse and prayed that it wouldn't spill.

"It's about time," a girl said when I came out. She was my age and visibly pregnant under a T-shirt printed with the words TOUCH MY BELLY AND LOSE A HAND. There was a baby in her arms and she looked like she wanted to strangle me. "You kept me waiting for fifteen minutes. Nobody around here ever hogs the bathroom for fifteen minutes."

I didn't answer. I just walked away because I didn't know the rules and I didn't belong here with tough-faced girls who were probably headed toward a life of food stamps and black eyes from worthless men.

"When should I call for the results?" I asked the nurse after I gave her my sample.

"We can't do it over the phone," she said. "You'll have to speak with the doctor in person."

"Why?" I said, but I knew. It was because the clinic didn't want to be responsible for what people might do while they were alone if their test results came back positive. They might get crazy ideas in their heads, ideas like swallowing a bottle of migraine pills.

"It's our policy. You can make an appointment at the front desk."

I went to the desk, where I found that I couldn't catch a break. Nothing was easy, not even scheduling my appointment. The receptionist flipped through her book and told me to come back in three weeks, which might as well have been three years.

I was helpless to do anything about it, so I just nodded. Then I trudged through the waiting room, where phrases like "my baby's daddy" and "my overdue child support" were being tossed around. They stuck with me even after I was outside in the dusky afternoon, listening to the morbid sound of church bells that reminded me of a funeral. I ignored them and kept going, feeling numb and trying to figure out how I'd gotten here.

On a Monday morning I noticed that the snow on our lawn was melting and the grass was growing in sparse clusters around Saint Anne's feet. Early spring was hideous. I couldn't stand the sight of it, so I decided to keep my bedroom curtains permanently shut. Then I gathered my books as Mom smiled at me from my doorway and used her delicate voice.

"Would you like a ride today, Ariadne?" she said.

She'd been asking that question every day since I'd gone

back to Hollister, and I shook my head like I always did. I didn't think it would be fair to make her drive to Manhattan—I was enough trouble already.

I left the house and stared straight ahead. I didn't want to see her standing at the living room window, clutching the curtain and watching me walk down the street. She was as worried about my future as she used to be about Evelyn's, and that made me want to cry.

So I didn't look back. I kept going even though my walk to the train station seemed to have expanded several miles and the ride to Manhattan was endless and claustrophobic. The subway car was warm and I spotted a *Safe Sex* pamphlet on an empty seat, and knowing that I had to wait another ten days for my test results made me panic. Everything felt small and cramped and I had to get out at a station that wasn't mine just to catch my breath.

That made me late for school. A pimply hall monitor stopped me at the front door; I considered wrestling him to the ground and threatening to snap his neck because he was shorter than I was and only a sophomore. But he'd probably accuse me of assault, and that might give Mom a legitimate reason to commit me to New York–Presbyterian, so I just let him fill out his stupid tardy slip, which led me to the principal.

I'd never even seen this woman before. I'd never been on academic probation and had never violated the dress code, so there had been no reason to see her.

"I hope you have a good explanation for being late," she said.

She was much younger than I expected, and she was using

Mom's teacher voice, which annoyed me. I belonged in the principal's office as much as I belonged at the clinic. Why was everything so upside-down? A few wrong turns had changed me into something I had never wanted to be. I felt like waving my second-place ribbon and my old report cards in her face and saying "See? This is who I really am."

"The subway stalled," I said, and the words fell right off my tongue because I was used to being a liar. "I was stuck in the tunnel for an hour."

She eyed me skeptically and dismissed me as if I was a total write-off. This put me in a crabbier mood and I couldn't pay attention in my classes because I was fed up with everything. It got worse later, when I was in the bathroom and heard some girls gushing about the senior prom and what kind of flowers they wanted in their corsages. They also talked about going away to college in the fall, to New England and to Midwest campuses with old stone buildings and football games where they planned to sit on bleachers while they were wrapped in blankets made of wool.

I didn't want to be reminded of wool blankets. I didn't want to hear about the prom and corsages and everything else that was passing me by. Those were once-in-a-lifetime things, things as special and fleeting as Halley's comet. And if you missed them, you could never get them back.

I rode home on the subway later that day, feeling irritable and disgusted and thinking about Blake. I was usually sad when he crept into my mind, but now I was angry about what he'd done and what I'd done and the big disaster it had all turned out to be. Then I shifted my anger to Mr. Ellis, because this mess was his fault. I wouldn't have had any problems if it wasn't for him. If he'd kept out of Blake's business, I would have been as happy and carefree as those girls in the bathroom whose biggest concern was whether they got lilies or roses.

The three weeks were finally over. Now I sat in the doctor's office at the clinic, sweating and biting my nails even though I never bit my nails. Then the doctor came in and I watched as she sat at her desk and skimmed through a folder filled with charts and notes. The suspense was killing me. I was about to leap across the desk and look at that folder myself.

"You're not pregnant," she said.

I didn't believe her. "But I'm late. My period is weeks late."

"Stress interferes with your system . . . it can make you skip a month." Her eyes rose over her bifocals. "You also tested negative for HIV and everything else."

"Negative?" I said with a smile that felt weird because I hadn't used it for so long.

"That's right. But you should come back in three months for another blood test, because HIV and some other STDs don't show up immediately."

"Oh," I said as my smile disappeared.

She looked at her folder. "I wouldn't be overly concerned, Miss Mitchell. From what I see here, you've only had two sexual partners . . . and one of them used protection every time. So AIDS, while not impossible, is unlikely."

Unlikely sounded good. *Two sexual partners* didn't. The thought of Del made me wring my hands, and the doctor got suspicious.

"The second man," she said. "The relationship was consensual, wasn't it?"

I sort of wished I could say that it wasn't, that Del had forced me by holding a switchblade against my throat, but he hadn't. His only weapon had been a shoulder for me to cry on.

I nodded at the doctor, who started offering me diaphragms and sponges, and I almost laughed because she seemed to think I needed those things. She didn't know that I couldn't let anybody touch me except Blake, and he was never going to touch me again.

"No thanks," I said, and left the clinic, breathing a huge sigh of relief.

March was almost over, the snow was gone, and daffodils were popping through the dirt around a tree that I passed on my way home. They were pretty and hopeful, and the church bells ringing a mile away didn't remind me of a funeral. This was the closest to normal I had felt since Christmas.

At home, I sat on my bed, opened my calculus book and tried hard to remember the method of integration by parts, because failing out of high school would be almost as bad as everything else that had happened recently. I didn't want to end up working at Pathmark or getting locked in a padded room at New York–Presbyterian, so I had to try to heal on my own.

The rusty wheels in my brain were slowly turning when I glanced away from the book and saw my teddy bear. It was facedown on the carpet, exactly where it had fallen after I'd slammed my door in February. I picked it up and brushed dust from its ears. I felt angry with Blake again, and I thought that I should move it, maybe hide it in one of those boxes in the basement, but I couldn't. It reminded me of things like soft kisses on the back of my neck and the idea that some-body loved me once. So I put it on my dresser because that was where I still thought it should be.

In June I decided to skip my graduation ceremony. Dress-ing up in a dopey gown and marching down an aisle past gawking strangers would be overwhelming; I didn't need to go through all that to get my diploma. Hollister could just send it in the mail. This was another letdown for Mom, even though she didn't say so.

"You still want a party, don't you?" she asked.

I didn't. But she'd been so considerate and patient over the past few months that I couldn't deprive her of everything. "A small one," I said. "Just family."

That was good enough for her. So on a sunny day at the end of the month, she cooked a big dinner and bought a chocolate cake with words written in pink icing: CONGRATU-LATIONS, ARIADNE, CLASS OF 1987.

I stood by the open refrigerator and stared at the cake. Mom was getting dressed upstairs, Dad was buying beer at Pathmark, and I felt awful. I didn't deserve a party. I hadn't gotten into college and I'd been moping for months, and Mom must have been out of her mind with worry because she still kept my migraine pills locked up. Then she was in the kitchen, wearing a cheerful flower-print dress and pearl earrings, and I thought I might cry but I didn't. I was completely cried out.

"I'm sorry," I said, my eyes on the cake.

"For what?" she asked.

I shrugged. "For everything."

"Ariadne," she said. "It's fixable. You can reapply to Parsons. You aren't in trouble and you didn't catch anything. Isn't that right?"

She sounded a little worried. "Right," I said, even though I was only positive about the pregnant part.

"So everything is fine. You've been going through a bad time, that's all. It's just a bump in the road. Someday it won't matter."

I couldn't imagine that day. "Then I'm sorry for not being what you wanted."

She took me by the shoulders and spoke in a serious voice. "You're *exactly* what I wanted," she said, her eyes firmly set on mine, and I was so surprised. Mom didn't think I was a disappointment . . . and I wasn't completely cried out after all.

"I think I'm getting a headache," I said, grabbing a tissue to dry my eyes.

She left the kitchen and came back carrying my migraine pills. "Here," she said, sticking the bottle in my hand. "You can keep these now, can't you?"

"Yeah," I answered. "I can. You don't have to worry anymore, Mom."

"I'll always worry," she said, and I knew she was talking about normal things, like worrying about me getting mugged on the subway. The possibility of her daughter overdosing on butalbital wasn't something she had to worry about anymore.

A few days later, I got a call from Julian at Creative Colors. He said he'd love to have me back this summer and so would Adam, who never stopped asking if he would see me again.

The idea of working was tiring, but I couldn't let Adam go on wondering if he was ever going to see me again. So I promised Julian I would be there next week, and that I'd work until September.

I hung up the phone and told Mom I was going for a walk, even though that wasn't true. I was actually heading to the clinic for another blood test to make sure I hadn't caught anything from Del.

The nurse at the clinic was getting better at finding veins—she only stabbed me twice. I went back a week later and the doctor showed me a chart—a list of diseases and the word *negative* typed beside every one. It was relief, but the chart was like the one Blake had shown me last year. The thought of him made me sink into my chair.

"What's wrong?" the doctor asked as we sat in her office. "It's good news."

I stared at diplomas on the wall behind her. "I know. I'm just thinking about someone."

She leaned forward at her desk. "Who are you thinking about?"

I moved my eyes to a credenza across the room. It was

covered with framed pictures of what looked like children and grandchildren. "My ex-boyfriend," I said, turning back to her. Saying it made me sink even lower.

"Well," she said. "You've been through a difficult situation . . . waiting to find out whether you were pregnant, worrying about lab results. Have you confided in anyone?"

I shook my head. "I can't do that. I don't want anybody to know."

The doctor nodded and reached into her desk. Then she handed me a business card with the name of the clinic's psychiatrist, and she said that I should make an appointment, but I didn't want to. I couldn't lie on a couch or sit in a chair and talk about Blake for hours. In my opinion, it was better not to talk about him at all.

Adam wanted me to draw all the same old things, but I didn't mind. My pictures made him smile a big smile that broke out two deep dimples, which made me happy and sad at the same time. I was happy that I could give him a little joy, and sad because he was even better-looking than last year. He was growing into a handsome man with a brain that would never keep up.

"You're a good artist, Snow White," he said at the beginning of July.

I smiled weakly. "I'm not an artist, Adam."

"Sure you are," he said, lifting one of my drawings by its edge as proof.

Maybe his brain wasn't all that damaged. Maybe he knew

more than I did. And his was the first face that had interested me in a very long time. So that night, I went into my studio and sat down at my easel. My pencils were dusty and my paper was discolored from being left alone by the window for so long, but it didn't matter. I still knew how to draw. Maybe I actually was an artist, because before I knew it, Adam's face was staring back at me from my sketch pad.

"Oh," Mom gasped from the doorway. "You're drawing again."

I couldn't match her excitement. I still didn't have the strength. I just nodded and she backed off, saying she had some silverware to polish, and I heard her walking away.

"Mom," I said.

She poked her head into the room. "Yes, Ariadne?"

"Don't polish the silverware. Work on your novel."

She rolled her eyes. "For what? I'll never finish. I'm not a real writer."

"Sure you are," I said, the same way Adam said it to me, and just as sincerely. If I could be interested in drawing again, then anything was possible.

We went to Queens a few days later for the Fourth of July. Dad drove Mom's Honda and I sat in the back, my hair blowing into knots because all the windows were open.

"You really should get the air conditioner fixed," I called toward the front seat.

"We will," Mom said. "We'll fix it when you start driving."

What was she talking about? I had only driven once, in

February, when Patrick gave me my first lesson. Then Mom said that Patrick had offered to give me more lessons and to take me to the DMV to get my license, and soon she was going to buy a new car and I could have this one and wouldn't I like that?

"Yeah," I said. "I won't have to walk everywhere."

"And it'll come in handy later on . . . when you start college."

Dad's head snapped toward Mom. "Nancy," he said in a chastising tone, as if I was hobbling on crutches and she was pressuring me to run.

That shut her up. I looked at Dad's gray hair, saw his fingers on the steering wheel, the wedding ring he never took off. My hand was at my side and it moved toward him, toward his shoulder, which I wanted to squeeze. But I didn't because we didn't touch each other much, and if we did, it wasn't in a mushy way. I just held the back of his seat instead, hoping he could feel me through the leather.

At Patrick and Evelyn's house, we joined a backyard crammed with off-duty firefighters, Queens housewives, and kids who played catch on the grass. Patrick spent the day slaving over his barbecue, so I didn't talk to him until the crowd thinned out. The sun had just started to set when he plopped down next to me on the Sears sofa and I felt something hit my ankle. Then Kieran chased a ball as it rolled across the patio, grabbed it, and held it up to my face.

"Remember this?" he asked. I did—it was the Red Sox baseball from Blake. "Your boyfriend gave it to me. Where is he?"

Kieran was too young for tact. I squirmed in my seat and Patrick rescued me.

"Don't ask nosy questions," he said. "And put that damn thing away before I make sure you never see it again."

Kieran was used to his father's tough talk. He skipped into the house and I felt a headache brewing. I rubbed my temples and Patrick stood up, reached into his pocket, and tossed his key ring onto my lap.

"I don't feel like driving right now," I said.

"Did I ask how you feel? You'll be nineteen in six months and you still don't have your license. That's wicked lame."

Wicked lame. I laughed a little and I swallowed two Tylenol in the bathroom before Patrick and I hit the road in his truck, where I had my second driving lesson. There were more lessons after that, through the rest of July and into August, and one day toward the end of summer he said I was ready for the DMV.

I wasn't sure how ready I was, but I gave it a shot and ended up with a New York State driver's license. I passed the test on my first try, and it gave me a familiar feeling, the feeling of pride I used to get from the letter A written on exams at school. I hadn't felt that way for months, and I hadn't realized how much I missed it.

The next time I felt like that was during my last day at Creative Colors. Adam was upset because I was leaving, so I gave him his portrait and it cheered him up. Julian looked at my drawing over Adam's shoulder and I felt very small, worrying that Julian might be one of those critical people who had haunted my imagination for years. But I was wrong.

"This is really good, Ari," he told me.

"It is?" I said.

He chuckled and gave me an invitation to his wedding, which was going to be in October on one of those rented yachts that sailed around New York Harbor.

Later that night, I was drawing in my studio when I decided to take the SAT again. Maybe I could do well enough to get into Parsons this time. But if not, there were other schools in Manhattan, and now I had the sense to fill out more than one application.

My decision made Mom very happy. After I told her, she made a squealing noise and spent hours scribbling in her perky pink notebook. And that made *me* very happy.

The next morning I cornered Dad while he was eating breakfast and Mom was taking a shower. I reminded him that Mom was working on her novel and that she'd finished six chapters already, and she couldn't possibly write the whole thing with a ballpoint pen.

"Let's buy her a typewriter," I said. "An electric one. You can leave work early today and we can go shopping together."

What was I thinking? Dad never left work early. But he agreed that the typewriter was a good idea and took some money out of his wallet, and I bought a Smith Corona that afternoon. Mom was thrilled and I acted like it was Dad's idea. Then she kissed him and typed until midnight.

Mom gave me her car the night before Labor Day, after she and Dad went to a dealership in the Bronx to pick up a brand-new Honda. It was a color called Desert Mist. Dad had finagled a good price because the salesman was his partner's wife's ex-husband or something.

The next day we took it to Patrick and Evelyn's house, where Evelyn told me and Mom that she'd signed up for a secretarial course at Queensborough Community College.

"It's only for a semester," she said. "To learn office skills and all that crap. I may try to get a job when Shane starts nursery school. Patrick thinks it's a good idea."

So did I. And so did Mom, who looked as if Evelyn had been granted a full scholarship to Yale. "That's fantastic, Evelyn," I said.

"But here's the thing," she began, and that worried me even though there was no need to worry. She just said that her classes were on Mondays and Wednesdays and she needed a babysitter and I wouldn't mind taking care of the kids, would I?

"Well, I have nothing else to do," I said with an unexpected laugh, and it didn't sound so tragic.

twenty-four

It was mid-September, the time of year when fall edges up on summer and the air smells of lighter fluid because everyone wants to use their barbecues before they can't anymore. Dad was busy figuring out who raped and murdered a girl in Battery Park, Mom was intimidating a brand-new pack of sixth graders, and Evelyn was learning how to type.

I was proud of Evelyn. Early on Mondays and Wednesdays I drove the Honda to Queens, where I found her waiting at the front door clutching textbooks to her chest. Then she sped off in her minivan, and I drove Kieran to second grade and spent the rest of the day taking care of Shane and studying for the SAT.

On one of those Wednesday mornings I filled out my second Parsons application, and my first for three other colleges in the city. Later I strapped Shane into his car seat and stopped at the post office to mail the four envelopes before I picked up Kieran at school.

That night, I drove home to Brooklyn and found the house empty. Dad was working, Mom was at a faculty meeting, and the red light on our answering machine was blinking. I pressed it and heard the raspy voice of a girl saying I should give her a call at the Waldorf. Room 163.

It was a warm night but I felt a nervous chill. I didn't want to think about the Waldorf or Leigh or anyone connected to her. I was afraid that if I did, it would pull me into the deep dark hole that had been so hard to escape.

"I could go for some ice cream," Mom said after dinner.

She and I were sitting at the kitchen table. She licked her lips and suggested a Carvel Flying Saucer or a pint of Jamoca Almond Fudge from Baskin Robbins, but I didn't want ice cream and I came up with excuses because I couldn't tell Mom the truth. I couldn't tell her that Leigh's voice had rattled my shaky foundation and now I couldn't stop thinking that it was much easier to recover from mono than from Blake Ellis.

"Come on," Mom said. "Food is one of life's simple pleasures."

Maybe she was right. Maybe something as simple as Jamoca Almond Fudge would help. So I smiled and stood up from the table. Then the phone rang and it was Evelyn, who wanted Mom to know that Kieran had won the second-grade spelling bee and that Evelyn had earned a B⁺ on a typing test, and I didn't want Mom to have to cut the conversation short.

"I'll run over to Baskin Robbins," I whispered. "I'll be back soon."

She nodded and I went outside. The warm air had been chased away by a cool breeze that rustled the trees, and there was a bunch of grade-school girls with braids and ponytails riding their bicycles in circles on the street. Our neighbor was standing on her driveway, talking to another woman with curlers in her hair who kept shading her eyes from the sun. They both waved as I drove past and headed to Baskin Robbins, where I bought a gallon instead of a pint.

I left my windows open as I drove home, enjoying the crisp air and the sound of kids laughing on street corners. I was almost there when a bicycle cut in front of me. I slammed on my brakes and heard my tires screech, and then nobody was laughing.

I'd never been in a hospital before. Of course I'd been *to* a hospital, but I'd never been *in* a hospital, where I was the patient and doctors asked me questions like *What's your full name?* and *Who's the president of the United States? Ariadne Mitchell* and *Ronald Reagan*—that was how I answered—and everybody seemed impressed even though the questions were so silly. For a minute I wondered if I'd finally gone nuts and I was in New York–Presbyterian, but it didn't seem that way because I wasn't tied up in a straitjacket. This was just a normal room with a television and a bed and a powerful smell of

Lysol. I was in the bed, there were sheets pulled to my waist, and I was hooked up to a machine that measured my heart rate and never stopped beeping. I was also wearing a gown that I didn't remember putting on.

"Where are my clothes?" I asked Mom, who was standing next to me.

"They took them off," she said. "You were unconscious."

The fact that some random strangers had removed my clothes was more disturbing than finding out I'd been unconscious. I tried to remember which bra I'd worn today. I hoped that it was decent, that it didn't have ripped elastic or holes, but I couldn't remember anything and my head was killing me. Mom kept talking, saying I hit the brakes so hard to avoid the girl on her bike that I had slammed my forehead against the steering wheel.

"Is she okay?" I asked.

"She's fine," Mom said. "A moron, but fine. Who the hell rides a bike in the middle of the damn street?"

Then I found out that I wasn't exactly fine, that I had a big bump and a purplish gray bruise growing and darkening across my forehead, and that I might have a concussion, but the doctor wasn't sure so I had to stay in the hospital overnight for observation.

I didn't think I had a concussion and neither did a matronly nurse who checked on me after Mom left. And I was starting to feel better. My head didn't hurt all that much by the time the ten o'clock news started, and I was settling into my pillows to watch a story about that dead girl in Battery Park when I heard the door open.

I thought it would be the nurse. But when I turned my head, I saw long red hair and eyes with gold flecks.

"Wow, you got banged up good," Leigh said.

I was nervous again. The feeling lingered while I listened to her talk. She said she hadn't been sure I'd gotten her message, so she'd stopped by my house but nobody was home, and my next-door neighbor had told her I'd been in a car accident and she could find me at Kings County Hospital. I wished my neighbor had kept her mouth shut, because now Leigh was sitting on the empty bed beside mine. She was smiling and telling me about UCLA, and I couldn't smile or answer. Her arrowhead charm swung from her neck and it brought back memories that kept me very quiet.

I felt guilty, too. I hadn't contacted her after Valentine's Day. I blamed her for having introduced me to Blake and Del when she was completely blameless, and yet here she was, acting like I didn't deserve the Worst Friend of All Time award. But maybe she was taking pity on me because she knew what it was like to lose someone you love.

"Uncle Stan had a triple-bypass operation," she said. "He's not doing so well."

Good, I thought. I haven't been doing so well either because of him. "Oh," I said, and nothing else, even though Leigh seemed to be waiting for something else, something considerate or encouraging. But I just couldn't give it to her.

She twirled her hair around a finger. "I'm glad you're okay. Accidents like this can turn into something much worse, as I know all too well."

She meant M.G. I wanted to ask if she still thought about

him, if she still missed him, and how long it took to be completely over someone, but I couldn't do that either. "I'm glad I'm okay too," I told her instead.

She nodded. "Listen, Ari . . . Blake is out in the car."

My heart skipped a beat. I wondered if it registered on that machine. "Why?" I asked.

"I told him you were in an accident and he wanted to see if you were all right." She touched her charm, and I couldn't take my eyes off it. "I'm not sure if that's all . . . but he wants to see you. Do you want to see him?"

Why couldn't she ask me one of those easy questions like *Who's the president of the United States?* That had been a cinch to answer. This one was so confusing. Part of me wanted to see Blake more than anyone in the world, and the other part didn't want to see him ever again because he had betrayed me and I had betrayed him and he would never betray his father, especially if his father was sick. So there wasn't any point.

"No," I said. That word wasn't easy to say, but I thought it was the best word.

"Are you sure?" Leigh asked.

"No," I said again.

She stood up from the bed. "I understand. Well . . . I'm sure you're tired. I'll get out of here and let you relax. Take care of yourself, okay?"

She headed for the door and I reached out and clutched her hand to stop her. I held it in mine for a moment, regretting that I'd never been the friend she deserved. She seemed to understand that, too.

"Take care, Leigh," I said.

She smiled. "Get better, Ari."

Leigh left without promising to call me the next time she was in New York. I think we both knew that I had to make a clean break from the Ellis family if I was ever going to forget about them.

A few minutes later, the nurse came in and asked me how I was feeling. When I tried to talk, my voice broke and a tear rolled down my cheek.

"What's wrong?" she said.

I wiped my face. "Someone came to see me but I decided not to see him."

She nodded. "We have mental health counselors here. Do you think you'd like to talk to someone?"

I wasn't even sure why I was talking to her. I didn't talk about Blake with anyone, although I was starting to think that keeping everything to myself wasn't such a bright idea. *Don't bottle up your emotions*—that was what the doctor who diagnosed my migraines had advised a long time ago. I really should have listened.

"Not tonight," I said. "But I'll be ready soon."

I didn't have a concussion and I didn't talk to a counselor at the hospital. Instead I made an appointment with a psychiatrist at the clinic. I went there the next Friday afternoon with a bruise on my forehead and spoke with a forty-something woman named Dr. Pavelka. She wore cat's-eye glasses and lipstick the color of Pepto-Bismol. She had a soothing Slavic accent and a comfortable couch in an office with plants on the windowsill. I liked her immediately. I liked her enough to tell her things I'd never told anyone else, such as how I had kept my curtains closed to block out the sight of Saint Anne's face and spring grass poking through slushy snow.

She bit the tip of her pencil as she sat in an oversized chair. "Since when do you feel this way?" she asked.

"Since . . . ," I said, searching the stucco ceiling for an answer. Then I looked back at her, at the strawberry blond hair that was piled on top of her head and secured with two chopsticks. "Since after kindergarten. I felt really good in kindergarten."

"I see. And this statue—this saint—you think it talks to you?"

"Oh, no," I said quickly, wondering if she thought I was schizophrenic and I heard voices coming from plaster. "No, it just . . ."

I stopped because I didn't know which words to choose. I needed some that wouldn't make me sound certifiably insane. Dr. Pavelka kept biting her pencil, and I waited for men in white uniforms to swoop in and take me away.

"Is hard to explain," she said. "It may take a while to figure out. Right?"

"Right," I said, thrilled that she didn't think I was a blathering lunatic.

She stuck the pencil behind her ear and crossed her legs. "Your migraines, Ari . . . there's no physical cause? Your physician said that they're brought on by stress?"

I relaxed into the cushions on her couch. "Stress," I

agreed. "Loud noises, being upset . . . and keeping everything to myself."

Dr. Pavelka uncrossed her legs. "Come back next Friday," she said. "I get feeling you should've come here long time ago. We have lots to talk about, no?"

I went back the next Friday. She didn't admit me to a psych ward or give me medication. All we did was talk, and we did have lots to talk about. We discussed Blake and my parents and Evelyn, and Dr. Pavelka wasn't shocked about anything. She acted as if feeling depressed was no different from having mono. And she wasn't the least bit disgusted when I told her about Del and that I used to have a crush on my own brother-in-law.

"Isn't that strange?" I asked. "I mean . . . the way I felt about Patrick?"

"Is normal," she said.

She made me feel normal. I saw her the next Friday afternoon, and the one after that, and soon the leaves on the trees outside her office window turned from green to brown.

"I still think about Blake," I told her on a crisp day in October.

"How much?" she asked. "On scale of one to ten."

I shrugged. "Maybe a six."

"Of course," she said. "He was first boyfriend. First love. Not easy to forget so quick. But you have to remember, Ari . . . you have future ahead. Yesterday is gone."

She stood up because our session was over. I stayed where I was, thinking that yesterday was gone and I couldn't get it back and that was really sad. But then I thought that going back to yesterday might feel like visiting elementary school, where the desks were small and you couldn't believe that you had ever fit in them, and you knew you didn't belong there anymore.

I walked home afterward, my mind on Julian's wedding and the fact that I had nothing to wear. That night, while Mom tapped away at her typewriter in the kitchen, I stood in my bedroom riffling through my clothes and trying to find something appropriate for a wedding cruise around Manhattan. I came across a black dress, the one I'd worn to Mr. Ellis's Christmas party, the one that had ended up on the floor after Blake's twenty-first birthday. I took it out, touched it and stared at it, and then Mom was beside me.

"I'll buy you a new dress," she said, gently detaching it from my hands. "Something that's in fashion."

That dress was still in fashion. A little black dress is always in fashion. But Mom didn't know any better, so I didn't correct her. Besides, I thought she might actually have a point. That dress was very yesterday.

We went to Loehmann's the next morning and bought a purple skirt set that matched the bruise that still wasn't completely gone from my forehead. It was small now, just a few speckles above my left eyebrow, but Julian noticed. He saw it after the ceremony, when he was officially married and I was standing alone, leaning on the yacht's railing and staring over the water at the skyline.

"Did you get mugged or what?" he said.

I laughed and told him about the accident. It was a beautiful autumn night with a clear sky and a cool breeze, and Julian wanted to know what I'd been up to since the summer.

I said that I hadn't really been up to anything except planning to start college next year, and he asked where I wanted to go.

"Parsons, I hope. I have to retake the SAT next month. I really blew it last time."

He laughed. "The SAT seems important now, but it won't matter later on, especially for somebody with your talent. You know, I showed that portrait you drew of Adam to a friend of mine—a guy who owns an advertising agency in the city—and he was impressed. He said he might have a part-time opening next spring if you're interested."

"An opening," I said, imagining myself answering phones or stuffing envelopes. "What kind of opening?"

"For an artist, Ari," he said, like I was a total ditz. "Are you interested?"

There was a time when I would have said I wasn't interested, when being an artist seemed big and scary, like something that would dissolve me into thin air. But now I didn't say I wasn't interested, because a lot of big and scary things had come my way lately and I was still here.

"What do you think?" Evelyn asked.

It was New Year's Eve and I stood behind her as she examined herself in her full-length bedroom mirror. She'd just slipped into a beaded party dress with an Empire waist, and she nervously checked her reflection from different angles. She studied the embroidery on her skirt, the showgirl-type shoes on her feet. We'd bought everything together at one of those hole-in-the-wall shops where they sold vintage clothes at affordable prices, and I knew she was going to out-shine everyone at the party she and Patrick were attending tonight. It was at a catering hall on Long Island, hosted by a neighbor who'd recently inherited some money and wanted to welcome 1988 in style.

"I think it's beautiful," I said. "And stop fidgeting."

She smiled. "Will you be okay with the kids? They just can't shake these colds."

I adjusted her hair around her face and smiled back. The boys had been sick since Christmas, coughing and sneezing and fighting low-grade fevers, but I didn't want Evelyn to worry. She and Patrick deserved a carefree night filled with shrimp cocktail and champagne.

"We'll be fine," I said, handing her the silver clutch purse that a saleslady had told us was made in 1928. "Just have a good time."

She gripped the purse with one hand and unclumped her mascara in the mirror with the other. "Call Mom if you have any problems," she said, and I nodded even though I had no intention of calling Mom. She and Dad were throwing their own New Year's Eve party at home, with brandy-spiked eggnog and throngs of NYPD and their spouses, and they deserved a good time too.

I pushed her toward the living room, where Patrick sat on the couch with Kieran by his side and Shane on his lap. He rubbed Shane's back and held a tissue for Kieran to blow his nose. He was dressed in a sleek black suit and a silky blue tie.

"You clean up nice," I told him.

He tugged at his collar. "I'm suffocating in this thing."

That comment reminded me of someone else who would have preferred a T-shirt and jeans to a fancy suit. It made me remember that I didn't have anyone to kiss at midnight.

I took the kids away from Patrick to distract myself. Dr. Pavelka had told me to distract myself whenever I felt the slightest hint of depression. *Don't dwell,* she said. Then Shane held my neck and coughed into my sweatshirt while Kieran used my sleeve to dry his nose, and the three of us stood in the front hall watching Patrick and Evelyn slip into their coats.

Patrick opened the door and held it for Evelyn. There was a Christmas wreath on the door and I heard its bells jingle. I also felt the cold air and Evelyn's soft cheek on mine when she leaned over to say good night.

"Thanks for taking care of the boys," she said.

It was something she said a lot more than she used to. "Enjoy the party," I answered.

When they were gone, I supervised Kieran playing with his new train set after Shane went to bed. Kieran finally fell asleep on the couch, and I moved him to his room with the Jets sheets that Dad had given him for Christmas. I laughed to myself as I closed the door, thinking that Patrick was going to burn them to a crisp when Evelyn wasn't around.

Then I plopped onto the couch with the remote control, but not for long. I heard Shane coughing in his room, so I raced upstairs and gave him a dose of medicine.

"Feel better?" I asked, pushing damp hair away from his warm forehead.

"I want to watch TV," he said.

So we sat together on the couch, and I was flipping through the *Daily News* when the doorbell rang. I scooped up Shane, walked toward the front hall, and opened the door. I heard bells and saw a petite girl with straight blond hair cut into a chin-length bob. She wore a cream-colored coat and matching gloves, and she smelled of L'Air du Temps.

"Hi, Ari," Summer said. "Happy New Year."

She looked so different. Her clothes weren't flashy. She'd lost six inches of hair. There was no shimmery lip gloss or indigo eye shadow. Her makeup was subdued except for the matte red lipstick on her mouth, and she was prettier than ever. She reminded me of photographs I'd seen of women in the 1920s, the ones who carried the sort of purse that Evelyn had brought to the party tonight.

"Hi" fell out of my mouth, in a weak voice that I could barely hear. I hadn't seen Summer since last year, and I had never expected to see her again.

"I stopped by your parents' house," she said. "Your mother told me you were here. She was having a party."

"I know," I said, my voice louder. I wished Mom hadn't disclosed my location, but I couldn't be angry with her. Even though Mom suspected various things, I had never told anyone but Dr. Pavelka about what had happened between me and Summer. It would sound too ugly outside her office.

Summer shifted her eyes from me to Shane. "Oh, you've gotten so big," she said. She reached out to stroke his cheek but I jerked him away.

"Leave him alone," I said.

Her smile disappeared and her arm fell limply to her side

as if she knew she deserved that. It made me feel sorry for her, even though sorry was the last thing I wanted to feel. Is this a new look, Summer? I thought. Are you new and improved? I tried that once and it didn't work.

"Well," she said, her breath hitting the air and changing into steam. "Can I come in, Ari? I mean . . . I want to talk to you."

I thought of slamming the door. I thought of kicking her down the stairs. But a nagging little part of me remembered Uncle Eddie's wake and a sweet-sixteen party and a box of art supplies, and the rest of me was curious, so I let her in.

She glanced around the living room—at the blinking Christmas tree, the messy pile of torn-open gifts on the floor. The place hadn't changed at all since the last time she'd been here, and I wondered if she was going to turn up her big-shot UCLA nose at everything, but she didn't. She just yanked off her gloves and sat on the couch.

I sat across from her in the new plaid La-Z-Boy that was Patrick's Christmas gift to himself. He said he planned to enjoy a lot of Red Sox games in it next season. Shane started rolling a toy fire engine on the kitchen floor while I stared blankly at Summer.

"I thought you'd be in California," I said, folding my arms across my chest.

She unbuttoned her coat. "I'm visiting my parents for the holidays."

Which holiday? I thought. Hanukkah or Christmas? Did you choose a religion yet, Summer? Make up your mind. "Oh," I said.

She seemed nervous and I wasn't going to do anything to put her at ease. I just watched as she leaned forward and selected a Hershey's Kiss from a bowl on the coffee table.

"Ari," she said, peeling silver foil. "Do you ever see Blake anymore?"

Blake. It seemed to echo against every wall in the house. I never said his name outside of Dr. Pavelka's office, and it was unsettling to hear it now, especially from Summer.

"No," I said, clutching Patrick's chair, terrified of the question I was about to ask. "Do you?"

"Me?" she said with wide eyes and chocolate melting in her palm. "No. I haven't seen him in a long time, and I don't want to. My mother doesn't even work for Ellis and Hummel anymore—she picked up a bigger account last spring, so she doesn't have time for them. She's expanded her business—she's got a few people working for her now."

"Oh," I said again, releasing my grip on the chair. "That's . . . good for your mother."

Summer nodded, abandoning her chocolate on the table. "Ari," she said. "I was wrong about everything. I thought Blake was a nice guy, but he wasn't. He wasn't a nice guy at all."

"Blake was a nice guy," I said, the same way and for the same reason that I'd protested when Patrick had said that Summer wasn't a *nice girl* and when Del had called Summer a *floozy.* "He just wasn't a strong guy."

"Yeah," she agreed. "You're right. His father really bossed him around. Honestly, I think Stan liked me more than Blake did. Anyway, Blake had the wrong idea about me. The whole thing was a huge mistake."

Where had I heard that before? And lots of people had the wrong idea about Summer. It gave me a satisfied feeling to know that both she and Blake regretted what they did, but I also pitied her again. I knew that Mr. Ellis had used her, that Blake had used her, that she'd been searching for a guy who would look her in the eyes when they made love, and I doubted that Blake had, even if he'd been right on top of her.

"Yes," I said. "It was a mistake."

She nodded once more, stood up, and brushed foil fragments from her coat. "Ari," she said. "I'm not better than you. And I don't think you're average."

I guessed this was her idea of an apology. I accepted a tiny fraction of it and gave her a half smile. Then she quickly changed the subject as if my silence equaled forgiveness. She started talking about her new boyfriend and she pulled a wallet from her purse.

"This is him," she said as I looked inside the wallet at a picture of an attractive young man. He stood beneath a palm tree with his arm around Summer. The picture was as perfect as the ones that always came with wallets—the photos of happy couples. I guessed that her new look was for him, for California, for starting over. "He's a little older . . . he graduated from UCLA five years ago and now he's working on his MBA. I think it's good to go out with older guys—they're more mature and they treat you better."

I could tell that the guy in the picture treated Summer better than Casey had, better than Blake had, better than any of those names in her diary, and I was surprisingly glad. I also got the feeling she wasn't seeking *experience* anymore.

"That's great, Summer," I said. "Really."

She smiled and we walked to the front hall, where I opened the door and smelled burning wood in the air.

"Goodbye," she said.

She walked down the stairs and I listened to her heels tap the sidewalk as she headed up the block. Shane ran out of the kitchen, I picked him up, and the two of us watched Summer's bright coat disappear into the darkness.

"Bye-bye," Shane said, waving a tiny hand.

Bye-bye, I thought, almost sure that I'd never see her again. But if I did—if we ran into each other someday—I knew we would smile and say polite things like *How are you?* and *Give my regards to your parents,* and we would secretly remember that we used to mean something to each other. And even if that never happened, if we never spoke again, I was grateful that we'd have tonight.

twenty-five

Parsons accepted me. In February, the mailman brought a thick envelope and then I had to take a portfolio of my work to the city and interview at the school, and soon they sent another letter that I tore open while Mom peered over my shoulder. *Dear Ariadne,* I read. *Welcome to the Parsons School of Design, Class of 1992.*

She was ecstatic and so was I, and we were both just as happy when I met with Julian's friend in May. He offered me a part-time job at his agency in Midtown, where I worked as an entry-level illustrator under senior artists and art directors, and none of them ever said I didn't have any talent. Sometimes people at the office would show me their work and ask, "What do you think of this, Ari?" and the idea that someone cared what I thought made me feel even more important than being given a ruby necklace for Christmas. The whole thing made Mom change her mind about the value of connections, just as long as there weren't any strings attached.

So I kept working through my freshman year of college, and soon it was the summer again. I spent three days each week in the city and two at Creative Colors, and I found out that Adam still liked drawings of lakes and mountains.

"Do you have that same boyfriend?" he asked one Friday afternoon in August.

I was filling in a lake with a cobalt pencil and I shook my head.

"Oh," he said. "That's okay. You'll find another one when you're ready."

I laughed because he was right.

The next day, my parents and I went to a citywide firefighters' picnic at a park in Manhattan with Evelyn and Patrick and the boys. It was warm and sunny, and we sat on folding chairs around a table covered with food. I was drinking a glass of lemonade when Kieran came running across the grass, panting and saying he had to tell me something.

"I saw your old boyfriend, Aunt Ari."

"Shhh," Evelyn said, grabbing his arm and shoving him into a chair. Mom shushed him too and Patrick kept his eyes on his hamburger. I knew they meant well, as usual, but they didn't have to protect me anymore. I didn't want anything from Blake. I just needed to see him one last time so that I would never need to see him again.

"Where?" I asked.

"It was probably just someone who looked like him," Mom said, lighting a Pall Mall. "Eat your lunch, Ariadne."

"Where?" I said again, staring at Kieran.

"He's over at the track," Dad said.

We all looked at him. He was sitting at the head of the table and he glanced down at his plate as if he hadn't just done the nicest thing ever.

I got out of my chair and dared to put my arms around him. "Thank you, Dad," I said, and he actually hugged me back. It wasn't for long—just a few seconds—but it was something.

I walked away, across the park, where I saw Blake. He was running laps on the track, dressed in black shorts and a gray T-shirt. I stood at the edge of the asphalt and called his name as he passed.

He stopped running. He turned around and walked toward me, and I saw his handsome face. Time had matured his features; he looked more like a man than a boy.

"Ari," he said with a smile I didn't expect. I wasn't sure he would want to see me, especially since I'd refused to see him at Kings County Hospital. But I hadn't been ready then. Now I was. "How are you?"

"Fine," I answered, nervous and not sure what to say next.

His eyes moved around my face. "You look good."

"I do?" I said, and he laughed as if I hadn't changed at all, but he was wrong. Then he asked if I was at Parsons and I said

I was. I also told him about my job, and nothing surprised him.

"I always knew you could be an artist," he said.

I smiled because that was true. He had always believed in me. "What are you doing these days?" I asked, hoping he'd tell me he was planning to become a fireman and was running laps so he could ace the physical portion of the FDNY entrance exam.

He shrugged one shoulder and tugged at the bottom of his shirt. It was damp and clinging to his chest. "I'm in law school now."

My heart sank, even though I wasn't shocked. "But you wanted to be a firefighter."

He paused for a moment, looking down at a rock on the track. He kicked it toward the grass before looking at me again. "You remember that?"

Of course I remembered. How could he think I wouldn't? But so much time had passed—I *was* starting to forget things, things like what kind of chocolate he'd given me when I was sick with mono. "It was so important to you," I said.

He nodded slowly and rubbed the back of his neck. "Yeah . . . I still think about it sometimes. But things took a different turn."

"They sure did," I said, struggling to keep sarcasm out of my voice. I wasn't sure I'd succeeded. "Well . . . I guess your father is happy you're in law school."

He ran a hand through his hair. It stood up straight just like it used to. "My father died a while back, Ari. He never followed the doctor's advice . . . he still ate whatever he wanted and he worked himself into the ground, even after he had surgery. Aunt Rachel's taken it really hard, but she'll be okay eventually. Time heals all wounds, as they say."

He was right. And I didn't feel the same as I had when Leigh told me that Mr. Ellis wasn't doing well. I didn't feel hatred anymore. I wanted to say something to make Blake feel better, but I couldn't think of what that would be.

"I'm sorry" was all that came to mind.

Blake shrugged as if he wasn't sad, but I knew better. He was still a bad actor. Then he moved closer, touching my hand as it hung at my side. "Me too," he said.

I knew he wasn't talking about Mr. Ellis. I knew this was the day Mom had told me about, the day when everything that had happened didn't matter anymore. I looked into Blake's eyes, remembering my lost marble and thinking that even though it was gone forever, there could be another match out there. There might be another guy who would kiss my forehead, a guy who was just as sweet but was strong enough to choose me over everybody else.

I nodded. He squeezed my fingers in his, stepped back, and changed the subject.

"Del sold his club and moved to California. He opened another place in Los Angeles. You know Del and I never got along . . . but he's doing well and I'm happy for him."

"That's great," I said, and I could tell that Blake had no idea what had happened in the loft on Valentine's Day. Del kept it a secret, like I'd asked—he wasn't such a pig after all. "But you're alone in New York now, aren't you?" I asked, thinking that his closest relatives were either dead or in California.

"I'm going to school in LA," he said, yanking his shirt

again. UNIVERSITY OF SOUTHERN CALIFORNIA was printed across the fabric in red letters. I hadn't even noticed.

"Oh," I said, surprised. "Do you like California? I mean—is law school okay?"

He sighed. "It's what I expected. So is California. But Aunt Rachel wanted me nearby. . . . I think I should be around my family for now. And my father always planned for me to become a lawyer."

I glanced at my sandals and back at him. "Your father is gone, Blake."

He stared at me for a second. "So you don't think I should do what he wanted?"

"I think you should do what *you* want. He isn't here."

There was a wounded look on Blake's face. He shook it off quickly and spoke in a determined voice. "I know he isn't—and that makes following his plans even more important. His partners are running Ellis and Hummel. I've kept an apartment here in the city, and I come back every month or so to check in at the office. I'll start working there permanently after I graduate. Eventually I'll be in charge of everything."

I remembered New Year's Day at the penthouse when he'd broken up with me. I remembered him standing by the elevator as I left, looking brave and dutiful, like a soldier. He looked the same way now, and I realized he hadn't changed much. It made me sad for him.

"Ari," he said. "Are you seeing anybody?"

"No," I answered, shaking my head. "Are you?"

He shrugged. "Since we broke up, there hasn't been anybody important."

I felt a little smug. I thought he should have realized

sooner that important people don't show up very often, and you should hold on to them when they do. Maybe I was smarter than he was all along, because that was something I'd always known.

From the way Blake was looking at me, I got the feeling he'd finally figured it out. Maybe that was one thing about him that *had* changed. But it had taken him too long.

I remembered the things we used to talk about, the things we'd planned, everything that had taken me so long to leave behind. But now I wanted other things, new things, like the career that people at work kept telling me I was sure to have. I'd probably want the house and the kids and the husband one day, but not yet. There were so many things I wanted to do between now and then. I also knew that Park Slope wasn't the only place to plant a flower garden. There were even better places out there somewhere.

Blake stared at me and I sensed what he was getting at— there wasn't *anybody important,* he was going to be in New York *permanently* after law school. As I stood there looking at him, Summer popped into my mind. I heard her saying *I don't think much about guys from the past. I'm glad I knew them, but there's a reason they didn't make it into my future.* Back then I had thought she was probably right. Now I was sure.

I took a deep, quivering breath. "Well," I said. "I hope you find somebody important. I hope you get everything you want, Blake."

He looked like I'd let him down. I didn't want to hurt him, and it wasn't easy to say what I said, but I knew it was right.

Blake sighed, gave me a faint smile, and wrapped his hand around my elbow. "Thanks," he said, holding me tightly. He still smelled like aftershave and toothpaste. "I hope you do too."

"Thank you," I said, and my voice cracked. "Goodbye."

He let me go. "Good luck, Ari."

He started running down the track and I turned away. I walked across the grass toward my family, feeling the warm August air against my face and the sunshine on my hair. I really meant it when I told Blake that I hoped he'd get everything he wanted. I hoped I would too.

That night, I cleaned my room while Mom typed in the kitchen. I sorted through wrinkled test papers from Hollister, and threw junk into garbage bags and everything else into boxes for Goodwill. I cleared off my dresser and got rid of dusty magazines and dried-up nail-polish bottles, and then the only thing left was my teddy bear. I picked it up and stroked its face and the smooth brown beads that were its vacant eyes.

"Ariadne," Mom said.

She startled me. I hid the bear behind my back and she didn't see it because she was too excited. She said she had just finished her novel.

"Oh, Mom," I said. "Congratulations."

"It still needs work. But it's done," she said, taking a seat on my bed.

"Your next goal," I said, "will be to quit smoking."

She gave me a half-annoyed, half-amused look. "Maybe," she said, so I didn't push it. At least she didn't say no. *Maybe* was progress. Then she looked down at the embroidered roses on my bedspread and rubbed one with her fingertip. "Ariadne," she said again, her eyes on the rose. "When you used to see that doctor . . ."

"Dr. Pavelka, you mean? I still see her, Mom . . . just not as much. Every third Friday."

"Right," Mom said. "When you see Dr. Pavelka . . . when you talk to her . . . does she ever say that . . . that when you went through that bad time . . . that it was because of me? Because of something I did? I mean . . . I always meant well." She glanced up. "You know that, don't you?"

Mom's face was tired. Her eyes were swollen from late nights bent over the Smith Corona. She couldn't know that Dr. Pavelka and I had spent countless hours talking about her, and about Dad, and about Evelyn and everything else, and that I had always known Mom meant well. I didn't blame anyone for that bad time—not even Blake.

"I know, Mom."

That made her happy. She stopped touching the rose and looked around the room. "Well," she said, standing up. "It seems like you're moving things along in here. I'll leave you alone to finish . . . I really need to get some sleep."

When she was gone, I went to the basement, found an empty box, and sealed the teddy bear and the NYU sweatshirt inside with heavy-duty tape. I started thinking about Leigh's ID bracelet and I imagined that one day, maybe years and years from now, I might open the box and say the same thing to my daughter that Leigh might say to hers: *This was from a boy I used to know. He was very special to me, but that was so long ago.*

And later on, when my room was clean and all the important things had been packed away, I carried two trash bags to the curb and saw Saint Anne on my way back inside. Her shawl glistened from the glow of the streetlight; her dress was a bright shade of blue. She didn't look lonely, and I could have sworn she was smiling.

Lorraine Zago Rosenthal was born and raised in New York City. She earned a bachelor's degree in psychology and a master's degree in education from the University of South Florida. She also earned a master's degree in English, with a concentration in American and British literature, from Northern Kentucky University. In addition to writing fiction, Lorraine enjoys reading, watching movies, and spending time with her husband. *Other Words for Love* is her first novel.